The Ex...y ...... ...evenson

"A haunting tale of timeless love. The vibrant voice of Hannah's heroine brings the lonely coast of Scotland very much to life, complete with the taste of oatcakes and the tang of smuggled claret. A surprising, rich, and rewarding novel."

—LAUREN WILLIG, author of *The Betrayal of the Blood Lily*

"An extremely original piece of storytelling with a thoroughly unique heroine."

—DEANNA RAYBOURN, bestselling author of *The Dead Travel Fast*

"This is a stunning debut: a haunting, extraordinary tale told by a born storyteller who combines humor, heartbreak, and real suspense."

—BERNARD CORNWELL, *New York Times* bestselling author of *Agincourt*

"Darci Hannah's debut novel has something for everyone: romance, mystery, humor, historical detail, a feisty protagonist in Sara, and a stunning Scottish setting."

—ANNE EASTER SMITH, author of *The King's Grace*

"Like the gales that sweep over the desolate north coast of Scotland, *The Exile of Sara Stevenson* gathers force and delivers an atmospheric tale of love, passion, and loyalty. Like the lighthouse lamp at the symbolic center of the novel, details of the story that at first seem inconsequential or mysterious gather into one great beam of light, illuminating a conclusion that shows the power of love to transcend death and even time itself."

—LAUREL CORONA, author of *The Four Seasons: A Novel of Vivaldi's Venice*

The

Exile of

Sara Stevenson

# The
# Exile of
# Sara Stevenson

A HISTORICAL NOVEL

## Darci Hannah

BALLANTINE BOOKS

NEW YORK

A Ballantine Books Trade Paperback Original

Copyright © 2010 by Darci Hannah

Published in the United States by Ballantine Books, an imprint of The Random House Publishing Group, a division of Random House, Inc., New York.

BALLANTINE and colophon are registered trademarks of Random House, Inc.

Library of Congress Cataloging-in-Publication Data
Hannah, Darci.
The exile of Sara Stevenson : a historical novel / Darci Hannah.
p.   cm.
ISBN 978-0-345-52054-8 (pbk.)
eBook ISBN 978-0-345-52055-5
1. Single mothers—Fiction.  2. Sailors—Fiction.
3. Scotland—Fiction.  4. Time travel—Fiction.  I. Title.
PS3608.A7156E95  2010
813'.6—dc22          2010005229

Printed in the United States of America

www.ballantinebooks.com

2  4  6  8  9  7  5  3  1

Book design by Caroline Cunningham

*For my husband, John,*

*and our sons, James, Daniel, and Matthew.*

*You are the pillars of love, wisdom, perseverance,*

*and humor upon which my life is built.*

*My heart and soul forever*

# ACKNOWLEDGMENTS

The author is positively ecstatic to finally get the chance to acknowledge publicly those very special and hearty souls who've helped make a most cherished dream come true. My deepest and most heartfelt thanks to:

Dave and Jan Hilgers, my wonderful parents, who were the first to suffer my wild tales and are still, unbelievably, my sounding board and most ardent supporters; Bernard and Judy Cornwell, my dear friends and benevolent mentors, whose support and guidance (and back-cover blurb!) have been invaluable, and whose love of toffee is truly inspiring; Linda Marrow, editor extraordinaire, for her insight and enthusiasm about this novel from the onset, and for the killer title; my agent, Meg Ruley, for being one of those rare and extraordinary people whose passion, influence, and expertise shape destinies; my husband and best friend, John, who might not always understand what I do but believes in me regardless, for saying things like, "Y'know, with a pot of coffee and a catheter you'd be good for at least another eight hours"; my son James, for being an extraordinary human being, and for building my computer and not requiring me to understand how it works; my son Daniel, another extraordinary soul, whose athletic ability and academic achievements inspire me, and whose tales from the locker room keep me laughing; my son Matthew, for his disarming combination of cherubic smile, sharp wit, and humor, his freakish knowledge of historic weapons, and for being the one to remind me, "Hey, Mom, are you almost done writing, because we're starving up here!"; my brothers, Randy and Ron Hilgers, who, aside from teasing me unmerci- fully, are waiting for the audio version of this book; my sister- in-law Brenda Hilgers, for books and pictures of Scotland (no, I've never been); my longtime best buddy, Jane Boundy, for all the calls, laughter, and cherished moments these many years; Jerome Boundy, for the English perspective on all things, and for sharing his coveted Christmas cake with me; Rachael Perry and Cyndi Lieske, dear friends and brave first readers, whose feed- back was invaluable; all the rest of the talented South Lyons Writers; the wonderful librarians at the Howell Public Library, for tirelessly fulfilling my every request; Junessa Viloria and all the other hardworking folks at Random House/Ballantine; Robert Louis Stevenson, Sir Walter Scott, and Robert Burns, the great Scottish men of letters whose works have captured my imagination; and a very special thanks to you, dear reader, for now holding my most cherished dream in your hands!

The

Exile of

Sara Stevenson

# ONE

## Cape Wrath

❧❦❧

$\mathcal{S}$omebody once told me that every tower had a ghost, and every ghost had a story. Certainly there's nothing more compelling than a well-told ghost story. They made for great fireside tales, tales devised to scare children so they'd lie awake in their beds late into the night straining to hear ghostly footsteps on the landing, the rattling of chains against the walls or, heaven forbid, the high-pitched moans of the unliving. As a child, tales of the ghosts of Edinburgh enthralled me—specters such as the immortal Wizard of West Bow Street ambling down the lane with his demonic thornwood staff, boisterously celebrating his hellish afterlife, or the Lone Piper playing his haunting lament in the secret tunnels beneath the Royal Mile. There were gray ladies wandering through castles by the score, and the White Lady of Corstorphine appearing in a virginal gown of white as she brandished the very sword used to kill her unfaithful lover . . . still dripping with his blood! I've heard tales from those who have witnessed for themselves the Death Coach—that notorious ghostly soul-collector, pulled by black, demon-eyed steeds who blew flames of fire out their nostrils—and lived to tell their tale, and fewer still were those who had actually seen the headless drummer boy at the Castle, beating his ghostly tattoo, an augury of a future attack on the city. It was marvelous fun, but just stuff. Besides, it was common knowledge that those who claimed to have actually seen an entity dangling between the living and the dead were those known to succumb to flagrant imbibing. Sure, some argued that excessive drink was a result of a frightening encounter, not a precursor to it, but this was just an excuse. Drink flowed too freely and rather cheaply in the ancient, terribly haunted, wynds and closes of Edinburgh.

My head may have been filled with stories and my imagination fertile, but I had never seen a ghost; therefore, I didn't believe in their existence. Still, I had to wonder if the forlorn, lonely tower I had been banished to was home to a lingering spirit.

I pondered death as we sailed along the treacherous coast— what it was, what it meant, how it felt. When someone dies, do they know they're dead? And can someone be dead yet still think they're alive? I believed I fell under this last category. But the wind, beginning to pick up, bit straight through my clothing, reminding me that I was indeed quite alive.

Yet I felt so dead inside.

The more forceful gusts began to lift the bitter cold spume off the sea, driving it into my face. I cursed it under my breath, damned it to hell and knew I had too much hatred inside me to be truly dead. I also cursed myself for choosing style over warmth and attempted to shrink farther inside the meager protection my soaking ermine-trimmed pelisse provided. Fog was also proving a menace, thick and damp, turning the air into a vaporous pudding where sea and sky were nearly indiscernible. I was sitting in the middle of a goddamned cloud being tortured by the elements!

And then I heard the tolling of the bell.

The deep, resonant din wafted through fog and sea to warn us we were near. But I had no idea how near we were. Another gust of wind and the fog peeled farther back, rolling like a woolly blanket off a newborn babe. It was then I saw the yellow eye. It hovered above me, suspended in the cloaking mist, only able to break through with its roving, searching, blind eye. I jabbed my elbow into the shivering body next to me and whispered, "Polyphemus. You'll know Polyphemus, Kate? The Cyclops who relishes the taste of human flesh? We've not landed on the Cape, we've been blown all the way to the Isle of Sicily! Isn't it marvelous? But don't worry overmuch, I hear the Cyclops only eats those with sweet flesh, not sour and rotten like yours. However, on account of my benevolent nature, I shall put in a good word for you nonetheless."

Kate, my lady's companion, glowered at me. There was real hatred there. She didn't bother to hide it, as would be proper for a person of her position. Because hiding things, as well as keeping secrets, were not amongst Kate's virtues, I had learned.

"You have spent what little sense God gave ye on unholy, pagan tales! How ever did your dear mother, a good, honest Christian forbye, beget such a wicked child as you?" she hissed through clenched, chattering teeth, shifting her gaze to the light.

"*The Odyssey* is literature, Kate, and I believe you know very well how one begets a child." At this she had the good sense to look affronted. And I would have smiled in triumph had I not been thrown from my seat.

"Clap a hand on the rail there, Miss Sara!" came the late warning from the helm. Captain Seumas MacDonald might have been a crack skipper, but he was no hand with hospitality. I hit the freezing wet deck with startling force.

It was the strong yet gentle hand of Robbie MacKinnon that helped me back to my place on the bench in the stern. Robbie was a good man, even if he was married to Kate, and knew very well the nature of the baiting that played out between his wife and me. Where once it had been mere folly and sport—all in good fun—it had recently taken a turn toward the malevolent. And why?

Because Kate had betrayed me.

There was a time when we had been very close, much closer than what was normally accepted between a servant and her mistress. At twenty-two, Kate was only three years my senior and could be charming good company when she wanted, but she also possessed a startling self-righteous streak. This morally superior air was why my mother had liked her so well, no doubt, both being cast from the same unyielding mold. Yet her high and mighty, dare I say tattling, ways had also been self-destructive too. After all, she was here with me freezing in the inhospitable elements and not in our warm, comfortable home in Edinburgh.

"There, now. Ye must take care, Miss Sara," Robbie gently chided. "'Twould never do to let go just now. Think on it. Think of your responsibility—nay, your duty to this place and to us. Aye?"

His words brought me once again to the problem at hand. "Oh, aye," I responded slowly, without emotion, forcing my eyes back to the light on the promontory, guarding that place on the sea so fatal to mariners. The sheer rock sides of the cliff dropped hundreds of feet straight into the icy water, where the breakers hungrily lashed at it and cliff-dwelling birds circled through the mist, awaiting their next meal.

And then I began shaking uncontrollably, because this time I knew that the yellow-eyed Cyclops was truly going to devour me.

Perhaps I deserved it. To use the exact words of my father, I had brought this problem on myself by being a "foolish, ignorant, ungrateful, ill-mannered, amoral, disobediently willful child" who had disgraced her family. And the real shame of it was my father's strong words hadn't caused me much pain. This was because his accusations were partly truthful, but also because I was too young, and alive, and gullible to believe I had made a mistake. My punishment for not conforming to the rigid standards of my family was banishment to this little purgatory—this little cape of hell. Yet even as befuddled as I was, I knew that banishment to the lighthouse on Cape Wrath was not what hurt me so, causing me to feel so dead inside. That was something altogether quite different, and the mere thought of it sent another wave of hurt and anger running through me, along with the now familiar ache in the pit of my stomach.

"Miss Sara, lass, Mrs. MacKinnon," Captain MacDonald called out from the helm, both hands firmly grasping the wheel. "We're gonna give Mr. Campbell a wee signal, let him know we're here, aye?" Assuming that was enough of a warning for us, he gave the signal and a cannon at the bow was fired. The sound was deafening, louder than any clap of thunder I had ever heard, especially so since it echoed off the cliff walls. This sent the sea birds exploding off their roosts, causing the air to be at once a swirl of gray fog and flapping wings.

"That'll wake the lad. Now, then," he continued, looking much better for firing his weapon, "if you ladies will please clap a hand on the railing and keep it there. We're about to head into the rough stuff."

"Rough stuff?" I parroted, spray hitting my face as the boat rocked more violently than I thought it could withstand. "How can it possibly get any . . ." But my words were whipped away on the wind.

I held on to the rail, as told, though there was a part of me that harbored a fantasy of letting go as we neared the angry breakers. The sea mirrored the turmoil I felt; we were kindred spirits—wild, unruly, a force to be reckoned with. The swells had grown, the sails were taut to the point of imprudence and the hearty little lugger was being pushed onto her side as she raced down the coast. It would be so easy, I thought. There was nothing any of them could do. And my fingers began to relax a measure.

I was startled by an ice-cold grip that came hard over mine. A warm breath hit my ear, carrying the stern words: "No ye don't!" I looked next to me and saw Kate.

"If I have to endure it, so must you!" And then came that look of pity, so distasteful coming from the likes of her. Purely out of respect for her husband, and none for my own comfort, I liked to believe, I let her hand stay over mine.

It wasn't long before we entered a barren gray cove not far from the towering light. The wind died down within the high cliff walls, the surf slackened until the waves were no more than a gentle, soapy, lapping presence. And then a lonely wooden pier arose beside us.

This was not the first time I had come to Cape Wrath. I had been here before, a mere six months ago. Yet somehow it seemed a lifetime away. It was the same unremarkable pier we had docked against then, only our boat had been much grander at the time. More people had been aboard her too. And it was the memory of one of those travelers that caused the tightening in my gut and the stabbing pain in my chest. As a sailor secured a rope around the piling that passed for a bollard, I felt the familiar sting of tears once again.

"Och, come now, lass," soothed Robbie, noting my reduced state as he extended a hand to assist me to the dock. "This is not the end of the world."

I stood on the unmoving wooden planking, cold water dripping off my clothes, and looked to the north. I then turned to the east and to the west. There was nothing but an unwelcoming gray sea sparsely dotted with more cliffs, towering stones and faraway islands. And to the northwest stood the Atlantic, unobstructed—a straight shot clear to America. "But it is the end of the world, Mr. MacKinnon," I corrected. "It is the very bitter end!"

It was true. Cape Wrath was the very end of my island home of Great Britain. It was the lonely, desolate, harsh northwestern tip of Scotland, located in a region known as Sutherland; and it was my father who had dared to build a lighthouse here. He was a civil engineer who had made a name for himself illuminating the dangerous coast of Scotland for all the worlds' mariners. I used to think it was a commendable business, for the coast of Scotland was so wild and dangerous that many sailors unaccustomed to navigating her waterways avoided going anywhere near her shores for fear of wrecking. But perhaps I had been too proud and too caressed by the wealth such an endeavor created to see it clearly back then. Glancing at the white tower on the cliff, sound in design, perfectly cylindrical and topped with a black domed cap, I felt a wave of foreboding shoot through me.

Perhaps some places on earth were not meant to be touched by man.

Pushing my unreasonable fears aside I looked once again at my new home, and then I smiled recalling a bit of ribaldry on the subject from my early youth. It pertained to a man named Willy Campbell, who, as fate would have it, just happened to be the current principal light-keep on Cape Wrath and the very man Robbie MacKinnon had come to assist. Mr. Campbell had been younger then; it was a good five or six years since he had emerged from my father's office at the back of our home at Baxter Place, winning the title of light-keeper. My sister and I were hiding in the garden. She was older than me yet we both liked to watch the men who came and went from my father's door. It was then a group of sailors came walking toward Willy, hailing him and asking where he was bound. "Bell Rock," Mr. Campbell had answered.

"Ye hear that? Why, if our ain Mr. Willy Campbell isn't off to the towering prick o' the waves!" one of the sailors declared, causing the rest to break out in raucous laughter.

"Mr. Stevenson's erect wonder! 'Tis a fine place for ye, laddie!" another added playfully.

"Though dinna expect to bows your jib for a while," they teased. "A man spending his days polishing a tower that size scares off the lasses!"

My sister and I giggled, she because she understood what was said, I because I liked the sound of men's laughter.

Poor Mr. Campbell, a fine-looking dark-haired gent, turned red with embarrassment. He narrowed his pale blue eyes and defended, "It is a feat of remarkable engineering, gentlemen. And you'd do well to remember it." He then strode off amidst more gales of laughter. It was only as I grew older that I realized lighthouses, for want of better design, did tend to resemble men's more private parts. The "prick o' the waves" the sailors had been referring to was my father's first and most remarkable lighthouse. It was built on Bell Rock and was a wonder of modern engineering—that men could build a solid, towering structure on a reef in the North Sea! It stood directly in the path of ships entering the Firth of Forth on a northern approach, and was designed to withstand high winds, crashing waves and partial submersion in salt water. It had sealed his fame; perhaps it had been the downfall of mine.

Captain MacDonald and a couple of his sailors began depositing barrels and crates on the dock. These were supplies for the lighthouse. Next came our trunks. When first I learned of my banishment to Cape Wrath I made no attempt to pack light and frantically stuffed my trunk, not only with every stitch of clothing I owned, but with books and paper, quills and ink and all the gold coins I could procure. I packed bed linen, bolts of fabric, thread, yarn and needles. I even threw in a couple of loose bricks from my old fireplace and a wrought-iron poker. Watching the good men of the tender *Pole Star* struggle under the weight of it caused me a pang of guilt, guilt I hadn't felt when my father's porters had struggled to haul me away.

"Never could I reckon how a lady required sae much to keep her in comfort," reflected Captain MacDonald, scratching his stubbly chin in wonder as his men bent their backs under the weight of my trunk—a trunk, I might add, that was twice the size of my companions'. "But therein lies the mystery of the fair sex, lads. The more they own, the fairer they are, eh?" Although the captain was mightily pleased with his own wit, his men forgot to chuckle. "There, now, given the wee dock holds under all this weight, Mr. Campbell should be down in a bitty with the wagon to haul her up. Until then, ye can either stay put or start up thon road."

"You're not going to stay, Captain MacDonald?" I asked, glancing at the dirt path he referred to as "thon road," which angled out of the jetty landing at a frighteningly steep pitch, disappearing into nowhere.

"Och, there's no need now that Mr. Robbie MacKinnon's here. You're in fine hands." He gave the new assistant keeper a nod and a grin. "Besides, Alasdair was the chatty one of the pair, and that's no' saying much. Campbell's fair brilliant but a wee on the closed-lip side. But never ye fash, Miss Sara, never ye look so glum. The lads an' I shall be back in a few months to check up on ye, drop off goods, deliver post an' pass along any gossip from Edinburgh I happen to glean. Aye?" He tugged on his thick woolen cap in a show of deference before turning to go. Then, remembering something, he turned back to me again. "Would ye be so kind, Miss Stevenson, to tell Mr. Campbell that his personal delivery is in that there crate?"

I glanced at the crate in question, a sizable, nondescript wooden box, nodded my consent and silently remarked that the men of the *Pole Star* looked a little too eager to cast off.

It was just as the stout lugger was rounding the point that the jingling of harnesses could be heard. Within moments two sturdy drays appeared, cresting the hill in perfect unison and pulling a low-sided wagon behind them. The driver, Mr. Willy Campbell, much to my astonishment, was the exact likeness of the young man I had seen long ago in the garden of Baxter

Place. I had seen him six months ago, under much different circumstances, but that seemed a lifetime away. He was sitting on the bench of the wagon, his dark silhouette much the same as ever—straight nose, firm-set jaw, a well-shaped head that was framed by dark, unruly curls. He was driving the team with a gentle touch that belied the powerful arms beneath slightly rounded shoulders. I believed Mr. Campbell had once been a sailor, and he still had much of a man-of-the-sea air about him, but that was all I knew of him. He was just another of my father's men. And although his appearance might have been familiar, he was in actuality a complete stranger—a man who preferred solitude and isolation over the comforts of community and companionship. He was at some remove a friend of the family's, I supposed; the exact circumstances were unclear, but he had sought my father out, specifically asking for this post. That fact alone said volumes about the man.

There had been another keeper here, another recluse like Mr. Willy Campbell. The two had manned the lighthouse since it came into operation nearly a year ago. Just last month the other keeper, Alasdair Duffy, had met with an unfortunate accident, the nature of which was unknown to me. Had I cared, I might have asked. But I didn't care. The man was dead, a new keeper was needed and my family wanted rid of me. That's when Robbie MacKinnon stepped in on both our behalfs.

Kate's new husband was an ambitious man, one eagerly seeking more opportunity than what was normally allotted a former ship's purser turned longshoreman. In spite of the fact he was married to Kate, Robbie was intelligent, hardworking, respectable and a proper Calvin. My father was also quick to point out that, barring a respectable family, Robbie had more to recommend him than I. And when my world crumbled around me, darkness and doom descending on me from all sides, the intrepid Mr. MacKinnon, perhaps out of sorrow, shame for his wife, or just clever opportunity, pulled my father aside for a private word.

The result of that conversation was the reason I was standing on this godforsaken strip of hell now—as a nominal keeper of the lighthouse on Cape Wrath. But the nebulous title fooled nobody. Robbie's new career was a convenient excuse to whisk two women away from the splendors of Edinburgh. This was my penance. And this was the price Kate was made to pay for the hand she had played in my downfall.

Pulling to a stop at the landing, Mr. Campbell alighted from the wagon and made his way toward us. He was taller than I recalled, and leaner, yet he still walked with the ease and grace of one comfortable in his own skin. However, the closer he got to us, the more the ease seemed to crumble away, leaving the telltale awkwardness of one unused to the ways of civility. He stood before us, staring with his odd pale eyes, his mouth agape, unspeaking. And then, remembering himself, he doffed his weathered hat, tucked it under his left arm and made a good show at a proper bow. But then, rather too quick for propriety, he concealed the mop of dark curls once again under the shabby headgear.

"I saw . . . I heard you coming," he corrected without preamble, alluding to the lighthouse. "Was unaware—did not expect ye so soon. Thick weather. MacDonald was set to come tomorrow, not today." Then, realizing he was stammering on, he made another bow and replied without any real emotion: "Honored. A pleasure. Truly."

The men introduced themselves, each one taking in the measure of the other. Men, I gathered, were not overly picky when it came to choosing a workmate. Considering the fact that they were total strangers and would be spending a good deal of time together in close quarters, I thought it rather remarkable. Once it was established that Robbie had all his limbs intact, good health and most of his God-given teeth still in his head, Mr. Campbell next inquired whether he could read and write.

"Aye," Robbie answered.

"And your eyesight?"

"Sharp."

"You are used to heavy lifting?"

"Very."

"Do ye take the drink?"

"Only when it's right and proper."

"Are you, by chance, scientifically or mechanically inclined?" Willy's pale eyes narrowed as he watched his new man with interest.

"Somewhat. And what I don't know I shall endeavor to learn."

"Very well, Mr. MacKinnon, welcome to Cape Wrath," he concluded, offering his hand.

Mr. Campbell next turned his attention to us women. If he had regained some semblance of humanity back while talking with another male, clearly it left him as he stood staring at us. His eyes narrowed in consternation, his ruddy face, hidden somewhat beneath the stubble of a day's growth, became pinched and pale, and his lower lip was clenched nervously between his teeth. It was then I believed he was trying to figure out which one of us was the unfortunate young gentlewoman he once knew. Although I had seen him briefly last summer, it appeared as if I hadn't made any lasting impression on the man.

"Mr. Campbell," I began, making a polite curtsey. "May I have the pleasure of introducing to you Mr. MacKinnon's wife and my dear companion, Kate MacKinnon? You must excuse our appearance, sir, for we've had a bit of a rough journey."

"Honored," he uttered, making another attempt at a polite bow. And then he turned his attention to me. It was a while before he finally spoke, but when he did it was more of an observation than any proper greeting. "Miss Stevenson, again ye have come to Cape Wrath. You've grown up a good deal since those days ye used to play in your father's garden."

"Well, I hear it does happen, given enough time." And though I meant no harm by my words, my reply had a very different effect than I had intended. He darkened and regarded me as if I were a pariah.

And a pariah I was, if my father had been forthcoming. "Forgive me," I quickly amended. "It was impertinent. All I meant was that time has a way of changing us all, though not always for the better, I find." His eyes, an indescribable pale bluish-green, widened at this and bore into me with surprising intensity. The proper thing to do would have been to look away. But I had gained a reputation for not behaving properly and continued to stare back. It was then I noticed the toll time had taken on him, things I hadn't noticed six months ago. Fine lines had marred the smooth skin at the corners of his eyes, while dark, sunken circles appeared under them, making the already pale irises seem paler still. And then again there was the visible loss of the flush of youth. Mr. Willy Campbell was an older man, already perhaps even in his thirties, I surmised. I believed I had struck a chord. "I trust you have received my father's letter?"

"Aye," he answered with an awkward, shifty gaze then lowered his head, unable to look me in the eye any longer.

"Then I must thank you, Mr. Campbell, for allowing me to accompany Mr. and Mrs. MacKinnon. It was most kind of you. Certainly Cape Wrath is a far cry from Edinburgh, but I shall endeavor to . . ."

He looked up. His piercing, pale eyes shot through me and I faltered. He then spoke very evenly. "I never allowed anything, Miss Stevenson. You should not be here at all. But I don't have any say in the affairs of the Board."

It was another blow to add to the many I had so recently received. Unwanted. It was becoming a plaguing theme. "Well then," I said, attempting to summon what was left of my pride. "I shall contrive to make my presence here as little known as humanly possible. Not many know, not many shall know, and when I leave here, your reputation as a stoic lighthouse recluse will go unchallenged." I turned to go. His iron grip stopped me.

"You misunderstand. All I meant was—"

I removed his hand from my arm. "I misunderstand nothing. I know very well what you meant. And for what it's worth, your point is well taken."

Mr. Campbell looked helplessly at Robbie. Robbie, dear man that he was, was recently married and appeared just as lost as he. I motioned for Kate to follow and started up the road, leaving the men to deal with the luggage.

"Miss Stevenson, your father, in his letter, spoke of ye being a hand in the kitchen . . . a fair cook, said he."

This caused me to falter. I stopped and spun around on him. "Did he?" I was shocked, then angered. Another humiliation. Having always employed a cook in our home, I barely knew where the kitchen was, let alone how to use one. And yet my father expected me to cook for this man—this recluse with the odd, unsettling eyes?

"A man . . . a man appreciates a warm meal every now and again. 'Twas all I meant," he added, going very pale again.

"Well then, Mr. Campbell, I shall endeavor to see that you get one!"

. . .

The long, low, one-story whitewashed cottage sat within the extensive lighthouse compound. Many other little buildings resided here, all protected by a high stone wall, which served to buffet the capricious, ever-present winds coming off the Atlantic. The great stone tower was only a short walk across the courtyard from our new living quarters, which was an abode that was unremarkable by all standards. The place was roomy enough, though sparsely furnished and shockingly untidy. Upon entering, there was one main room; the focal point, if one was to go beyond the mess, being the great stone hearth at the center, serving both as a means of heat and a place to prepare the meals. On one side of the hearth was the scullery, separated from the main room by a long wooden worktable. From the blackened pots, dirty plates, bowls, cutlery and half-filled mugs, it had the appearance of an untidy laboratory belonging to a third-rate scientist more than a place where meals were to be prepared. Behind the overflowing counter, cupboards lined the walls, yet they were suspiciously bereft of dishes. And under the empty cupboards was more counter space—messy counter space—as well as a basin for water. The other side of the room, I was given to understand, was for leisure, for there was a rather pretty settee and two wing-back chairs placed near the fire. Yet great cobwebs dwelled in the corners, books and papers cluttered the dining table and the wood-planked floor was nearly hidden under a layer of dust. On a brighter note, a smoky peat fire blazed away in the hearth, taking the chill out of the air. And although there was a yellowish linen sark, a thick woolen sweater and some equally thick woolen hose draped over a rack to dry, it was a welcome sight—enough to warm an icy body, if not enough to melt a stone-cold heart.

I stood beside the laundry and held my hands toward the flames, sighing with pleasure. Mr. Campbell, having already unloaded his wagon and tended the horses, came up beside me and began hastily removing his personal garments.

"There's no need to remove those on my account," I assured; but he removed them nonetheless.

"I've not had time to clean properly," he said by way of apology.

"Pray, don't tell me?" I turned to face him. "My father wrote and told you what a hand with a mop and broom I am!" But the sarcasm was lost on my new host. The pale eyes burned into mine with frightening intensity, his face, rather dark and not unhandsome, blanched. He curtly excused himself, said something under his breath to Robbie and left the cottage, shutting the door behind him. I turned and watched out a dirt-smudged window as he skulked through the blustery courtyard, his long oilskin coat billowing out behind him, until he disappeared into the safety of his tower.

"By God, where are your manners, lass!" chided Kate. "The man's been out here over a month now—on his own—standing watch day and night without a soul for company and no one to help! His last mate died on him! Have ye no shame at all?"

I turned to my companions. Both were glaring incredulously at me. "You sound just like my mother, Kate. And as for shame, I've had more than my share lately. You don't know Willy Campbell. I don't know Willy Campbell. He could have killed the man himself for all we know!" An awkward silence fell over the room, enhancing the soft crackle and hiss of the fire.

It was Robbie who intervened. "I know this has been hard on ye, Sara. And things will likely get harder still, but you must tone down the venom if we're to get along out here. Winter's nigh, and we'll be stuck in this place for a great long while. I beg ye, as a friend, give the man a chance."

"Have you considered, Mr. MacKinnon, that perhaps this time the fault does not lie with me?"

He held me in his unwavering gaze, and without so much as doing me the courtesy of pretending to consider, replied with a curt and resounding: "No."

Surrounded by hostile forces on all fronts I retreated to the relative safety of my sleeping quarters to further wallow in self-pity. Two hallways came off the main room, one off the "scullery" side, where the MacKinnons were to live, and another off the "parlor" side, where my room sat, halfway down the hall. Yet when I came to the designated door, and then entered, I was overcome. In even the most barren, bereft places on earth beauty unexpectedly appears, and I was touched that I should be the recipient of this kindness. Mine was undoubtedly the largest room in the cottage, warmed in advance of my arrival by a soft fire and void of any semblance of dirt. The oak bed frame had been polished to a rich luster; the windows sparkled in the settling dusk; a table and oil lamp had been placed beside the bed, along with a bookcase and rocking chair. The bed was covered with down pillows, and soft quilts sewn in shades of pink and

lavender to rival the heather-covered moors. But it was beside
the hearth where my attention came to rest; for along the wall,
pushed nearly in the shadows of the corner, sat an empty cradle.

"Damn him!" I swore under my breath, tears coursing down
my cheeks. "Damn him!" Yet I wasn't at all certain which "him"
I meant.

# TWO

## *The Light*

❧❧❧

*A* person must indeed endure many changes and adapt as best they can if they are to survive in this world, and for the first time in a great while survival was in the forefront of my mind. Napoleon and his army had been ravaging the continent for so long, and so much of the world had been lured into war, that at times I failed to see how precious life was. Hundreds of thousands had been killed, thousands more displaced. Since the signing of the Treaty of Chaumont last March, Napoleon had been driven back into France—where, at last, in April he finally abdicated and was imprisoned on the Isle of Elba. And although the Bourbon monarchy had been restored, France was still trying to recover from years of devastation and war. With so much of the world on end, and so many families touched by Napoleon's atrocities, did I really think I was impervious to change? A mere three months ago I had longed for change. I had planned for it. And in my heart, no matter how hard I tried to expunge the thought, I still believed he would come and change my world— even when every sign pointed to the contrary. "How stupid are you not to understand?" my mother had scolded, boiling with anger and indignation. My father was little better. Where I had once been the apple of his eye, he barely had the will to look at me, I was such a disgrace. Was I really so void of intelligence? There was a real possibility I was. But then again, they didn't know him like I knew him.

I recalled a time not so very long ago, walking down crowded Leith Street with my friends Jenny and Mary Ferguson. We had been returning home after another day of indulging our vanity in the burgeoning shops of Edinburgh, when we happened to fall in behind two gentlemen going our way. They were older gentlemen—scholars, from the look of them, dressed in somber frock coats of dark gray, knee britches of a lighter shade, white silk stockings and black buckle shoes. They wore powdered perukes on their big round heads beneath plain tricorne hats, and each one brandished a silver-capped walking cane. Yet what struck me most was not their unremarkable dress or silver-capped cudgels, but their loud conversation. The men were debating intelligence. I nudged my friends, indicating that we should listen to these intellectuals of Edinburgh.

"Alas," began the taller of the two, "I'm inclined to report, due to my extensive observations on the subject, that intelligence, especially in males, skips generations."

"My good fellow, could we, in fact, be discussing the same case?" the shorter man stopped to inquire. The three of us paused as well.

"Young Thomas Stevenson?"

"The very same. It pains me tae think it! His father's a brilliant man, quite the engineer; mother's a fine, God-fearing, well-bred woman tae boot. But the poor lad has not a chance . . . nay, not a prayer of achieving anything like success in any field, engineering or otherwise."

Here I had to leave off because I was giggling so hard. The gentlemen had been discussing my older brother Thomas. He was the youngest of the boys, the closest to me in age and perhaps the most blatantly unambitious of our brood. It wasn't that Thomas was slow or dim-witted; he just failed to see the point of schooling. Nor did he see the point in teachers being so liberal with the cane! School was drudgery to him, subjects such as arithmetic and science eluded him and it was his very nature to rebel. He did, however, have a rather brilliant imagination fed by an insatiable desire to read books unsuited for a young man of learning. He was a teller of tales, a spinner of stories and a supplier of forbidden gothic romances to an impressionable girl.

Later that same day, and much to my surprise, the two gentlemen of Leith Street showed up at our house for supper. They were guests of my father, professors at the university where Thomas was studying, and although I knew my brother was failing miserably (due to their earlier conversation and his own admission), neither gentleman had the courage to tell Mr. Stevenson of their discovery. It was shameless pandering. Had it been money that made them so reticent, or fear? It was actually a bit of both, I discovered—for my father, a patron of the university, told them at length what high expectations he had for his children. Perhaps if he hadn't been so preoccupied with running the lives of his many employees—the supreme high ruler of his personal empire—he might have taken notice that his own children were falling short of the mark. Amazingly, and much to my chagrin, Thomas had turned out rather well. I, however, was the miserable failure of the family.

"Kate," I said with a yawn as I walked into the main room after a sleepless night pondering my predicament and firming up my resolve. She turned to look at me, eyes narrowed; I turned to look at the pile of unwashed plates, bowls, mugs and pots she was stooped over.

"Aye?" she replied.

"I believe I have a plan."

"Pray tell, I long to hear it."

There was mockery in her tone, mockery she likely picked up

from me during her stint as my companion. I chose to ignore the gibe and asked if the men were about.

"No."

"Well, do you know where they are, then?"

She pretended to ponder this before answering, "As it's well into the afternoon I should think they're out."

"Out?" I questioned, going to the window. "Could you be more specific?" The sun was low in the sky, the western sky. We were far north. It was late November. "I must have dozed off," I said as much to myself as to Kate.

"The men have a lighthouse to keep, Miss Sara. Lighthouses, I'm told, don't exactly keep themselves."

"No, I don't suppose they do. And that's what I want to talk to you about, keeping the house . . . assigning duties."

"Really? And here I was thinking our duties were already assigned, you being the privileged layabout, and me being your maidservant."

Oddly, her anger pleased me, yet instead of baiting her I smiled sweetly. "Kate, I mean no disrespect, but I think *I* fall under your long list of duties. I may be a nominal keeper of the light, but *you* are *my* keeper, if you know what I mean."

"Your keeper?" Her cheeks flushed with palpable ire as she spat the words in my direction. I kept smiling. "I may have been your companion—"

"And my moral compass," I added softly.

"Aye, and that, but I am neither of those any longer! I'm the wife of a lighthouse keeper, and you are a . . . a . . ."

"Yes, yes, I know very well what I am. Mr. Campbell might even have some inkling on the matter. But that's neither here nor there. I just thought . . . perhaps we could lay aside our differences for a moment. You must know how truly sorry I am that it has come to this. If Napoleon hadn't caused such a mess, I'd likely be in the South of France by now, at some 'girls' school,' not in a little cottage teetering on the far tip of nowhere. But here we are, and there's naught more to say on the matter."

"The South of France would have been warmer!" she blurted with real passion.

"Yes, indeed. But France is not Scotland."

"I don't give a fig for Scotland!" she spat, her pretty face blotching red and white with anger, matching the knuckles of her hands as she tossed the pot she'd been scrubbing back into the tub of brownish water. "But I do give a fig for warmth!"

"You don't mean that, Kate," I added quietly, because try as I might, her very real hurt and fear began to soften my cold-hearted pleasure at seeing her suffer with me. And I knew, somewhere deep down, that she didn't entirely deserve all she had suffered because of me. "And what about Robbie?" I added, looking into her troubled eyes. "You are blessed with a husband who loves you, God only knows why, and keeping this lighthouse, even if it is in the middle of nowhere, is a good deal better for him than working on the docks of Leith. Don't you agree?" To this she did not reply but uttered a forlorn: "I miss Edinburgh."

"So do I," I agreed, glancing again out the dirt-smudged window, where my gaze was met with whitewashed brick beneath a fathomless milky sky. "And with any luck we shall be there again someday. But for now we are here and we should stop bemoaning our misfortune and make the most of it."

Although I felt I was helping to smooth over our unsavory situation, she scowled and turned on me like a rabid mongrel. "That's easy for you to say. But I wouldn't have to make the most of it if you didn't contrive to sell your love so cheaply! For a highborn lady, I find a common tart has nothing on you!" And if insulting me weren't enough, a challenge issued forth from her narrowed, dark brown eyes.

It was then I understood the exact nature of Kate's hatred. It was not the fact that Robbie had been given a promotion and had taken a post tending the lighthouse on Cape Wrath; if he had done so under any other circumstances, Kate would have been, if not mildly happy, then at least very proud. But because her plight in this desolate location was so intertwined with my downfall, and there was no recourse but to succumb to the mundane and belittling chores of scrubbing dishes and doing laundry, I was the obvious one to blame. However, she had to realize, at least on some level, that the blame was not all mine.

Sure, I wanted to hit her for her biting insults, but I refrained. I was not generally known for my stellar control of emotions—or any amount of self-control, for that matter—but for the sake of our friendship and the fact that we would be living together under this small roof for quite some time, I would try. I took a deep breath then let it out very slowly, half closing my eyes. "All I was going to say is that if you think you can manage the cooking, I shall tend to the cleaning. Perhaps we can both lend a hand with the laundry. I realize, as much as we might lament it, this is our home now, and it would be in both our best interests to take a little pride in the keeping of it. Now, if you'll excuse me, I have some work to do." I brushed past her, making for the door, but turned, unable to resist. "Oh, and if 'tis not too much trouble, I did promise Mr. Campbell a warm meal. Perhaps ye could manage a roast, done to a turn . . . or succulent meat pie? Why, I believe the poor man would even relish a good Scotch broth! See what you can do."

Her eyes grew wide as her scowl deepened to a spiteful leer. "I am not a cook! That was never part of the bargain!"

"Please, I've a headache," I said, rubbing my temples from the shrillness of her voice. Then, "I'm surprised by what you tell me. And here I was under the impression you knew everything there was to know about the running of someone else's home. Very well, try a flummery, then." I smiled at this taunt and made to grab a fur pelisse before deciding on a more weatherly looking old boat-cloak.

"Don't make light of this, Sara, as you do everything else! I wasn't employed to be a cook!"

"No. You were employed to be a lady's companion. And since you've made it perfectly clear that there are no ladies to companion, you'd best seek out a new trade."

"But why me be the cook and not you?"

"Because, whereas I'm a mere dilettante, you, Kate, have a moral righteousness that will not let you fail. Prove me wrong if you like," I offered, pulling the thick oilskin around me and then leaving the cottage.

The great white lighthouse, when standing at the base of it, was an impressive-looking tower. The stone I knew to be hand-cut and strong enough to support the cylindrical shape. It rose well over sixty feet in order to suspend the great light-room at the top, where at night the giant lamp would be lit, burning brightly beneath the black iron cap. Hundreds of panes of glass had been specially cut to create the light-room window, placed in a diamond pattern so the great light could be seen on all sides as it slowly rotated. Sitting just below this giant window was a narrow balcony that ran the circumference of the tower. It was while looking up at this balcony that I happened to catch a glint of sunlight reflecting off a long copper tube. Either it was a sizable gun, which I highly doubted, or the barrel of a powerful telescope. And I imagined the view from so high was quite spectacular. How far I could see! What details could I glean on a passing ship! Perhaps I could even see faces, maybe even his face. . . . I had peered through perspective glasses before, those marvelous instruments mariners used to help them see farther, but never had I looked through anything so powerful.

I scanned the little courtyard that was nestled between the thick white walls of the cottage and the tower structure to see if anyone was about. It appeared I was quite alone. I pulled open the heavy iron door, walked past the storerooms where the broom and bucket I was looking for were most likely to be had and began climbing the eighty-one steps that spiraled into the tower.

As hard as I tried to be quiet, my footsteps echoed off the dark, brooding walls; and before I had gone halfway up my breath was coming a little heavy. My clothes felt tight as well and my head was spinning a wee bit from lack of food. But I would be damned if I passed on the opportunity to peer through the glass; for if there was a ship out there somewhere, I would be certain to spy it. I pressed on through the dark spiral, climbing the thick stone steps one at a time, until at last, panting and growing a bit faint from the effort, I reached the landing. I hadn't expected the door, though thankfully it was unlocked, and when I went through to the room on the other side it was as if I had entered another world altogether.

A huge apparatus sat in the middle of the room, attached to a complex structure of glass and mirrors that rose up through the ceiling into a tower of glass. It was the great lens. I had seen this before; it was my father's own design. When the Argand lamp was lit, a huge parabolic sheet of silvered copper placed behind the flame would catch the light in its focal point and increase its power tremendously. From there the light would pass through many prisms of specially cut glass, magnifying its power all the more. Then an explosion of white light would burst forth, hit the yellow-tinted glass surrounding the structure, giving it its distinctive color, and bound into the darkness, where it was able to be seen nearly twenty-five miles out to sea. To compound matters further, a hand-wound clockwork motor was employed to ensure the light would revolve slowly. It was a marvel of engineering, yet as amazing as it was, it was nowhere near as impressive as the view from the lantern room.

I stood near the base of the light in awe, watching out the window as the steady westerly breeze pushed striated clouds across the sky. The sun, on its descent, poked out every now and again, touching the barren landscape with splashes of light. Sunlight and shadow rippled across the cold Atlantic, illuminating the crests of waves and creating every shade of blue imaginable. One might almost term it beautiful if one was in a more benevolent frame of mind. But I was drawn to the tower for another reason altogether; I was drawn to the tower because of the telescope.

I made my way to the balcony, passing a table and chair in the corner of the lantern room. I paused. It was his chair. There was no reason to stop and examine the curious leavings of the mysterious recluse other than perverse curiosity. And, God help me, I was possessed of perverse curiosity.

There were more books here, as in the cottage, piled on the table along with paper, a quill and an inkwell. A black enameled pot sat atop a little spirit stove near the edge, and next to this was an earthenware mug still containing remnants of the most recent brew. I sniffed at it, stuck a finger in and tasted. Coffee. So this was how the man stayed awake during his long shift! I picked up one of the books and flipped it open. It was a ledger of sorts, remarking the date, weather conditions, temperature, ships sighted and all manner of boring work-related entries, though it did give me a good indication of Mr. Campbell's writing. His letters were very small and neat, perfectly formed and, from what I could tell, spelled correctly. But his words were uninteresting: *November 22, 1814 Temp. 42°, wind NNW at 10-15 knots, patchy fog. Three local fishing rigs sighted between 5 and 7 a.m. Five herring busses sighted around the hour of noon, heading for the Grand Banks. 2 p.m. tender* Pole Star *sighted at jetty bringing supplies, stores and new keeper.* I flipped back a few pages, and then a few more, and saw the writing of another hand. It was the other keeper's writing. Interesting, I thought, noting it was nowhere as neat, nor were his entries as thorough. I put the book down, searching for another, more interesting read.

I passed over one on ships, another on maritime signals. There was the novel *Candide, ou l'Optimisme* by Voltaire, which, from the look of it, had never been read, and the novel *Robinson Crusoe* by Defoe, which, I gathered from the little paper marker stuck in the middle, was currently being read. A forlorn sailor, shipwrecked alone on a desert island, was not a tremendous leap of the imagination for a recluse. Yet for all intents and purposes, it could not be a very uplifting tale for a light-keeper stuck on so desolate a post. The next book I came to was a thick, pedantic volume with a distinctively Latin title. The cracked spine, the dog-eared pages, indicated it was a frequent favorite: a light read for a light-keeper, I mused. However, it was the book on the very bottom of the pile that caught my eye. It was larger than the others, leather-bound in a shade of deep vermilion and boasted no title. When I flipped it open the reason instantly became clear.

My hand flew to my mouth in a feeble attempt to stifle a cry. The image confronting me was as ghastly as it was spectacular, and I had never seen its like. It was a very detailed, lifelike sketch of a woman—a naked woman—laying herself bare with a disturbing boldness—arms out to her sides, legs slightly parted. She was full-breasted, full-bodied, with plump, rounded hips and a patch of woolly darkness to shade her genitals. Yet her face was expressionless, her eyes dead. Horrified, I flipped the page.

It was another sketch of yet another naked woman. The body was the same but the position different, prone on her back, head lolled to one side, eyes dead and expressionless. There was some scribbling at the bottom of the page, notations in Latin I descried (although I could not read Latin) and a smaller inset sketch that upon closer inspection proved to be the most secret, the most deeply private part of a woman. "Oh sweet Jesus!" I breathed, all aflutter, and flipped the page again.

There was yet another woman, this one not only naked but with a swollen belly. There were three views of her—back, side and front—and more indiscernible words. The next few pages documented a progression of swollen bellies, from merely thick to bursting ripe. And the page after that was so brutal and ghastly, it nearly undid me. The woman, eyes dead, belly swollen, was cut open and skin splayed wide to reveal the curled, lifeless fetus inside her. My God! What horrors—what vile demons lived in this man's mind?

My heart was beating so loud and so fast that I never heard a thing until the shadow fell across the page. At first thought, I believed it was just clouds crossing the path of the sun again . . . until I heard an exhalation of breath from directly behind me, as if someone had gotten the wind knocked out of them. I slammed the book shut and spun around, feeling his burning gaze before I saw it. He too appeared frightened, perhaps more so than I, but then his pale eyes narrowed beneath his dark brows. Anger, cold and implacable, had come upon him.

"What are you doing in the light-room?" he demanded harshly. He was a terrifying sight—red-faced, eyes glowing, hair that perhaps had been tamed earlier but now had gone wild, swirling about his head. And he was all the more terrifying to me because of the knowledge I had gleaned of what filled his mind. I jumped to my feet and stumbled backward into the table, knocking the little kettle off the stove. I made a grab for it, coming around the table, and so did he. Our hands collided; the mere touch of his skin caused me to jump back. I fell against the base of the great light fixture, crashing into it with enough force to cause the entire housing to shudder and protest with a clanking of glass and mirrors.

"If you'll . . . if you'll just come away from there now," he almost pleaded, contriving to sound rather calm; but his look was as wild as his hair. "Please, dinna touch the light, I beg ye," he uttered, his well-controlled accent growing thick in his tempered distress. "'Tis a verra . . . complicated . . . piece of equipment," he added a bit breathlessly while putting up a hand to caution me. He then gently set down the coffeepot with the other. "I dinna mean to startle ye, but you're not supposed to be up here. The light-room's forbidden for all but the keepers. Aye?" He looked at the books strewn across the table then back at me. "Now tell me, Miss Stevenson, what exactly were ye doing up here?"

"I . . . I," I stammered, thinking of a logical explanation. I turned and saw the brass telescope pointing out to sea. My heart sank. Damn my insatiable curiosity! I had risked the tower for the chance to look through the eye of the telescope and was waylaid by the tantalizing thought of glimpsing into the mind of this enigmatic man. God, but I wished I hadn't done it. I hadn't peered through the telescope, but I had gotten a glimpse into his perverse and demented mind. I felt sick and knew Mr. Campbell was staring at me. I looked up and saw that his eyes, sharp and piercing, were taking in everything. I cleared my throat, fought to regain my composure and began again. "I . . . I was looking for a broom."

The man didn't say a word for a good long minute, instead he just stared at me with an odd, puzzling expression. "Was it not in the broom closet?"

"Broom closet?"

"Aye."

"And where . . . where might that be?" I inquired softly.

"In the cottage, back hall off the scullery side of the main room."

I nodded nervously, performed a slight curtsey and turned to go.

"Miss Stevenson." His voice, soft and low, stopped me. "There are some places on this earth, and some people, that are best left alone. You'd do well to remember it."

I caught the look in his eye, the warning, and then I bolted out the door and down the eighty-one steps with a heart racing so fast that I feared it would surely explode.

• • •

I burst through the cottage door on a gust of wind, fought to secure it behind me and then leaned against the solid barrier until I had mastery over my fears. And afraid I was, for a lone man in a tower had spent his long nights sketching pictures of women, women in humiliating positions, all naked, all dead. When my breath was again coming more naturally, I looked up and saw my companions. They had been enjoying a wee respite beside the fire, sitting close, heads bent together, talking softly . . . until my abrupt appearance.

"Sara, what is it?" cried Kate, springing out of her chair and coming to my side. "Dear heavens above, child! You look as if you've seen a ghost." Her hand on my shoulder was comforting, as was her look of real concern. I had missed her, my old friend, but the wounds of betrayal, I found, were the slowest to heal.

I patted her hand and reassured, "Nay, it was no ghost. You know very well that I don't believe in such things." A shadow of doubt touched her dark eyes, and I added by way of explanation, "'Tis just the wind. It blows harder up here, colder." I forced a smile. "I shall get used to it in time."

"Where were ye?" asked Robbie. "Where did ye get off to?"

I looked at him. He was a good man with an honest face, clear blue eyes and bright ginger hair. I realized it would never do to lie to such a man. "I, umm, I went to see the lighthouse," I replied with a hint of ambivalence.

"Och, the lighthouse," he repeated, and raised a brow. "And?"

"And what, Mr. MacKinnon?"

"Did it meet with your approval?" he questioned, eyes twinkling with curiosity.

"Well, I'm no sort of an expert on these things, you understand, but I'd have to say, given what I've seen, it is rather remarkable."

"Oh aye?" he said and offered a quizzical half smile.

"Aye. A sound, if not practical, piece of engineering."

"And did ye happen to see Mr. Campbell on your wee visit there?" Here his question was met with dead silence. I looked at Kate for some guidance, but there was none to be had. She was as curious as her husband. Robbie added, "When we parted a short while ago, he said he was on his way to the lantern room—or light-room, as he calls it—to take the first watch. He should be lighting her up at four o'clock."

"Yes, yes, I did run into him. Kind man," I added out of sheer nerves. But both my dear friends knew what a liar I could be.

"Well, while you were gallivanting with Mr. Campbell in the lighthouse, Kate, good lass, has contrived to make us a wee supper," Robbie informed me with a proud grin.

"There was no gallivanting, Mr. MacKinnon!" I snapped, for

my nerves were still raw from the experience. They both stared at me with wide, unblinking eyes. It was then I looked away and saw the remarkable change. The far side of the room that housed the scullery had been scrubbed clean, dishes and cutlery placed back into the cupboard, while a suspect whitish lump inhabited the now clean wooden counter. A blackened pot hung over the fire, and although I could not discern what it was by the smell alone, I did detect a hint of oats. I realized then that I was starving.

"'Twas only a jest, Miss Sara," Robbie uttered softly, chastened by my harsh reaction. "I did not mean to imply—"

"'Tis quite all right, Mr. MacKinnon. I'm just peckish from lack of food. Kate, dear Kate, you are a good woman in spite of what I say," I remarked, and for once I meant it. She had upheld her end of the bargain. I would have to do better to carry out mine.

"Aye, we can all do with a little supper, and I told Mr. Campbell that you'd be bringing his up once it was ready."

"Me? But cannot he just come down and get it himself?" I reasoned, for I was not about to tell these people that I would never go into the tower while *he* was in there.

"He cannot leave his post," said Robbie. "Not until I take over at eight. The light needs watching, the gear needs to be cranked every two hours. And then Mr. Campbell's back on at midnight, and off again at four. The schedule's been worked out."

"Was . . . was he all right with me going up there—I mean, once you told him I would?"

"Aye," he replied slowly as his ginger brows furrowed in question.

"He didn't complain or forbid it?"

"No. The man's a bit protective of his lighthouse, Sara, but given his post, it's only natural. He has to answer for her in the end, should anything be found amiss."

"And how do you find Mr. Campbell?" I inquired softly. "What kind of a man is he?"

"Well, he's a quiet gent, diligent, conscientious—"

"Do you find him a bit odd?" I demanded abruptly.

"A bit. But 'tis only to be expected. He's been here alone for a good long while."

"And you'd . . . you'd send me up there . . . with his food?"

Robbie leaned back in his chair, his face quite serious now. "He's not going to hurt ye. Why, I'm more afraid of what you'd do to him, or say, than what he'd do to you."

I looked at them both, knowing they believed I was the crazy one, not Mr. Campbell. It was little use to tell them what I had found out about the man, for they wouldn't believe me if I did. Again, and quite literally, I knew I was utterly alone. "Well, you know I'd love to be of service," I lied blithely to my companions, "but I find I'm not feeling very well just now," which was not a lie. "I think it best if I take my supper in my room. I'm certain you'll find some other way to get Mr. Campbell his food tonight. Now, if you'll please excuse me."

Without awaiting a reply I headed off down the hall, shaking uncontrollably. And while I stood before the door to my only sanctuary on this horrible rock, placing my hand tentatively on the knob, I heard Robbie's voice softly echoing down the narrow passageway. "You're right, Kate, she's not the same girl at all, and more's the pity. I swear it, if I ever lay eyes on that bastard again I'll . . ." But I didn't wait to hear what Mr. MacKinnon had it in mind to do.

·  ·  ·

My huge trunk sat at the end of the bed, unpacked. It was a reminder that my stay here was only temporary. Cape Wrath was not to be my permanent home, but dear Lord, could I last that long? Likely not. I would die before I ever saw my home or family again; for there was a madman—intelligent, though totally deranged—living with me; a man who harbored a perverse fascination for dead women. Naked dead women.

It was not that I particularly wanted to see my family again, I reflected. They were a disappointment to me. They hadn't turned out to be the people I imagined them to be. Hardworking, God-fearing, maybe, but even Jesus had it in him to forgive. He championed the wayward and the lost, those of us who are blindsided by the excitement of life. Perhaps it was because we were the greatest challenge, or perhaps, when refocused, our passion had the greatest potential, not unlike the great lens in the light-room, where one little flame, reflected and refracted, passed through prisms, bounced off mirrors and properly aimed could burst forth with a light seen twenty-five miles away. I didn't pretend to understand how it worked, my mind did not lend itself to such machinations, but I had grown up with it, and accepted that it does happen. Just as I had accepted his words as truth when he told me that he loved me.

In a burst of anger and frustration I threw open the lid to my trunk and dug through my belongings. There was a lot there. Damn me, but I had been spoiled! I flung the many beautiful gowns of colorful, rich fabric and stylish design aside, rooted through the pile of cambric shifts and silk stockings, tugged at the cashmere shawls, woolen capes and two little, prettily embroidered spencer jackets. I yanked out a couple of stiff, slim-waisted stays—a contraption that when pulled taut not only cinched my waist to the point of absurdity, but also boosted my breasts to an unfathomable plumpness. Ha! I spat and chucked them so hard they almost landed in the smoldering peat fire. I found a pair of long kid gloves, which would be little use when one was to sweep and scrub floors all day in the wilderness. I flung shoes, boots, pattens and some floppy lace caps, desperately searching for that one little treasure. I knew it was here. I knew I had packed it. When I was almost at the bottom where the books, bricks and wrought-iron poker lay, my hand came to rest on a velvet sack. It was in here, along with many combs, hairbrushes and a tarnished silver mirror, that I had placed it. How cruel of me, I thought, and then pulled the little frame out of its hiding place.

My heart stopped at the sight of him, sitting there, smiling at me. The frame was mother-of-pearl, fresh from the sea; just like him. Yet even its wondrous, iridescent beauty could not begin to hold a candle to his luster. "Damn you," I said to his miniature golden-haired, blue-eyed oil likeness. "You have no idea what you've done to me, Thomas Crichton! Damn you for a cold-hearted, honey-tongued, misbegotten, blackguardly liar!" And then I placed his portrait against my pounding, aching heart, because I did not possess the strength or the courage to push him away.

# THREE

## Thomas Crichton

*H*is name was Thomas Crichton, and his was not a remarkable story, no more so than any other young man growing up and struggling in the shadows of a great city. He was born the son of a fisherman, a poor, honest workingman, and had not the advantage of a mother's love and care to guide him. What few advantages he did have, besides the thorough knowledge of his trade, were obvious the moment one saw him. At least that's how it was for me that day, not so long ago, when first he came to my father's house in Edinburgh.

It was late spring, and a rather typical day at Baxter Place. Men of all trades seemed to be traipsing through our gardens on their way to my father's office and workrooms out back. It was busy, more so than usual, because my father was interviewing sailors for a few vacant positions that had opened up on a yacht owned by the Northern Lighthouse Board. He was preparing for an important tour of the Scottish coast, where the yacht and all her dignitaries would visit many of his lighthouses and de-termining places where more were needed. I was especially in-

terested in this because, being the youngest and the only one left
at home, I had begged and connived my way onto the tour.

It was after my daily devotions, a fruitless hour on the spinet
and a trip to the market with Kate that I was allowed a little
respite. The sun was out and the day was splendid, with just a
slight chill in the air so, naturally, I couldn't resist indulging in
my favorite pastime: pretending to read on the garden bench
while covertly watching all the men walking by. Many of them I
already knew, for they were frequent visitors—civil engineers,
stonemasons, lighthouse keepers, sailors on the tender—and
they hailed me with cheerful greetings of: "Good day to ye, Miss
Sara. A fine bright mornin' 'tis!" to which I would reply, "Indeed,
a day could hardly be finer!" Sometimes, if the men weren't too
harried with work or urgent matters, they would come over and
strike up a conversation. Captain MacDonald had been a frequent visitor and, if the tide was not about to turn, I could always be assured of a ripping yarn.

He liked to tell me tales of the fabulous sea creatures that
lurked around the Scottish coast, creatures like the giant serpent
that dwelled in the cold waters of the Moray Firth. This same
serpent was often seen in Loch Ness, but when truly hungry it
would travel out to sea, sometimes feeding on sailors who were
plucked off their ships when no one was looking, much the way
a fat lady plucked the choicest shrimp off a platter! There was
the fabled Leviathan, the largest of sea creatures, lurking beneath the waves. But his favorite stories by far were tales of the
beautiful mermaids who frolicked off the shoals of Skerryvore.
They were so compelling, he told me, with their lustrous auburn
hair, "very like yours, Miss Sara," and eyes as green as emeralds,
which again, according to Captain MacDonald, were very like
mine. He would go on and on about their beauty, flattering me
shamelessly with, "again, very like yours, Miss Sara," until he
got to the part where the poor sailors, blinded by such beauty
and grace, were lured so close that they drove their ships
aground on the jagged rocks and drowned.

"Captain MacDonald," I'd say teasingly, "if sailors are so foolish as to be blinded by beauty, perhaps they deserve what they get? After all, a sailor's first responsibility is to his ship and crew, not indulging in mythical water-nymphs."

"Och aye! An' dinnae I kennit!" he would exclaim in a thick brogue. "I'm still a sailor, forbye, an' no woman, mermaid or ither, has gotten her hooks in me yet!"

I was pondering sailors and their fascination with mermaids when I cracked open my book, an uninteresting essay on the importance of healthy soil and the proper cycle of crop rotations. I had meant to grab something a bit more to my taste but I didn't want to waste precious time searching for a book I had no intention of reading. I took the little octavo with me and sat beneath a cherry tree, still full of pink blossoms, which had a perfect line-of-sight to my father's office door. It was closed. Someone was already in there with him. Poor soul, I mused, and began educating myself on soil.

It was a real struggle keeping my eyes open; the sun felt so wonderful and warm against my skin, the book so pedantic and vapid, that when combined acted like a powerful sedative. My eyes became unfocused of their own accord and my head was being lulled by gravity. And just when the garden was fading to a blur of soft green and then to blue—ocean blue, as in a dream—the sound of my father's door pulled me back. I continued staring at my page for a moment, gathering my composure, but when I didn't hear the telltale sound of feet retreating to safer quarters, I turned to look.

Perhaps I was dreaming, I remember thinking; for staring directly at me was a vision only the inner-workings of my subconscious could conjure. He was a golden Apollo, with hair of yellow ringlets and eyes the color blue of my half dream, luminous and mischievous. His cheeks, clean-shaven and well defined, were touched with red that seemed to transcend his deep tan . . . and he was not turning away. Our eyes seemed to be locked, as if drawn together by the magnetic force of a compass, he being the arrow and I the force that held it steady. I have no idea how long we stared at each other, so bold, much too bold than was proper. And when his hand finally moved up to remove his cap, a smile playing on his firm, sensuous lips, I had to look away; for my heart was beating so loudly that I feared not only he would hear it, but my father as well.

I would not look at him again, though I knew he was still there looking at me. I felt thrilled that I could captivate such a man, and the thought caused me to smile. That he saw my smile was almost a certainty, but still, I would not look at him. Once was enough. He had made my time in the garden complete. And though I could hope, the odds were not likely that I would ever see him again. I kept my eyes focused on the page before me; hesitantly, he drew away. I followed him down the walkway with my ears, listening as he strode with a jaunty briskness. My self-control crumbled, I was weak, and so I chanced a glance at him once more. My eyes took in the sight of him, savoring his image with the same wonder one looks upon a masterpiece. He wore a plain russet coat that stretched taut over broad shoulders. Worn black breeches clung to the bulging muscles of his legs. His modest attire suggested he was no dandy, nor even a proper gentleman. But what it did reveal, beyond the question of a doubt, was that he was a true Roman god. Only when he disappeared through the garden gate did the breath I had been holding escape my body. It came out as a pathetically wanton sigh. And it was with real sorrow that I closed my book.

The young man in the garden haunted me throughout the day. I couldn't seem to get him out of my mind. It was at night, during dinner, that I finally gathered up enough courage to ask after him. Three gentlemen were dining with us and all four men were discussing business. The youngest among them was invited on my account, a wealthy, prominent man of my family's acquaintance, a Mr. John Graham, who just happened to harbor notions of courting me. I smiled politely every now and again but largely ignored him. My mother, as always, was the good hostess, listening attentively, nodding her approval where needed and keeping the food circulating. Ours may not have been the most interesting table in Edinburgh, but no one could claim that they ever went hungry.

I pushed a piece of dry gristly beef around my plate with my fork, navigating cautiously through the hard peas and mushy boiled potatoes. I had not the stomach to eat, not because the food was bland, which it was, but because the fate of my Roman god was a mystery to me. His image hung in my mind. His voice, which I never had the honor to hear, called to me, talking to me, whispering things in my ear only a lover had the right to say. Yet he continued to plague me, and he was more delightful than Mr. Graham by far. Who was he, I wondered? Why had he come to our home? What was the outcome of his private interview with my father? And then I could bear it no longer. "Papa," I blurted, causing all four gentlemen to stop discussing the famous astronomer Herschel and the proper method of lens grinding long enough to stare at me. Apparently they had all forgotten I existed.

"Yes, Sara?"

"I was just wondering, sir, if you've found a skipper for the yacht yet?"

He leaned toward me, a kind smile on his lean face, and replied, "Indeed I did. And I believe you already know him."

"I . . . I do?" I replied with a like smile, thinking of my young man.

"Aye, Captain MacCrea."

"Captain MacCrea?" I parroted, trying to hide the disparagement in my voice. "But isn't he a bit old for such a voyage? I mean no disrespect, sir, but sailing such a coast requires the utmost vigor, I should think."

"MacCrea's only forty, Sara, and forty's not so old at all. Why, I'd give my left arm tae see forty again!" A resounding "hear,

hear" followed. "MacCrea's a good captain, and you'll be safe aboard with him at the wheel."

"I'm certain I shall, Papa. 'Tis just that he looks so much older," I mused aloud while looking pointedly at Mr. Graham. I then commenced stabbing at the crinkly peas with my fork.

"Well, 'tis true he's no young buck any longer, and the sea does take a toll on a man. Perhaps you'll be happy to know I hired another man to assist him."

I looked up. "Another man? What . . . what other man?" I questioned, trying to sound merely interested and not hopeful.

He thought for a moment, brows drawn together in deep concentration, before coming to some conclusion. "Crichton, I believe the lad said, a Thomas Crichton."

"A new man, Robert?" Mr. Graham politely questioned.

"Aye. Every now and again, John, I make it a practice to give a leg up to an honest fellow of humble station and low birth who might not ordinarily get the chance to better himself. The lad came all the way from the docks of Leith, humbly asked for an interview, conducted himself well, appeared a good Scotch Calvin and was able to recite scripture when asked. And so, being in a benevolent mood, I gave the lad a job on the yacht."

My mother looked admiringly at my father, a good Christian; a friend to humanity. I, however, believed that a man like young Mr. Crichton would do well in the world of his own accord. "Papa." I broke the silence of suspended adulation. "Pray tell, what scripture did Mr. Crichton recite?"

"I believe it was Psalm 107, God the savior of men in distress. He recited it rather prettily too: 'He hushed the storm to a gentle breeze and the billows of the sea were stilled; they rejoiced that they were calmed and he brought them to their desired haven,'" my father mimicked in a deep, resounding voice. "And then he added a passage from Revelation, the one where the sea shall give up her dead and every man shall be judged according to his conduct recorded on the scrolls. It was prettily done, I should say. The man was also well versed in the plight of Jonah."

"Indeed, Papa," I concurred with the general mood of the table, "Mr. Crichton seems a lucky man to have landed such employment." And then I smiled to myself, recalling that every sailor worth his salt, good Calvin or no, would certainly know the codices of the sea—the maxims of the mariner, as it were. Mr. Crichton was not only handsome; he knew the right words to impress the right men.

. . .

The next time I saw Mr. Crichton was dockside. The very moment my foot crossed the threshold between the boarding ramp and the deck of the yacht, he appeared, like a hero's timely entrance in a play, his hand reaching out to take hold of mine. I was shocked at the warmth of his skin and the firmness of his grip. The mere sensation caused a delightful tingle, starting in my hand and racing all the way to my heart. To the casual observer, his was a gesture of deference for a lady traveler, polite and chivalrous. However, those with a sharper, more discerning eye might have picked up on something else, something covert and hidden; something very like animal desire.

It was the second time that our eyes had met. The luminous blue orbs nearly burned into mine, his gaze was so intense, yet I would not look away. I was not in my garden any longer. There was no blossoming cherry tree to shade my modesty; there was no great house to which I could run for shelter. I was a grown woman in the bloom of her youth and beauty, and I would not shy away from the rush of life that I felt. I tightened my grip on his hand as my foot hit the deck and said, "Thank you, Mr. Crichton."

At this mention of his name his eyes widened with shock, and then smoldered with wonder. I couldn't help from smiling at my advantage.

"'Tis my pleasure, Miss Sara Stevenson," he replied softly, letting me know that he too had inquired after my name, before bowing his head. "If there is anything I can do, any way I might serve ye on this voyage, all ye need do is but ask."

"Thank you, Mr. Crichton. I will certainly keep that in mind."

It was my father's authoritative voice that finally broke the spell that had settled over us, pulling both Mr. Crichton and myself back to the present. "Ah, Mr. Crichton," he said, stepping aboard while assisting one of his dignified guests, Mr. Walter Scott, who was not only a member of the Faculty of Advocates in Edinburgh and Sheriff-Deputy of the County of Selkirk, but also a celebrated writer and poet. "I see you've met my daughter, Sara. Be so good as to take Mr. Scott's dunnage below and stow it in the guest cabin next to mine. Take care with the writing desk, lad," he cautioned as a porter handed the cumbrous mahogany piece over. "Mr. Scott will be needing that, as he's told me he's gathering notes on a new novel he's writing."

"A novel, sir?" Mr. Crichton asked, looking upon the man with wonder. For although my father did not read much in the way of poetry or literature, and did not regard those who dabbled in such endeavors very highly at all, apparently the young man did. I too had read some of Mr. Scott's poems, unbeknownst to my parents, and found that I liked them very well.

"Do ye read much, Mr. Crichton?" the author inquired, walking over to the young man. I noticed Mr. Scott had a slight limp, a lameness in his right leg, yet it seemed not to impede him at all. He was a tall, broad man, nearly as tall as the young sailor, and he looked at him not with superiority or condescension, as a man of education often regards the working class, but with real interest twinkling in his intelligent blue eyes.

"Whenever time allows, sir."

"And what is it ye like tae read, lad?"

"Why, sir, I find I like . . ." and words began to form on his lips as his eyes shone with the interest of one who devours books.

But then he must have felt my father's eyes upon him and humbly replied, "Why, sir, only the Bible or the Book of Common Prayer."

"Good man. You could scarce do better than that!" replied the writer, smiling kindly. "But Mr. Crichton, if I might be so bold, may I press ye to take a keek at some pieces I have by me— rough sketches and fragmented thoughts, though they might be? I find it helpful to an author tae have a reader's opinion."

"I'd be honored, sir, truly," he replied shyly, and then turned to attend his duty.

"Mr. Scott, may I be of service as well?" I asked, much to my father's chagrin. At my inquiry I heard Mr. Crichton's footfalls slow to a halt on the hard deck. I looked past Mr. Scott and saw that the golden sailor had paused briefly and then, without turning, he continued on again. Shifting my attention back to the writer, I listened as Mr. Crichton went to the gangway and then took the steps going down, down to the deck below, only to disappear somewhere aft. "I may not possess a vast knowledge of literature, sir," I said, smiling sweetly at my father. "But I am always willing to offer my opinion."

• • •

It turned out that the writer was new to sea-travel, as was I, and took great interest in everything around him. I often sat with him while the other gentlemen were busy with their charts, designs and making great plans for the coast. Whenever Mr. Scott had questions about the curious doings of the sailors, the handling of the sails, the steering of the yacht and so on, Captain MacCrea often obliged him. But when the captain was not available he sent his first mate to be of service. It was in this way that Mr. Crichton and I had cause to be together. Mr. Scott took a genuine liking to the young man, who was always amiable and willing to share his knowledge of his trade. I, for my part, never tired of watching Mr. Crichton go about his duties. Early on in the voyage Mr. Scott picked up on this, and though he was never so crass as to comment on my covert glances at the young mariner, he did contrive to leave us alone. In fact, it was on the second day of the voyage that Mr. Scott called Mr. Crichton over to explain the curious terms of the rigging on the ship.

"Well, sir, Miss Stevenson," he added with a lingering smile, "we happen to be sailing on a small barky, which is a three-masted, square-rigged ship, one of the most complex of all the seagoing vessels." And then, smiling broadly to reveal his star-tling white teeth and mesmerizing blue eyes, he launched into a diatribe of the ship's virtues, in the manner only a man with in-timate knowledge and passion for his craft can. "Those long lines are part of what we call the standing rigging, meaning they don't move about like the running rigging, or at least in theory they shouldn't—unless they get sprung, which is not supposed to happen—and each line, or rope, has a specific name. For example, that long line running from the mast here—what we call the mizzen, as it's the farthest aft—we call that, sir, a mizzen backstay, as it keeps the mizzen from toppling forward, and is counterbalanced by the mizzen stay, over there," he pointed to the line in question. I looked in the direction he indi-cated, pretending interest, when really I was just watching him, marveling at his classical looks, thinking him the model for every magnificent Roman statue and sculpture I had ever seen. "Like I said, every piece of rigging has a specific name," he con-tinued, "depending on the part of the mast she's supporting . . ." And he then proceeded educating us quite thoroughly and with great enthusiasm as he rattled off the names and functions of every tedious little rope and piece of canvas hanging from the massive wooden structure overhead. Mr. Scott seemed perfectly enchanted by Mr. Crichton's descriptions; my interest, rapt and utterly focused, was in reality focused purely on him, not the ship he so beautifully sailed.

"The next one up is called the mizzen topmast shroud. D'ye see?" he said to Mr. Scott and pointed to the sail in question. We were nearing the end, having reached the last mast on the ship already. Although I had no idea what he was saying, I did know that I didn't want him to stop talking. Mr. Crichton gave a brief description of the sail and its purpose, which to me sounded exactly like every other sail, and was about to continue when Mr. Scott kindly broke in, interrupting the young man.

"Mr. Crichton, ye are a wellspring of knowledge, forbye, but I find my landsman's memory will never grasp such a concept without I don't get some paper and a pen to help me. Will ye please keep Miss Stevenson company while I go to my cabin to fetch them?"

"Forgive me, sir," replied Mr. Crichton, blushing slightly. "I didn't mean to run off like that . . . I'm certain ye could have done without the great windy lecture . . . especially you, Miss Stevenson." He looked at me and his fine tanned face turned even darker.

"Nonsense, Mr. Crichton!" proclaimed Mr. Scott. "I'm a man devoted to details. But I'll never remember a word without putting it down. Will ye be kind enough to sit with Miss Stevenson until I return?"

His answer was a heartbreaking smile and the words: " 'Twould be an honor."

It was the first time the two of us were left alone, face-to-face. Certainly there were others about, sailors mostly, attending to some duty or another while a man, not the captain, was at the wheel. Captain MacCrea was belowdeck going over charts in his cabin with the men of the Northern Lighthouse Board, my father included.

Thomas, after so lengthy a lecture—and one delivered with obvious passion—seemed at a loss for words. It was unsettling, yet I too didn't know how to begin, for he was after all a complete stranger. But I would not sit beside him in silence when so many questions—and a real desire to know him better—burned inside of me. In retrospect, I should have given a bit of thought before blurting the first bubbling utterance that came to my lips,

but then again, I was never much of one to think before I
jumped. "So, you only read the Bible, do you?"

This caused him to start. But then, when he saw the look in
my eye, he realized I was calling him out. "Sure if I didn't learn
to read from the Bible. My father saw to that. But alas, I soon
learned that man cannot live on bread alone."

I smiled at that. "No. I suppose that's very true. But if man
needs more than bread for his sustenance, what else might strike
his fancy?"

"What else, Miss Stevenson?" he retorted with a teasing grin.
"Why, Burns of course."

"Burns!" I exclaimed. "But Burns is so . . . so blasphemous!" I
chided, feigning indignation, though knowing full well that I too
devoured him.

"Oh aye, he can be. But he was also brilliant."

"So he was," I concurred, and then in a softer voice I prodded,
"And what else, what else does a man need, Mr. Crichton?"

He leaned in closer, his magnetic gaze locking with mine.
"Well, I find a man also needs Fergusson," he said, indicating an-
other questionable Scottish poet. "And sometimes Pope. Some-
times he seeks out Ramsay, Sheridan, Fielding and Smollett.
But he can never go amiss with poems from Mr. Scott, like
'Marmion' and 'Lady of the Lake.'"

"No, he certainly cannot," I concurred. "So, you are a reader,
Mr. Crichton, though you hide it well enough. But I too must
hide what I choose to read."

"Oh, really? So I take it ye were not reading the Bible the
other day in the garden?" I grew hot at his question and the
mention of that day not so very long ago. "Might I inquire after
what ye *were* reading?"

"I'm not really certain myself what it was, Mr. Crichton, or
who wrote it." He raised his eyebrows at this. I dropped my gaze.
"Oh, very well. It was a treatise on the importance of good soil
and the proper rotation of crops." This admission caused a
hearty chuckle to escape his rather full and wonderful lips.

"Why, that was very scandalous of ye. I now see why ye must hide such things from your father. Do ye, Miss Stevenson, have a hankering to till the soil?"

"Good heavens no!" I replied, and gave a small shiver of disgust. This caused him to smile.

"I see you're passionately against playing in dirt. I find that reassuring in a strange way. But if ye have no interest in soil and crop rotation, why were ye reading it, if you don't mind me asking?"

"I wasn't reading it," I stated honestly. "I only grabbed it because it would have taken too long to search for the one I wanted."

This truthful admission caused a thoughtful look to cross his handsome face. "I find it fascinating that ye sit in your father's wee garden pretending to read a book ye have no interest in reading at all. Tell me, what was it ye wanted?" Although he asked this rather innocently, his eyes were mischievous, belying his gentle question.

"I wanted peace and quiet," I replied, which was not exactly a lie. "If I had found something more to my liking, and my father took a hard look at it, he might have gotten upset. Once he found me reading *The Mysteries of Udolpho*, and he took it from my hands and said that a lady should never fill her head with such drivel—that it was improper, and that it filled the mind with all manner of unsavory thoughts." This caused Mr. Crichton to crack a conspiratorial smile.

"Well, if it's any consolation, my father's cut of the same mold. Once he found me with Burns. I was but ten-and-four, and we were fishing . . . way out to sea. I had bought the little octavo with my own money, saved up for months just to get it, and he took it from me, read the cover and, without so much as a word, tossed it into the sea. He said the only thing Burns was good for was to fuel the fire or feed the fishes. I never forgave him that."

"It sounds like our fathers are very similar men."

At this remark his brows drew together in consternation and

his whole face seemed to darken. "My da is nothing like yours!" he averred. "He's but a lowly fisherman; a man who works his hands raw harvesting whatever the sea chooses to give over. Your da is one of Scotland's greatest engineers. He's a great man, Miss Stevenson. And men like him make men like me."

"I think, perhaps, you overestimate my father," I said softly, looking at my gloved hands in my lap.

"Did he no' put the lighthouse on the Bell?" he stated. We had just visited the Bell, took a tour of it the day before. I looked into his face—a face that was better suited to a prince than a lowly fisherman's son—and saw there a desire that I seldom saw on any man. It was raw determination. It was the desire to rise above one's station in life. "The Bell's saved many a mariner, Miss Stevenson. Your father is to thank for that. And ye, Miss Sara Stevenson," he whispered, captivating me by using my Christian name. "Ye, lass, are not only beautiful, but very lucky indeed."

I could not speak, but it was just as well. A bell rang out and Mr. Thomas Crichton, performing a polite bow, turned to go.

"Why, Miss Stevenson," said the writer, appearing as if from nowhere to take his seat beside me. His eyes were fixed on the retreating back of the young mariner, and a curious expression transformed his face. "A sailor's life is governed by bells, I find, more's the pity," he stated rather wistfully before turning his attention to me. "Are ye all right, lass?" A bemused sort of concern seemed to overtake his sprightly features. "Perhaps ye should go below and take a wee rest, aye? Why, bless me, but your cheeks are as red as a rose in bloom!"

. . .

My voyage on the yacht with the men from the Northern Lighthouse Board was as full of wonder and excitement as any journey I could have ever imagined. The Scottish coast was wild, majestic and magnificent. The waters were gentle and the weather mild. I was surfeit with interesting conversation, good food and fresh air. My new friend Mr. Scott was entertaining, delightful and cunning, while my father kept busy being important and industrious. He still had plenty of time to govern me, as a good father governs a dutiful daughter, but his days were long and tiresome, making him a sound sleeper at night. Mr. Crichton assisted the captain for a good part of the day, conducting the business of sailing by relaying the captain's orders for the adjustment of sail, taking soundings, going over charts and taking a turn at the wheel. He was kept very busy, but always had a warm smile and kind word for me. Sometimes he would find time to join Mr. Scott and me as we sat on deck discussing books, authors and works we admired. It was during one of these discussions that Mr. Scott inquired where it was that Mr. Crichton got off to, disappearing just after supper?

"Why, I sleep, sir," he replied very matter-of-factly.

"Sure if all the running about and climbing ye do, combined with this fresh sea air, works like a soporific on your constitution! Why, bless you, Mr. Crichton. There's nothing like a good night's sleep to set a man up!"

Mr. Crichton smiled kindly at the writer, giving the man a dazzling white-toothed grin. "I don't sleep because I want to, sir. I sleep on account I've the middle watch."

"Middle watch? Whatever is that, Mr. Crichton, and why would it cause one to drop off directly after supper?"

Here Mr. Crichton chuckled at the writer's candid questioning. "Forgive me, Mr. Scott, but having the middle watch simply means I've command of the ship between the hours of midnight and four in the morning. If I don't catch some sleep whilst I can, it makes for a long, long night." And as he said these last words his eyes met mine.

"How . . . how do ye stay awake?" I asked, processing this new bit of information.

"Any way I can, Miss Stevenson, any way I can."

. . .

As fate would have it, it was always half-past midnight that I found it hardest to sleep. I tried to tell myself that this punctual insomnia was not brought about because of the knowledge that Mr. Crichton was on deck . . . alone. But instead I was nearly convinced it was due to my overactive imagination. I would lie awake for hours in my little bunk, conjuring up images of what sea creatures might be lurking beneath the ship, a mere two-inch plank separating me from the Leviathan. I'd strain to hear cries from the ship's crew—or perhaps, perhaps I was listening for a deep, melodic voice giving an order somewhere above me. Either way, sleep had a way of evading me.

The first time I actually sought solace on deck, beneath the star-filled sky, was just after our stop at Cape Wrath. It was there the gentlemen toured for the first time the lighthouse. Cape Wrath was one of the most remote locations, with a history of maritime disaster. After inspecting the grounds and light-room, the keepers, Mr. Willy Campbell and Mr. Alasdair Duffy, told us of the local population. According to Mr. Campbell the region had suffered greatly during the last century's clearances, forcing many a farmer off the land to make way for the sheep industry. The poor dirt-farming locals and kelp harvesters had made a healthy practice of supplementing their meager incomes with the spoils washed up from the many wrecks that occurred yearly. The lighthouse, with its intruding bright yellow beam, was the first step in preserving these ships, yet the locals hadn't taken its presence very kindly. It interfered with their livelihood, Mr. Campbell had told the Board, dead men be damned!

It was his description of these creatures, the human scavengers picking through the bloated, lifeless bodies that washed ashore, that haunted me. I could scarcely get them and their grubby, kelp-stained hands out of my head as I tried to sleep on my tiny, undulating bunk, and so, I decided that a stroll on deck was the very thing to soothe my nightmares. No one heard me slip from my cabin; no one saw me as I melded into the dark passageway, swaddled in a black boat-cloak. And certainly no one would have ever dreamed that the daughter of Edinburgh's brightest civil engineer would blacken her father's name by consorting in the dark of night with a poor sailor, right under his very nose. I don't know what I was thinking that first night I went on deck, but I did know that if anybody could quell my nightmares it would be Thomas Crichton.

I saw him standing at the helm, his face illuminated by the soft glow of the binnacle lamp as he bent to study the compass. He looked more the golden-haired god than ever before; strands of his sun-bleached hair had escaped his queue and now framed his chiseled face. The breath caught in my throat, and so, unable to speak, I just stood and watched him for a moment. He seemed to sense my presence. Before I ever took a step forward or spoke a word, he turned to me. It took his eyes a while to focus in the blackness beyond the lamp, for he squinted and fought to discern who the dark shadow was. But then, I believe he already knew, for he said very softly, "Miss Stevenson?"

"Aye, 'tis me," I replied in a like voice, and stepped from the darkness into the soft light cast by the binnacle lamp.

"Whatever are ye doing here, lass, out of bed?" he inquired, though there was no hint of surprise in his voice. He softly excused himself from the man at the wheel, and came forward. We were not alone. There were a few other sailors on deck, but they all seemed to have a polite, though tacit, understanding of the special relationship I shared with Mr. Crichton. None came forward but he.

"I can't sleep," I began to explain.

"Neither can I. And if on the off chance I did, Captain MacCrea would string me up by my thumbs, he would!" This caused me to giggle slightly, while he merely smiled.

"Mr. Crichton, please forgive me," I said, attempting to rein in my racing nerves while straining to absorb every minute essence of him. He was very close to me, so close I could smell his earthy muskiness. He smelled of the sun, and the sea, and the wild westerly wind. There was just a tang of sweet watered rum on his breath, and I was sorry to think that I wanted a taste of him. I longed for a taste of him. Dear God, but I was a hopeless wanton! "I should not be here," I uttered by way of apology, my distress at being so close to him rising by the second. "I don't know what I was thinking."

"Aye, but ye should be here," he whispered. I could taste his sweet breath. "Ye should, Miss Stevenson, for there's nothing like the star-filled sky to soothe one's mind. Look," he said, gesturing to the billion sparkles of light overhead. "Have ye ever seen anything so grand?" It was a rare uncommon night. It was a night where dreams are made and then realized. "Come," he commanded. "I shall give ye a better view."

"Mr. Crichton, I really should not," I protested as he took hold of my hand and began leading me forward. We were heading toward the bow of the ship, away from the helm; away from people.

He turned to me and smiled. "Please, call me Thomas."

"I . . . I really should not," I protested again, letting him lead me like a needy little lapdog.

"Aye, but ye should," he insisted, "though only when we're alone. And may I beg the same favor from ye?" He paused and turned to look at me. "May I, Miss Stevenson, call ye Sara?"

Stunned by this intimate request, all I could do was nod, while secretly wishing I could hear my name on his lips a million times more. In response to my consent he flashed a resolve-melting smile, causing me to blurt rather suddenly, "But are we . . . are we to be alone very often, Thomas?"

"Only if ye wish it. And I must be honest, Sara, I have wished for this moment ever since I saw ye that day in the garden."

"You wished I'd have a nightmare and come on deck?"

"Never!" he averred, taking my face between his warm hands. "I would never wish for an angel to have a distressing thought.

And ye, Sara, are an angel. You are my angel." His words were as sincere as the solemn look on his face. "I only wished that ye would find some way to come to me, without the watchful eye of your father, or the kindly presence of Mr. Scott, to intervene. I wanted to see ye alone so that I might tell ye that ever since that day I first saw you, I have no' been able to get ye out of my mind. I know I should not ask it. I know ye are likely bespoken for already. And I know a woman like you deserves so much more than a man like me could ever give, but I will say it because I am not a coward. I love ye, Sara Stevenson."

"Oh Thomas," I uttered, pulling away from his tight grip; for his words were as shocking for me to hear as they were for him to admit. "Thomas Crichton, what are you doing?"

"I'm digging my grave, I am," he quipped with a roguish grin.

I shook my head, attempting to clear the tumultuous surge of thought and emotion. "Let's just say . . ." I began at last. "Let's just say, for the sake of this argument, that I too feel the same about you. You know that my father would never agree to such a thing."

"Aye. I believe I've surmised that much about the man. As Captain MacCrea keeps reminding me, I'm but a goat turd to Mr. Stevenson . . . no more than insignificant muck accidentally stepped in and easily kicked aside."

"Captain MacCrea says that to you?" I was shocked. And then I grew a little indignant by this treatment of the man that, although I would deny it, I knew that I loved.

"Oh aye. He's an observant sort, is Captain MacCrea. He may appear daft as a loon and three sheets to the wind on occasion, but the man is no fool. He knows what's going on between us and he's warned me to lay off. Says no good can come of it. Perhaps 'tis true. But I'm also a man willing to take a risk for what he believes in. And I believe in ye, Sara Stevenson."

"Dear Thomas," I said, daring to touch the warm skin of his face, marveling at his rugged beauty. "I'm afraid Captain MacCrea is right. He knows my father well. My father is successful at what he does because he bends men to his will. And those who will not bend, he replaces. I do care for you, Thomas Crichton, more so than any other man I've ever met, and that's why I'm telling you, it could never be."

"Fair enough," he replied, covering my hand with his, yet his words held no conviction. My heart was pounding with frustration and desire as he pressed my palm to his smooth, warm cheek. He held it there, daring me to pull it away. And when he saw that I would not, he slowly brought my fingers to his lips, overwhelming me with chaste kisses of daunting passion. "If ye honestly believe that obedience surpasses true God-given happiness, then I will acquiesce. All I ask is that ye think on it, and that from time to time ye allow me to chase away your nightmares."

Alive with desire yet speechless from an awakening I had never before known, I nodded helplessly.

"Now, then," he spoke calmly, shifting my attention to the moon-kissed waves beneath the star-strewn sky. "Do ye know the story of Orion?"

I shook my head as he gently turned me toward the rail. He was standing behind me and bent low to whisper in my ear, "He's just over there." He pointed to the sky, indicating the stars in question, but my eyes were closed, reveling in the feel of his warm breath against my cheek. It was then a soft moan escaped my lips. He slipped his arms around my waist and held me tightly to his hard body. I covered his hands with my own, afraid to let him go. "Do ye see the giant hunter, lass? Close your eyes and picture him, and I shall tell you the story of the poor mortal Orion, and of the beautiful goddess Diana, who loved him."

. . .

Since that night many, many months ago, I have often recalled the story of Orion. I cannot help but think of it and of Thomas whenever the giant hunter appears. Sometimes I gaze upon his brilliant stars with the same bittersweetness with which the story was told to me. Other times his image inspires hatred. Yet more often than not, Orion sparks in me a longing so fierce that I have to turn away, and it is those times I think of Diana and how she wept for her lover—wept for him and for what she had done.

# FOUR

## For Pride's Sake

$\mathcal{I}$t started one month after my arrival on the Cape. At first I was able to sleep; in fact, I slept like a baby, for I felt so tired all the time. I was still getting used to my new surroundings, the weather had turned very harsh and I was encumbered with so many domestic responsibilities that I felt exhausted the entire first month. And so I had slept. But all too soon it came back to me, and once again I found it hard to sleep at night knowing he was out there . . . somewhere.

The first night that I had heard the tolling of the bell I awoke with a start, thinking I was on the ship again. It was the same bell, calling out in that familiar ding-ding, ding-ding. It was not a loud bell, not like a warning call with its fervent pounding of ding-ding-ding-ding-ding, or even the constant, steady, far-reaching din of the fog bell with its resounding dong . . . dong . . . dong . . . dong. No, the bell that awoke me sounded off at midnight in the same manner as the bell on the ship, signaling the changing of the watch with a little ding-ding, ding-ding, followed by silence. And in this silence I waited anxiously for

Thomas to appear. I sat up in bed, staring at the blackness of my room, trying to remember where I was. I had been dreaming of him again, dreaming it had all been a mistake—a terrible misunderstanding that was now resolved. He was coming for me. I knew that he was, for he had whispered the words in my ear. And so I sat up in bed waiting for the sound of his footsteps. Excitement coursed through me; I was awash with bliss, and when I heard his approach my heart quickened. It was faint at first, sounding far-off as if in a dream, yet it was undeniable that he was drawing nearer. And I sat up a little straighter, eyes fixed to the door, awaiting him.

The footsteps came closer, each one hitting the wood with a purposeful stride. There was confidence there. Thomas, if he was anything, had always been confident, I thought, and my heart began to quicken in anticipation. But as the footfalls drew closer to my door the confidence of his stride seemed to dwindle and I could feel his hesitation and uncertainty. "Come," I beckoned in a breathy whisper, clasping my hands together as if in prayer. "Come, my love, I am ready." And to my astonishment, come they did, stopping just on the other side of my door. I peered into the darkness and saw the soft glow of his lantern seeping through the hairsbreadth of space. It drew my attention like a beacon. He was close now, so close I could feel him. Desire and longing consumed me, and without another thought I slipped out of bed and ran to him.

I flung open the door, ready to launch myself into his waiting arms, when the lantern revealed the horrific trick my mind had played on me. It was momentum, combined with sleep-induced stupidity, that carried me into him when my mind screamed to the contrary. Fear-struck and with heart pounding like a deranged smith attacking his anvil with an oversized mallet, I found myself in the arms of Mr. Campbell, not Thomas Crichton! Still unable to speak, my eyes took in the sight of him—the dark tousled hair, the black, three-caped cloak emitting the faintest scent of pipe smoke and cold night air—but it was his eyes, those odd, mesmerizing pale orbs that seemed to glow from the depths of his shadowed face, that caused real panic to consume me.

At first he was merely startled, like me, for he had hardly expected the greeting I gave him. And then, to my astonishment, he smiled. But when I began to scream from the rank shock of it, he became confused. And then anger took him.

Of course screaming in the dead of night was unwise, but I couldn't help myself. I was terrified. The thought that perhaps I was being irrational did flash through my mind, for Mr. Campbell, besides being aloof, distant and at times rather harsh with me, had, for the most part, kept to himself for the last month. Since our arrival on the Cape Mr. Campbell had been slowly coaxed into something resembling humanity. It was a precarious transition, like making a pet out of an ill-used cart horse, a task to be approached gingerly and with caution. And though he was used to our presence by now, having been forced to live under the same roof with us, he was nothing like tame, no more familiar to me than he had been on that inauspicious first day. Never willingly would he come to the fence; he disclosed little about himself, always evading polite conversation and ignoring any direct questions that might delve deeper into his person than his working title of principal light-keeper. Had I not learned for myself his dark secret I might have regarded him as merely caustic and unsociable. But fortunately I knew better, and what I knew about Mr. Campbell had never left me.

He was always there to remind me . . . staring at me with those odd pale eyes.

Now, unavoidably, plagued by the harsh weather, shut in together on an inhospitable coast and forced to eat Kate's stomach-churning, barely edible meals, the man had indeed cracked. I knew it would happen. Human beings can only take so much. Cape Wrath was enough to try the most patient of saints, let alone a reclusive light-keeper with a taste for the dead and naked. And it was just after the tolling of the midnight bell that Mr. Campbell had finally snapped.

His eyes darkened and he tightened his grip on me, shaking me and hissing for me to be quiet.

But I kept screaming.

He set down his lantern and brought his hand over my mouth, pushing me inside the bedroom, where he shut the door behind us. And while holding me in his viselike grip as he pressed my body firmly between his and the door, he demanded that I be quiet.

"Hush now! For God's sake, lass, be quiet or you'll wake Mrs. MacKinnon!" Indeed that was my intent, and I tried to bite the palm of his hand. "Jesus Christ!" he swore when I had managed to nip him. And then he pressed harder, covering my nose as well, attempting to take the breath from me. It was working. As I struggled against his surprisingly strong, hard body, wriggling and kicking to break free, my head began to grow light from the lack of air. He leaned close to my ear and whispered again, "I beg ye, calm yourself, lass."

I really had little choice in the matter, for I could not breathe, nor could I fight against such strength. And so, helpless against him, and threatening to lose consciousness, I nodded my consent.

"All right, very good. I'm going to let go now and you're going to be quiet. Aye?" He was breathing very heavily, pressing his body firmly against mine, and then slowly, very gingerly, he removed his hand from my mouth.

"Please," I uttered, gasping for breath. "Please, Mr. Campbell, do not kill me. I'll do as you wish. I swear it. But I beg you, let me—"

"What in God's name are ye talking about?" He cast me a dark, confused glance. "May I remind ye that it was you who jumped out at me and no' the other way around?"

This, of course, was true. "Well . . . well, what were you doing

outside my door?" I demanded, slightly confused and fully indignant.

He paused. I could see this question bothered him. "I . . ." he
began, then halted. It was his turn to come clean and I took a
small pleasure in the fact that he did not like answering my direct question. "I was . . ." he continued, then paused again. He
stared at me, his unsettling pale eyes willing me to back down
and look away, but I would not. I stared right back, indignation
emboldening me, and I could see he did not like that. "I was on
my way to my room!" he finally said, visibly irked that he was
made to answer. "I thought I should sleep before I was called out
again."

"Your room?" I replied skeptically.

"Aye," he replied bitterly. "Ye'll know it. 'Tis just down there,
at the end of the hall."

Indeed it was, and it was the only room in the entire cottage
I was forbidden to enter. "Yes, yes, I know where your room is.
But you stopped outside my door, Mr. Campbell. Why did you
stop?"

He looked a little ashamed by this, because it was true. "I
thought," he mumbled, unable to look me in the eye. "I thought
ye might be awake. I heard ye . . . I know sometimes that ye read
at night." I looked at him, not comprehending what he was saying and waited for him to elaborate on this roundabout explanation. "Well, I wanted . . ." He paused. "I just thought I should
apologize to ye. I believe . . . it comes to my attention that I may
have been a little hard on ye this evening during supper." I
cocked my head and stared at him in disbelief. "I never meant to
belittle your efforts . . . What I mean is . . ." And then his tone
hardened, his pale eyes darkened and he continued. "I expect ye
to understand, Miss Stevenson, that we must ration our supplies
up here. The coast is dangerous this time of year; storms flare
up, making the weather too risky for the supply tender to come
out. We cannot depend on it. And if we run low on food, we'll

have to go without. We cannot just run down the lane to fetch a pound of flour or a pinch of salt on a whim. There are no markets or shops to be had here."

It was then I realized what Mr. Campbell was doing. He had been caught red-handed lingering outside my door. He might have made a habit of it, lingering about as I slept, entertaining all manner of insalubrious thoughts, but tonight I had caught him. And now he was ashamed. To cover for his debased behavior he would have me believe he had come to apologize for his rank bad manners. Yet Mr. Campbell was often rude, habitually rank, and now he expected me to believe he had come to apologize for his unseemly tirade at dinner? It all started because I had been unable to bear any more of Kate's unorthodox cooking and had nobly volunteered to make the evening meal myself. Having no idea what I was about, I failed spectacularly on my first attempt at a stew, burning our allotted ration of stringy mutton. To cover the mistake I added flour and water, and only succeeded in creating a stringy, grayish, gelatinous, tasteless sludge that was not fit for man or beast, and so I threw it, along with a burnt, lumpish, doughy breadlike substance, onto the dung heap and tried again—the second time with a wee bit more success. When Mr. Campbell realized that some of his precious stores had gone missing, and later learned what I had done with them, he become furious with me for throwing out the first supper, declaring that all kitchen stores were meant to be eaten, no matter what form they may take. He had lit into me then like a Dutch uncle, going on and on about my flagrant ways, my devil-may-care attitude and my flippant behavior, until finally, unable to bear his choler any longer, I got up and left the room. And he was doing it again—now—in the dead of night!

"Are you serious?" I questioned when he had finished his pathetic apology.

"What d'ye mean, am I serious?" he rejoined, growing a little chuff. "Am I serious about our survival? Am I serious about the running of this lighthouse? You seem to think it all a great game, carrying on about all your scented soaps and your wee soothing rosewater baths, your three-hour teas with your fancy friends and the fine shops you once frequented. Ye take a stab at the cooking and when it doesn't meet with your high and mighty approval ye toss it away without a care or thought to anyone but yourself!"

"On the contrary," I corrected, my anger matching his. "It was precisely because I think of others that I threw that chamber-pot carnage away!"

His eyes, now appearing dark in the scant light, scanned my face. And then his gaze dropped to my neck, coming to rest just below the top of my nightdress, where the tie had come undone. His gaze lingered. I was conscious that I was breathing heavily, riled by indignation, and suddenly, under his unflinching gaze, I felt very vulnerable. I fought the urge to cover myself, steeling my nerves, attempting to show no weakness. And then he spoke very softly.

"It takes a bit more to survive up here than money. You're not in Edinburgh any longer, Miss Stevenson."

I cleared my throat, hoping to draw his attention a bit higher than my exposed, heaving bosom. "For your information," I began, summoning a well-practiced haughty air, "I have never once complained out loud about the very real lack of decent ne-cessities up here. I'm not the selfish, spoiled young lady you seem to think I am. But what I am, Mr. Campbell, is proud, and my pride absolutely forbade me to serve that meal!"

"There are some forms of pride I find very admirable in women, Miss Stevenson, but self-indulgent pride is no' one of them," he whispered very closely, so close I could smell the cof-fee and sweet tobacco on his breath.

Bristling with indignation, and a strong distaste for coffee, I pushed him away. "I don't really care what you find admirable in women, Mr. Campbell, and what I meant when I asked if you were serious was, did you seriously come here, standing at my door in the middle of the night, to berate me for my ineptitude, my unbecoming ways and my flagrant misuse of lighthouse supplies?"

He paused, breathing heavily, his dark face suddenly looking confused and tormented. "No. That was not my intent."

"Good, because to be brutally honest with you, I would have rather you'd just come to kill me and be done with it. It may have not gone so well for either of us, but I assure you, I would at least have respected the effort a whole lot more than a churlish lecture!"

"Kill you?" he breathed, looking truly wounded. "Kill you." And then he added haltingly, "I pray, for your sake, it doesnae come to that."

I was still breathing heavily when he left my room. I leaned against the door, fighting to catch my breath, for I felt as if I had just run the gauntlet—uphill and against a headwind. Whether it was fear, anger or something darker that stirred me so, I knew not. All I did know, for a certainty, was that try as I might, sleep would not come.

. . .

I'd be lying if I said I wasn't angry with Mr. Campbell, because I was, and I had just cause. His words, delivered in the dark of night and under the guise of an apology, were irritating and hurtful. It wasn't that I even cared what the man thought of me; for he was indeed an odd creature, straddling an unforeseen chasm between civility and savagery, with often that look in his pale eyes warning me that he could flip at any moment. And although I should have taken the warning—as logic would dictate—I now was utterly convinced that I was bereft of all logic, and instead of being scared witless into submission by what I knew lay under the seemingly tame exterior, my self-indulgent pride (as Mr. Campbell had called it) rallied against all higher thought and reason. The man had insulted me, and no man, prince or pauper, had that right. Damn Mr. Campbell for his insolence! Damn me for my pride! And as I lay awake at night picturing him in his tower, poring over books so distastefully horrific and execrable, I listened for the bell. And then I waited. I waited for the sound of his footsteps, willing them to pass me by. Sometimes they would; other times they were hesitant, as if he toyed with the notion of assaulting me again. When this happened I would sit up in bed and hold my breath, praying that he would walk away. And when I heard him retreat to his own quarters farther down the hall, only then would I allow myself to fall asleep. But my dreams of Thomas Crichton, the man I loved, began to fade, only to be replaced by more disturbing dreams—nightmares of a light-keeper with haunting, pale bluish-green eyes.

For all that Mr. Campbell was a mystery to me, plying me with covert looks when he thought I was not looking and unconcealed disapproval when he knew that I was, I became filled with the desire—merely for the sake of my contumelious pride—to prove him wrong about me. And while I worked hard to illustrate that I could survive on Cape Wrath, I also sought to find fault with him. I wanted to pick and chisel away at the man, exposing his weakness, yet unfortunately all I discovered, aside from his dark secret, was a dauntless, tireless worker. Begrudgingly I was forced to admit that he was a rather commendable light-keeper. Nothing was wasted under his watch, not fuel, not food nor even something as inane as soap. And although such pinchbeck staunchness annoyed me greatly, I had to admit that I rather admired his particular kind of fortitude, for it took a great amount of self-control to be so thrifty.

In the morning, after sitting the last shift of the night, Mr. Campbell would come to the cottage, stoke up the fires with just the right amount of peat and then head back outdoors to draw the morning water. He'd return to hang a pot over the fire to boil, warm up his hands, and once he saw to it that Kate and I were beginning to stir, without so much as a "good morning" he'd turn around and go right back outside to tend to the animals in the stable. It wasn't until Robbie awoke that Mr. Campbell would venture inside again, bearing another armload of peat. With all souls awake and about, the men would then sit down to breakfast and eat Kate's watery oat porridge without a hint of protest. How they stomached it, day after day, was a mystery. Yet not to be outdone by this stoicism, I too learned to hold my tongue, and one blustery cold morning in January I even found myself proclaiming that the porridge was the best I had ever eaten. Of course this was a blatant lie. Yet noting how this statement shocked my companions, I affected a blissful smile and attempted another spoonful, most of which dribbled off the shallow utensil before ever reaching my mouth. Both men just stared at me with mouths agape. Kate merely crossed her arms on her chest, looking perturbed.

"No, really, I find it just the thing to set one up. In fact, after I finish this lovely tea," I said, looking into the chipped cup that contained a tepid liquid resembling dirty bathwater more than a hot, sustaining drink, "I'll be ready to face another of God's glorious January days! Can anything be finer than all this snow and ice?"

Mr. Campbell slowly set down his cup, having already drained the dregs, and stared at me from across the table with disbelief. "Miss Stevenson, although I'm glad to see you've finally come to accept your new home, I must admit, I find your cheerfulness offensive."

"Offensive?" I questioned, and smiled brighter, attempting the exact opposite posture as the light-keeper. "I'm sorry, sir, but I do not understand. How could my happiness at being here possibly offend you?"

"First, because it's not real. And second, had ye bothered to look outside this morning you'd have seen that a storm has blown in, and with it—with all the snow and ice that seems to amuse ye so—comes great responsibility. The light still needs to burn. The road to the jetty needs to be cleared, and any ship that's caught unawares today will have a fight on its hands. That, Miss Stevenson, is no reason for cheer."

I lowered my head, feigning shame, and peered up at him through my lashes. "Forgive me, Mr. Campbell. I never meant to offend you. But I beg to differ, sir." His eyes were boring into mine—trying, no doubt, to detect my sincerity. I had to turn away. "No one can deny that you work very hard, and for that we are all grateful. But I do think you have a very real absence of cheer. There's none in you. You're totally void of it. Perhaps if you smiled more . . ."

"You mock me!" he stated defensively.

"I would never," I countered, challenging him. "It's just that you're so serious all the time. I thought . . . perhaps if you—"

"You're not here to think, Miss Stevenson!" he averred, slamming down his cup. "'Tis my job, like it or not, and I'll thank ye to remember it. I never asked ye to come here, just as ye never intended to be here, but here ye are, and we both must bear it as best as we can . . . and I'll thank ye to do it without mocking me or using me for your own wee sport!"

"Forgive me, but how can one mock something one has no understanding of? And sport? I'm not that desperate! The mere accusation is execrable!"

"Execrable? I find your behavior to be execrable, not my accusation."

"Oh, that's coming it a bit high, even from a reprobate like you." I threw down my napkin.

"I may, in fact, be a reprobate, but perhaps I'm not the only one here."

"Mr. Campbell!" It was Kate, coming to my aid for the first time since we arrived on this godforsaken coast. "We're all a bit tired of being cooped up together in this wee cottage, and perhaps you are being a bit hard on Miss Sara. I don't believe that angering you was her intent at all. Miss Sara is a woman of very high spirits. And you must remember, sir, she's been through a great deal in the past few months, and she *is* trying. Perhaps not by your standards, but you must bear it in mind that she's a lady born and bred, and to her credit, she's done more here in the past two months than she was ever wont to do at home in her entire life!"

This statement, delivered with passion and good intent, was not flattering by any means; but it was true enough. And I *was* trying. I may not have owned the skills required for the job I took, but at least I went about them with a willingness to learn and a decent amount of humor. And I was attempting to understand the light-keeper, who kept us all in the dark.

"I'm well aware that Miss Stevenson's a lady," he replied softly, in a voice void of all emotion. "Just as I know that Cape Wrath is no place for her kind."

"For my kind? Whatever is that supposed to mean?"

Ignoring the looks from our companions, Mr. Campbell stood and replied, "I believe ye know very well what that means." And then, as if unable to bear our company any longer, he excused himself from the table, beckoning for Robbie to follow. "Come, Mr. MacKinnon, we've plenty of work to do." And with one last look behind, both men headed off for their duties at the lighthouse.

"Heavens save us, but I don't understand it! Whatever has gotten under that man's skin? Why . . ." Kate paused, her large brown eyes turning on me with naked question, "he's usually very pleasant, kind even . . . until you show up."

I cast her a reassuring smile and sat back in my chair. "I'm afraid that what troubles Mr. Campbell is very simple, Kate; he's a classic misogynist—the man doesn't like women."

"Doesn't like women?" She leaned across the table, peering at me with her wide brown eyes. "Just what are ye suggesting?"

"I'm suggesting nothing," I replied, and shifted my attention to the window, where I could better watch the men stomp through the snow on their way to the tower. "I'm simply stating a fact. That man has it out for me, and perhaps women in general. You're lucky." I looked back to her. "You're properly wed and under the protection of Mr. MacKinnon, a fine, upstanding gentleman in his own right, but I'm not and Mr. Campbell is well aware of it. Some men don't take kindly to women like me."

"I think you misjudge the man. I think," she continued, apparently going to tell me what she thought regardless of whether or not I wanted to hear it, "that you made a muckle mess of it from the get-go and now you are too bloody stubborn to apologize."

"Too bloody stubborn? Did I not just tell the man a few moments ago that I was sorry?"

"You were toying with him, Sara! Toying with him like a cat toys with a mouse. Men don't like to be toyed with."

"Well, if you think so, perhaps I was," I demurred, pushing my bowl away, unable to stomach the weak porridge any longer. "But I assure you, Kate, that man is no mouse."

. . .

I was rather grateful that there was so much work to do, because the men were kept plenty busy. While we cleaned up after breakfast and the men were off tending the lighthouse—measuring out the oil needed for the next lighting, placing it into buckets and then lugging it up the many steps to the great lantern— I was silently mulling over a plan. Both Robbie and Mr. Campbell would be a while yet up in the light-room, keeping the mechanism in perfect working order, for Mr. Campbell took his responsibilities very seriously. The great lens needed cleaning, the wicks would be trimmed and the reflectors would be polished to a shining brilliance, or so Robbie had told us, for neither Kate nor I dared venture up the tower uninvited. Supplies were also carefully monitored and then the logbooks were gone over, transferring the information from the night before into another book, which would be sent to the engineer at the end of the month. And when the men were done with their morning duties they often took a nap. Today, however, there would be no nap, for they would be out clearing the road to the jetty, attacking it with both plow and shovel. And while the men were toiling behind the one horse needed for the task, I had it in mind to take the other out for a long overdue ride.

It came to my attention that we were not entirely alone on the Cape. Cape Wrath was indeed desolate and inhospitable where weather was concerned, but there were a few hearty families that lived on this side of the Kyle of Durness, or so Mr. Campbell had told us one night—that body of water that stood between the village of Durness (the nearest outpost of civilization) and our windswept cape. We had neighbors and I was anxious to see other faces and hear other voices than just the three I was forced upon. I knew Mr. Campbell would never abide my using one of the lighthouse horses for my own pleasure, but he need never know. I had been on the Cape for over two months and still had no word from my family, friends—or civilization in general. I felt closed in, never more so in my entire life, and I was growing restless and fractious. An opportunity to venture beyond the lighthouse boundaries had shown itself and, damn me, I was not one to let such an opportunity go by.

It was indeed a glorious January day, in spite of what Mr. Campbell thought. Certainly it was cold, and a storm might be brewing out in the Atlantic, but from all accounts it wasn't a bad one. The snow was a refreshing change from the freezing rain of early December and it was falling in large, delicate flakes. There was a slight wind, to be sure, but there was always wind blowing about our barren little outcrop. Besides, I could tell it wasn't a great amount of wind because the snow was falling straight down, making a perfect blanket. And a blanket of white against a landscape of white was just the thing to conceal my departure . . . mine and Kate's.

The men had barely made it to the road before we slipped into the stable and saddled Wallace, the lucky one. Unlike his partner, Bruce, he had escaped the plow and was happily munching on his allotment of oats . . . until we came and employed him on another task.

"Are you certain we should be doing this?" Kate questioned, her face pinched and looking nervous as I pulled her up behind me.

"Very," I replied. "'Tis a perfect day for it too. Why, the ground's soft, the wind's fair and we're on an important mission."

"Aye," she agreed begrudgingly. It took a little effort on my part to coax Wallace out of his warm stable and into the snow, but he was an obedient creature. And as we slowly made our way into the courtyard, Kate bent forward and said loudly in my ear, so as to be heard above the mild wind, "I should really tell Robbie where we're going."

Kate was always saying things like that—"I should tell Rob," or "I should let Robbie know about that," or the dreaded "Robbie would be most interested to hear it!"—and I found it very weak-minded of her, not to mention annoying. Because Kate was a married woman, it appeared she had no mind of her own anymore, and that disturbed me. Was it normal? Could not my own mother make a decision without my father's approval? No. Apparently not. And so, being the only independent thinker amongst the three of us, I yelled back, "No, you should not tell Robbie. This is to be a surprise, Kate, and you cannot surprise someone if you tell them everything."

"But should we even be out on a day like today? Maybe we should wait until the weather turns milder?"

"Wait for milder weather?" I questioned, turning my head to better look at her. "Sure, and we'd be waiting until June with that attitude, and even then my guess is that the summer storms will start to blow in, and we'll have to wait some more. No. I believe today is our day. We have to get used to this weather sometime, Kate. We cannot be afraid of it; this is our home now." And although there was logic in that statement somewhere, apparently it was lost on both my companions.

"I'm not so sure. I think we should wait." I pulled Wallace to a stop and I turned to look at her again. "If you want to stay here, that's fine with me. But I, for one, believe it's important. There are homesteads out here where women not only raise their children and care for their husbands, but also do all that's necessary for their survival. We're in the Highlands, Kate. These people are hearty and ingenious! You and I can barely manage the wee cottage, but these people have learned to survive and thrive here against all odds. I think we could learn a little something from them."

Perhaps it was wrong of me, but I had convinced Kate that we were on a mission to better our domestic skills. There was some truth in it, for I was now driven by the insatiable need to appear capable in front of Mr. Campbell, merely to prove the man wrong about me. But the real reason I had saddled the horse and sought to brave the elements was driven equally by a mixture of boredom and curiosity; for who would choose to live in this wild, desolate place, and why?

Kate was quiet behind me, no doubt weighing the advantages and disadvantages of our mission. And while she silently mulled over my words, I dug my knees into Wallace, clicked twice and the big bay gelding obediently trudged ahead.

I knew there to be a croft house about two miles beyond the jetty, at a place called Kervaig Bay. There, apparently, sat the dwelling of our closest neighbor, Mr. Campbell had told us, and the family went by the name of MacKay. He apparently knew the man, but he seldom talked of the locals. People, I noticed, didn't make a habit of coming to visit the lighthouse keeper. He alluded that there might be a wife and children there as well, but he had said no more on the subject, only that there were a few crofts he passed whenever he traveled the lonely road built by the Lighthouse Board that crosses the moorland—or the parve, as it was known—on his way to Durness. I took it Mr. Campbell was none too fond of children either by the way he spoke of them. Perhaps they too mocked him and laughed as he went by, for children have an uncanny knack of seeing through adults. But it was this kernel of knowledge that there were others here that had set me wondering, and now we were on our way to see this family for ourselves.

The men were only intent on clearing the road to the jetty, which was long enough. I felt it to be a fruitless task to begin with, for the snow was still falling at a steady rate, but who was I to argue with Mr. Campbell? We traveled a little distance inland to skirt the men unnoticed. Once I felt we were safely past, we headed back in the direction of the road and continued southeast. It took a bit longer than I had imagined. I was unused to traveling on horseback through such open, desolate country, and just when I thought that perhaps I had overestimated my abilities by misjudging the storm and its lack of intensity, which clearly I had done, I was harboring the thought of turning around and heading home. But then I smelled something. Permeating the air, heavy with wet snow, was the smell of something quite delicious. I hadn't smelled anything remotely like it in some time, and I knew, without a doubt, we were close. "Can you smell that?" I asked Kate.

"No. I smell nothing because my nose is frozen . . . along with my fingers and my toes!"

"Well, you can cheer up, then, because very shortly I shall have you properly thawed," I promised, and steered the horse in the direction of the rising smoke, praying that it was not another lie.

We found the little croft shortly after smelling it. It was a long, low building of gray fieldstone with a roof covered by a foot of snow, making it almost invisible against the landscape of white. If it weren't for the black smoke pouring out the chimney we might have missed it altogether, but thankfully we had arrived. Kate stood beside me as we knocked on the door, and for a second the thought did flash through my mind that perhaps it was an odd time of day to be out for a visit. But then, realizing that it was too late for second thoughts, and that I too was cold, I continued pounding on the door until it opened.

The face of a little boy, topped with a mop of fiery red hair and liberally smudged with soot, poked out and asked very frankly, "Who are ye?"

"Good day, kind sir," I greeted him with a show of good cheer. "My name is Miss Stevenson and this is my friend Mrs. MacKinnon . . ."

"Weel, go on, what do ye want then?"

"Ah," I said, thinking of a way to reply, for this was not the greeting I had envisioned when I came up with the daft plan. I looked to Kate for inspiration, but she was just staring at the little creature, agog and shivering. "Why, we don't want anything," I assured him. "We've just come for a wee visit and to introduce ourselves."

The boy looked at us, looked beyond us, and then looked back to us again as if we were mad. "Ye want tae introduce yourselves . . . today?" It did sound rather absurd coming from one so young and so unkempt. "Well then, get on wi' it, who are ye?" the boy demanded, placing balled fists on his slight little hips, looking strangely like an underfed terrier assuming the work of a properly bred guard dog.

"Well, so much for Highland hospitality," I said to Kate, who was still stupid with cold. I was again about to explain who we were to this scrappy sentry-from-hell when, to my relief, another voice called out, chidingly, "Hughie, for God's sake, lad, who is it?"

" 'Tis some ladies, Ma. Says they've come for a wee visit," he replied skeptically, never taking his eyes off us.

"Ladies?"

"Aye, on the lighthouse horse."

"Weel, mind your manners, laddie, and let them in!"

The boy opened the door just enough to let us pass. And then, with a sideways glance at me, he uttered in a sigh of exasperation, "I best go fetch your horse, or 'tis likely ye'll never find 'im when ye have it in mind tae leave us again."

Puzzled, I looked back to the horse. He was hobbled, sure enough, but a fine layer of snow had already begun to gather on his coat. "Yes, thank you. That's very good thinking."

"Hughie!" the voice scolded. "Make your leg to the ladies and dinna forget to pull on your coat." The boy hastily did as he was told and then dashed outside.

The moment we entered the croft my heart sank, for it was the smokiest, darkest little hovel I had ever seen. There was hardly a window in the place and the only light to be had came from the peat fire in the hearth and the few tallow candles on the little table in the corner. It was enough to illuminate the squalid dwelling. There looked to be two rooms at best, the sparsely furnished main room we had just entered, and perhaps another room beyond the door to our left, which I guessed contained the sleeping quarters. The thought that I was indeed a fool, as so many had tried to convince me of late, rang out in my head, sounding off like a mighty fog bell. What had I been expecting? An afternoon lounging in a fine parlor, stimulated with interesting conversation while downing pots of imported tea and tiny finger cakes? I had risked the inhospitable climate and the wrath of Mr. Campbell for this? And then as quickly as the thought came upon me it went, dispelled by the sight of the woman who appeared before us.

She was a petite little thing, perhaps a head shorter than myself, but for all her diminutive size I could see she possessed a great boundless sort of energy. Maybe it was the look in her eyes, that disarming mixture of kindness and curiosity with just the hint of mirth, or perhaps it was her plain dress of sensible blue wool poking out under a stain-smudged cotton apron depicting the telltale signs of her trade—she was a mother. Under her floppy mobcap poked tendrils of ginger hair, and though it was the same color as her son's, as well as the toddler in her arms, her greeting was more welcoming by far. She set the chubby little girl-child down and came forward to greet us.

"Do forgive wee Hughie. He's the manners of a heathen, he does, but ye see, we dinna get many visitors out here, especially on a day such as this."

"Yes. Oh yes, I'm sorry about that. I know it must seem odd . . . we shall not keep you."

"Never think it! What a pleasure 'tis to see new faces, truly. You'll be from the lighthouse, I expect."

Kate and I looked to each other. "Yes," I answered. "How did you know?"

"Well, as you're here on this day, in the middle of January, you'll be from the Cape side, for the ferryman willna be taking folks across from Durness in this weather. And since I already know everyone on this side of the Kyle, that leaves the lighthouse."

"Indeed," I replied, smiling at the woman. "That is very logical. I'm impressed."

"Och!" she exclaimed and waved a hand. "There's really no logic in it. Hughie said as ye were on the lighthouse horse." Her smile was like a breath of fresh air. "The truth is, I've heard rumors that the new keeper has come all the way from Edinburgh, and with him two pretty ladies. I would have come to introduce myself sooner, but things being the way they are . . ." She trailed off, as if uncertain of what to say. But then, recovering, she smiled and asked, "So, which one of ye is the man's wife?"

"She is," I said, indicating Kate. The woman looked her up and down with just the hint of pity touching her lively blue eyes, then she reached out her hand and said, "Well then, 'tis a pleasure, Mrs. Campbell."

Stunned, Kate stopped in midshake. "Ooo no, no, no! You have it all wrong! I'm Mrs. MacKinnon, the new keeper's wife."

"Oh, please, do forgive me. So your husband has come to re-place the other gent. Mr. Duffy was a kind man, rest his soul." Then, turning to me, she blurted, "Then ye'll be his wife?"

It was Kate's turn to stifle a guffaw. I threw her a chiding look before answering, "I'm sorry to say, but your powers of logic have failed you. You were doing quite well too. But I'm not Mr. Campbell's wife either."

"His betrothed then?" she quirked, her brow poised in a comical gesture of intrigue.

"Once again I'm afraid I must disappoint you. My name is Sara Stevenson," I introduced myself, taking her proffered hand, "and my husband has not yet come . . . but he will," I added confidently. It was then I made the mistake of looking at Kate, for she was glaring at me with an incredulous expression, her dark eyes growing even darker. "And until he does," I continued, shifting my attention back to our hostess, "I'm here helping my dear friend become adjusted to her new life."

"Well, 'tis quite an adjustment, I'm sure. But I'm happy to finally make your acquaintance, all the same. And I welcome ye to Cape Wrath. My name is Mary MacKay, but please, call me by my first name, and may I beg the same favor from ye?" It was agreed, and our hostess drew us to the little wooden table by the hearth. Pulling the little girl onto her lap, she stated, "Now, tell me, I'm ever so curious, what brings ye out on such a day as this?"

Mary MacKay knew the feeling of being "cooped up" all too well, for she herself had suffered from the same affliction when she first arrived on the Cape a little over five years ago. Both she and Mr. MacKay were from a village to the south, but when the Countess of Sutherland and her English husband began evicting her tenants from the lands they had lived and worked on for hundreds of years to make way for her sheep runs, the MacKays felt it a good time to move north and help Mary's husband's great-uncle with his sheep, lest they become victims of the countess as well.

"They can do that?" I questioned, thinking her story of such heartless eviction—from a clan laird, no less—a bit overdramatic.

"Aye, they can, and there's naught anyone can do about it. They have that power. My Hughie saw it comin', but others refused tae believe it. My own brothers had to join the countess' own regiment to avoid eviction. She promised my parents that they could stay on their farm if my brothers would serve the king in her colors. They did, and were both sent to the continent to fight Napoleon. My brother Jamie died shortly thereafter in a bloody battle in Spain. And my other brother, Fergus, well, when he heard about what was goin' on here, he got it in mind to stay on the continent awhile longer, because all the time they were away fighting for king and country, the good Countess of Sutherland still managed to evict my parents off their land, burned their home to the ground with a' their belongings still in it and forced them into an early grave."

"Oh how terrible!" I interjected with real outrage. "How can that be? Isn't that illegal or something?"

"No' up here. This is the Highlands. 'Tis a different way of life and a different law altogether than in the Lowlands. There was a time when the clan laird used to look out for his kinsmen, but now he just cares about filling his own coffers, no matter what the cost. Anyhow, I dinna mean to bend your ear tae my ain troubles, but what I was trying to get at is that living up here, in this desolate, harsh place, is certainly better than having no home at all. And for that, and my Hughie, I'm grateful." Hughie, I gathered, was also the name of her husband. And then, placing the little girl on the floor, she went to fetch the tea.

I watched as she deftly removed the blackened kettle from the fire and poured it into a little earthen pot to steep. She then rootled around a cupboard, finally pulling down a little corked jar and a plate of flat cakes. The little girl, adorable and apple-cheeked, followed her mother along, holding her apron and tugging on it while begging, "Mama, I help! I help!" She lifted the little girl up and placed her on a stool. "There, now, Maggie, will ye please tae put these on a plate for the ladies?" The child looked delighted with the task and set about putting the cakes onto a wooden plate with her chubby, dimpled hands. I smiled at Kate and both of us became enthralled watching them. While these preparations were under way, the boy, wee Hughie, came back inside.

"Your horse, if indeed he is your horse," the boy drawled skeptically, "is fine now. I gave him some hay," he said pointedly while hanging his coat on a hook by the door. And then, like quicksilver, his attention shifted to his mother. "Are ye makin' tea, Ma? May I have some too?"

"Why, of course, Hughie, this is a special occasion. Miss Kate and Miss Sara are from the lighthouse, and they've come for a visit."

"Why, I knew where they were from, Ma!" he said, coming to stand beside her. "They're ridin' one of his horses!" And then he turned to us, looking suspicious again. "And I bet they dinna even ask before they took 'im!"

"Hughie! Mind your tongue or ye'll get no tea! Please excuse the lad," she asked, looking plaintively to us. "His father's been gone a few days now and he thinks whenever his da's away that he can act like the man of the house."

"Well, I, for one, think it commendable," I said, looking at the boy. "Young Mr. MacKay seems a fine, capable young man. Wise too."

"Aye, a bit too wise for his mother!"

We sat around the table drinking sweet tea with oatcakes and jam. It was, undoubtedly, the best-tasting meal we had eaten since we arrived on the Cape. There was nothing fancy about the little croft, nothing imported or store-bought anywhere to be seen. And for this—this little pile of stones, capped with a wad of thatch and sitting in the middle of nowhere—Mary MacKay was grateful. And then I thought of my own home in Edinburgh. Mine was a fine home, a grand home, and because of its grandness I had sneered at this little dwelling. This croft was everything to Mary MacKay, and with an unfamiliar longing, while looking at this happy little family—a family who struggled to eke out a living on a forgotten strip of land—I realized that Mary MacKay had so much more than I. She was loved, and needed, and fairly worshipped by her children. And the look in her eye as she spoke of the unseen Mr. MacKay, who had gone to town to visit some fishermen, told me she fairly worshipped him as well. Her home was clean, her children clothed, fed and happy and she could obviously cook, for the oatcakes were delightful. There was also a wonderful-smelling stew cooking over the fire. And the irony was that none of these skills Kate or I had yet managed.

"May I ask you something?" I said to our hostess when I had finished my tea. "Whatever you have cooking over there smells wonderful. One of the reasons Kate and I took the horse and ventured out on such a day, unbeknownst to the keepers," I added for the sake of young Hughie, "was to gather some insight on cooking. Neither Kate nor I know what we're about in the kitchen and we were wondering if you might give us some advice?"

"Ye dinna know how to cook?" the boy blurted, looking at me with incredulity dripping from his wide blue eyes.

Again I felt the fool. "No, I've never learned," I admitted frankly, and flashed a self-effacing smile. "We try all the time but with little success, I'm afraid."

"Why, what sort of a woman canna cook? I never heard the like!"

"Hughie! That'll be enough out of ye!" Then turning to me, "Why, of course I'll help. I'd be honored. But do ye mind me askin' how it is ye've survived all these years without being able to cook?"

"Well I guess I've never had to."

"Ye never had to?" she repeated, ruminating over this little admission. "If ye dinna have to cook, what is it ye do, then?"

I was stunned by this question, humiliated even, and while I thought of an answer—looking at my hostess and her precocious little boy, who was staring at me with mouth agape . . . as if I were a traveling oddity at a county fair—Kate replied for me. "Why, she shops. She's very good at it too. And when she is not shopping or drinking tea, she reads books and writes love letters."

"Kate!"

"Is it true?" Mary asked, looking evenly at me.

Unable to lie to this woman, a woman who was the paradigm of domestic industry, I nodded and hung my head. "Yes, I'm afraid it is."

"Ye can read and write?"

I looked up. "Ah, yes. I can."

"Tell me, if I gave ye a letter, could ye read it to me?"

"A letter? Why, of course. I'd be happy to." And without another word she got up and went through the door to the other side of the croft. Hughie, for all his ten years, remained at the table and held me in his scrutinizing gaze.

She came back a moment later with a letter in her hand. "Hughie, will ye be a dear and put Maggie down for her nap?" The boy looked as if he would argue, then thought better of it, and carried the little girl through the door, casting one more arched glance behind him. Mary looked a bit nervous as she handed the letter across to me. "It came a week ago," she explained. "My Hugh read it, said it was from my brother, and then he left for town the next day. I asked him to read it to me, and he did too, very kindly, but I've the feeling he dinna read it all. There looks to be more to it than the words he read, and what was in the letter that made him leave so hastily, I canna tell. I'm no' sayin' that my husband's a liar, mind ye, but perhaps he's keepin' something from me?"

"Well," I began, looking at her, "have a seat and I shall read it, then you can decide for yourself."

The letter began, as every good letter should, with a salutation, and I read:

*November 5, 1814*

*Dear Mary and Hugh,*
  *'Tis been a long time on the continent and I've grown very fond of it here. France is particularly lovely, and since the war, with old Bony safely in Elba, there's plenty of opportunity for those who seek it. I have handed in my musket and now turn my sights on other ventures. Yet even more alluring than profitable business opportunities, I've found a special person who makes me very happy. Her name is Isabella and she speaks very fine English.*

I looked at her with raised eyebrows; she smiled and urged me to continue.

  *Her family has long been supporters of the Bourbons and so they are happy now that their king has been restored. But that makes little difference to me. I am happy and look forward to peace as well as a long life with Isabella beside me. We plan to wed this winter. Hopefully we can manage a visit next summer. Wish me well, sister.*

*All my love to you, Hugh and the children,*
*Fergus*

"Well, it seems your brother's quite happy in France," I denoted, stating the obvious.

"Aye, 'tis grand, certainly, but is that all . . . is that all it says?"

"Ahh . . . no. There's more, an aside really or postscript, though it's not indicated as such," and I read the rest of the hastily scrawled lines at the bottom.

  *Brother: I will be arriving in March as planned on the spring tide, and hope to make a run every month thereafter if it can be*

*arranged. The signal, as always, remains three. Tell the lads. Be
ready.*

"It looks as if your brother will be coming this March," I said
cheerfully, but Mary was not smiling.

"That last part was the part Hughie dinna read . . . But why?
Why keep it from me?"

Kate and I looked to each other. "Well, what do you suppose it
means?" Kate inquired with her fine dark brows pulled close together.

"I dinna know," Mary mused, shaking her head softly.

"Ma," came wee Hughie's voice. The boy poked his head in
the doorway, the sound startled his mother out of her reverie
and she spun around. "I dinna mean to interrupt, but they are
plannin' to leave today, are they no'?" He indicated *they* by jerking his bushy head to us. "I just thought I should ask because the
snow is no' letting up and 'tis comin' on to blow."

"Blow?" I uttered stupidly.

"Aye, a right nasty storm," he said with a sly twinkle in his
eyes. "The kind what makes travel aye muckle difficult, especially with such weight and upon a stolen horse forbye."

After a wee word in her son's ear, followed swiftly by his awkward and ingenuous apology, and after several futile attempts to
convince us to stay, Kate and I were packed onto poor Wallace,
with a crock of strawberry jam, a dozen hen's eggs and plenty of
good instruction for a quick, failsafe supper. After learning that
Mary could not read I insisted on teaching her and her son, realizing it was a way I could be useful to the people here. In exchange for this service, which Mary seemed eager for if only on
her son's behalf, she would bequeath to me her knowledge on
the domestic arts, concentrating on the more useful skills of
cooking and making preserves. She was hopeful, more so than I,
and we parted with a budding friendship and the promise of
meeting again soon. Just before we left the safety of the little
barn, Mary hastily passed us two dark green bottles containing

some type of spirit, stating that it was a present. She then said a blessing over us in the Gaelic, and we were on our way.

We were indeed in need of a blessing, I realized as soon as, heading back to the road, we crested the little hill leading from the MacKay croft, for the wind had picked up and the snow was driving into us at a near horizontal angle. The weather was bad enough, not one of God's creatures dared stir on such a day but us, and to make matters worse Kate sat behind me berating me like a daft granny, swearing that I was the most foolhardy person alive. Why had she gone with me in the first place? she wondered aloud. Robbie was going to be right furious! What had we been thinking? We were both going to die! And at one point, when we had to get off the horse and walk up a steep snow-covered hill with heads bent against the biting wind that nearly tore the coats off our backs, she even cried. But I did not. I grabbed her mitten-covered hand, shouted for her to keep moving and pulled her along, smiling all the while because I now had a friend. Mary MacKay and her precocious children were a breath of sunshine in this land of chilling darkness, and if I was made to suffer for my foolishness, then so be it. We had just made it to the top of the hill and were getting ready to mount back up when I saw a sight that knocked the breath from me.

He was there, appearing like an amorphous dark shadow behind a veil of white, sitting on a horse that mirrored my own. It was unbelievable. Had we been gone for that long? And if the weather was not enough to frighten me, the sight of him was.

"I've been looking for ye," was all he said, his voice as cold and biting as the wind. "Your husband's been very worried, ma'am," he added, coming closer, directing his comment to Kate. But it was I who felt inclined to answer.

"You forget, I don't have a husband, and therefore am answerable to no one but myself," I replied defensively.

"Aye, and if there ever was a woman who needed a husband, it would be you."

"And what's that supposed to mean?"

"Get on the horse," he ordered, ignoring me. "Help Mrs. MacKinnon up and give me the reins."

"I can manage just fine!"

"Sara, for God's sake, please be a good lass for once and do as Mr. Campbell wishes!" cried Kate, very near tears again. "I'm frozen clear through, I cannot feel my legs, and I want to get home and see Robbie before I die!"

Mr. Campbell dismounted and came storming over. He took Kate by the waist and lifted her into the saddle with a gentleness that belied his anger. "You," he said, turning to me, and there was nothing gentle about it, "climb up behind her and grab hold of her. She's freezing. Use your body to shield her from the wind and give her whatever warmth ye can." He laced up his hands to assist me. Without question I did as I was told and swung up behind the saddle, holding tightly to Kate. And without another word, Mr. Campbell led us home.

When we arrived, Robbie was there waiting, and came running over to us, pulling his wife down before we ever made it to the courtyard. He took her in his arms and carried her into the cottage, leaving me alone with Mr. Campbell. "I'll take care of the horses," he said plainly as we dismounted in front of the stable. "You get yourself into the cottage, take off those frozen clothes and climb into bed. I'll be there in a minute to have a word with ye."

"I'm not tired," I stated boldly, even though I was, and walked past him to retrieve the little sack Mary had packed for us.

He grabbed my arm and yanked me around. "I'm not asking you! I'm telling you! You get into the cottage, take off those clothes and get into bed! And then you're going to tell me why it is ye feel ye can do whatever it is ye please around here."

"Mr. Campbell, sir," I replied haltingly, fighting not to lose my temper, "it was my decision to leave the lighthouse grounds, and though I took longer than I intended, I have not forgotten that I have duties. And I intend to fulfill them."

He gave me a piercing look with his crystal aquamarine gaze.

"Och! I dinna want ye to make supper! What I want, Miss Stevenson, is for ye to do as I tell ye and get into bed! By God," the expletive exploded from his mouth in a breath of frustration, "is it not enough that ye coerced poor, guileless Mrs. MacKinnon into going with ye on your daft errand? She could have died! You could have died out there too! This is not Edinburgh! And Wallace is my horse! Ye had no right taking that beast! He's lighthouse property and therefore none of your own. A woman in your condition ought to have more sense . . . ought to have more respect . . . ought to be more mindful . . ."

"I understand," I replied with ambivalence and left him to his angry tirade. I could hear him breathing heavily behind me, trying to expel his pent-up anger as he stood beside the two steaming horses. A pang of guilt shot through me as I trounced through the deep snow of the courtyard. Yet like my cold, shivering body, I pushed it aside; for my self-indulgent pride was much stronger, nearly impenetrable, I thought, and it was all I had left to me, to defend myself—to keep me warm in the night. And I would show Mr. Campbell I was not a woman to be pushed and prodded like a malleable, docile heifer.

Thankfully it takes a good deal of time to rub down a horse properly, and more still to stable two, and Mr. Campbell did everything properly. Thankfully for me, because I used this time to my advantage by hanging a kettle of water over the fire, changing my clothes and then starting on supper. I fried a rasher of bacon, as Mary had instructed, mixed a spoonful of the fat into the oat flour, added enough water and a pinch of bicarbonate, until I had a sticky dough. It was a good dough, I thought, especially so since it didn't require the use of yeast. I pulled the bacon from the pan when it was done and put it in a tray, keeping it warm near the fire, and then I fried the little disks of dough, keeping diligent watch over them lest they burn. They didn't, and these I removed to make way for the eggs. I scrambled and fried them in the rest of the bacon fat, mixing them until they were thoroughly cooked. And these too I kept warm by the fire. I washed and set the table, put out the pot of jam, poured the boiling water into the teapot to steep the tea. And then I made up a tray for Kate. I found her in bed with a warm brick by her feet and Robbie sitting beside her talking in a soft, soothing voice.

"May I come in?" I asked, stirring them from their moment of marital privacy.

"Sara," said Robbie, a look of displeasure in his eyes until he saw the tray in my hands. "Why are you not abed?"

I smiled and offered contritely, "Because I thought it more important to bring food and hot tea for my dear friend. I think it will help."

"Aye," he agreed cautiously. "Come in."

I set the tray down and sat next to Kate. She was all bundled in a flannel nightgown and cap, tucked into bed with the coverlet drawn to her chin. Seeing her there, under the tender concern of her husband, made me slightly jealous and I secretly longed for Thomas. Would he have fussed over me so? Would he have put me in flannel, placed a hot brick in my bed and used his body to warm me? Or would he have treated me with scorn and derision, berating me for my stupidity like Mr. Campbell? Never in life. Thomas Crichton loved me, and damn me, but I missed him!

"How are you not cold? How are you not frozen straight through? "

"Because the thick layer of foolishness I wear keeps me from it." She smiled at this. "I'm truly sorry, Kate. I used poor judgment and hopefully I've learned my lesson. But look here, do you see? I made those."

"Truly?" she said with the right mixture of astonishment and disbelief touching her eyes. She sat higher and admired my golden-brown oatcakes. "Oh Sara, why, they're lovely!"

"They are." I beamed with pride. "Yours are on the table, Robbie, and there's a bottle of ale for you as well."

"Ale?"

"I think. Why don't you go see?" With a gentle kiss on his wife's forehead, he left us.

"So was he very angry with you?" Kate asked as soon as her husband was out the door.

"Angry as the devil, hotter too. He's not unlike my father, Kate, a tireless despot. But whereas my father has the divine right to govern me, me being his daughter and all, Mr. Campbell has no such right."

"He is the principal light-keeper."

"I understand, but he's not my keeper. Now, eat up. I want to see his face when he realizes that I disobeyed another of his orders. I slaved over the fire rather than lounged in bed."

Kate giggled. "My, how very unlike you."

"Yes, isn't it?"

I was not disappointed. Mr. Campbell was stunned. He looked at the table, smartly set and displaying plates overflowing with delicious-smelling food, and seemed at a loss whether to chide me for my willful disobedience or commend me for my efforts. Yet so late in the day, and having had nothing but watery oat porridge for sustenance, his growling belly held mastery over his finer sensibilities. He looked at me with his mesmerizing eyes and there I saw an expression quite foreign to him: heartfelt appreciation. But as quickly as it came it went and he frowned, stating, "I thought I made it clear ye were to get to bed."

"And so I shall, sir, just as soon as I've eaten." I then sat down at the table that for once seemed pleasantly welcoming instead of rudely repellent, beckoning for both men to join me. As they silently helped themselves to the rashers, eggs and oatcakes (or bannock, as Mary had called them) from the overflowing platters, I pulled from the bag Mrs. MacKay had given me one of the bottles. With all eyes on me, I poured out three glasses of a dark, purplish liquid and handed them around.

"What's this?" Mr. Campbell asked, picking the glass up and regarding it with due skepticism.

"A token of my sincere apologies. And I am apologetic . . . to both of you for my actions today."

"Aye, ye better well be, for they were—"

I held up my hand to stop him. "Really, sir, there is nothing you can say that I've not already thought of myself. I beg you, just enjoy the meal." Begrudgingly he picked up his glass and took a sip. So did Robbie. The reaction to this Highland drink was enchanting, for both men looked at their glasses as if they had never tasted anything so delightful. I smiled as I watched them sip again, and while Robbie kept sipping, Mr. Campbell turned to me.

"What . . . what is this?"

"Heather ale, I suppose," was my answer. For although I had never tasted the legendary drink myself, being a Lowlander, I assumed it was the nectar of the Highlands—along with whisky of course.

"This is no' heather ale. Where did ye find it?"

I tilted my head and then took a sip. Indeed, there was nothing heathery or honeyed about it. The liquid on my tongue was crisp and fragrant, piquant even, bursting with the essence of vine-ripened grapes under a blissfully hot sun, combined with something darker—earthy, perhaps, spicier. In a word, it was ambrosia. "Dear lord, this is just about the finest claret I've ever tasted!"

"Aye, 'tis. Where'd ye get it?" he asked again, pouring himself another glass.

"Why I . . ." and while I thought about the absurdity of the little croft on the edge of nowhere producing such a fine Bordeaux wine as this, I recalled Mary's letter. Her brother was in France, exactly where I was uncertain, but why not Bordeaux? He spoke of finding a profitable business venture. He had left a cryptic message for her husband, who immediately went into town to talk with the local fishermen. "Dear lord," I uttered aloud. And then, recalling the responsibilities of a lighthouse keeper, a man who not only illuminated the coast but was also encouraged to report suspicious activity, I replied, "Forgive me," and set my glass back down.

"What is it?" Robbie asked, finally digging into his eggs and bacon, between sips of wine.

"Nothing. I just . . ." and then I looked to Mr. Campbell and said very softly, "I'm sorry, sir. I'm afraid I haven't given you any reason to have a high opinion of me, and what I'm about to tell you will not help my case in the least. The truth is, I took these from my father's house. He didn't know. It was wrong of me, but you must understand, I was not in a very benevolent mood when I left."

"Ye stole wine from your father's house?" He cocked his head and studied me with narrowed eyes. I couldn't tell exactly what he made of this, but surprise wasn't in it, yet neither was thorough disappointment, and when he finally picked up his glass again he drank the liquid with the finesse and relish of a man who had known better times.

Robbie, with mouth still full, and drinking without much thought, felt inclined to add, "Wouldn't be the worst thing she's done of late. In fact, I'd say 'twas a rather brilliant move. And I highly doubt Mr. S. will ever notice this has gone missing. Touché, Miss Stevenson!" he toasted, raising his glass to me before draining it completely.

The men ate with wolfish hunger, devouring every last morsel, and when they were done, Mr. Campbell sat back and said very softly, "Thank ye for the meal. 'Twas grand. But now I must insist ye get to bed. The cold . . . the damp, biting wind is apt tae give ye a chill. It is not good for ye. Promise me you'll retire?"

I looked at him, wondering if he was going to treat me to another longwinded lecture on my previous stupidity, but he remained silent. He had no more to say and so I nodded, feeling benevolent and grateful.

He stood and for a moment just looked at me. I could not imagine his thoughts, for his face gave nothing away. Did he

dare me to disobey him again? Was he marveling at my willingness? Did he concede my victory after so foolish an adventure?
And as he stood there, silently studying me as I was studying
him, I realized that I was perhaps as much a mystery to this man
as he was to me. Then, breaking the silence, he softly excused
himself, plucked two oatcakes off the platter and stuffed them
into his pocket. He then grabbed the second bottle of wine, now
half-empty, and turned to go, taking the token of my sincere
apologies with him to his tower.

"Well, ye heard the man," Robbie said, turning to me. "Go.
Get yourself off to bed and I'll clean up here tonight."

"Thank you, Robbie, but I'll clean up. Go to Kate. Keep her
warm for a bit. I'll retire when I've finished."

"Are ye certain?" he questioned, looking curiously at me, as if
I had become a stranger.

My answer was a gentle smile and a reassuring nod.

· · ·

It was dark when all the dishes were finally put back into the
cupboard and the pans scrubbed clean. Aside from the warm,
crackling fire, the cottage was deathly quiet. The wind had
picked up measurably in the last few hours and it howled outside
like a lone wolf calling in the darkness for a mate. Exhausted,
and overcome by events of the day, I sat down in a chair and gave
myself over to the tiredness I had battled, pausing to listen to
the raging elements. The way the wind hit the windows with a
gust of force, how it seeped under the door with a shrill screech,
was as if it were talking to me, trying to reach me in my cell of
isolation. And though the mere sound of such wildness should
send shivers down my spine, forcing me under the comforters of
my warm bed, it didn't. It reminded me again just how far away
from home I was. Strangely, sitting alone by the fire, it was not
home I longed for. Truthfully, I didn't care if I ever laid eyes on
that place again. No, it was Thomas Crichton who stirred me. It
was thoughts of him combined with extreme exhaustion that

caused a near debilitating bout of self-pity to emerge, engulfing me entirely. Without another thought I grabbed my coat off the hook, pulled on my mittens and hat and headed into the night— alone.

The snow had stopped; the storm, being swept away by the persistent wind, had left a blanket of swift-moving clouds in its place. I could see a full moon trying to peek out when the thick clouds gave way to thinner layers and then peeled away alto- gether, revealing the bright orb. But as quickly as the moon was revealed it became hidden again, and the speed of the clouds be- came a dizzying game. My head was already light from the wine and so I walked out of the courtyard, intent on gazing at the fathomless sea. But as I did, I happened to glance at the light- house, and there, beneath the stalwart beam, I saw Mr. Camp- bell's noble silhouette in the observation room. His head was bent in concentration, as if he was reading or writing. I stood, compelled to watch him for a moment, studying his movements. He appeared to be playing with something in his hand, twirling the instrument point down. He then took a sip from a glass and stood up, an act that brought the object into view. It was a knife of some sort, smallish and slender but sharp all the same, for a glint of light reflected off the blade. The sight of it caused a shiver to run up my spine. Still holding the object, he walked to the other side of the room, disappearing from view. I took a few breaths to steel myself and then slipped past the towering light, undetected, to better gaze at the mighty Atlantic, over which the raging wind blew.

I stood on the high cliff looking out at the black sea, over- whelmed with the inexplicable feeling he was out there. Thomas was a sailor after all and the sea was the domain of the sailor. And so I searched. Overhead, the clouds ripped open again, and this time when I saw the light shining through it was not com- ing from the moon, but from him—Orion: the mighty hunter of the skies. He was there, unabashedly bright as his glinting stars mocked me with their brilliance against the crisp, black sky. And just the sight of him, alone amidst the racing clouds, caused tears to well up in my eyes. And the story came flooding back once again . . .

Diana, Thomas had told me that night on the ship, was madly in love with the mortal Orion. For like Diana, Orion was a remarkable hunter, the best mortal at the game, and Diana, the huntress that she was, could scarcely take her eyes from him. The two fell in love, and as their love grew Diana became so infatuated with her lover that she began to neglect her duties, which were, of all things, pulling the moon across the night sky. Diana's brother, Apollo, who himself was charged with the pulling of the sun, was tired of his sister's negligence and so, one day, he spotted Orion fishing on the sea, and the sight of the handsome man, unaware of the gods above, gave him a plan. Knowing his sister's vanity, Apollo focused his bright light on Orion, making him appear no more than a speck of seaweed floating on the sea. The god then pointed to the scrap and called out to his sister a challenge: "You who are so great a huntress could never hit a target so small as that, I'll wager." Diana, like the true goddess she was, was unable to resist such a challenge and pulled out her bow. She put the nock of her arrow to the string, and without another thought she took aim and shot the target straight through the middle, teaching her brother never to doubt her skills. Then, happy with her victory, and happy to have proven her brother wrong, she went back to work, while Orion's dead body plunged straight to the bottom of the sea. That night, as Diana went to the beach to meet her lover, she found he was not there. She waited and waited. She walked along the water's edge searching for him, calling out his name, certain he would come. She waited all night and was about to give up when his body suddenly washed up at her feet. She saw the arrow in his heart and knew instantly what had happened. She was the one who had killed him! Heartsick and desperate, she picked up her lover's body and took him to an empty spot in the night sky. There she placed him, the mighty hunter, immortalizing him and their love for all eternity. And every night, as she pulls the moon across its path, she and her lover, Orion, are together once again, if only for the brief space of a few hours.

It was a touching story, and the mere fact that Thomas had told it to me that first night made it all the more poignant and beautiful. I watched the stars slowly fade away, being covered by a gauzy haze of clouds. Orion had left me, just like Thomas. And when the magnificent stars had vanished altogether, I dropped to my knees in the soft snow and began to cry.

How long I had been there I do not know. It could have been minutes or hours, for time had no meaning for me anymore. I cried four months' worth of tears, finally realizing that he was never coming for me. How could he? He had no idea where I was. And I cried some more, until I saw a light coming up behind me. Someone was there. Yet instead of turning around to confront whoever it was I crouched down deeper, as if to meld with the snow in one freezing ball of ice.

I felt his hand on my shoulder; his strong grip pulled me around. "Jesus God," he uttered. "What the devil?" he said, and then stopped when he saw my face. "What . . ." he finally breathed, "whatever are ye doing out here, lass?"

"Please," I cried, tears streaming down my cheeks. "Please just let me be!"

He knelt so that his eyes were level with mine, holding up the lantern to better see my face. "Now, that I cannot do. This is my watch. I let nothing go amiss on my watch if I can help it." And without another word he picked me up, like a father picks up a sleeping child, and commenced carrying me back to the cottage.

"Please," I cried, feeling outraged. "I can walk just fine. Let me down!"

"But I dinna trust ye to walk," he said huskily. "I thought I told you to get to bed."

"I was on my way," I stated through hot tears.

Here, I believe, he stifled a laugh, readjusted my weight and continued on. "Well then," he said, "I can see ye do not know where your own bed lies, for you've missed it . . . by a long shot."

It was useless to argue with the insane and so I let myself be carried into the cottage and all the way to my room, my tears of heartache and sorrow long since turned into futile tears of frustration.

He put me gently on the bed and bent over my prostrate body, placing his hands on either side of my head. "Miss Stevenson," he said, his face hovering inches over mine, and because he was so close I grew afraid. I could smell the claret on his breath, mingled with something darker. He continued. "I dinna pretend to understand what drives ye, nor do I know what torments ye so. What I do know is that while ye are here on Cape Wrath ye are my responsibility. I dinna like it any more than you do, but even ye, I believe, are aware that I take my responsibilities very seriously. I am trying," he said earnestly, his brilliant eyes appearing more brilliant under the wavering lamplight. "And I expect ye to do the same. Now, take off your clothes and get into bed."

"What?" I said, thinking I didn't hear him correctly.

"I said, take off your clothes." There was a no-nonsense air about him that suddenly chaffed me and I flat out refused.

"I . . . I will not!" I uttered, and attempted to pull away.

I could see my obstinacy had an equal effect on him and his face darkened a measure. "By God, ye will!" he countered, and grabbed hold of my coat. And then, to my further humiliation, he began pulling it off me. It was remarkable on his part, but even with my thrashing unwillingness to obey, he succeeded in uncloaking me, and with great success too. Emboldened by his success he next attacked my boots and my wool stockings. I was kicking, fighting him off, knowing that in his current mood he would not stop until he had bared me completely. He was attacking my frock, his large hands snaked behind me, where he proceeded to wrestle with the buttons. And then, much to my horror, he flipped me onto my stomach, sat astride me, pinning me helplessly to the bed.

"Mr. Campbell!" I hissed, fighting to get away from his industriously probing hands, but to no avail. "No matter what you think of me," I cried into the pillow, "no matter what you've heard, I'm not that sort of woman! Mr. Campbell!" I cried again, this time exceptionally loud. "I SAID I AM NOT THAT KIND OF WOMAN!"

"What?" he stammered, as if hearing me for the first time. I could feel his grip on me relax, allowing me the opportunity to roll around and face him. Still confined between his hard, muscular legs, his chest heaving as if he had run for miles, I looked earnestly into his face and saw an expression there that shocked even me. It was as if he had seen me for the first time, my harsh words piercing his primal desires until his fists, knuckles white, relaxed and the folds of my woolen frock slipped from his grasp and fell to the bed around me. "I . . ." he stammered, his eyes looking wild and fearful at once. "Holy Christ!" he blurted, and looked truly abashed. "You misunderstand . . ." he said, and attempted to straighten my rumpled skirt, which had been wrenched up around my bared thighs. With great haste, as if burned by a white-hot poker, he sprang off the bed and stood there. His hands were at his sides, clenching and unclenching nervously as a scarlet flush overcame his strong features, making his pale eyes positively burn as he stared at me. It was then I could see the torment in his face. This was not a man who had mastery over his emotions. He was as volatile as the sea, placid one moment and raging the next. How was I ever to survive here with such a creature?

He backed away, slowly, looking at me all the while as if I were a pariah. He next scanned the room with jerky movements of his head, looking for God knows what. He was at the door, bumped into the frame then backed over the threshold. "Please," he uttered with a wild, off-kilter look. "Please just get to bed. I willna trouble ye any longer." And then he left, shutting the door firmly behind him.

I stared after him, incredulously, and found that I too was breathing heavily. My mind was awash with colliding emotions, and I saw that once again I was alone in my room, scared and lonely, wound too tightly to sleep, with only the memory, the very dear memory, of Thomas Crichton to keep me sane.

# FIVE

## The Broken Promise

𝒯he voyage aboard the yacht of the Northern Lighthouse Board was the grandest adventure of my life. There was a real sense of freedom as the little barque filled her sails and careened forward, cutting through the waves, eating up the miles and miles of sea that surrounded Scotland. There was the excitement of seeing places I'd only heard of, places like the romantic Isle of Skye, where Flora MacDonald disguised Bonnie Prince Charlie as a woman and helped him escape the English after the Battle of Culloden; Iona, the little island where Saint Columba founded his monastery back in the sixth century and converted the people of Scotland to Christianity. And we even found the rocky shoals of Skerryvore, where Captain MacDonald's mythical mermaids frolicked.

Try as I might, none of those beauties were to be seen; yet we were not immune to their siren song. As we left the Isle of Tiree, heading for Skerryvore, the wind suddenly shifted and a storm blew up, threatening to blow the yacht onto the rocks. I soon learned that in perilous times the skill of a sailor is measured.

And Thomas fought the malevolent wind like a hero-god. Many of the gentlemen from the Board thought the voyage was done for, doomed to the fate of so many ships before us. They raced about with wild eyes, cursing the ship, the wind, the rain, and even the stalwart sailors. When one gentleman had the audacity to order Captain MacCrea to "Turn the ship around this instant!" believing his engineering skills and high education gave him jurisdiction over the dogged mariner, I thought the captain was going to lose his temper and clock him in the chops, as he deserved. But the captain refrained. I would have laughed outright at the impotence of such a statement if I hadn't been terrified as well. For even I, a sheltered young woman in the throes of her first love, knew that a ship at sea was ultimately at the mercy of the wind. Our only chance at escaping destruction, if indeed it was possible at all, was to be determined by the cunning of her captain and the skill of her crew.

It was then Captain MacCrea calmly ordered everyone below. My father turned to me in the same instant and demanded that I get to my cabin and secure the door. His face, streaming wet in the downpour, held the concern of a loving parent. I was about to disobey, protesting that I felt safer on deck, knowing that I felt safer when Thomas Crichton was in my sights. I shook my head and began to form the word *NO*, when his firm grip dug into my shoulders. "Ye get below, Sara. Now! I'll have none of it, lass!" It was then I looked beyond my father and saw him. Great rivulets of water streamed down his tarpaulin coat and hat as he stood staring at me. I was captive in his gaze. He looked at my father and then back to me, his eyes vibrant and alive. And then he nodded slowly. I understood. He wanted me to obey; he wanted me to go below. I hesitated, relaying my fear for him with the intensity in my own eyes. His answer to this was a glorious smile, smug and confident, a little too confident, I thought, and frowned in response. He cocked his head to one side and performed a mischievous wink. Thomas Crichton would have me believe that he was enjoying this perilous sailing. I fought a smile and frowned again, letting him know just what I thought of his flippant attitude toward his own safety. Yet before I could see his reaction, I felt my father's fingers dig painfully into my shoulders, calling my attention dutifully back to him. I had forgotten myself for a moment. And his look of reproving suspicion caused me to panic. He turned his head and was just in time to see the back of Mr. Crichton as the sailor made his way toward the bow of the ship. My father looked back to me, none too pleased.

"I should be going now" was all I said, and shrugged off his tight grip, nearly running to the slippery gangway, where I raced a torrent of water to the lower deck.

I burst into my tiny cabin and shut the door, leaning against it as the ship rocked violently beneath me. It took everything I had to maintain my balance. My heart was beating wildly and I fought to bring it under control, but I was scared. I wasn't afraid for the ship, because Thomas was on deck. I knew enough about the young man to know that if there were a chance of escaping being torn to pieces on the rocks, he would manage it. No, I was not afraid for the ship or for my life, I was afraid for my happiness with Thomas Crichton, because for the first time since the voyage began, my father was looking upon his new employee with suspicion. He hadn't seen us together before, but for the few times we were with Mr. Scott talking of literature, yet he'd never made a remark about it. But I feared that was all about to change. Although Thomas and I were utterly discreet, carrying on our clandestine, and rather chaste, courtship under the stars, I was scheming in my head about what to do—what lies to conjure—when a soft knock came upon my door. I took a deep breath and opened it, ready to face the man who so dominated my life. Yet to my surprise it was Thomas.

"Whatever are you doing here?" I gasped, stupefied, and then thinking more clearly I pulled his rain-soaked body inside my room before he could answer, and shut the door.

My cabin aboard the yacht was the width of my little bunk,

with barely three feet to spare between the bed and the door. I owned an armoire at home that was bigger. Yet at that moment the tiny cell was a godsend, for Thomas and I were pressed close together, so close that I could feel the warmth of his body radiating through his cold, wet clothes. The feel of him, the contrast of the cold and heat, both thrilled and terrified me, yet I didn't push him away. There was no room. "Dear God, Thomas!" I chided his audacity. "If my father found you in here he'd be none too pleased!"

"Well, I wager he won't. He's still on deck with the captain. Hush now, love; I've not much time," he whispered, bringing his finger to my lips. "I just came to tell ye not to worry. All the glories of heaven will not make me give up my treasure without a fight, and I'm a man who knows how to fight Old Poseidon."

"Treasure?" I repeated, thinking he was referring to the ship, or perhaps alluding to some mysterious valuable in his sea chest.

"Aye, my treasure." He must have seen the blank look on my face, for he then elaborated on what he meant by *treasure*, stating that *I* was his treasure. "I have never asked the Almighty for riches or glory," he said plainly, looking into my eyes. "I'm not a man who chases such things. And though the Lord kens I've been plenty wicked, He's still managed to bestow on me something glorious. He's given me ye, Sara. Deny it if ye will, but as long as I shall live, I will let no harm come to ye. Now, listen, lass, I've no' much time. Kiss me." And with that said he took me in his arms and convinced me, beyond the shadow of a doubt, that I was indeed his treasure.

I had never before kissed a man. I had dreamed of it many a time, to be sure, especially where Thomas was concerned, and I had always imagined it to be quite wondrous. Yet even I was not prepared for the searing force of such a kiss. Although the storm raged around us, and the ship rocked violently with every successive wave, I had never felt safer or more loved. He enveloped me in his steamy cocoon of ice water and searing passion, with lips coming over mine that were both soft and fierce at once.

And though it lasted only a moment—out of necessity—it was a moment that changed my life, for I no longer could deny that I loved him. He felt this, knew it to be true, and with reluctance pushed himself away, breathing as heavily as I. And then he smiled. It was a sublime grin that lit his face, a face that radiated pure joy, to match my own. "God, but I dinna want to leave!" he uttered, still grinning and still fighting to catch his breath. "But I'm afraid I must. However, I believe ye now know I'll be back." There came a shout on deck. His eyes flashed to the low beams of the ceiling, where hurried footfalls scampered overhead. And then, with the hint of apology in his eyes, he left with the same abruptness he had entered my room.

When my father came by a while later to tell me of the remarkable maneuver performed by the captain at the behest of Mr. Crichton that saved the ship, I was just beginning to recover from my surging emotions, as well as the raging sea. My father, seeming in awe of what he had just witnessed on deck (he being the only man allowed to stay there), relayed to me a risky maneuver called clubhauling, where one anchor is sacrificed to drastically change the direction of the ship. Thankfully the excitement on deck and the near destruction of the Lighthouse Board's precious yacht had pushed his earlier suspicions about myself and the young sailor far from his mind, nor did he comment on the state of my deeply flushed cheeks. He simply told me that the ship was in the clear; I had no more need to worry. Captain MacCrea had shifted her direction just enough to avoid destruction. We were now heading out to sea to ride out the storm.

The storm blew over within twenty-four hours, yet there was another storm brewing, building silently within the confines of the little brig. It wasn't obvious to the casual observer, but the tension was there nonetheless. Ever since the incident on deck where my concern for Mr. Crichton had been so plainly written on my face, my father harbored a suspicion that my dealings with the young man were anything but casual. Much to my chagrin, he kept me close, involving me in many of his boring affairs, with ever an eye on the young mariner. For four days I humbly complied, being as charming as circumstances dictated, with never a direct look at the man who possessed my every thought. I stayed in my cabin at night, prayed for sleep, and when it would not come, I took to dosing myself from a bottle of Captain MacCrea's heady port wine. For all my discreetness, Captain MacCrea seemed to know very well what demons plagued me. He handed me two bottles of wine from his private stores, declaring with a conspiratorial wink that my secret was safe with him. Whether he thought I was a closet lush or merely a young woman who couldn't sleep knowing her lover was on deck, I was not entirely certain, and I was not about to correct him if he happened to have the wrong impression.

Thomas, at first, did not understand my odd behavior—my blatant shunning of his kindness—thinking it a result of his bold kiss that day in my cabin. This he indicated in a note entrusted to Mr. Scott. When I was handed the note by the writer, and read it, I felt sickened by his assumption. Without another thought I borrowed the writer's pen, ink and a scrap of paper and scribbled my own hasty reply, assuring Thomas that my avoidance of him was to divert my father's suspicion, and in no part due to his visit to my cabin, which, I underscored, had been the pinnacle of my trip thus far! This he was relieved to read, and although he did not agree with my drastic measures, he understood my motive and refrained from talking to me on deck, contacting me only by notes passed along through Mr. Scott.

It was childish and perhaps wrong of us to implicate the great man so, but Mr. Scott seemed tickled to be the mediator of our clandestine courtship. "Good day to ye, Miss Stevenson," he greeted me on the fourth day of my little charade. "Ye appear a wee peaked this morning. I hope you are not unwell?"

"No. I'm well, sir, very fine, thank you," I affirmed, stifling a yawn from yet another sleepless night. Mr. Scott smiled at my transparent statement.

"Och, there's naethin' sae grand as young love, forbye! 'Tis a pity yours need be shoved down a mine shaft, concealed in a subterranean warren for only the creatures of the night to see, and not allowed to shine forth like one of your father's great lights. Perhaps we'd all benefit from such a glow as the one hidden beneath the wan skin o' your face."

I narrowed my eyes at him. "You obviously don't know my father, or you'd understand why the glow you seem to think I possess need be hidden."

He replied with a hearty chuckle. "Ye are no' the first fair maiden to be stricken with Cupid's arrow, nor, I pray, will ye be the last."

"You sound very familiar with love, Mr. Scott. If it's not too impertinent of me, may I ask if you speak from experience?"

"I will tell ye a wee something about young love, Miss Stevenson. The very day I first laid eyes on my Maggie was the day it struck me daft. Changed my life forever." He looked at me with his kind, sharp eyes. "Clouds a man's mind, it does. Makes him foolish, bold and daring! But alas it also gives a man purpose; gives his life direction, which is no' such a bad thing for the young chiels, I find."

"And did Mrs. Scott give you direction?"

"Why, as to that, sure she did—and still yet does. For ye see, I'm still findin' my way in the world. But the journey's been all the smoother with dear Margaret by my side."

"And if," I began searching his twinkling eyes, "if Mrs. Scott was forbidden to marry you, what would you have done then?"

"Weel, being daft, and on account of young love, I'd likely have done what many a good Scot has done before me." I leaned forward, anxious for his answer. "I would have swept her off tae Gretna Green or gone across the border."

I liked Mr. Scott's answer. It was bold, daring and daft, yet ever so romantic! I then scanned the deck and found what I was looking for. But before he saw me I dropped my gaze to my lap, aware of my father's eyes upon me.

"Is something amiss?" Mr. Scott inquired.

"My eyes are just tired, sir. The men were discussing the Isle of Iona at breakfast this morning, thinking of making a stop there to see the ruins of St. Columba's monastery and the burial place of some ancient Scottish kings. A map was then fetched, the tiny island spotted and some calculations were made. Tides were discussed and then Captain MacCrea was consulted as to the approach the ship should take. I was quite perplexed by it all. I'm certain I shall never understand nautical navigation!"

"Nor should ye, my dear. What a pity you were made to suffer through it. Your head should be filled with a' the sights and sounds of the sea, a marvel of God's handiwork forbye, as well as take in a little poetry every now and again. And speaking of poetry, it just so happens I have with me an interesting little piece from what I would call a budding young poet, an honest man, a workingman, perhaps reminiscent of Rabbie Burns." Here he paused to look above and beyond me, where I caught him wink. I turned and saw said young poet, perched halfway up the ratlines, propped in the rigging like a giant, golden-haired monkey. He appeared to be advising a topman to shake out a reef in the great sail, but in reality he was watching me. I shifted my attention down the deck to where my father seemed to be engaged in conversation with the captain. I looked back up at Thomas and took the note from Mr. Scott's hand, then proceeded to read the words Mr. Crichton had so painstakingly written. "To the Young Lady of my Dreams," it was titled, and thus began the first of many love poems to come that Thomas Crichton had penned specially for me.

> *Leave me not alone tonight*
> *To stand the wrath of dawn's first light,*
> *Beneath the stars that shine so bright,*
>     *All alone.*
> *Without your smile and warm embrace,*
> *The beauty of your angelic face,*

*A body sae full of artful grace,*
   *A' the night's sae lang.*
*O' Sara, I beg, torment me nay longer,*
*My will is weak, my passion stronger,*
*'Tis for your lively spirit I hunger,*
   *Come satiate me!*
*While Orion awaits all through the night,*
*For Diana's arrow true in flight,*
*His heart she pierced with blinded sight,*
   *O' still he loves her!*
*So be not afraid to come, my love,*
*From questioning eyes we'll stand above,*
*Then scatter in the morn' like the winged dove,*
   *Above suspicion!*
   *My love for ye's without condition.*
       *T.C.*

"Oh my," I uttered, nearly breathless, a hand over my heart, so touched by his words. The poem was so intimate, the sentiment so bold, and yet it was so wrong of me to even consider endangering him by frolicking beneath the stars! And yet . . . and yet I could not deny that I felt the same as he did. I looked again to the ratlines where Thomas was perched and saw that he was staring intently at me—as if he was afraid of how I would react. With his gaze still on me, I took the little piece of paper and carefully folded it. I then placed it gently in the top of my bodice and snuggled it against my bosom, where it would remain close to my heart. I knew he would understand this small gesture, and my reward was a glorious smile solely focused on me; a smile that radiated through every fiber of my being. Damn me, but I was indeed under Thomas Crichton's heady spell!

With my father placated as much as could be, and through my ambivalence toward Mr. Crichton whenever in public, doubt was beginning to spread over his previous suspicions. He slowly began to relinquish my tether. This was a blessing. For I had been given a taste of love by a man who thrilled me beyond reason, and I was not about to let so precious a gift slip by unopened. I would continue to meet Thomas Crichton beneath the stars.

It was a glorious time. And because Thomas had a job to do, and because I would have been mortified if my presence distracted him from his duty, I only visited him for an hour or so, weather permitting. But it was enough. We spent our stolen moments with heads bent together, talking of family, of our lives, of our dreams, while holding hands under the cover of our boatcloaks. We carried on like a pair of moonstruck children, grinning and giggling over nothing much at all, while attempting to be as discreet as possible. It was under the stars that I learned Thomas' mother had died shortly after giving birth to him. He was raised by his father, a poor, honest fisherman who had struggled to give him as decent an education as he could afford. But by the age of eight his formal education had ended, and Thomas went to sea with his father. Yet from the start he hadn't been satisfied with the life, always wanting more. And when he had turned sixteen, the two Crichton men had a falling out—over literature, no less!—and Thomas left home, never to look back. His life on the streets of Edinburgh had been hard, he confided, but he managed well enough. He worked the docks, worked the shipyards and eventually found employment on the seas. And though he had steady work, he never felt truly blessed, had never felt the presence of God—the God his father had incessantly preached to him—until that day in the garden of my home. I smiled at this, thinking it was just stuff, but Thomas insisted it was true. And, of course, because he was Thomas Crichton, I believed his every word.

After we had shared an hour together, holding hands and talking softly, Thomas would pull me to him, wrap me in his arms and kiss me. It was the only time—just once a night—and it was all I would allow; it was what I lived for. When he was done and at last we parted, I knew I would sleep like a baby: for I'd be dreaming of Thomas Crichton.

. . .

As all good books draw to an end, so too, I learned, do voyages. And just like a story that sweeps you away, one becomes ever conscious of the dwindling pages, feeling a bit sad that the end is drawing near and praying that it would go on well after the last page is turned. But such is not the case with books or voyages. Nothing so perfect was made to last forever, and so, the closer we came to the Firth of Forth, the deeper our silent melancholy grew. I thought it an emotion palpable only to us, but my father sensed it as well and began studying me in his cold, disjointed way, as if my feminine sentiments were a problem to be solved by mathematic equations and astute calculations. And on the second to the last day of our voyage he called me out, questioning my blatant lack of *joie de vivre*, as he had termed it, stating that it was something I had possessed in such great quantities all along. To my horror and disbelief he chose the very public forum of the dining table, addressing me for all to hear with his demand, and wishing to know the cause of this drastic shift in my temperament.

"I'm just tired, Papa. It's been a long voyage," I replied, hoping this explanation would be enough.

"Tired?" he questioned. "'Tis no wonder you're tired when ye leave your cabin in the dead of night to wander the ship!" he countered in a voice loud enough for all to hear.

"Leave my cabin, Papa?" I could feel the heat of shame rise in my face as all eyes settled on me, and prayed that I could think of some way to explain my scandalous behavior.

"Aye," he said slowly, piercing me with his parental eye. "I've noticed on several occasions that ye've left your cabin after midnight. Tell me, child, where is it ye go so late?" His voice was stern, his eyes accusatory.

"I . . . I . . ." I stammered, trying hard to think of a viable answer, yet knowing that any answer I could give would not please him. "I sometimes cannot sleep," I uttered meekly.

"Really? And where is it ye go, may I ask, when ye cannot sleep?"

"Ah, Mr. Stevenson, sir," Captain MacCrea broke in, noting my extreme discomfort. "If I may be sae bold, I've noticed Miss Stevenson sometimes suffers from the insomnia—not all landsmen take to sleeping aboard a rollicking ship sae easy as ye, sir, and when Miss Stevenson cannot sleep, I often give her a wee dram o' port from my ain locker. Nothing lulls the mind and soothes the body, I find, like a good dosing o' the Frenchies' water!" he added, and punctuated his sentiments with a disarming grin.

"Is this true?" my father demanded, turning to me.

"Yes sir."

"Then why did ye not say so? Why not tell me of it?"

"Because I know how you regard spirits," I replied a little defensively, for his feelings on the subject were hardly a secret.

"Well, I've not changed, Sara! Nothing good can ever come from the bottom of a glass. I expected ye to know that, just as I expect ye to find another answer to your insomnia. Try reading the Bible or the Book of Common Prayer next time."

"Yes, Papa," I humbly acquiesced.

"Och, why, if nothin' puts ye tae sleep faster than the Good Book!" injected Captain MacCrea, with good-hearted cheer. Yet for all his goodwill and kindly intentions, it was a sentiment lost on the rest of the table.

I had escaped, but just by the skin of my teeth. I flashed the captain a look of gratefulness and excused myself from the table. Dear Mr. Scott had been standing near the threshold of the door, our friend and confidant, observing this troubling discourse with a detached calmness for one so entangled in our plight. And as I walked past him, not daring to meet his eye, he spoke softly.

"Oh, what a tangled web we weave when first we practice to deceive!"

I stopped and turned to face him, his blue eyes twinkling with mischief. "Marmion," I uttered softly, recalling the phrase from his famous poem. "Mr. Scott, I am no Marmion!"

"Nor was that implied, my dear. Ye are far too pure of heart to be anything like Marmion," he whispered closely. "I simply meant that when one is perpetrating deception, one must take great care, especially when one is attempting to deceive one so astute and penetrating as Mr. Stevenson."

I stared at him, knowing the truth of his words yet sickened by them all the same.

"It can be done," I challenged, thinking of my brother Thomas and how his little deception had gone unnoticed by our father for years. However, my words sounded much braver than I felt. But damn it all! I was young and determined; the world was awakening all around me and I believed I was invincible. I turned from the writer and stalked off down the hall, vowing to myself that no force on earth was great enough to keep me from my chosen destiny!

I dared not go to Thomas that night, knowing my father was monitoring my every move. It was our last night aboard the yacht, a night that was supposed to be spent planning our future together—how and where we would see each other once we went ashore. I didn't even know where Thomas lived, for he always evaded the question whenever I asked him. He dwelled in a part of town where a lady should never venture, he told me, and that was all. And by not telling me, he said he was assured I wouldn't disobey his wishes and come find him, which, in all honesty, I might very well have done.

He obviously knew where I lived, and that was a comfort, but meeting in the garden of Baxter Place was not an option either of us would dare to consider. No, we needed a trysting place, somewhere neutral, somewhere private—a place where we could be alone together, safe from the watchful eyes of the many nosy Edinburgh citizens. And as I lay awake that night, listening to the sound of his footsteps as he paced the deck above me, I could feel his impotent, pent-up desire with every step. I was about to rap on the ceiling, letting him know I was there, when a distant voice called out, drawing him away.

It was two in the morning as I sat on my bunk, thinking how to get word to him, and not wishing to employ Mr. Scott with so important a message. And then a place came to mind. I sprang out of my bunk, grabbed a quill and scrawled *Midnight, Thursday, Ferguson's barn* on the edge of the paper containing Thomas' poem. I blew on the ink, tore off the corner, waved it in the air to dry and pressed it to my heart, praying he would come.

It was just before the hour of noon when we came to dock at the quay in the Leith estuary. It was a busy harbor, crowded with people, suffused with the familiar stench of tar and tobacco that mingled with the more putrid odor of pelagic decay. And although the sun was high, shining its blissful rays on the good people of Edinburgh as well as the many sea birds that circled and swooped, I felt dark and empty inside. My extraordinary adventure was over and I was to return to my commonplace life. The only glimmer of happiness for me lay completely in the hands of Mr. Thomas Crichton.

My mother was there with the porters, awaiting us; her joyful smile and eager waving momentarily belied her dour Scotch Calvinism. My father, also losing himself to the moment, returned her greeting with mirrored excitement. And as my parents were thus occupied, waving and gesturing to each other like a couple of schoolchildren cut loose, Mr. Crichton appeared at my side.

"May I assist ye ashore, Miss Stevenson?" he asked politely, though his eyes were hungrily devouring me. He wanted to say something; his mouth was forming the words when I boldly squeezed his hand. He was shocked into silence. Surprise flickered across his face, and then I saw that he understood. Without another word he helped me across, holding my hand with the same fervent force that I held on to his. And when my feet were firmly on solid ground, only then did he let go. I released the note, leaving it in the palm of his hand. He quickly concealed it in a tight fist, not daring to look at the little missive, only at me. His eyes held that familiar twinkle as his lips fought off an encroaching grin. "'Twas a pleasure serving ye, Miss Stevenson. I hope that our paths shall cross again someday." He bowed.

My response was a maidenly smile, warm and hopeful, with the soft utterance of: "I too hope for the very same thing." And then I turned to go, never once chancing a look behind me.

. . .

A day had never felt so long, I thought, as I awaited the hour of midnight. It had been a trying few days back in the fold of my mother and Kate. Kate's constant presence began to annoy me. She had endless questions about our travels and I found myself growing a bit short and fractious. But when after dinner she began prodding me about handsome sailors I might have taken a fancy to, I began to understand the game. This bold line of questioning—from Kate, no less—was suspicious indeed, and I surmised my mother had learned of my suspected dealings and employed my dear companion for the task of drawing out any damaging information.

"Honestly, Kate," I began, looking at her reflection in the mirror as she brushed my hair, patiently suffering her nightly ablutions, "I fancied all the sailors. Had I known men of the sea were so amiable, handsome and kind, why, I'd have taken to loitering around the harbor months ago! Many women do, I hear, hang around the harbor, that is," I teased, feigning seriousness.

"Aye, an' they're called harlots!" she scolded, as I knew she would.

"But isn't that where you landed Mr. MacKinnon? Wasn't he a sailor or longshoreman . . . or something of the sort? And did you not, in fact, speak of how you saw him coming off a ship, and swooned with desire at the dashing figure he cut? Certainly you are no harlot, Kate . . . are you?"

"Of course I am not! And Robbie was a ship's purser," she corrected with a scowl. "That's much different than a common sailor. And you know very well I met him here, not loitering around the harbor like a common whore!"

"Are whores very common, then?"

The brush stilled in her hand. "Common enough, I should think, and they make a good living off men of the sea, or so I hear, but that is not a conversation proper young ladies should be having!"

"No . . . no, you're very in the right of it." I smiled sweetly at her reflection. "Please forgive me."

"Now, back to my question. Certainly there were some intriguing men aboard the yacht? Tell me, Sara, as a friend, did any man happen to strike your fancy?"

"As a matter of fact, one did," I admitted, relishing the way she was leaning forward, her doelike eyes wide and imploring. I remained silent.

"Well, did he have a name, then?" she prodded, growing impatient.

"Yes, as a matter of fact, he did."

She let out an exasperated sigh and dropped the thick strand of auburn hair she was coaxing into a radiant sheen. "I'm asking his name, not if he had one, which by the by, everyone does!"

"Oh very well, then. But you mustn't tell a soul! Promise?" She nodded, looking the very image of virtue. Apparently lies came easy to my mother's spy. "His name is Mr. Walter Scott, and I found him to be very engaging company."

With satisfaction, I watched Kate in the gilded mirror of my dressing table as her lovely face contorted with distaste. "Mr. Scott the writer? Surely not the writer."

"Yes, the writer-poet. You know him?"

"I know of him. And he's an old man. Married too." Her eyes narrowed with suspicion as the realization that I was playing with her began to take hold.

"Yes, I know he's married," I replied, and smiled coyly at her perturbed reflection. "But I found him intriguing, all the same."

"Young Mr. Graham came by quite a bit while ye were away," she felt inclined to add, knowing how to ruffle me as I knew how to ruffle her. "Did your mother happen to mention that to you?"

"As a matter of fact, she did say something on the matter." I smiled as if I didn't care.

"Mr. Graham fancies you, Sara. He made that quite clear while you were gone. The man's a good catch. Why, any young lady would be flattered by his attention. He has a living of five thousand pounds a year and is hoping to pass the bar very soon."

I took the brush from her hand and turned to face her. "Just what Scotland needs," I proclaimed with a hint of sarcasm, "another lawyer! Though I'm afraid I wouldn't make a good wife for an advocate. Perhaps it's escaped you, Kate, but I find many of the laws tiresome and superfluous."

"Perhaps," she agreed. "But for five thousand pounds a year, anything can be tolerated, even the law."

"How about his looks? Is it worth five thousand pounds to suffer that great beak of a nose, the yellow, misshapen teeth and a backside that's constantly flatulent . . . in my presence? Imagine what he's like when he's not in the company of a lady!"

"So his diet needs adjusting. And his teeth can be filed or pulled. He's a kind man, Sara, and sweet on you," she equivocated.

"Sweet? How nice. I suppose I'll have to grasp the nettle, as they say, sometime, Kate, but not tonight. I'm very tired tonight. In fact, why don't ye get along to Mr. MacKinnon early? I'm certain he's not a man to mind his wife before her due."

"You've no more need of me?"

"Kate, I shall always need you, but tonight I'm very tired. I'm going to bed now," I assured her, placing a gentle pat on the back of her hand. I could see she found the thought of joining her husband early titillating.

"Very well, I shall leave you alone, then. But, Sara, if you do wish to talk about men, about someone you fancy, you will come to me? I have no wish to see you get hurt by someone who might not be everything they appear, nor do I wish to see your parents suffer on the off chance that you do."

"Kate, dear Kate, when have you ever known me to be so foolish as that?" To this she had no answer, only a forlorn shake of her head. "Go, then, and do give Mr. MacKinnon my kindest wishes."

I waited until the house grew quiet, until all footsteps retreated to their proper quarters. And then I waited some more. When at last the time had come, I crept out of bed, pulled a shawl around my nightdress and slipped out of my room, tiptoeing barefooted down the hall. All was going well until I turned the corner, heading for the stairs, for my parents' room was here, and before their door slept the family collie, Flora. Excited to see me awake, she scrambled to her feet, making a great noise on the hardwood floor with her sharp claws and hitting my parents' door with the great bush of her tail as it fanned in delight. She dashed to my side. I made a quick grab for the scruff of her neck and attempted to calm her with a hushed whisper. Flora, bless her, was not the most intelligent of God's beasts, and she thought this a great game, whining, and pawing the floor in delight. I hushed her again and made to pull her with me, away from the door, when I heard the creak of a bed coming from the other side. I froze. And then I heard heavy footsteps approaching. With my heart in my throat, I jumped back around the corner and pressed my body to the wall, praying Flora would not give me away. The door opened and I heard my father's voice.

"Flora, what's afoot, lass? Is it time for our milk already? Aye, so you've missed me, I see. I've been away a long time, but not so long as to forget about that." The dog, amazingly, seemed to understand this prattle and began pawing the floor again. "Very well, then, we shall have our wee nip, but don't tell Mother." And then, to my relief, I heard my father begin down the stairs. The dog, however, hesitated.

"Go on, go on," I urged under my breath.

"Flora, what is it?" my father questioned, and a moment of dead silence followed.

I was frantically thinking of what excuse I could give for lurking around the halls in the dead of night, and while my mind raced, I thought of Thomas. Was he already at our trysting place? Would he come at all? And was he right now sitting all alone, wondering where I was? How long would he wait for me before giving up? And then, while still holding my breath, and growing evermore nervous, I heard the dog descend the stairs, the promise of food winning out over the excitement of discovering me. Thank goodness the beast was a slave to her belly! And with the two coconspirators thumping around in the kitchen, I slipped down the stairs. I had no choice but to pass the very door where they were, for the kitchen was down the back hall . . . which led to the back door, which led to the garden. A shaft of soft light poured from the opening, illuminating part of the hallway. I could see their distorted shadows moving about on the far wall as my father continued to engage the dog in soft conversation. From the look of it, both man and beast were about to partake in a good deal more than a wee dram of milk. I pressed myself into the shadows as I listened to the man's one-sided conversation, thinking I had never heard him talk so candidly before. I was lulled by the sound of it as I began making my way slowly toward them. I was just about to cross the opening to the kitchen, focusing on my destination at the end of the corridor, when a mouse skittered past, right over my foot, clinging to the same wall as I. The sudden shock of it, the unseen violation to my naked foot, nearly caused me to scream, and I shook it, as if it were palsied, trying to rid myself of the distasteful feeling. I feared it was up—my little game, over—and I pressed myself to the wall again, watching the mouse continue on as I waited with a heart beating unreasonably fast from so small a creature. Yet all I heard was the clinking of glass and the glug of some liquid falling into it. The sharp smell of cheese and the tang of spicy sausage hit me then and I knew the night-raiders were too preoccupied to hear the likes of me. With a silent sigh of relief, I followed the path of the little mouse, past another room and then to the back door—where, to my amazement, I watched the tiny creature squeeze under the threshold.

I hated mice; I loathed them, but at the moment I would have given anything to be able to enter the garden without the business of opening the door. I held my breath and slid back the bolt. I then tried the door, opening it just enough for my body to squeeze through, then shut it behind me with the touch of a downy feather. I caught my breath. I was through! And I took off at a dead run, barefooted, through the dewy grass, with only the light of the full moon to illuminate my way.

The Ferguson barn was just beyond our orchard. It was a place I had often played as a child, and Mr. Ferguson, our neighbor, kept a fine stable with a team of four sprightly bays to pull his coach. I had told Thomas all about this special place and hoped he remembered how to find it. Yet as I approached the side door, nerves overtook me, and for some unexplained reason I was shaking. I told myself it was just a chill from the night, but even I knew what a liar I could be. I was afraid. I was afraid he would not come. I was afraid that perhaps Thomas was not quite what he appeared, as Kate had warned, and that our risky courtship on the yacht had just been a way for him to pass the time. He was a sailor after all, and sailors were notorious rakes! What if I was a fool—a young woman with fanciful notions of her own creating? I was tempted to turn away; I half thought I might, for the risk I was taking was so great. But then my arrogance and imprudence prevailed, and with a thrust of force that surprised even me, I pushed open the door.

He was there. He had been waiting for me. And at that first sight of him, sitting on a little three-legged stool in the soft glow of a lantern, clutching his hat nervously between his hands, my fears faded. And the hopeful delight, glistening in his night-darkened eyes as he saw me, melted my heart. "Sara," he uttered, then alighted from his seat to sweep me up in his arms. "Oh, Sara, I was afraid ye wouldna come."

"I ran into some difficulty," I whispered, holding on to him just as tightly as he held to me, allowing my nerves and fears to fade away in his warm embrace. "My father, I discovered, has a habit of visiting the kitchen at night. He almost found me out. Thank goodness he has a habit of talking to the dog, or else he would have heard me for certain."

"He talks to the dog, does he?" He let out a soft chuckle. "Pray, what does the man say?"

"They talk about engineering mostly, though when I walked past tonight they were discussing the smelting of iron—you know, how to make it stronger."

Again he laughed; it was a deep, throaty, mesmerizing laugh that caused a frisson of pleasure to ripple under my skin, while at the same time sent the horses shifting anxiously in their stalls. He lowered his voice. "Smelting iron? And what were the dog's views on that?"

"I don't think she had any. She was more focused on the wheel of Stilton they were pillaging."

"Aye, Stilton," he agreed with a knowing grin. "Well, sneaking past your father's a very brave thing, indeed, Miss Stevenson, but I fear 'tis too great a risk for ye to take. What if he caught ye? I have to tell ye, Sara, the man's asked me to his office tomorrow, to discuss further employment, and his motives are a puzzle."

"You're coming here tomorrow?"

"Aye. One o'clock sharp."

"I shall watch for you," I whispered, and kissed his golden-stubbled cheek. "And you must tell me what he says—everything, Thomas."

"Aye, I shall leave ye a wee note of the whole affair under thon bench, the one beneath the cherry tree. The one ye were sitting on the day I first saw ye. I shall tell ye of it and more. I shall tell ye how I love thee."

"I shall leave one for you as well," I said, and delight swept through me. It was another line of surreptitious communication.

"Aye, I shall look forward to it. But now, Sara, now we are together, just you and me, all alone, and it is an opportunity I willna waste. Come, sit with me," he said, pulling me gently to his lap. He wrapped me in his arms and whispered, "Sit with me and tell me, how are we to do this, lass? How are we to be together? For I willna always be satisfied skulkin' around in strange barns to steal a moment with ye, ever fearful of your father's watchful eye. I want more than that, Sara. I want you for my own. How are we to do it, lass?" he asked again, his whisper husky with emotion as his luminous eyes pleaded the same question. I had no answer. Thankfully I didn't have need of one just yet, for his lips, hungry and succulent, began nibbling my neck. It was too much for me; the thrill of him was too much, and I turned to him, meeting his hunger with my own while diverting his thoughts further from a question to which I had no answer.

We stayed in the barn, whiling away half the night talking, touching and kissing. He was careful not to press for more, reining himself in, never daring to go beyond that point we both longed for but I was not yet prepared to give. Thomas Crichton, for all his humble station in life and great disadvantage in the world, was a true gentleman, or so he made me believe. And when we had a decent understanding of each other, our intentions clear, he took me by the hand and walked me through the garden, nearly to my back door.

"Someday, I pray, I'll be able to stand here in the broad light of day, boldly holding your hand for all the world to see. However," he stated, casting a doleful look at the house, "that day has not yet come. Now, be careful," he warned, "and perhaps I shall see ye tomorrow."

"Why of course you'll see me," I teased, and blew him a kiss as I stood with my hand on the latch. He watched until I was through, and then silently left, making his way back to wherever it was he had come from.

• • •

The next day, precisely at one o'clock, I stood at my bedroom window and peered out into the garden, watching for him. He was prompt. He came through the garden entrance and walked down the path to the office door, where he paused to remove his cap. He then turned around and scanned the house, finally spotting me in a second-story window. Our eyes met, and I caught his smile, though it was only for a second, because just then the office door opened and my father appeared. I jumped behind the curtain at the sight of him. When I thought he could not see me, I peered out again, and caught him looking directly at my window. He then shifted his gaze to Thomas but said nothing to the young man as he ushered him inside. Yet his eyes returned to my window—as if daring me to appear.

Not more than a quarter hour later Thomas emerged. My heart sank, because I thought so short an interview could not bode well for a young man looking for further employment. What was more, I couldn't read the expression on his face, for his head was bent and his cap back on as he walked to the garden bench. There he sat for a good while, appearing to contemplate some thought, and when his contemplations were done he withdrew a little piece of folded paper from his coat pocket. On this he made a note, scribbling something quickly with a little pencil and then refolding it, placing it gently in a little tuft of grass near one of the back legs. It was there his hand found another piece of paper, a paper that he discreetly stuffed into his pocket. And then he turned to me once more. This time he knew exactly where I was, and when our eyes met, he delivered to me a smile of sublime puzzlement—one of wonder—as his hand came over his heart.

I had no idea the exact meaning of this look and gesture, and longed to inquire further from behind the glass, but I didn't get the chance, for just then two more men emerged from the same door, men I recognized: Captain MacCrea and another sailor from the yacht. They walked over to where Thomas stood, said something to him, and the three left the garden together.

It was only later, when I finally had the courage to retrieve my secret message, that I understood the meaning of Thomas' expression. After some touching lines written to me came the scrawled message:

> *Unbelievable! Still employed. To stay on with Capt. Mac on the tender and given a raise of two pounds six pence more a month! Perplexed but did not dare question. Huzza! I owe it all to you— my Love, my Luck, my Treasure!*
>
> *T.C.*

I remember thinking that this was tremendous good news, for not only would Thomas be remaining close by, it also meant that perhaps my father liked him. And if my father liked him, it wouldn't be impossible to persuade the man to see Thomas as more than a mere sailor, but as a man worthy of his daughter's affections as well. My heart careened ahead with hope; yet intuition warned to proceed with caution.

We continued meeting clandestinely in the Fergusons' barn whenever we could, and when we could not, we contrived to leave letters for each other beneath the garden bench. Thomas became a frequent visitor at Baxter Place, charged with delivering reports to my father. And as much as I would have liked to believe things were going well between the two of them, I found this was not the case. Besides, things were growing more difficult for me as well.

"Sara?" came a whisper through the darkness as I snuck through the barn door.

"Nay, 'tis Sara's father," I teased, and Thomas opened the cover on the lantern just enough to reveal a soft glow.

"Do not joke about a thing like that," he chided, pulling me to him and nuzzling my ear. "Did I happen to mention the man truly frightens me? By the way, you're late. I was beginning to think ye were not coming."

"I was waylaid a bit. Kate's been asking far too many questions lately, probing me about my blithe spirits, my rude behavior toward Mr. Graham, my inability to concentrate on what she's telling me and the mysterious disappearance of my writing paper! And if that weren't enough, Flora's taken to lying outside my door every night now, knowing she'll get a nice bit of cheese if I happen to be leaving my room. It was a precaution I took at first—keeping a stash of cheese in my linen drawer—but the daft creature's caught on, and now my father's growing suspicious."

"Suspicious?" he questioned with a frown. "I pray he doesnae treat ye with polite disdain also."

"Polite disdain?"

"Aye, a polite tone of voice accompanied by a cold-hearted look in the eye. 'Thank ye for the report, Mr. Crichton. Anything else? That'll be all.' And I'm waved awa' like a wretched fly on a jam tart."

This was a little disheartening and I sighed. "Oh, whatever shall we do?"

He looked at me a moment with eyes that glistened in the wavering light. "Ye should come awa' with me. Be my woman."

"Thomas, be serious," I reprimanded.

"Oh, but I am, lass," he said, pulling me close—so close his lips were nearly touching mine—and I knew that he was, for his look was one of naked desire. Gone was Thomas Crichton the polite, patient gentleman and in his place stood a man of daring adventure, filled with dangerous thoughts and dangerous needs.

This hot-blooded urgency both frightened and thrilled me. My knees grew weak and tingly, my pulse quickened. "Dinna be afraid, lass," he whispered to my lips. And I found his voice, as well as his soft caresses, soothing. "Surely ye know that I want ye as a man wants a woman? I want to love ye, to make love to ye; I want ye for my wife, Sara. May God help me, but I do."

"But . . . how?" I uttered as tears of helplessness stung my eyes.

"I shall get a job on a merchantman. I'll pay a visit to the lads at the East India Company and beg a job on an Indiaman heading for the Cape! Your father might even be kind enough to write me a recommendation. What d'ye think?"

I sniffed and forced a smile. "I think if he knew it would get you out of his garden, he'd write you the best recommendation in the history of recommendations. But, Thomas, I could not bear it if you went away—and to the Cape of Good Hope, no less!"

"Och, dinna fash. I'll be taking ye with me. 'Tis the whole point, aye?"

I nodded. "But how, Thomas? How can we? What do we do about my—" But his finger stilled my lips.

"Trust me," he said, and then he added with all the sincerity I had ever heard him use, "I will move heaven and earth if I have to so that we can be together, ye do know that?" The words—the very sentiment of rearranging heaven and earth to fit our needs—sent a crackling, electric tingle throughout my body, quite inexplicably, radiating from head to toe. It was not unpleasant, yet I shivered all the same, for I had never felt anything like it. I touched him then, willing him to feel how the magic of his words affected me. For I believed him and trusted that what he said was true.

"Dear Lord," he uttered, his eyes wide with wonder. I knew he felt it too. "Are ye all right?"

"I want you, Thomas Crichton," I stated with conviction,

"and I too will move heaven and earth for you." And then I fell into his awaiting arms.

I knew Thomas was a man that my parents would forever shun and repel. He was nothing to them—a goat turd, as he once said—that unpleasant muck beneath the boot one sometimes steps in. But to me he was everything. And I would be damned if I traded true love and happiness for a smelly, pompous man and five thousand pounds a year—including an estate in the country! To reassure myself, and Thomas, I drew him to me for a kiss, one that I knew would take the breath from him.

"Dear Lord above," he uttered when he could. "Marry me, Sara Stevenson, marry me and I shall endeavor, for all my days, to make ye as happy as ye make me." And to add more fuel to an already burning fire, he shamelessly recited Burns' "A Red, Red Rose," whispering the poem in my ear and delivering it with a passion I seriously doubted had ever touched it before.

> "My love is like a red, red rose
> That's newly sprung in June;
> My love is like the melody
> That's sweetly played in tune.
>
> "So fair art thou, my bonnie lass,
> So deep in love am I;
> And I will love thee still, my dear,
> Till a' the seas gang dry.
>
> "Till a' the seas gang—"

I didn't let him finish. I didn't want him to. Because I was his for the night; I was his for all eternity.

I was as eager for Thomas as he was for me, and we made love that night in the hayloft of the Fergusons' barn. I didn't know what to expect, for I had never been told, only that it was a vile, amoral, sinful act to behave so licentiously with a young man. But I was young and wild and naive, and if I thought his desire would tame me, I was wrong; it made me ravenous for more. Thomas was a Roman god, young and virile, gentle yet eager, and he was mine. And when later we lay naked, entwined in each other's arms, I knew that whatever evils the preachers preached on the sins of the flesh, and however horrid my mother made sexual love out to be, the reality of it was something really quite miraculous and spiritual. How could it be wrong, I thought? How could such a thing be so reviled? And then I had an epiphany; it was the great secret. How else would one control and stifle so magical, so intimate an act between two people? And I smiled then, nuzzling deeper into Thomas' neck, knowing that he was my secret.

It was four days before we could meet again, and this time I had a surprise for him. In response to my acceptance of his proposal of marriage, and tired of hearing me complain of how I missed seeing him when he was out to sea, he managed to leave a miniature oil likeness of himself before he left again, under the garden bench, with a note attached stating that it was only to tide me over until I had to suffer seeing his face every day. But he had insisted he would never tire of mine. I clutched the little picture to my bosom and ran inside, where I placed it directly under my pillow so I'd be near him as I slept. It was his gift, and I was grateful for it. Yet now I was in pursuit of a gift of my own, one especially for him.

I was scanning the windows of the many shops in the Luckenbooths, as Kate, Robbie and I walked placidly along the Royal Mile. It was a glorious day in early autumn and most of Edinburgh's residents were out enjoying it, or so it seemed as we weaved our way in and amongst the throng. I didn't know exactly what I was looking for, but when I passed the window of a watchmaker, I knew. It had been a long day, and I could tell Robbie was growing bored with our women's demands, looking into all manner of flouncy shops, where we fawned over outrageously colorful fabrics, silk ribbons and bows to match and thoroughly impractical hats that were all the rage in France.

I had done a good job of lulling my companion and her amiable husband through my compliance and good cheer, talking of the smelly Mr. Graham in the kindest light while professing how agreeable I found him during his last visit. At first, naturally, both Kate and Robbie were skeptical of my change of heart, knowing what a stubborn creature I was. But my acting skills were greatly improved since my adventures with Mr. Crichton, and they were finally pulled into my web. I sent them ahead to the little pub where we were to have refreshments, feigning that I had seen some silk ribbon in the window of Lady Rebecca's that I absolutely must have. Given Robbie's aversion for shopping, and how tired he must have been, he promptly agreed and pulled Kate with him down the lane, despite her protests. I stepped into the storefront of Lady Rebecca's and watched them go, assuring them I wouldn't be long. As soon as they were out of sight I slipped back into the street and made my way to the watchmaker.

It was a narrow, woody shop I entered, filled with the scent of lemon oil, varnish and sweet pipe smoke. The many timepieces and case clocks ticked and chimed away as I walked past; but my eye was intent on one in particular, the one that had caught my eye in the window. I didn't know anything about timepieces apart from the fact that they usually kept time. And I didn't know why the little watch in the window struck my fancy the way it did. But the truth was that I could see—no, feel—the joy of owning such a smart-looking piece reflected in the eyes of the man I loved. It was not a gaudy, gilded piece to constantly cause him worry if he should lose it, nor was it too plain as to surpass notice. The watch that caught my eye was a strong, solid piece, handsome but not flashy and encased in brilliant polished silver. In short, it reminded me of the man I loved: it reminded me of Thomas.

Quickly, and with no time to spare, I found the little watch and bent to pick it up, yet before I could grasp the object in question a voice near my ear stopped me.

"Either ye are the destined owner of that watch, or you have very fine taste, m'lady." I turned, shocked to see the curator of the shop standing directly behind me. Realizing that I had likely been so absorbed in my arrant quest that I had not heard him walk up, I stood and offered him my kindest smile in apology. The watchmaker, gray-haired and bespectacled, was industriously polishing a tiny circle of glass in his hands. He performed a few last wipes and then dropped the corner of his apron and thrust the lens in a large pocket on the front. He then peered at me with owlish blue eyes from behind his spectacles. "That," he said, shifting his gaze from me to the timepiece still sitting in the window, "is a rare fine chronometer. Came in just two days ago, all the way from London."

"From London?" I questioned. "You didn't make this, then?"

This caused him to chuckle. "I can see," he began, and bent to pick up the watch, "that ye have little experience with chronometers. So maybe ye are the destined owner of the wee watch after all?"

I smiled, for I was not unused to sly salesmen. "Dear sir, I don't believe that inanimate objects have destined owners. However, I am in need of a special gift. And that pocket watch certainly caught my eye. Can you tell me about it?"

"But of course, m'lady. Why, if this isn't a very special watch indeed." And with a twinkle still in his eye he flipped the watch over. "Eighteen-oh-five it says, only one previous owner, an astronomer forbye."

"So it's not new?" I said and scrunched up my nose at the thought.

"No, 'tis not new, but that does not matter with a chronometer as fine as this. The previous owner was a meticulous man. I was told," he added, bending close so that only I could hear, which was just silly because I was the only other person in the shop, "that he was attempting to measure eternity, certain that

the heavens had no end and that God lived just beyond the reach
of his mighty lens." He quirked a wiry brow. "He believed in an-
gels too! But for all his peculiarities, he certainly kept this in fine
working condition. Ye could hardly do better than a John Roger
Arnold detent chronometer like this."

"John Roger Arnold," I repeated. "That was the name of the
astronomer?"

"Heavens, no," he replied, and let out another chuckle. "He's
the one what made the watch. Why, he's quite a reputation for
the making of such pieces. In fact, in the year this fine piece was
made, the Arnolds received a handsome cash award for their
work on such chronometers by the Board of Longitude. Tell me,
miss, did ye have anyone in particular in mind for this?"

I looked at him and replied very truthfully, "A mariner."

"Well then," he said with all seriousness, "this is just the thing
for a man of the sea! Deadly accurate, none more so, and handsome! Why, if kept well oiled and promptly wound, this little
chronometer will keep ticking away forever!"

"Forever . . ." I repeated softly as my mind turned to the notion of eternity and God living beyond the reach of a lens. The
watchmaker, with keen eyes on me, let my little chronometer
slip from his hand, where it dangled and twirled at the end of a
long silver chain. It was a marvelous thing—a mesmerizing
thing—and I believed it was the perfect gift for Thomas. After a
long moment, the old man flicked the shiny object back into the
palm of his hand. He then opened the front, revealing two little
hands beneath a piece of polished glass; they moved smoothly
across the white face, denoting the hour and minute. Their
movement, unbelievably, was dictated by an intricate array of
tight springs and oiled gears. A soft, melodious chime sounded
at the top of every hour, while a window displayed the phases of
the moon, somehow also calculated through the ingenious
mechanism. I knew, for a certainty, that it was an instrument designed to measure the elusiveness of *forever*. "How much?" I
asked cautiously.

"Twenty guineas, six shillings" was his reply.

It was a good deal of money. It was the kind of money one spent on a very, very fine gown, and I had to think for a moment if it was worth it. But then the clever man put the little pocket watch in the palm of my hand, and once again I felt that strange, enlivening tingle travel the length of my body. At the same time the tingling came, heightening my sense of touch, I was struck by the feel of the little timepiece—by the solid weight of it, and of a presence it seemed to have, as if it were a living thing. Its little mechanical heartbeat pulsed in the palm of my hand with an implacable rhythm that sent tiny ripples traveling in the opposite direction as the tingles; and if that weren't enough, the silver housing grew warm and alive . . . as if it were Thomas' skin. Perhaps I was dreaming, but I ached—physically ached—to give the frivolous little gift to the man I loved. I looked up and saw reflected in the eyes of the old watchmaker that he knew, just as I knew, I would pay whatever price he asked.

"Very well," I said, reluctantly handing over the watch. "I'll take it. But for twenty guineas six shillings, do you think, good sir, you could contrive to engrave a message on the back for me?"

"But of course, my dear lady," he said with a twinkle. "That would be my greatest pleasure."

. . .

For once, it was I who got to our secret place first, waiting patiently on the little stool. I had no lantern with me, never thought to bring such a thing, and so I sat in the dark barn waiting. A barn at night is not a silent place, I learned. The horses could be heard shifting in their stalls down the breezeway, making soft snorting noises every now and then. Little shuffling noises and the scurrying of tiny feet denoted that there were plenty of creatures about, no doubt being stalked by the two cats that patrolled the barn. I pulled my feet off the ground and hugged my legs close to my chest, balancing my body on the tiny little circle of wood. I was growing uncomfortable and thinking of leaving, thinking that Thomas was detained, when a loud screech rang out from the hayloft overhead. The sound startled me, throwing me off balance. The door creaked open at the same instant I tumbled off the stool. The barn owl swooped low, aiming for the opening and nearly grazing the top of Thomas' head.

"Sara?" he uttered in surprise and helped me to my feet, dusting the hay from my shift. The soft glow from his lantern showed me he was startled to see me already there. "The auld owl makes a habit of clouting my head whenever I come. 'Tis his wee game," he explained with a soft smile. "Are ye all right, lass?"

"I am now that you're here," I said, and took him in my arms. But when he kissed me I tasted the sweet tang of rum. "Thomas, have you been drinking?"

"Aye, 'tis why I'm a wee bit late," and he kissed me once more.

"Well, are you drunk, then?" I asked, slightly piqued when at last I had the will to push him away.

"Nay, I dinna think that I am. But if I am, would it make any difference?" he asked with a disarming grin, and made another grab for me. This I averted and stood with arms crossed, waiting for an explanation.

"Weel, if ye must know," he drawled, his speech growing thick with passion and drink, "I was takin' a wee nip at the request of Captain MacCrea. I talked to him, Sara. Told him about my intention to work on an Indiaman."

"Did you?" I said, uncrossing my arms. And then, alarmed by his silence, I took an anxious step forward. "Well? What did he say?"

Amused at my change of heart, he leaned his long body gracefully against the post before he laconically replied. "He asked me a few questions, poured me a few drinks, then asked if this notion dinna spring from my dealings with a certain young lady. When I hinted that it very well might, he was all in favor of me jumpin' ship. For auld Captain MacCrea, hard tartar that he is, admitted that he liked me and hated to see me make a mess of my life over a pretty face in a skirt." Here he gave me a mischievous grin. "The good captain was under the impression that I'm runnin' awa' from a lass, not *with* a lass. And by the by, 'tis all settled."

"What's all settled?"

"I'm comin' tae take ye away tae Gretna Green!"

"Gretna Green?" I questioned, recalling the place Mr. Scott had told us about where young lovers often went to elope. "But that's awfully far away, Thomas. How are we to get there?"

"I shall come for ye with a horse."

"A horse?" I questioned, then giggled, for the image of my brave mariner on the back of such a beast was mightily amusing.

"Aye, ye giggle? Do ye no' think I can manage?"

"Thomas, can you even ride a horse?" I challenged, still giggling.

"No, I never have," he admitted quite frankly, shifting his weight against the beam while crossing his arms. "But how hard can it be? I can sail any ship known tae man, and a wee barmy horse willna lay Thomas Crichton by the lee!"

He was being cocky. He had little notion what he was about, but I loved him all the more for it. Besides, if worse came to worst, I could always take over, whisking him away to Gretna Green. And after another hearty, heady kiss, I decided it was time to give him my gift.

I watched as he untied the little box and then pulled from it the little wad of jeweler's cotton. And when he unwrapped the chronometer, and beheld it with awe and wonder as it rested in the palm of his hand, I saw that tears had welled up in his magnificent blue eyes. "Oh . . . Oh lass . . ." he uttered. "Oh Sara, my love, what have ye done?"

"Turn it over," I instructed, and watched again as he read the tiny inscription. "To my beloved Thomas, eternally yours, Sara 1814." He looked at me. "Eternally yours," he whispered, still too choked up to say much else. "For all eternity. I like the sound of that." And he pulled me to him again.

We stayed in the hayloft, entwined in each other, until nearly dawn, neither of us willing to relinquish the other to the separate lives we lived. "Soon," he whispered in my ear, "very soon we shall be together as man and wife under God. Remember, Thursday, one o'clock, the observatory on Calton Hill. I shall be there, waiting with my trusty steed."

Filled with excitement and a terrified thrill, I nodded, promising I wouldn't be late, and to pack very light, as Thomas so sagely advised. We parted with a kiss at the foot of the garden. I watched as he slipped back into the darkness, his golden locks melding with the gray as he walked with the silence of a man used to living in the shadows. I would pull him from the shadows, I vowed, and then I too turned, and headed for my own door, my heart still thumping with the exertions of our lovemaking.

I went to slip inside as I had done for the past few months, but the door was locked. I tried it again, unable to believe that someone had locked it after I had left. I twisted the brass knob again unproductively. I stopped, afraid I'd wake Flora. "Damn!" I uttered, at a complete loss for what to do. I was not good at situations like this. I was a mess, all tussled and rumpled, with bits of hay clinging to my shift and unbound hair. I smelled too, not badly, but I smelled of him. His scent lingered around me, and until I had a good wash in my basin with a dash of lavender sprinkled on my linens, what I had been up to was a dead giveaway. What was I to do? Sit on the stoop until one of the servants came to open the door for me, looking upon my figure with the suspicion I deserved? And then, in a moment of loss, I thought of Kate. The room she shared with Robbie was across the hallway from the kitchen. It was on the first floor. I could rouse her out of bed, confide to her my secret and swear her to secrecy! She of all people understood love. She knew how it took hold and possessed a person. Was she not herself a slave to it? I would go to Kate and tell her to let me in, make her understand, and then swear to any god she wished that I would not do it again. For I wouldn't, I would never again be sneaking to the Fergusons' barn in the dead of night. I was beyond that now, but this I would never tell.

I stood on my tiptoes and rapped on the window. "Kate," I hissed under my breath, praying she would hear me. "Kate, open up." A few moments later the curtain fluttered back and a face appeared in the window. It was not Kate's face; it was Robbie's. The look he gave me, the puzzlement in his eyes at seeing me there, was enough to sink my heart.

"What in the name of God?" he uttered, quite stupefied and aghast at my untimely appearance.

"Robbie, get Kate to open the back door. I've been locked out."

I spent the next hour in my room attempting to explain to Kate just what I was doing out-of-doors at four in the morning. "By God, Sara, it's unseemly! I've never heard the like. Sneaking out of bed to consort with the devil's bucky! He's evil, is that one! All smiles and charm on the surface—it's how he snags his victims."

"Mr. Crichton is an honorable man!" I countered in a heated whisper, afraid of waking the house.

"Does an honorable man coax an innocent maid to a barn in the dead of night so he can have his way with her? He ought to be hung for such base debauchery!"

"It was nothing like that! I love him! I've loved him ever since the first day I laid eyes on him! You of all people should understand."

"Mr. MacKinnon would never dream of luring me out into the dark night to take advantage of my innocence. He's a gentleman—a respectable man—unlike that randy sailor who's taken you into his net." She paused to let her venom sink in, and then, looking me up and down, she decried, "He's had you, hasn't he?" She sniffed at my rumpled chemise and jumped back. "Holy mother of God, what have you done, Sara?"

"I've done nothing I'm ashamed of!" I defended. "I've loved a man who loves me in return. How can that be wrong? Why can't you see it?"

"Because he doesn't love you!" she uttered, truly believing her own words. "He's only using you because you're your father's daughter! He's a man looking for a way up in the world and he's landed on the magical rung. A young woman filled with such romantic notions is an easy target for one such as yon Mr. Crichton."

"How dare you speak of him so? You don't even know him! He *is* an honorable man, Kate!"

"Then how come he's never come forward with his notions?"

"Because my father has already made it clear he wouldn't approve."

"He won't approve because he's a wise man."

"Kate," I said, grabbing her wrists, forcing her to hear me. "I swear to you, I will make it right and prove to you once and for all that Mr. Crichton, though of humble birth and station, is an honorable man. But you must swear to me that you will never, ever mention any of this to my father! Swear it, Kate, as my friend. Swear it, for you know I would do so for you."

It took her a moment. I could see the struggle play out behind her brown eyes as she fought the temptation to divulge so juicy a morsel as she had just stumbled across.

"Very well," she finally agreed. "If you are truly convinced that this sailor is honorable, then so be it. But don't come crying to me when you find out he only used you, used you like a whore he didn't even need to pay for!"

Her words cut deeply. Yet I would gladly accept them in exchange for her silence; for I knew that very shortly I would be proving her wrong. I would be free of them all, gone, whisked away on the wind to a life of my own choosing. And that thought alone made me smile.

· · ·

On Thursday at one o'clock I made my way to the observatory on Calton Hill as planned. I had with me a little bag stuffed with the few things I thought to take. I didn't want much. I didn't want the reminders of what I had once been. And so I chose mundane things like a comb and brush, a mirror, a change of clothes, some money, and my little painting of Thomas of course. And that was all. I walked the pathways, climbing the hill, marveling at the spectacular view of the Firth of Forth on one side, the Palace of Holyrood to another, with the many spires and rooftops, cathedrals and castles that made Auld Reekie look more magnificent than ever before. The air was full of autumn splendor, with a crispness that enlivened the senses making every leaf and flower pop with color and purpose. My heart lifted at the sight of it all, and at the thought of Thomas. I walked around a great deal, searching through the couples that wandered the pathways with me, always on the lookout for a sailor with a horse. But none was to be seen. I sat on a bench beneath the observatory building waiting for Thomas to come, and after an hour of this waiting, I thought perhaps I had missed him, and continued to walk the paths again. Another hour passed and I decided to wait on the bench, certain he would eventually come by.

I waited and waited.

Soon dusk came, and with it a soft maudlin rain; and still I waited. I sat there on the bench, clutching my little bag of belongings tightly to my shivering chest as the chilly water drenched every fiber of my being. I was certain he would appear. I had dreamed it. I had willed it. Yet still there was no sign of Thomas.

It was well after dark when a man came by, holding a lantern to my face, the flame hissing in the damp.

" 'Tis dangerous for a young lass tae be out so late on a night, unescorted."

"I'm waiting," I told him curtly, and continued hugging my bag for warmth.

"Aye, I see," he said gently, and took a seat beside me.

I ignored him, unwilling to look at him, and started to harbor the notion of running away, until his words stopped me.

"Your name wouldn't happen to be Sara Stevenson, by any chance, would it?"

"It is," I said, and turned to look at him. He was middle-aged and dressed in a dark blue uniform. He was one of the magistrate's men charged with keeping the streets of Edinburgh safe. I had seen this man before, and this recognition made my heart sink. "I believe it is time to go home now, Miss Stevenson. Your parents are worried sick about ye." And without any consent from me, he took my hand and led me home.

They were all there, gathered in the parlor, waiting for me—my father and mother, Kate and Robbie, even my brother Thomas and my sister Jane and her husband. One look at the many pairs of eyes beholding me with expressions ranging from pity to disdain and I knew they knew my secret. While I was gone missing Kate had spilled all, breaking her promise to me and forfeiting our friendship.

"So, Mr. Crichton has shown his true colors after all," my father stated coldly, getting to his feet. "Was only a matter of time, really. Ye can put a beggar on a horse and he'll ride to the devil. Mr. Crichton has proven himself to be exactly what I thought him to be, a poor, uneducated, debased reprobate."

"He's nothing of the kind!" I cried in my lover's defense. "How dare you sully his name! You don't even know him! Thomas Crichton is a good, honest man!"

"Does a good, honest man take another man's daughter and treat her like a common whore, coaxing her out after dark to consort in amoral behavior? And you," he said, pointing a shaky finger at me, unable to quell his rage. "How could ye bring such shame upon your family. You're too old to be behaving like a spoiled child." Here he paused, and then, becoming a bit lachrymose, he stated more softly, "You're a grown woman; I see that now. And that is why tomorrow, Sara, I will be calling on Mr.

Graham to tell him that you will happily accept an offer of marriage."

"I will not marry that man, Papa!" I cried, oozing all the rage and frustration I felt. "I will not marry any man but Thomas Crichton!"

"Are ye so daft that ye cannot even see it!" he cried back as all eyes held to our quarrel. "I would never allow such a marriage! And Mr. Crichton, for all his foolish stupidity, was at least bright enough to know that! But you, my own daughter . . . ? How it shames me. He left ye, Sara, and I doubt that he'll ever be back again. Mr. Crichton was a common rake and a coward, and I pray that you've learned a lesson from it. Now, then, I shall not hear another word from you. You will marry Mr. Graham and we'll hear no more of this foolishness, this . . . this disgraceful affair!" He took my mother by the hand and they turned to go, both unwilling to look at me any longer.

"Mr. Graham?" I said mockingly to their retreating backs. "Dear Mr. Graham? Go ahead, Papa, and ask Mr. Graham if he'll take for a wife a woman who's carrying another man's child." It was the last card in my hand, and like the fool that I was, I played it.

The room fell silent as all of them stared at me with mouths agape. And then my mother began to scream.

It was while I stood there, bravely reveling in the knowledge that I indeed carried the fruit of Thomas Crichton's love, that the reality of my situation began to sink in: Thomas Crichton had left me, and he had left me in a state where no respectable man could ever want me again.

# SIX

# Inner Demons

*M*y little foray through the snowstorm to the MacKay croft was not without its price, and that price was extracted in flesh—not exactly lopped from my body as in the proverbial *Merchant of Venice* pound of flesh, although I'm certain Mr. Campbell was tempted. Instead, and fortunately for me, mine was extracted slowly, melting from my body first in the form of a wracking, bone-shaking chill followed shortly by days of fever and delirium. My body burned so that I believed I was close to conflagrating the very blankets and quilts Kate insisted on piling on me. And while I lay in this vapid, lifeless state, hovering on a thread between consciousness and unconsciousness, unable to talk sensibly or comprehend what was going on around me, the fevered dreams took over. It was in them I first saw his death.

Dreams are horrible things when they go against our innermost wishes, and mine were terribly contrary to my deepest desire. The first time he appeared he was standing on the deck of a ship. He turned to me and smiled. He was so close, only a few feet away, and held out his hand, beckoning to me with his magnetic eyes. Without hesitation I began to walk toward him. I reached out my hand, filling with happiness at the thought of being with him again. Yet before we could touch, a billowing cloud of gray smoke rolled in, obscuring his golden form from my view. My hand frantically searched the acrid smoke, trying to find him. I walked into the cloud myself but could see and feel nothing but air. And when at last the gray fog receded in the same direction and manner from which it had come, all that was left was a pool of blood. I stared at it, dark and sticky on the deck, seeping in the caulked spaces between each plank. The sound of waves lapping against the wooden sides filled my ears along with the gentle groaning and popping of slack lines moving against block and tackle. Except for this all was still and quiet. I knew he was gone. And I half screamed, half cried from the pain of it.

A voice came, calm though insistent, attempting to pull me to the surface, yet I resisted, yearning to follow Thomas. It came again, urging more fervently, unrelenting in its tone, until at last I was forced to obey. I believe I was still crying when I finally opened my eyes, and when I did I was shocked to find him sitting there.

If he was angered by my surprise, he didn't show it. The soft glow from the lamp on the nightstand illuminated his features, revealing an expression contorted by deep concern or, perhaps, pity. Just how long Mr. Campbell had been sitting in my room watching me, I had no notion. "'Tis only a dream, Miss Stevenson," he offered calmly. "A very frightful dream." Yet when he bent forward, looking more closely at me, he breathed, "Jesus God, what is it that haunts ye so?"

I looked at him, not understanding what he was saying. It was then I felt it. Deep within me, from the confines of my budding womb, the baby quickened for the first time, fluttering in my stomach like the wings of a trapped butterfly. I gasped from the feel of it. I had never felt such a thing before, regarding the stigma I carried as something inanimate and isolated from me as a person. But suddenly, in one fleeting moment, everything changed. I reached my hand under the sheets, smoothing it over my thickening belly, straining to detect the little tremor that moved my body so. But I could not feel from the outside what I felt on the inside. And then the thought that I carried this life, this child of Thomas Crichton's when I saw his death, made the tears keep streaming from my eyes in an unrelenting flow.

"Hush now, hush now," Mr. Campbell soothed, noting how I was unraveling right before his eyes and growing a bit suspect. "What is it? Are ye in pain, lass? Where does it hurt?"

I didn't know how to answer this, for I was in pain. I was hot, flushed and tormented. My body burned and ached, yet it was my heart breaking that caused my breath to come in gasping half sobs and my fists to clench and unclench the tangled coverlet under which I slept. The physical pain was nothing in comparison. And still too, even more baffling than all these symptoms put together, was the small glimmer of something alive buried deep within me. It was not pain but something quite contrary to it, something I had no name for. Mr. Campbell was staring at me, his eyes looking puzzled and a bit wild. I both nodded and shook my head.

"I don't understand. Ye are in pain?" he questioned, eyes narrowed as he attempted to puzzle it out.

Again I gave an incoherent mumbling gesture.

"Ye are not in pain? Och! But I dinna understand! What will ye have me do? What can I do? By God, what is it, lass, that makes ye cry out so in the dead of night?"

I reached up a hand to wipe the tears and sweat from my eyes, fighting to shake the lingering dream and become master over my emotions once more. He didn't move. He sat very still and kept watching me, studying my face in a disjointed way, his pale eyes hidden in the dark shadow of his brow. And then, with a voice trembling from disuse and lingering sorrow, I answered his question in aught but a whisper: "My baby's father."

He sat quietly processing the words I had spoken. His face

grew distant, his focus inward; and then without any warning his hand came forward, reaching for my neck. Still fevered, I flinched but possessed neither the strength nor the will to fight him. His long fingers, rather elegant and fine for a lighthouse keeper, were cool against my hot skin. They came around me, thumb on the opposite side as the deftly probing fingers, and then, gently, he tilted my chin back, exposing the long white column of my throat. Still watching him with my fevered eyes, I swallowed, then waited, almost willing him to continue.

I had so little to live for. I was completely at his mercy, and this he most certainly knew. His eyes scanned my neck with singular interest as the fingers pressed into my flesh almost painfully. They were moving around, searching for the right spot for which to end my life, and as I waited—my heart thumping ungodly fast, aware of a new life fluttering within me and feeling just a glimmer of remorse for it—his roving fingers stopped. He pulled out a pocket watch, held it under the lamp and continued feeling my pulsating neck. "Dear God," he uttered softly after some moments had passed. "'Tis as skittish as a hare and as feeble as a wean. Give me your arm."

I had no choice; he took it. It was a thing of wonder and horror how swiftly he moved. My arm was pulled flat along my side, propped over a little bowl, palm up, with the sleeve of my nightgown pushed over my elbow. His hand dipped into his pocket and drew forth a little knife, the exact same knife I saw him twirling in the window of the lighthouse. Without another word he gripped my arm, squeezed tightly and pulled the blade across the tender white skin of my forearm. It burned where he cut me, and I flinched, half from the pain, half from the violation of it.

"There, now," he said, relaxing his grip while making certain the blood dripped into the bowl. "We'll just draw off a bit. That should help balance the humors enough to break the fever."

"But I'm not out of humor," I protested weakly, hating the practice of phlebotomy and fighting the urge to pull my arm away.

"From all my observations, Miss Stevenson, ye are very out of humor." I was about to protest this offensive statement when I saw the corner of his mouth twitch upward ever so slightly. He found this amusing. Mr. Campbell was baiting me. Fevered as I was, I would not bite. "Be a good lass now and relax. I'll be back in a moment." And then he left.

I had no choice but to lay my head back on my pillow, being too hot and weak to move. And as I felt the blood drain from me, dripping steadily into the little copper bowl, my heart began to slow down as well, beating at something like normal while the fluttering of tiny angel wings inside me also ceased. Mr. Campbell reappeared.

He took my arm and placed a strip of gauze around it, tying it off in a neat little knot. And then he propped me up on a mound of pillows and insisted I eat some of the broth he had brought with him. "I can manage," I said, when I saw that he meant to feed me like a child.

"Aye, perhaps ye can, but I don't trust ye overmuch. I've little reason to do so."

"I'm not going to run away," I replied a bit testily, and made a pathetic grab for the spoon.

He pushed my arm back to my side, glared at me and retorted, "I don't expect that ye would. You wouldna make it as far as the door. Now open up." I had little choice, and so I did, suffering in silence the humiliation of being spoon-fed by a man who despised me.

"Ye need to eat. Ye need to remain strong. You'll not get better otherwise," he advised sternly as he kept the watery broth coming. There was an unnatural tension in the air that arose between us as he diligently worked the liquid into me with the same fortitude he might set to polishing the great lens. There was naught for me to do but sit and obediently open my mouth on cue, accepting the meal I had little stomach for. He was nearly finished with his unsavory task when all of a sudden his gaze dropped to the bowl cradled in his hand. His mood changed. He appeared introspective, or, perhaps—dare I think it—embarrassed? But whatever chimerical wind had come over him he felt compelled to ask in tones soft yet probing, "Tell me, your baby's father . . . did he . . . did he assault ye, then?"

"What?" I blurted, causing the last spoonful of broth to dribble ignominiously down my chin. I wiped it with the sleeve of my nightgown.

"I asked if he . . . if he forced himself upon ye?"

"No!" I said more than a little tersely.

He looked up. "He did not take advantage of ye . . . forcing himself upon ye . . . committing an act of rape?"

"No!" I was thoroughly indignant at the notion.

"But I thought . . . ?"

"Well, as usual, you thought wrong! It was nothing of the kind!"

This seemed to confuse him and he asked, "Then why is it . . . why is it ye act so skittish and daft all the time? Your willful disobedience . . . your hatred of men. Why do ye cry out in the middle of the night? Often when I walk past, I hear ye, I hear ye weeping into your pillow and, by God, it unnerves me."

"Well, I'm sorry for it, Mr. Campbell! And I'm sorry too that you have no notion what it's like to love someone and then realize that the one you love so deeply, so completely, has truly left you! I cry, sir, from the pain of it, and because I'm still waiting for him to come. But I'm afraid he will never come because he doesn't even know how to find me!" It was said with more heat and passion than I intended.

This admission startled him and he grew suddenly quiet and morose. His face seemed to darken while his lips pulled taut into a pained sort of grimace. And then he cradled his head in his hands, raking his long fingers through his unruly dark hair.

He suddenly looked up, his eyes pale and piercing. "Is that why . . . is that why ye were up in the light-room that day? Ye were looking for the telescope? Were ye looking for him?"

I was a little riled, perhaps overly defensive of my previous behavior, and quipped, "Why? Does that sound so daft to you . . . to look for someone in a place as lonely and forlorn as this? Yes, I was trying to reach your telescope. It intrigued me. I thought . . ." Here I trailed off, believing he really didn't care what I thought. "I'm sorry," I added instead. "I'm sorry for breaking one of your 'lighthouse rules.' I really didn't know."

He was quiet, watching me as I talked, saying nothing, not even a nod in acknowledgment of my apology. And then, abruptly, he stood to go. "Ye need your rest, Miss Stevenson," he said coldly as he bent to turn down the lamp. The light played on his features, slowly receding like the setting of the sun, casting the landscape of his strong, rather handsome face into shadow. It was dark again but for the soft glow of the banked fire in the fireplace. "I'll send Mrs. MacKinnon by in the morning to check on ye. But now, I believe, 'tis time ye went back to sleep." He picked up the copper bowl containing the blood he had drained from me and carried it to the door. Yet there he paused, stood thinking for a moment and turned around. "If ye like . . . when you're feeling better, I can show you how to use the telescope."

I propped myself up a little higher and looked at him incredulously. He was silhouetted in the doorway; the dangerous look had left him. His odd pale eyes that could pierce with the points of daggers when they wanted to seemed quiet and distant.

"But ye must promise not to touch anything, of course, like the great lens or the housings. But if ye are careful, and if ye are still interested, I can take ye to the observation room and ye can have a look."

"Really?" I uttered, slightly suspicious of this change in him.

"Aye, really. Now, good night to ye, Miss Stevenson," he said, and left the room, still carrying the little basin of my blood, a palpable air of tiredness and defeat lingering about him.

. . .

There were indeed many changes that happened as the harshness of winter receded. As I recovered from my illness, trying to regain my strength from the fever that had ravished my body, I was forced to drink many malodorous and putrid infusions and decoctions prepared by Mr. Campbell and served up by Kate, she insisting that they were not poison but medicinal substances. This I doubted, especially since it was Mr. Campbell who prepared them, but I was in no shape to argue and so I drank what I was given, mainly to appease Kate and Robbie, who would not let me out of bed until I complied. And I was growing all the more restless and irritated, confined to my room as I was. There was also an upside to this forced assault and methodical destruction of my taste buds, and that was that Kate's cooking wasn't nearly so hard on the palate as it once was. At least my stomach didn't rebel as often as it had when I first arrived.

There were other changes too, not just the minor culinary improvements of our cottage, but changes in Mr. Campbell as well. He never came to sit with me again, never attempted to bleed me or probe my neck, but he did look in from time to time, standing at the threshold of my doorway, daring to go no farther. He was fleetingly polite with conversation, asking few questions and answering mine with monosyllabic words. His eyes, those marvels of nature, seemingly pellucid one minute then calculating and cunning the next, were not nearly so harsh and captious. He kept his distance; he kept his anger in check, yet there was an air about him that bordered on desolate. I'd like to say it didn't bother me, but I found that it did. And the reason for this was that I believed I was the cause of it.

There was also a change in my body. Where for so long I had been slender and lithe, hardly believing my own words when I proclaimed to my family that I was pregnant, and wishing it more than feeling it, only suspecting it by the skipping of one menstruation cycle, it was indeed true. Once I began to take solid foods again I could feel my stomach thickening with a pleasing roundness. There had been, of course, the word of the examining physician back in Edinburgh, a neighboring country doctor with no ties or knowledge of our family. He had confirmed for my parents their worst fears and preserved me from a loveless marriage. Kate and my mother still implored me to marry the good Mr. Graham straightaway, advising that I beguile him with wedding-night passion and then pass the fruit of another man off as his own. This was downright amoral cuckoldry and they knew it! How good, God-fearing Christian women could think of it was in itself disturbing, but that they should both approach me with the same solution on their own was yet more telling and damning by far of the cunningness within the fairer sex. How often was this particular *coup d'état* employed? Of course I rejected this notion out of hand for personal reasons, taking the moral high ground, which was rather pathetic coming from a fallen woman. Yet only now was I certain that Thomas' child lived within me, and its presence—felt in the stillness of the night with heavenly caprice—both thrilled and inspired me. And I longed for its father all the more.

It was late February, a mild day on the Cape, with a cloudless sky and the sun shining forth with diminished midwinter intensity. The ground, covered by two feet of snow, sparkled like so many diamonds, while great arrows of gannets passed overhead. It was still plenty cold outside, but there was a hint of spring in the air and I chose this day to approach Mr. Campbell with my request. He looked up from his plate of eggs and biscuits, his pale eyes scanning my woolen-frocked form as a stableman might check a mare for soundness. Unable to abide such scrutiny—my pride absolutely forbidding it—I stood where he could better see me, performed a graceful pirouette, then bobbed a courtly curtsey to him. He dropped his fork. Kate giggled.

"Well, ye look healthy enough," he finally said. "At least you've the strength to mock me. But can ye manage the climb?"

"Why, of course I can," I insisted, sitting back down. "And hardly a day could be finer. Besides, I distinctly heard you say that the fishing fleets would be starting out for the Grand Banks very soon now. I wouldn't want to miss that."

"Aye, I spied a few lights last evening from passing ships. The weather was grand enough for it, but it will not last," added Robbie, reaching for more biscuits, no doubt relishing the change in breakfast fare from the usual watery oat porridge.

"I said they'd be starting, Miss Stevenson. Besides the navy lads, what you'll be seeing now is yon gallant adventurer or your more intrepid tradesman, but little else. The real shipping traffic won't start for a few weeks yet."

"Then I'll be ready," I stated with conviction. Although Mr. Campbell had some inkling of what drove me to the tower, Kate and Robbie had remained ignorant until that moment. They both looked at me, then at each other. There passed a look between them that went beyond my understanding, and when their eyes came to rest on me again, I got the feeling they were both displeased with my motives.

It was a peculiar phenomenon that four people could live in such close proximity for nearly as many months and still be largely ignorant of the many secrets we carried. Certainly we had a grasp of one another's unique personalities and idiosyncrasies—for instance, which of us preferred milk and sugar in our tea, and which of us did not, who enjoyed reading outdated copies of the *Edinburgh Review* over a shot of whisky by the fire at night, and who preferred to chat about Edinburgh and dredge up old gossip over a cherry cordial. Kate assumed I had forgotten the man I loved and that I was now living peacefully with the foolish choices I had made. Robbie was so fully absorbed in his new role as light-keeper and busy keeping a thumb on his own domestic affairs that he had little time for much else. Yet it was he that knew Mr. Campbell better than any of us, spending hours at a time cooped up with the man, or out hunting together on the parve when time allowed. However, both Robbie and Mr. Campbell were of reticent dispositions and aside from the occasional conversation about lighthouse affairs and small talk over a glass of whisky at night, they were nearly strangers.

It was Mr. Campbell who finally spoke out, inviting Kate along to the tower with us to investigate the telescope once the morning chores were attended to. But for whatever reason, even though she knew what drove me to the observation room, she declined and sent me on alone with Mr. Campbell.

The observation room of late February was the same lofty chamber it had been when I first ventured up the many steps months ago, with the exception of the table where the man on duty sat. It still contained the makeshift spirit stove designed to keep a pot of coffee or tea warm, I noticed, but it was now scrubbed clean and empty of all books and papers except for the few nautical volumes, ledgers and signal books required. Mr. Campbell was waiting by the window, his tall, powerful form silhouetted by the sunlight shining through. Upon hearing me enter, he turned around. His appearance struck me at once, for he had changed. No longer was he wearing his rough and ragged work clothes of the morning but had on a respectable greatcoat, stock, clean linen and fine-fitting tan breeches, along with polished black Hessian boots. His attire was better suited to the streets of Edinburgh than a lighthouse on the edge of the world. His hair was also different, not loose and wild about his head but brushed to a deep chestnut sheen and pulled back into a proper queue. The transformation was remarkable and it did wonders for his luminous eyes. "Good, you've come," he said without preamble, beckoning me over. "Mind the light, aye?" This he cautioned as I rounded the housing for the lamp, and then continued: "I was hoping you'd be along soon, for I've something of interest to show you. A small contingent from Ireland, I believe, is making its way down the Minch and should be rounding the Cape in the next hour or so, wind and tide permitting."

"Really? How fascinating," I replied, and went to stand next to him at the window. I looked in the direction he pointed and saw nothing but a few little triangles of white on a vast undulating sea. "How can you tell who they are when they're so far away?" I questioned, thinking it unbelievable.

"Well, have a look and see for yourself."

Eagerly I put my eye to the eyepiece attached to the swiveling scope, yet all I could see was blue—just a big circle of blue everywhere I aimed. When I said as much to Mr. Campbell he smiled slightly and instructed that I needed to sight the target properly first, then make small adjustments with the knob on the side, bringing objects far away into better focus. This I did, and once I had the ships in my sights, the difference was even more astounding. I could see there were five in all, remarkably similar three-masted vessels that seemed rather low in the water. And though I could not make out faces I could definitely tell there were people aboard them, and just that knowledge alone—that I could see something so far away with such detail—thrilled me. "What are they, do you think?" I questioned.

"They look suspiciously like transports to me. Do ye see the way they're rigged? Shorter masts for stability, not speed."

"You can tell by the way they're rigged?"

"That, and the more telling fact that they sail under the colors of the Transport Board—with the Union Jack flying at the mizzen. They're the king's ships, sure enough, but what business they're about, I haven't a guess."

"Transports? Are they going home, do you suppose?"

"Nay, they're heading in the wrong direction if they are. Perhaps they're for the continent. Maybe they have it in mind to invade Scotland? One never knows with the Irish aboard."

"Why do you say they're Irish when those are British ships?"

"Because if they were transports from west England or even southern Ireland they'd not take this route. They'd head south by way of the Irish Sea and round Land's End to the English Channel. It's easier and safer than threading the Minch, though I've known some to prefer it. No, those lads there are most likely heading to the North Sea, or even the Baltic, maybe for supplies—but to what end, I wonder?"

"You like watching ships, Mr. Campbell," I stated, still marveling through the sight of the telescope.

"Sometimes" was his reflective answer.

We stayed like that in the observation room watching the ships move closer, standing in compatible silence while noting aloud every now and again further details that struck us. Mr. Campbell was awed by the notion of soldiers being shipped back to the continent when so many, after years of terrible fighting in the peninsula, were now at home. Were they going to the Baltic? he wondered aloud, but what a time of year to brave that sea! I was finally able to see faces of the men milling about on deck, soaking up the winter sun. But there were so many of them, and they were all dressed in the red coat of the British Army, and still they were too far for any proper recognition. I must have given some indication of my disappointment, for Mr. Campbell asked softly, "Miss Stevenson, where is it ye believe your baby's father to be?"

I stood up, forgetting the telescope entirely, and looked at him closely for the first time. There was no anger or malicious intent about him. He looked handsome and cultured, his face set at an earnest tilt, his question polite as if he truly cared. Yet he was a man of such volatile constitution that I was hesitant to trust him with my secrets. He stood with hands clasped behind his back, waiting.

"The truth is," I heard myself saying, "I'm not entirely certain."

"Ye do not know where he is?" he questioned softly.

I shook my head, uttering the word "No."

"Did he leave ye, then?"

I thought on this, recalling vividly the pain and humiliation of that day on Calton Hill. I could feel the familiar stinging behind my eyes and cursed myself silently for not being stronger. "I . . ." I began, and then looked away, pretending to watch the ships again while covertly wiping the budding tears. "I cannot believe that he did. He promised he never would . . ."

"And why is it ye believe he'd be on a ship?"

"Because he's a sailor," I replied matter-of-factly, still looking out to sea.

"Ah, I see," he uttered softly. "And if . . . if ye did happen to see him one day, by chance on a passing vessel, what is it ye have it in mind to do?"

I never thought of this. Ever since Thomas Crichton came into my life, common sense and reason seemed to have left me. What would I do? What could I do? I lived on a cliff hundreds of feet above the sea; often the promontory was cloaked in fog. Even if I did run to the cliff's edge and jumped up and down waving my hands frantically, it was unlikely Thomas would see me. I was invisible. And alone. And hidden from the world behind a roving yellow eye.

"I'm sorry, lass," he said, and I could see that he really was. He was about to say something more, when a voice came echoing up the tower stairs. "Willy man, are ye up there?" It was Robbie. Mr. Campbell replied that he was and Robbie called up, "'Tis the wee lad Hughie come to see ye. Says his da's on his way."

"Och, I almost forgot!" he uttered, then called back through the doorway, "Tell the lad I'm on my way down." He turned to me, a conspiratorial smile on his lips, and said, "At least the wee fiend's good for something, aye?"

"Mr. MacKay's coming to the lighthouse?" I thought it odd after the way Mary had acted that day.

"Aye, and his wife too."

I studied him closely, detecting a somewhat smug look on his face as he delivered this message. The fact that he was dressed in a manner to receive company was also noted. "You asked them here . . . intentionally? That's why you look so fine today!" It was blurted in a half question, half accusation.

"Ye think I'm fine-looking?" he quipped, his demeanor slightly teasing. He did look fine in his own way; Mr. Campbell was a handsome man, but I shook the question off and repeated, "You asked them here? When?"

"Aye," he admitted, his face turning serious again. "I saw the lad out on the parve near a fortnight ago when Robbie and I were stalking that buck," he answered, making reference to the poor, thin creature we had been dining on for the past two weeks. "The lad had taken a fine brace of hare that day and came over to see what's afoot. He told us of your wee visit to his croft and was very chatty where you were concerned. Seems he'd taken the measure of ye quite well, from all accounts." He regarded me with an odd look of amusement so foreign to his serious demeanor. "The lad's got an ingenuous manner about him both MacKinnon and I found quite disarming, but he also happened to mention that his mother was especially taken with ye and Miss Kate, and was anxious for another visit. I told him ye were unwell at the time but at the next fine day they should come out for a visit. And what day could be finer than this?"

"You asked them here on my account?" I was astounded. I didn't think he had it in him. And I was certain my voice failed to hide the gratitude I felt. I walked over to the other side of the observation room to peer out the window. There, on the great expanse of undulating moorland, still covered in glistening snow, were two horses pulling what one might almost term a sleigh, but, in fact, looked more like a dogcart on runners, that was most definitely making its way toward us. There was also a horse in the courtyard hobbled to the flagpole; Robbie and the boy, wee Hughie, were leaning against the low wall, talking.

"Actually, Miss Stevenson, I'd be lying if I said yes." I turned from the window to look at him. He bent his head slightly, dropping his gaze to the floor. "I had a wee incident with Mr. MacKay last summer and haven't spoken to the man since. Haven't spoken to anyone on the Cape, for that matter. I thought perhaps it was time to clear the air between us."

"Incident?" I questioned. "What incident?"

He ignored my probing curiosity and came to stand beside me at the window, watching the little wagon as he spoke. "Truthfully, I wasn't certain they'd come at all, even if Mrs. MacKay had taken a liking to ye. Highlanders can be a bloody stubborn lot. It was a bit of a long shot, really. But ye see," he said softly, his magnificent eyes locking on to mine, "I employed a tactic, low though it may be, that was certain to bring them out eventually."

Mr. Campbell was standing in his observation room, his personal domain, and it was in here he was willing to reveal himself to me, opening up just enough for me to get a glimpse inside his complicated and contradictory mind. Eagerly, perhaps a little too eagerly, I awaited his confessions. "Why . . . would that be, sir?" I prodded hopefully, placing a hand gently on the sleeve of his jacket. "Why wouldn't they come, Mr. Campbell? And what sort of tactic did you use to bring them here?"

I truly believed I was winning him into my confidence with my unfeigned sincerity and interest, but he drew away. My touch, gentle though it was, made him flinch. His brows came down, his gaze darkened and I felt as if the door that had just begun to crack open between us was again slammed shut. He walked over to the base of the light and pretended to examine the complicated gears and clockwork mechanisms that when cranked by hand would cause the housing to rotate.

At length he turned to me, and with a sardonic smile said, "I promised the lad I'd show him all the workings of the great lantern if he came, Miss Stevenson—told him I'd let him stand in the observation room to peer through the telescope at passing ships on the sea, titillating his interest all the more. Because I knew a lad like that, a bit wayward, headstrong and coddled in the bosom of his family, would drive his parents positively daft with his incessant begging, with his singular focus on his own desires."

In his words and dark tone, I felt the personal reprimand. Indignation was rising and I wrestled it back, but I could not refrain from lashing out. "So you used the child for your own end," I said coldly. "How magnanimous of you. And here I thought you were actually beginning to have a heart."

"That was *your* mistake," he said evenly. "And I will tell you now, Miss Stevenson, so you don't make the same mistake again: I do not have a heart."

. . .

Puzzled and wounded by this mix of kindness and cruelty Mr. Campbell seemed to wield at will, I ran into the cottage, only half-heartedly returning wee Hughie's friendly greeting. Kate was already hard at work on refreshments, making a mess of the little scullery and fully aware that we were expecting guests. "You knew!" I stammered, coming through the door.

"Aye. Robbie told me," she confirmed in an offhand manner, and after stomping the snow from my boots while shaking my head deprecatingly, I went to my room to make the proper transformation required for receiving guests.

Thankfully I was in possession of many frivolous and fashionably high-waisted Empire gowns, every one of them thoroughly unsuited for remote cottage living. I chose a particularly enchanting one of deep rosy silk, accented with creamy satin ribbons and a matching spencer jacket. It turned heads in Edinburgh and it would likely suit my purpose here. And while I was disrobing, shucking off my ugly, soot-stained blue and cream work frock in exchange for the more elegant attire, I silently seethed with anger, knowing Mr. Campbell had played on my weakness. He knew what I wanted. He had seen the desperate look in my eye that first day he had found me in his tower. And he held the telescope before me like a carrot dangled before a starving cart horse. Foolishly, and apparently with no more control over my desires than wee Hughie, I had jumped at the chance. What was worse, Mr. Campbell now knew why. He knew what drove me. He knew what demon tormented me, yet I was no closer to discovering his. However, secrets revealed themselves slowly. And one secret of Mr. Campbell's was set to arrive very shortly!

It was a genuine pleasure to see the face of Mary MacKay again. It had been weeks since we had first met, and that under rather suspect circumstances, yet it hadn't diminished Mary's desire to renew her acquaintance with us. She bounded out of the sleigh and ran over to Kate and me, grabbing me up in a warm embrace while exclaiming how sorry she was to hear of my illness. "Grab m'bag, Hugh, will ye?" She directed the order to her husband, a tall, broad, fine-looking man with the same shade of effulgent hair as his namesake. He had his little daughter in his arms and was making his way toward us when he stopped, turned and went back to the cart for the bag in question. "I've brought some things as ye should have to see ye in better health."

"Why, thank you, Mary. How kind, truly. But as you can see, I'm much improved."

"Aye, perhaps. But ye caused me a terrible fright, Sara, when I heard what happened. I would ha' never forgiven myself. Especially since I told Hugh all about your visit and he being so anxious tae meet the both of ye."

Hugh came forward with child and bag in hand and introduced himself. He was definitely his son's father, for wee Hughie was the man's miniature. Yet the father's manner was more polished by far. "So ye are the ladies who ventured out in a blizzard tae meet my wife?" he began with a disarming smile. Put like that, our little escapade sounded rather foolish, and both Kate and I humbly acknowledged that we had. "Well, I'm certain ye've already had an earful for your efforts, but I, for one, am impressed, and grateful too. My wife has talked endlessly of your wee visit. Ye made a long winter brighter for her and the children, and for that ye have my deepest respect." He performed a slight bow.

"How refreshing to finally meet a man of reason!" I exclaimed impulsively, taking his proffered hand. "Because on our end here, Mr. MacKay, respect wasn't in it. An earful, however, was. Welcome to the lighthouse. We're overjoyed to finally make your acquaintance, and honored that you saw fit to visit us on this fine winter day."

We ushered our guests into the cottage, anticipating an afternoon of leisurely pleasure. Yet as soon as Mr. MacKay poked his

head through the doorway, scanning the main room with a scrutinizing gaze, he paused. "Where has wee Hughie gotten off to?
I'd expected him to be here waiting, as he promised he would
when he begged to be let to ride ahead."

"Why, sure he's here, never you worry, sir," offered Kate. "My
Robbie took him up to the light-room a short while ago to have
a look around. The wee lad was most anxious to see it."

"He's in thon tower?" the powerful Highlander exclaimed,
looking none-too-pleased, his ruddy face going a few shades
ruddier. "Is Campbell up there too?" It was more of a demand
than a question, and before I could answer he exclaimed, "Och!
But o' course he is, thon wicked glib-tongued gomeral, luring
my boy here like the canny de'il he is! He's got the lad up in the
tower filling his wee impressionable mind wi' all manner o' dark
notions. By God—"

"Hugh, please!"

"No, no, 'tis quite all right," I assured Mary, while silently admiring her husband's venomous tirade and willing it to go on
and on. But that would never do. The poor dear had gone nearly
as red as her husband, though out of embarrassment, not anger,
and was grappling the sleeve of his coat as one would rein in a
spooked horse careening toward the edge of a cliff. "Mr. MacKay,
please allow me to take you to the light-room myself. By no
means should you be excluded from Mr. Campbell's tour. Why,
he told me himself how eagerly he was awaiting your arrival.
I'm certain he's looking forward to having a word with you."

"Aye, I just bet he is," Hugh MacKay replied, breathing a little too heavily for a man engaged on a friendly visit. He thrust
his wiggling daughter into his wife's arms and then, excusing
himself civilly, stalked off in the direction of the tower.

That Mr. Campbell was expecting Hugh MacKay was a certainty, yet he took great care to look nonplussed at our arrival,
leaning his tall, elegantly dressed frame laconically against the
casement of the window and talking to the boy, whose eye was
bent to the telescope, with avuncular familiarity as the two dis-

cussed the ships rounding the Cape. Robbie was seated at the table, silently scribbling in the log. Both men looked our way as we entered. There was a moment of awkward silence, the cold air alive with a palpable tension, and then Mr. Campbell's eyes rested on me. He clearly had not expected my return after so inauspicious an exit only a short while ago, an exit spurred by hurt, anger and absolute frustration. He was also not expecting my transformation from dowdy pot-scrubber to Edinburgh debutante, and the flicker of appreciation crossed his luminescent eyes. Yet before his predatory gaze could linger I cut him off with a mocking smile.

"Why, Mr. Campbell! Here you are, dear sir. I came to let you know that the MacKays have arrived . . . But forgive me, you must already know that, having such a vantage point over us all. Mr. MacKay was most anxious to speak with you, especially so after learning his son had ventured into the lighthouse without his permission. I believe you are acquainted with Mr. MacKay?"

The men regarded each other warily from across the room. Robbie stood smiling politely while awaiting a formal introduction. Yet before introductions could be made, a pleading reproach came from across the room, interrupting the silent standoff with a resounding "Daaa!"

"Step away, Hughie. I thought we discussed that ye would wait until your mother and I arrived."

"But, Da, ye were taking a muckle long time about it. And the ships were passing, coming about in a line! 'Twas a grand sight indeed." His blue eyes widened, expressing the wondrous sights he'd seen.

"Do not argue, lad! Step away." Wee Hughie looked in my direction and crossed his spindly arms over his spare torso. The look of displeasure he gave me was comically reminiscent of Mr. Campbell's.

"Da, please! Ye said I could, and Mr. Campbell was only telling me about those ships. Surprisingly, the man knows a lot."

"Aye, that he does," replied Mr. MacKay as he walked over to the telescope. He then took his son by the arms and, squatting before the boy so as to better look him in the eye, said evenly, "But ye disobeyed me, Hughie, and a good lad never disobeys his father." This had an instant effect on the boy and he hung his head in shame, all the infantile bravado deflating from his youthful frame with those few reproachful words. I found it a strangely moving scene, very telling of the powerful relationship between father and son, and fought the urge to wrap my arms around the little creature and comfort him myself.

Mr. Campbell pushed himself away from the wall in one lithe move to stand closer to father and son. "I believe the fault is mine, MacKay, not the lad's. I'm sorry. I didn't know he was to wait. He's a good boy, bright too, and he's welcome back whenever he wishes. Aye, Hughie? Now, may I introduce my new man, Mr. MacKinnon, come late last fall to the lighthouse?" The men shook hands, but the tension between Mr. Campbell and the Highlander was still very much alive and dangerous. Then, turning to me, he said with a sugary smile, "Miss Stevenson, would you be a dear and take this young man back to the cottage for some biscuits and tea? We'll be along shortly. I believe Mr. MacKay and I have some matters to discuss."

It was apparent that neither wee Hughie nor I wanted to leave so promising a scene, one that might reveal something of Mr. Campbell's dark nature and why Hughie's father was so wary of the man. All eyes followed us to the door as I led the boy by the hand, waiting for us innocents to be safely out of earshot before they unloaded. Yet once over the threshold, with the door safely shut behind us, I sat on the top step and shooed Hughie away. "Go," I whispered. "Go back to the cottage. I'll be along in a moment."

The boy didn't budge.

"Hughie, go," I seethed. But the boy just looked at me, a sly smile playing on his ten-year-old lips.

"Come away with me or I willna go at all," he threatened.

"You'd not disobey your father again? Good lads do not disobey their fathers."

"What about ye?" he whispered back. "Ye are disobeying your man. He told ye to get to the cottage, but ye stay. Why?"

"I stay because he's not my man. And I'm not a child. And ye should not be arguing with adults. Now go," I shooed, and turned to listen, placing my ear to the door.

"Campbell, what the hell are ye thinking!" boomed the voice of Hugh MacKay. "Using my boy like a pawn in your wee sick game. Goddamn ye, ye soul-sucking gomeral!"

I looked beside me. The boy was still there, looking as intrigued by these words as I felt. I made to reproach him again, insisting that he leave, yet before I could he put his fist in front of the door, holding it an inch away and threatening to knock.

"What kind of ill-mannered devil-spawn are you?" I chided in a hushed whisper.

He slid down beside me, fist still poised by the door, looking at me with his wide blue eyes. "My da doesn't like Mr. Campbell owermuch, yet I find I like the man very well. I want to know why, Miss Sara, there is such distrust."

"Me too," I whispered back. I thought a moment. The child had me in a stalemate. "All right," I conceded, unwilling to miss the conversation. "You can stay. But I warn you, we must be quiet and say not a word about this to anybody."

It was agreed, and we sat squished together on the cold top step with our ears pressed to the door, straining to listen.

"I was not using your boy, MacKay. I said he's a smart lad and I meant it. But I did want to talk with you. You and the rest of the men on the Cape have kept your distance, and I respected that. But things have changed. Shipping will be picking up, and I have no wish to repeat the events of last fall."

"Nor do we. But ye have little respect for our wishes; ye have no personal involvement here."

"What makes you say that?"

"When I heard that two women were living at the lighthouse I thought that maybe perhaps I was wrong. Mayhap ye do have a vested interest here, bringing a wife—a budding family. But then I learned from my own wife that the young woman, that rather brave and comely child ye let ride to my croft in a blizzard, no less, was no' your wife! Could ye no' even commit to a lass as fine as that? Do ye flaunt the fact that she's living with ye, tending your home . . . sleeping under your roof? And yet ye will no' even give her the protection of your name? What kind o' man are ye?"

Mr. Campbell's voice came dark and even. "I'll thank you to leave Miss Stevenson out of this discussion. And her character is above reproach. She is indeed a very fine, very beautiful young lady, but she is not my woman, nor is she 'living' with me. She is only under my protection until her husband returns for her, and that is all." I put my hand over my heart at this seamless recovery, thankful that Mr. Campbell was as convincing a liar as I.

"Poor thing. Well, take care nothing happens to the lass. Ye have quite a reputation for disaster, and I wonder at the man who would put her under your care. May I suggest, for a start, not letting her ride across the parve in a snowstorm?" I felt a jab in my ribs. I looked next to me and saw that wee Hughie was intimating his father's exact sentiment with an expression that was insulting coming from one so young. I ignored him.

"That was her own doing. We had no idea the women were gone. And I ask you to leave Miss Stevenson's affairs to me." I reciprocated in kind to the boy next to me, making my own painful point.

"Well, I shall pray that ye let no harm befall the lass, because my wife speaks mighty highly of her. But ye see, I know all about ye, Campbell. Jamie Chisholm had a cousin what sailed with ye in the year oh-seven. The death ship they called it, aye? Ye lost, what?—over half your men?"

"That was different."

"Was it? And when three men of the Cape die doing your bidding, including one of your own, how does that affect ye? Apparently no' much. Ye risked nothing personally. Ye barely flinched over your own man's death, and nary a tear was shed over the others. 'Twas inhumane! Did ye even care that those men's families were ruined? Poor Mrs. MacDonald no' only lost her husband and son, she lost her croft; she lost everything! And now the poor wee creature is reduced to toiling in a weaver's mill just so she willna starve! Three men died that day, Campbell, two families ruined, and yet ye press us for more. We dinna ask ye here. We dinna want ye here! We were fine enough without your wee tower invading our land."

"I know that you did not ask me here. But here I am, and all I ask is that ye rethink your position. There were four wrecks last year, seven the year before. Many died. If we could but send a boat out, just to pick up the survivors, we'd at least save some lives."

"Aye, perhaps. But you're a cursed man, Campbell! Everyone knows it," came a voice wrought with extreme passion. "Can ye no' see it? By God, I pity ye. I pity thon poor, sweet young woman in your care, and I pity Mr. MacKinnon here and his wife! Because every venture ye touch—every path ye cross—ends in death and disaster. Do ye think that by sitting in this tower, saving mariners' lives, ye'll buy back all those wretched souls ye lost? We are no' your redemption here, man! The men o' the Cape canna save ye! Your job is to illuminate the coast, and that is all! Keep the light if ye must. But keep to yourself!" It was a scathing speech, one that even I was sorry for, and I wondered at the meaning of it. Could such a thing be true? Was Mr. Campbell truly cursed? And in the silence that followed, my heart went out to the heartless creature, for no one deserved such treatment. When at last he did reply, I was shocked. He sounded so nonplussed—his character had been raked over the coals yet he remained calm, nonchalant even.

"So you'll do nothing? When a ship wrecks off your coast, you'll sit back and watch men die?"

"We do what we've always done, Campbell. They're foreign ships, none of our own."

"And for centuries your people have made a profit by their loss. I know. I know all about it. But what if they were Scottish? What would you do then?"

Mr. MacKay replied a bit defensively. "Our lads know these waters. They know the tides, the currents, the risk o' the breakers. I have no fear for them."

"Like you know these waters?" Mr. Campbell riposted. "Och, I've seen ye, MacKay. I've seen the way ye handle a boat. You were not always a shepherd, were ye?"

It grew quiet.

"How long have you lived on the Cape? Five years? Seven? Why did ye come here, MacKay? Certainly there's not much appeal for a man like you to coddle a flock of sheep all day."

"What do ye ken of life in the Highlands?" demanded the booming voice. "What in God's name do ye know of trying tae keep a family alive? Ye have no family, Campbell! Ye Lowlanders live in another world altogether, and I wouldna expect ye to understand our ways here."

"Perhaps not," came the voice of well-schooled control, "but I'll put the question to ye again, all the same. What if ye had a vested interest in a ship cruising these waters, MacKay? Shall we say a French ship, for instance, coming in the dark of night, perhaps dropping anchor just off Kervaig Bay?"

Again Mr. Campbell's question was met with silence.

"If anything were to happen to such a ship, would ye not want to be prepared? To at least be able to preserve the life of her crew?"

"What are ye saying?"

"I'm saying that I have a fine view of these waters and the ships that cruise them. I know a lot more of what goes on here than ye might think. For instance, I know how hard it is to eke a living off this barren land."

"Are ye using the blackmail on me, then?"

"Nothing of the kind. I'm simply asking for your help. The men listen to you, MacKay. Persuade them that it's in their best interest to show up at the jetty early on the morning of the tenth of March. I have two boats in dry-dock there that I'd like pulled around to Kervaig Bay. Mr. MacKinnon has also expressed his wish to me to be a part of such an endeavor. I admit that I've used poor judgment in the past. Perhaps the jetty is not the place to stage a rescue, and I deeply regret the incident last autumn. I do grieve for them, you know," he reflected softly. "But perhaps with you in charge of the rescue boats, the men will have more confidence in their practice."

"Me? In charge? But I dinna want to be in charge! I want nothing to do with ye!"

"Nor do I want to see men die needlessly. Come, now, take my hand, Hugh, and let us pretend, for the sake of the womenfolk, that the air is clear between us."

Silence fell over the room. I envisioned two wolves, huge and male, teeth bared as they circled each other, hair bristling as they struggled for dominance. And then suddenly came the scuffling of feet. Hughie gave a tug on my sleeve. "What?" I hissed, my ear still pressed to the door.

"Take off your shoes, quick!" he ordered, and his were off in a trice. He then began tugging on my own. I understood. The men were coming and we needed to leave in silence. I unlaced my white little half boots and carried them with me as Hughie and I raced down the tower stairs in stocking feet. We were not a quarter of the way down the spiral when we heard the door open. Heavily booted feet wasted no time hitting the steps, striking the cold stone with a solemn force, the loud, purposeful strides shadowing our retreating forms. Hughie grabbed my hand and pulled me along, willing me to move faster. We reached the bottom landing and bolted out the door, onto the shoveled walkway. I was not as fast as I had once been—my lungs were short of air, my body heavy—and poor Hughie was terrified of being found out by his father, though no more terrified than I. We suffered the cold, wet gravel with aplomb, because we had little choice. And when we came bursting through the cottage door, causing some amount of alarm as two startled faces stared at us over teacups poised before their lips, I covered for our unprecedented entrance by exclaiming, as I doubled over to catch my breath, "Whew! I should really know better than to challenge a boy half my age to a footrace! Congratulations, you win, Hughie!"

"And ye should know better than tae be so foolish for a woman in your delicate cond . . ." Kate chided on cue, though she trailed off rather unheroically when she realized what she was saying. Yet she was too late with her recovery. Mary MacKay was a perceptive woman and knew how to put two and two together. She looked at me, looked questioningly at her son, who, for all his trickery, was no good at hiding guilt, and then took a sip of tea.

"Tell me that you two were not really engaged in a footrace?"

"No, Mama. But we were running." This frank admission, coming from such a cherubic face—the wide, guileless blue eyes, the rosy cheeks flushed nearly to the color of the tousled hair— was, admittedly, disarming. It became evident to me then why parents didn't eat their young, when all logic suggested that they should. By God, I would have forgiven the little heathen anything if he had looked at me that way!

While wee Hughie was working on his mother with his practiced, doe-eyed look, Kate peered out the window. The men were emerging from the tower, their faces set in reflective grimaces, not one of them looking as if they had fully enjoyed their experience together. She cast me a quizzical glance, came to some conclusion and said, "Well, take off your coats and come to the table. You'd best be sitting down when they enter. For I don't think they'd take very kindly to the knowledge that you two were eavesdropping."

"Kate, I commend you. You're growing sharper by the day."

"Only because you insist on playing with fire!"

· · ·

The men were remarkable in the fact that although wee Hughie
and I had overheard their heated and biting discussion, illustrating somewhat the problem between the keepers and the men of
the Cape, the three gentlemen put aside their differences and
continued through the rest of the afternoon with a stoic calm,
eventually reaching something like cordiality, and at the end,
even daring to venture into realms of neighborliness. While we
women had no end of topics to discuss, the men talked of inane
things like sheep-dip, the speed it should take to shear the fleece
(which, according to Mr. MacKay—or Hugh, as he begged us to
call him—should take something like under a minute) and the
fall-time activity of culling the herd, which I found a little distasteful, especially since wee Hughie took such pleasure in describing to me his personal experience of hacking off the head of
a ram that refused to die.

Because of our wayward adventure, where we huddled together on a cold step, listening furtively to a conversation neither of us had any right to hear, a sort of friendship had
developed between us. Yet what titillated the mind of a ten-year-
old boy was seldom apt to garner the same emotion from a ma-
ture woman of nineteen. Hughie was a bright lad. He knew this,
and took a perverse pleasure in describing for me his exploits.

"The first blow I delivered tae the beast only gashed him in
the neck, and the pain o' it caused him to bolt like a frightened
hare," he exclaimed, wide-eyed, while illustrating the speed of
the ram by shooting out his hand. "I chased him round the pen,
and he was spurting blood like the de'il spews fire, and me not
doin' a verra good job of it, for the blood was muckle slippery
and I fell quite a few times. Yet I continued on, round and round,
chopping at him with my bloody axe. Finally, my da wrestled the
beast to the ground so I could finish him proper! Seven bloody
tries and I'd done it! 'Twas the completest thing, though my da

wouldna let me keep the heid on account I made a muckle mess of one of the eyeholes."

"Oh my," I declared unenthusiastically, my heart going out to the unfortunate beast that fell under this misguided child's hand. "What a rich pastoral life you paint for me, Hughie. Certainly such experiences are telling of a young man's character."

"Aye, the lad's persistent!" Mr. Campbell asseverated before I could reply, and he gave his new young friend a conspiratorial wink. Mr. Campbell had insisted on sitting beside me, feigning a warm and healthy relationship for the sake of our guests. I commended him. He was a fine actor, and I, for the sake of appearances, upheld my end admirably well. Hughie sat on my other side while his parents—mother Mary beaming with parental pride and father Hugh staring stone-faced at the smartly dressed pariah next to me—were seated directly across from us. Kate and Robbie took up the ends, performing the duties of host and hostess with commendable fortitude, although their eyes did give away, from time to time, the incredulity they felt at the interplay between Mr. Campbell and me.

"Actually," I whispered to the transformed light-keeper, purely for wee Hughie's benefit, as the boy was listening, "I was going for the opposite of thorough—something perhaps closer to: sloppy, inhumane, boyish zeal. But perseverance is perhaps more encouraging for your new little friend."

Willy Campbell flashed a wry smile in my direction. "Actually, culling sheep takes a great deal of perseverance, Miss Stevenson. And, for what it's worth, killing your first ram is no easy task."

"Oh, and you have experience killing such things, do you?" I replied a little too loudly. As soon as the words left my mouth I regretted them terribly. His congenial smile faded. He looked across the table and, holding the boy's father in his gaze, replied, "In that line, Miss Stevenson, I'm afraid I outstrip you all."

He was about to get up. I could feel his defeat, the tenseness

in his body straining as he made to push back from the table, yet
no matter what I thought of him, I had no wish to see his plan of
manning rescue boats—even if he had resorted to blackmail of a
sort—fail. I grabbed his hand under the table to quell the notion. And squeezing forcefully, while smiling bravely for all to
see, I said sincerely, "Please do forgive me, Mr. Campbell. Why,
of course you do. How foolish of me to forget."

His pale eyes held to mine, looking almost frightened, uncertain where I was going with my apology.

But for once I was on his side. Mr. MacKay was a fine, charis-
matic man, enjoyable company even, but he held to a different
set of rules where lives of sailors were concerned, and I, for one,
being wholeheartedly in love with a man of the sea, could not
abide such a selfish notion. And squeezing even harder, unable
to let the keeper pull his hand from my grasp—as he so desperately tried—I continued, "But I'm certain your record of distin-
guishing yourself on the battlefield, however bravely you may
have fought, still cannot compare with slaughtering sheep.
Though your record is impressive," I added with a look of adulation. "My father spoke of your bravery often. Quite admires
you, I believe, which is saying a lot since he's a man who admires
very little. There is nothing to be ashamed of when one takes so
many lives in the name of king and country."

"King and country," Hugh MacKay reiterated, as if he found
the notion amusing. Yet there was also approval there—in the
way he beheld me—as if admiring my ability to lie so glibly.

"Ye were a soldier, Mr. Campbell?" Mary asked with unfeigned interest. Her son leaned across me, positively gawking
at the keeper with newfound respect.

"Apparently" was his bold reply, though his reproving eyes
never left mine.

"I had no idea," she marveled, smiling kindly at the light-
keeper.

"You wouldn't," I replied, breaking the chiding gaze to look at our guests. "Mr. Campbell is a very modest man, and keeps such personal exploits and horrors to himself." The hand, so firmly in my grasp under the table, jerked away. And at once the coldness settled in.

"Really?" came the skeptical challenge from the visiting Highlander. Yet before the two men could square off once again, Robbie was quick on the draw and pulled from the cupboard the "big gun."

"Ladies, gentlemen," he began, placing the bottle of single malt whisky and six glasses on the table. "I was going to save this for later, but I think now would be the perfect time. Will ye drink a toast with me?" He poured a measure in each glass and handed them around. I had to wrestle mine from wee Hughie. "May the past stay in the past . . ." he declared, holding his glass high before him, ". . . while the future looms brightly before us! To Cape Wrath," he declared. *"Slàinte!"*

*"Slàinte!"* all replied, and then attempted to drown the past— which was obviously harder for some than others—with the heady tang and burn of single malt whisky. Some, I noticed— particularly the adult male contingent—required more than one glass to accomplish this feat.

The meal, and the entire visit surprisingly, ended on a hopeful note; hopeful for Kate and me because we now had a commitment from Mr. Campbell that would allow us to visit the MacKay croft on a regular basis, and hopeful for the light-keepers because as Mr. MacKay shook hands to leave he conceded, "I guess I'll be seeing ye gents at the jetty come the tenth o' March."

.  .  .

I waited until I heard the bell, and then I waited some more. At last I heard his footsteps traverse the floor of the hall we shared. But he didn't pause before my door this night. Perhaps he had nothing to say to me, no interest in my motives whatsoever. He went straight to his room; and I waited until I heard the door close behind him. I was nervous. I had never visited a man's room before in the dead of night, especially a man who seemed to have a dark curse hanging about him. And so I stayed awake in my room, dangling my feet off the edge of the bed, thinking of every reason under heaven why I should leave him alone with his own demons. But I couldn't. Behind his dark, brooding exterior there appeared a glimmer of kindness that showed through every now and again. But he was afraid of kindness. That was evident. Whenever kindness appeared he cast it aside, covering it with cruelty. That he was toying with wee Hughie MacKay was also a certainty, for I did not believe a man like Mr. Campbell cared a fig for children. Yet he was good at pretending. His manner appeared genuine, and he had a way of reeling a person in without them ever knowing it was happening. He had done it to me on several occasions, and just when I was beginning to let my guard down, he cut me again. I hated him, truly. He was a vile and debased creature. Yet strangely I wanted to see him succeed in this one mission of manning lifeboats. And so, with this final notion, I set off on my task.

He had been in his room a good half hour before I gathered the nerve to go by. He should have been asleep, the light coming under his door should have been extinguished, but it wasn't, and so I was obliged to knock. The door sprung open immediately, startling me with its abruptness. He was standing before me, fully clothed yet disheveled, with a glass of spirits in his hand and a pen between his teeth. "Come," he uttered with a jerk of his head and stepped aside to let me enter. Puzzled and unnerved, I obeyed.

Crossing the threshold of his room was like entering a foreign country altogether and it was with great trepidation that I did so. What struck me first was the smell. It was not a bad odor, just a wee bit pungent, earthy even, with a decidedly male muskiness to it. The room was nothing near the immaculate state of the observation room. In fact, it was the opposite side of that coin. Clothes were scattered harum-scarum about the place, a discarded shirt rested on the post of the bed here, breeches draped over the back of a chair there, boots and stockings kicked off before the fire. He had what looked to be a chest, very like one a sailor might use, along the far wall, with names burned into the top of it—ships he perhaps had served on? A basin rested on a stand in the corner beside the chest, along with a razor and strop, and a tiny mirror hung on the wall above. Sketches adorned the walls, drawings of ships, each with a name under it and looking as if he had perhaps drawn them with his own hand. I next came to the desk, which was also an organized mess, all cluttered with books and papers. Samples of various plants, taken from around the Cape I presumed, had been tacked to the wall and sat drying on little hooks. Why he had such a collection was beyond my powers of deduction. On either side of the desk were bookcases, perfectly overflowing with well-worn volumes. And on the top shelf of each of these cases sat jars— clear glass jars—containing hideous creatures of various forms, suspended in grotesque postures as they loomed from their aqueous prisons. The mere sight gave me a start.

"Do they frighten ye?" he asked without the slightest hint of curiosity while setting his glass on the desk. He placed the quill pen back in its holder. "I figured they might."

"What are they?" I uttered.

"Just beasts I've collected over the years."

"Did . . . did you kill them?"

"Some. Others were gifts."

"Oh how very charming," I replied with a lack of enthusiasm and saw the corner of his mouth twitch in response to this sarcasm.

"Perhaps I should have covered them before ye came."

"How were you to know I would ever come?"

"Oh," he breathed in a voice that held the edge of darkness, "I knew you'd be coming to me tonight." He turned to face me then and leaned his powerful frame against the desk, crossing his arms over his chest in a gesture that exuded conceit. "That was, once ye mustered the courage."

I could feel my face go red. "You were expecting me?" I asked, incredulity thick in my voice. "But that's impossible!"

"On the contrary, my dear, I was counting on you. A woman of your spirit and driving curiosity is hardly able to let such a chance pass by."

"What? What's that supposed to mean?" He obviously knew that this predictability in my nature—one that was so smugly pointed out—would embarrass and chafe me. And he looked mightily pleased with himself for the discomfort he caused me, perhaps more so than the delight he took in my slavish commitment to my curious nature. The look on his face, the sardonic satisfaction, made me despise him even more. "Well," I said, mustering all the resolve I had left, "I'm not staying, so don't get your hopes up. I only came to apologize, and I'm not certain I even want to do that anymore. I was going to say that I was sorry for what I said at the table, and for making up that preposterous lie about you being a brave soldier and all . . . covering for your morbid proclivities." I cocked my head, mindful of keeping a safe distance from the man, and taunted, "Do you even want to know why I did it?"

"One can only imagine," he replied laconically, and I found his cruel smugness infuriating.

A burning desire welled up in me, one that insisted I taunt him, causing the same discomfort he caused me. And then I too smiled a smile that did not reach my eyes. "I think I'm going to tell you anyway. I don't normally lie for other people, Mr. Campbell, but I lied for you today because I . . . I happened to overhear you in the light-room." There, it was out. Now he knew that I knew his secret, and I held it over him, smirking and growing ever prideful.

"Happened to overhear me?" he repeated, his cruel smile returning. "Dear lass, a woman like you doesn't *happen* to do anything. Hearing the conversation between MacKay and me was your original intent. Am I correct?"

The man was either a remarkable guess-maker or he knew more about me than I cared to fathom. Either way, I felt my short-lived bravado crumbling. "So, you knew I was listening to you?"

"I suspected ye would; I might have even been a wee disappointed in ye had ye not. Anyhow, my suspicions were confirmed when I saw your face after ye asked had I much experience killing things. Ye knew the answer to that very well. Yours, dear lass, is a face that cannot lie."

"I believe I lie very well, Mr. Campbell," I parried a little indignantly, grasping at whatever I had left to me. "I've experience there. I'm shocked by what you tell me. However, it was no love of yourself that forced me to it. I listened because I was curious, yes. But it was your plan to man rescue boats in order to save the lives of drowning sailors that induced me to lie. Mr. MacKay has his reasons for opposing you, of that I'm certain. But your plan, however it chafes me to admit it, is a good one and I have no wish to see you fail. I will tell you plainly, I think your effort to be noble, no matter what sordid methods you choose to employ."

"Really? What a coincidence. A woman who would risk so much just to peer through the lens of a wee telescope, hoping against hope to see the face of her lover—a man, might I add, who left her in a shocking predicament—on board a passing ship, would approve of such a scheme?"

"How dare you mock me!" This time he had gone too far.

"Mock you? On the contrary, lass, I applaud you. Ye, Miss Stevenson, are a woman of extreme passion and strong conviction, however misguided it may be."

"Misguided? I'm seldom misguided, Mr. Campbell! I know very well what I'm about! You have no right to say such things."

"Be that as it may, did you also happen to hear the part where Mr. MacKay reminded me that I'm cursed?"

"I did," I admitted plainly. "But I don't believe in such nonsense as curses. You're a troubled man, Mr. Campbell, we all know that. But what troubles you is more of a perversion than a curse, I'd say." Although the thought of getting that off my chest seemed fine while I was speaking, in reality the effect my words had on him was frightening.

The magnificent, piercing aqua eyes burned into mine with a mixture of pity and loathing. And then, slowly, he uttered, "That's very interesting. I suppose you don't believe in ghosts either?"

"No. Again, I'm afraid I have to disappoint you. I've never seen a ghost, therefore I do not believe in them."

He pushed away from the desk and began walking slowly toward me. I backed away just as slowly. He kept coming. I hit the wall and was forced to stop. "Let me tell you a little secret, Miss Stevenson," he whispered dangerously, standing a hairsbreadth away—much too near for comfort. "I believe in ghosts. Call it a perversion, if ye like, but I see them all the time . . . the ghosts of those who were once flesh and blood, constantly reminding me they are no longer. And as for curses, you had best believe in those too. You may think my attempt to save mariners' lives noble. But MacKay's right. It's not the saving of lives that concerns me. I'm merely seeking redemption, for I cannot stand the sight of the ghosts that haunt me any longer."

"When . . . when you say you see ghosts, sir," I began tentatively, "I hope . . . I pray you are speaking figuratively?"

He didn't answer.

"Perhaps you should cut back on the liquor?" I suggested in an earnest attempt to be helpful. "I've known cases where those who imbibe too much begin to see things that aren't really there."

He placed his hands on the wall, flanking either side of me. I flinched. "I wish it were the case," he whispered thickly. "But I do not drink much. And when I do, I never really get drunk enough. That is another curse altogether."

"If your intent is to frighten me, Mr. Campbell, you can rest assured," I uttered softly. My heart was pounding with a fierceness that threatened to undo me, yet I found I could not look away from the startling eyes in so tormented a face. "You have succeeded in frightening me since day one. All I wanted tonight was to help you, you know. Why must you insist on being so horrid all the time?"

There was a moment of silence—of contrary reflection—and in one great pained gasp he admitted: "Because I like you, Sara Stevenson; I find I like you very well and have no wish to see you end up like the others."

The others. I recalled the book again, and all the sketches of those poor women, dead and mutilated. I swallowed. "There may have been a time when death had its appeal for me, but I assure you, that time has passed. I have my child to think of."

"Aye, ye do. That is why ye need to take extra care. Cape Wrath . . . it is an unchancy place here. I will not attempt to explain it to you, but why is it do ye think that ever since man has lived on the Isle of Britain no one has ever dared live on this point . . . until your father thought to put a lighthouse here? There's a reason for it. Unholy things dwell upon Cape Wrath."

"You're mad," I stated, and attempted to push him away, but my body was quivering uncontrollably.

He remained steadfast. "Perhaps," he agreed without emotion. "At times even I believe it myself. But I'm also very sane too. I came here for a reason; I chose to be here. But you," he shook his head, "I cannot figure it out."

"You . . . you know very well why I'm here!" I protested in a somewhat stunned utterance. My hands unconsciously moved to protect the budding life within my womb.

"Aye," he breathed, looking all the more puzzled, scanning me from head to toe with his pale eyes. Then, abruptly, he raked his fingers through his dark hair. "Aye," he repeated again and backed away. He went to his desk and took a mighty swig from a bottle resting behind some books, totally ignoring the glass. "The conversation in the light-room, I meant for you to hear."

He took another pull on the bottle then wiped his mouth on his sleeve and turned to me. "I wanted to see how you'd react to sending men out into the breakers, risking their own lives for the sake of others. Men have died here, Miss Stevenson. Many. My reasons for taking such risks are selfish, what about yours?"

Reasons? I thought about it. Was my willingness to help this creature driven by some general benevolence toward human-kind, or was it instead only a perverse desire—a grasping attempt in case one of the sailors pulled from the breakers some-day should be Thomas? I gasped suddenly, realizing it was the latter.

"I thought so," he said, seemingly able to read my thoughts with his pellucid eyes. "So singularly driven! Absorbed in naught but your own desires! Indeed ye are your father's daughter. Per-haps we two creatures, cast from society, are not so different after all?"

"No. No, you're wrong there. I'm nothing like you," I affirmed desperately.

At this he smiled, though it was a smile of bitter irony. "No. Indeed not. Whereas I'm merely a harbinger o' death, ye, lass, ye are a giver of life. I just pray that the forces that drive you are strong enough to defy the curses here."

"I don't understand you, Mr. Campbell. What is it you want from me? Why do you toy with me so?"

"Because I believe, Miss Stevenson, after observing you for the past few months, that we might be able to help each other."

# SEVEN

## The Letter

❦

It was before dawn when I awoke, coaxed gently to the surface from a blissful dream of Thomas. I didn't want to wake; the dream was so vivid and pure, so satisfying in every way, and the evanescent vision of him smiling lingered in my imagination as I came to consciousness, filling me with a resounding peace. I was aware of emitting a soft sigh as my eyes opened, staring into the darkness. And lying there, bathed in the memory of happier times, I brought my hands to my tumescent stomach under the quilts and gently caressed the restless little life within me. "Did you see him too?" I whispered, imagining that the little life we created—those many months ago—actually had. It was a busy thing, seeming to always flutter and roll whenever I was at rest. I toyed with the idea of going back to sleep, yet knowing such a dream would be impossible to recapture, and knowing that the entity in my stomach was awake, I sat up, threw on a dressing gown and left the room.

The house was still dark but for the glowing of the fire.

Robbie and Kate were asleep, as they should be, and Mr. Campbell was well into his second watch of the night. I placed a couple bricks of peat on the glowing coals to stoke up the fire, and then, with the thought of a nice pot of tea to cheer me, I threw on a coat and went to fetch a pail of water from the cistern.

I was used to the cold by now, but I didn't like it much. I longed for warmer days, which I knew lay just around the corner. There was, however, a perceivable mildness to the air, and its presence was indicated by the thin gauzy fog that had settled in. Yet I had no trouble seeing the lighthouse or the room that sat just beneath the great lantern. I looked at the window, awash with light, but could not see Mr. Campbell sitting there. I continued on my errand, and on my return I looked again. This time I caught a glimpse of him as he paced the room, dark head bent in consternation, jerking every now and again at some unseen interruption. He appeared a hungry predator trapped in a cage.

Dawn was just beginning to show itself as I swung the kettle over the gentle flame. It wasn't a very hot fire. I thought of adding another brick then thought again, recalling Mr. Campbell's example of thriftiness, and decided to wait patiently for the water to boil. It would never do to stare at the kettle, which, to my humiliation, I have done many a time without success. Water would take its sweet time to boil and no amount of wishful thinking could alter that, so, after preparing a pot with the correct measure of tea leaves standing at the ready, I decided to pull my coat back on and head to the edge of the promontory, to a place I sometimes went to gaze at the sea.

It was an eerily still morning on the Cape, gray and foggy. Gannets and kittiwakes were beginning to stir, rending the air with their echoing cries. The sea, far far below me, was a dark, undulating mass and, as I stared at it, marveling at the hypnotic movement, something in the east caught my eye.

It was a little skiff, close into the coast and coming out from what looked to be the cove to the jetty. The sight of it, the suddenness of which it appeared and the pristine beauty of the small craft against the dark water evoked in me a strange, disjointed feeling—a feeling heightened even more by the sudden prickling of my skin. I had never seen this particular boat before, but I did hear that at times fishermen would come to the lighthouse jetty in the warmer months to drop off post from Durness, or to sell the light-keeper a basket of fish. I watched the little skiff for a moment as it sailed, seeming to glide effortlessly on the undulating water, and then it turned from the coast in one elegant, sweeping motion. The white sails adjusted then filled. And the little boat headed into a wall of murky fog. Only when it had disappeared completely did I look up at the lighthouse to see if Mr. Campbell had seen it too. I could see his silhouette still pacing between the three windows in my view, head still bent in deep concentration as he silently worked out his demons. Excited, and filling with hope, I had no wish to disturb him—no desire to confront the man—and so, without another thought, I headed straight to the jetty.

I saw there a little package sitting on the end of the pier next to the postbox. It was an odd sight; a little unnerving even. The jetty was a lonely, desolate place but for the few birds and gray seals that called it home. As I walked out to retrieve the package—the first form of post to arrive in the four months I'd been here—I felt an odd sensation of foreboding, a sensation that magnified tenfold when I saw that the package was addressed to one Sara Crichton, Keeper of the Light, Cape Wrath. At the sight of these words, my hands started to tremble uncontrollably.

Crichton.

It was with great effort that I picked up the package and, as if carrying the most sacred of relics, brought it back to the cottage, having not the will to open it yet. I walked along the frozen road through the open moorland while the morning sun attempted to break through the mist. Every step of the way was shrouded in mystery and a terrible, perplexing feeling I had no name for.

The great light apparatus had already been extinguished by the time I reached the courtyard, and the smell of burnt toast hit me as I came through the door of the cottage. Oddly enough this had a calming effect on my nerves, for it meant that Kate was about preparing the morning meal.

"Where did you get off to?" she questioned, still bent near the fire, pulling the blackened toast out of the iron. "Hell and damnation, I scorched it again!"

Robbie, who was studiously reading an outdated *Edinburgh Review* at the table, as if the old news was news to relish, looked up at his wife's outburst. "I have no idea what you're complaining about, love, 'tis the same every morning. If you put a thick enough layer of those currant preserves that kind woman Mrs. MacKay brought by, you don't even notice the taste. Come, now, Kate, Sara's arrived." Then, noticing for the first time the package in my hands, he exclaimed, "Whatever have ye got there?"

This brought Kate from the fire and, dropping the scorched toast in front of me, next to the pot of fresh brewed tea, she observed, "Why, Sara, if you're not shaking like a leaf! Dear heavens, sit down! You're cold," she stated, eyeing me suspiciously. And then, concern flooding in, she called out to her husband, "Robbie, pull the wee blanket from the settle and wrap it around Sara. If you've gone and made yourself sick again," she warned me in a frighteningly similar manner my mother would have used, "I'm not responsible!"

"No. I assure you, I'm fine," I replied, still trembling.

She cast me a skeptical glance then poured out a cup of the strong tea. This she pushed before me then relieved my hands of the package. As I sipped the hot liquid, willing it to soothe my tumultuous insides, she took one look at the inscription, set the box down and crossed herself in the manner of the Catholics. "Sweet gentle Jesus," she uttered, attracting her husband's full attention. "'Tis from that devil's buckie! That wicked lad!" she breathed, and then held me with her accusing brown gaze. "How . . . where did ye come by it?"

I grabbed the package back and held it protectively. "I . . . I saw a little sailboat leaving the jetty this morning."

"A boat? When?" demanded Robbie.

"At . . . at the hour of dawn," I uttered, and at the thought of it my skin came alive again with the same indescribable tingling.

"You were out on the promontory watching ships at the hour of dawn?" he questioned, looking rather disturbed by this. There was no need for me to reply. He already knew the answer. "And did Mr. Campbell happen to see this wee boat as well?"

"I . . . I . . ." I stuttered, and shook my head. "No, I do not think he did."

"So ye went down to the jetty alone?"

"I'm . . . afraid that I did, Mr. MacKinnon," I admitted, feeling a welling of guilt at my impulsivity; for Robbie was a kind, decent soul and I truly hated to disappoint him. "But the moment I saw the little boat," I felt compelled to explain, "I knew that it carried something special." And though it made perfect sense to me, Robbie MacKinnon failed to understand this.

"Was anyone else about?" he probed with furrowed brows.

"No. The place was deserted. There was just this package."

A derisive look passed between husband and wife. But this time the meaning was not lost on me. "You do understand, Sara, that Mr. Campbell has absolutely forbidden you to venture beyond the lighthouse bounds unescorted?"

"I believe he said something on the matter to me, yes."

"And still ye went down there alone, in the frozen light of dawn . . . and in your delicate condition forbye?"

"When you put it like that, sir, you make it sound very ignoble and grasping. The truth was I had no wish to disturb the man. He appeared busy, and you must know how he hates to have anyone invade his tower uninvited."

"Could ye not have called up to the man? Sound does travel up the tower marvelously, you know."

"No sir, the thought never occurred to me." Which, unfortunately, was the truth.

Disgruntled, Robbie stood up from the table and walked to the window. After meditating on the view for a moment he turned to both Kate and me. "Campbell's coming. I suggest you open the wee package before he arrives. And then you can explain to him why it is you went down to the jetty alone, when by all logic and reason ye should have told one of us what ye were about."

I needed no more prompting than that to open this intriguing piece of mail.

Aside from the disturbing inscription linking my name with Thomas Crichton's, it was an unremarkable package by all standards: small, square, wrapped in brown paper and tied off with a length of twine. Robbie handed over his knife and I hurriedly cut the string and gently peeled back the paper. Before me sat a polished wooden box, cherrywood, by the look of it. It was not familiar to me, and for that I was slightly relieved. Yet when I lifted the lid my heart stopped. For there, peeking up beside an ink-splattered page, was a link from a silver chain. Ignoring the note I grabbed the link, knowing instinctively what it was. Again I was taken with the now familiar tingling—the touch of my skin against the silver link igniting my every nerve. And then I pulled from the nest of wood shavings a silver pocket watch—my silver pocket watch: the exact same one I had given Thomas in the hayloft of the Fergusons' barn. As it slowly revolved on its chain, reflecting the golden light from the candles, my hand began to tremble.

"What is it? What is it, Sara?" uttered Kate as all eyes were fixed on the watch. Yet I had not a voice with which to answer her, for the watch had turned enough to reveal the inscription on the back: *To my beloved Thomas, eternally yours, Sara 1814.*

A sound, odd and foreign to my own ears, escaped my lips— like the sound a wounded animal makes at the moment of death. I was in agony. Something in me had died. And tears of hurt and rage coursed down my cheeks unchecked. Thomas Crichton had returned my watch! Goddamn the bastard and his blackguardly soul to the depths of hell!

On impulse, as if out of some deep, primitive, atavistic response, I emitted a shockingly vulgar grunt and flung the object of pain from me, without heed, at the door. I was anticipating the impact of silver and glass on wood, followed by an explosion of gears and springs, yet instead all I heard was a muffled expulsion of air followed by a resounding: "What the devil?"

Mr. Campbell, to my astonishment and great embarrassment, stood in the doorway, windblown and dark hair askew, holding Thomas' watch by the chain while regarding me with an odd mixture of curiosity and chagrin. "Tell me, Miss Stevenson, is it a gift or a curse that ye bestow on me this morning?"

The man could see from my face, and the faces of our companions as well, that I was too distraught to speak. In one deft move he yanked the chain, sending the silver disk airborne, and caught it in the palm of his hand. Then, without another thought to the object that had assaulted him, he walked over to the table and stared into the box. He examined the brown paper, took note of the name inscribed in black ink and saw how the little gift had upset the whole mood of the cottage. "Oh? It is a curse, I see." He had spoken plainly, but his words held a deeper meaning for us both. And then he looked into my eyes with his own incandescent ones. "Do you mind telling me, lass, where it is you found this?"

"Did you not see it?" I asked, looking just as intensely at him. "Did you not see the little skiff this morning?"

"A skiff? Here? When was this?"

"This morning . . . at the jetty!" Yet I could see from the look in his wild eyes that he had not.

"Was it the tender ye saw?" he inquired, his eyes squinting in puzzlement. I shook my head. "Well, what did it look like, this little skiff of yours?" he demanded, a little too sharply.

Obviously he was more concerned with having not spied the little craft himself than the fact that I had just witnessed the return of a sacred gift. "I . . . I don't know!" I spat, shifting marvelously from hurt to anger. His look of impatience, combined with the unwillingness to move on, spurned me to add, "Well, it wasn't big, just a mast and a jib, I suppose. I didn't get a good look at it, at any rate. It was foggy, as you know. And I'm not nearly as adept at recognizing such things as you are."

He raised a sardonic brow and continued his chuff interrogation. "You saw a strange ship at the jetty this morning and you went there alone without saying aught to me on the matter?" Yet instead of berating me, as would have been normal for him to do, he schooled his baser emotions and nodded his acceptance of the fact that I had. And then, thankfully, he turned his attention to the watch.

He held it gently in his hands, almost lovingly, admiring the work of the master watchmaker, Mr. Arnold. From the little I knew of Mr. Campbell, I was well aware that he was a man who appreciated science and mechanics, and the work of artisans who could combine such complex things into a highly accurate, utilitarian object of beauty and wonder were not lost on him. I watched as he flipped the timepiece over. His pale eyes scanned the very personal inscription, and although he knew the nature of the demon I battled—was now, in fact, holding a piece of the man in the palm of his hand—he gave nothing away. He turned the watch over again. At last he looked me in the eye and softly said, "I wonder at a man who could forfeit such a treasure." And the way his eyes locked on to mine, the pointed way with which he spoke, made me to understand he was not speaking entirely of the watch. It was a kind sentiment, yet kindness from Mr. Campbell came at a dear price, I had learned. Warily, I took the watch from his hand, and as I did he asked, "Surely he'll have explained it in the note?"

"I . . . I . . ." I stammered, looking dumbly at the light-keeper.

"She hasn't read the note yet, Mr. Campbell," interjected Kate, watching us keenly. Although I had never made mention of this watch or its significance before, Kate, dear Kate, was a canny one, sharp and suspicious, and she added with due weight, "The sight of the watch and the mere fact the package was addressed to Mrs. Sara Crichton was a wee more than the poor dear could bear just now."

"Perhaps . . ." began Mr. Campbell, sitting down for the first time, and pausing just long enough to pour a cup of tea, "perhaps it would be best if you read the note. Maybe there's a reason the watch came back to you, aye? I find it never pays to jump to unnecessary conclusions." And then he put the cup to his lips and took a long sip, all the while still watching me. I could see that even he—an emotionally costive man, on all accounts— knew that any reason that would compel Mr. Crichton to return such a watch would not be a satisfactory one to me. However, fate had played its hand. It was now my apposite torture that I find out. Without any relish of my task, I excused myself from the table, collected my package and took it away to the quiet haven of my room.

. . .

I had to read the letter twice, it was so unbelievable. Yet in the end I believed some terrible mistake to have taken place; I didn't know how else to put it, and I was hard-pressed to find another explanation for so bizarre a tale.

The letter, written in a small, neat hand (thankfully, not Thomas'), began with an introduction. The author was one Alexander Seawell of Oxford, who not only stated he was a scholar of history at the university there, but a collector of antiquities as well, and most recently finished a stint as a soldier fighting on the continent. He apologized for the delay, the appalling notice, and offered his deepest condolences, stating that the chronometer was so beautiful and rare that he had been in half a mind to keep it for himself, and would have too if it were not the wish of a dying man that it be returned to his young, pregnant wife, presumably me. When I read these words my chest grew so tight it was nearly impossible for me to draw breath. It was as if a great crushing weight were pressing down on me, forcing life and breath from me, while the pulse in my heart dropped to my stomach, lurching and retching with every involuntary thud. For the words the man wrote were proof that Thomas was indeed dead, and the rest of the letter was lost in a blur of tears and half-breath, hiccuping sobs.

I allowed myself more than a few shameful moments wallowing in this deprecatory state before I forced myself to stop. It was then I reminded myself that I was pregnant and living on Cape Wrath, a cruel predicament brought about by the very man I was crying over—a man who had used me shamefully, professed his undying love by stating he'd move heaven and earth so that we could be together and then fled to the safety of the continent when the yoke of responsibility proved too much, no doubt forgetting all about me until guilt and death finally caught up with him. I dried my eyes and read further.

It was then I discovered Mr. Seawell was not writing of Thomas but of another man, a James Crichton, who was a soldier (not a sailor) and had fallen in battle many months ago on the fields of France. From that point on, as I continued to read the letter, I grew ever more curious and felt a deep resounding sadness for this Sara Crichton, to whom the letter was addressed. For I was Sara Stevenson, not Crichton, and the man who I once believed I loved was not James but Thomas . . . a renegade sailor and debaucher of women, damn his soul! Yet oddly enough the pocket watch was definitely the one I had purchased at the watchmaker's shop in the Luckenbooths that day long ago on the Royal Mile. It was indeed the fine silver detent chronometer by the renowned John Roger Arnold. How it had found its way into the hands of a soldiering Englishman, I could not venture a guess, but it had, and that very fact called for a letter to be written in return, demanding a bit more detail than a flippant allusion to the request of a dying soldier on the fields of France! And so, filled with questions, raging passion and more than a little discordancy, I plucked a quill from the holder, stirred the ink in the pot a measure and scribbled out my first letter from Cape Wrath to a Mr. Alexander Seawell of Oxford.

*Dear Mr. Seawell,*

*I regret to say I am Sara Stevenson, not Sara Crichton, the woman you intended your letter to reach. Though curiously enough, I was the very one who purchased the timepiece and foolishly had it inscribed with such a sentiment. You can imagine my surprise when it came back to me through the hands of a stranger and not the man it had originally been commissioned for—only a short while ago! How it ended up in the possession of that poor soldier boy, I shan't venture a guess. It seems a great mystery, and one, I hope, in which you will oblige me by helping to fill in some of the gaps. First off, how did you know where to find me? I was under the impression that not many knew of my whereabouts. Certainly not many women, respectable or otherwise, would keep a lighthouse on so desolate a coast, and I've not been here more than a few months. Secondly, was James Crichton any relation to a Thomas Crichton, formerly of Leith, Scotland? I know he was not a brother, for Thomas had none, but cousins of such a race might very well abound. By any chance, was this James fellow a man of disreputable character—perhaps a cowardly libertine? And would he have had access to a port where he would have been able to purchase such a thing at a pawnshop, or from a besotted, philandering lout of a sailor at quayside? It would not surprise me in the least if the man were a scoundrel, given the family name, and the poor woman he was trying to reach might well have been just an allusion to some wild, preconceived fancy he had conjured up before he was so grievously wounded. Well, I believe those to be all the questions I have at the moment. I would forever be grateful if you would see it in your heart to help clear up this troubling matter.*

*Sincerely and respectfully yours,*
*Sara Stevenson*
*Lighthouse, Cape Wrath, Scotland*

Without another thought I hastily sealed the letter and addressed it to the sender. Then, only then, did I allow the breath

I was holding to escape, bursting forth in one long cathartic huff. I picked up the watch and lent half a mind to hurling it against the bricks of the hearth, smashing it and every memory of Thomas Crichton once and for all. Yet the silver, at first cold to the touch, warmed quickly in the palm of my hand and as it did I felt the silent, pulsating beat. It was unfathomable. Trembling, and swept up again in that strange tingling wave, I flipped the timepiece over and beheld the face. It was still ticking. "Dear Lord," I uttered with a heart thumping twice the rate of the little watch and tenfold louder, and then I ran out of the room.

My companions were still lingering over breakfast, discussing, no doubt, my misfortune. Ignoring them I went straight to the case clock in the corner and checked the time against Thomas' watch. It was dead-on.

"Mr. Campbell," I said abruptly, turning to face him. "When you looked at the watch did you happen to wind it or reset it in any way?"

"No," he replied, looking up from the table. "Why do you ask?"

"Any of you? Did any of you touch this watch?" The faces regarding me were all startlingly blank; Robbie and Kate shook their heads mutely in answer to my question. I took a hard look at Kate. The simpering smile, the eyes that would not meet mine directly, told me she had done her best to apprise Mr. Campbell of the scandalous relationship I'd had with the previous owner of the timepiece. Pushing the thought aside I continued. "I ask because the watch is still working; the time is correct!" This revelation, whose meaning escaped the MacKinnons, both husband and wife looking on with faces that expressed pleasure that the gift, fine and expensive, was still in working order, was not lost on Mr. Campbell. He set down his fork and beheld me with questioning eyes. "The watch needs to be wound regularly, right? Once every day. I doubt very much it could make a lengthy journey and still keep the correct time, yet somehow it has."

"Lengthy journey? Aye, it would be odd indeed," he agreed,

and came over for another look. He took the watch, examined it closely and said rather softly so the others could not hear, "I take it the letter did not contain hopeful news."

"Why do you assume that, sir?" I whispered back rather curtly.

"Because your eyes are that red and swollen."

Without thinking I brushed my fingertips along the high edge of my cheeks, feeling the sticky residue and puff of recent tears. I cleared my throat. "Well, it wasn't from *him*, if that's what you were wondering."

He studied me for a moment, attempting to gauge my mood, I assumed, for when he finally spoke he did so with caution. "When ye say 'lengthy journey,' Miss Stevenson, exactly how lengthy are ye speaking of?"

"Oxford," I uttered, still perplexed by the whole notion. "And, for that matter, it came by way of the sea. Yet how it came to be in Oxford, England, and why, I haven't a clue."

"And is it your young man's watch?"

"I bought it myself, yes. It's the same one I gave to him."

He handed the timepiece back, no closer to an answer, and uttered, "Well, ye have very fine taste . . . in chronometers, at least. Do ye mind me asking who the letter was from if it wasn't from *him*?"

"Normally I would mind very much," I began a bit acerbically, then reined in my pride and continued. "But unfortunately I have no idea who the letter writer is. It's from a complete stranger . . . an antiquarian from the university, or something of the like. Tell me, sir, were I to post a letter, how would I go about doing that here?"

He cocked his head and regarded me curiously through his spectacular crystal-eyed gaze. And then a wry smile threatened to overtake his lips. "A stranger from England? A university man? And you have it in mind to answer his letter?"

I lowered my voice and, looking beyond the light-keeper to make sure Kate and Robbie could not hear, explained, "Under the circumstances, it appears I have little choice in the matter. There was a mistake. I might not be . . ." I lowered my eyes, unwilling to look at him, "I might not be the woman the watch was intended for."

"But you say it's your timepiece," he added quizzically, as if attempting to puzzle out the logic I used.

"Yes. It is."

"This Thomas of yours, could it mean that he did the honorable thing, then?"

"Don't speculate!" I hissed, not only to quiet him but to quell the familiar ache in the pit of my stomach at the thought that Thomas had willingly left me. I thought I had mastered my fears; I had even begun to forgive Kate for her betrayal of my secret, until this unsuspected belonging of Thomas' arrived. "I've done enough speculating on the matter," I added. "I just need a few questions answered, is all."

He looked as if he were about to ask after the nature of the questions and then thought better. "On Friday I was planning to take ye and Mrs. MacKinnon into Durness." This surprised me, and he added, "To see the doctor there. Ye can post it in town. However, there's a wee chance the tender might come sooner. We could take it to the jetty today and leave it in the postbox on the pier. If it's still there by Friday, we'll take it with us."

"The jetty? That's right!" I said, remembering what day it was. "Mr. MacKay is coming, isn't he?"

"Aye. I hope that he is. I was counting on you to remember it. Ye do remember our wee bargain?" I looked at him, looked into the eyes that had battled one too many demons of their own, and nodded silently. "Good," he whispered, and I thought I caught the hint of a smile. "Now that you've a timepiece, and we've determined it's a remarkably reliable one, I'll expect ye to not be late. Now, if you'll excuse me," he said, and headed in the direction of his room. Watching him retreat, I held Thomas' chronometer tightly in my hand, reveling in the feel of its steady tick and vowing I'd not be the one to ever let it stop.

· · ·

The nature of the bargain between the light-keeper and myself was simply that I use my one true God-given gift (as Mr. Campbell had so tactfully put it), and do my utmost to persuade the good men of the Cape that it was in their best interest to preserve the lives of imperiled mariners. Mr. Campbell, though perhaps deceiving himself on most things, was at least introspective and honest enough to know that he was no hand at wooing people over to his cause through personality alone. Being a recluse and uncommonly burdened with the pall of death, he admitted that a little help from me might do wonders for both our causes. My one and only God-given gift, as Mr. Campbell saw it, was merely my outward appearance. I found this, of course, to be extremely offensive, yet held my tongue. Mr. Campbell had been drinking when he said it and was extremely vexed by something. If he were erratic on a good day, certainly these extraneous conditions would only serve to undo the creature further, and so I said nothing to defend my character. He went on to say that my inquisitive nature, my prideful female bravado, my tendency to giddiness and my tongue I would have to repress, for I needed to act the part of a sweet, biddable, engaging young woman.

"I'm as good an actor as yourself," I riposted through a sneer as he leaned close to me. "Perhaps even better. People actually *like* me."

"Exactly my point," he replied with a derisive leer. "And because our goals are one and the same, you wanting to see the father of your baby again and me wanting to redeem some of my misdeeds, I trust ye will succeed where I have failed."

"Under normal circumstances I'd say it's a surety. However, have you bothered to give any thought to my current condition? You know I'm with child."

He looked me up and down with a jaundiced eye. "Aye, ye are. Some find it alluring in an unmarried woman. Others, it may give the wrong impression." He grinned with a hint of lechery. "But 'tis not obvious yet to the untrained eye, and many of the lads here are yet untrained where women are concerned. If anything," he continued, studying my figure beneath my satin robe, "I'd say the extra plumpness improves your looks overall. All ye need do is use your wiles to inspire the lads. Look fetching. Then ye and Mrs. MacKinnon can go visit Mary MacKay while the good men of the Cape and I pull the boats around."

"Well," I answered, gracing him with a forced smile. "If that's all you need me to do, rest assured. I shall make even your heartless soul proud."

. . .

Mr. Campbell and Robbie were already at the jetty by the time Kate and I were ready to leave the cottage. She took one look at me and grinned.

"Well, do I look fetching?"

"Not particularly, no," she said, eyeing the old calash bonnet I had pulled up over my hair, a calico relic I had pilfered from my mother. "And is that a riding habit you have on—for a visit? I thought I heard Mr. Campbell say this morning that you were to have a word with the men before we set off. He seemed to think that your well-bred elegance and charm would impress upon the men the importance of their help in his cause. But you are not very well attired for a visit, nor are you dressed to impress anything elegant upon any man. That habit, though perhaps well cut for its day, looks a wee bit tight on you now. What you are about to do, I suspect, is infuriate Mr. Campbell!"

It was accusatory . . . and she was only partially correct. "On the contrary, Kate. I'm about to give his cause a new purpose. And this jacket is not tight, just snug. Now, be so good as to hold my bag for a moment—be careful," I warned, pulling on a pair of black leather gloves after she took it. "It contains some books and a letter."

"Letter?" she intoned with a twang of disapproval.

"Never worry," I said, shrugging into an old boat-cloak before taking back the bag. "It's for another man . . . not Mr. Crichton." I teased her further with a dreamy smile and, biting my lip to keep from giggling, left the cottage intent on making my way to the jetty. Kate, unable to help herself, plied me the entire way for answers to her many questions, none of which I had any intention of answering truthfully.

At the top of the road that led down to the jetty landing we found wee Hughie sitting on the bench of a rickety old hay cart; the boy, capped, cloaked and chewing on what looked to be a twig from a bilberry bush, was intent on something transpiring at the jetty landing. "Good day, fine sir," I called out. Hughie spun around to face us.

"Ma'am. Ma'am," he said, removing the well-chewed fiber from his mouth long enough to make his greeting. The horse, which had also taken the opportunity to chew on withered moor grass, looked up, a clump of yellowish-brown weeds dangling from its velvety lips as they continued smacking. "Miss Sara, I'm tae take ye an' Miss Kate to my home."

"You're driving?"

He nodded with a defiant grin, willing me to challenge him.

"And have you much experience driving a cart, young Master MacKay?" I asked, coming beside him. I looked up at the little carrot-topped creature and beheld him with a scrutinizing stare.

"Aye, I have. I've been drivin' this auld rig and the Duchess of Sutherland since the verra day I was breeched." He said it with a straight face, proclaiming his prodigy-like strength and cunning with aplomb. I sized up the dun-colored cart horse, noting that the Duchess of Sutherland (a rather shabby-looking creature to bear such a noble title) had barely enough spunk in her to overpower a toddler.

"Very well," I replied amicably, "I shall take you at your word, Master MacKay. And what is more, I shall entrust Mrs. MacKinnon into your good care as well. Kate, will you be so good as to climb aboard next to young Master MacKay here? I shall be with you both shortly." At this Kate hesitated, looking skeptically at the rickety old cart as well as the precocious little boy gallantly lending his hand. With a nod of my head I urged her to take it, fighting back a smile as she did so. I then took out the letter I had written to the Englishman and handed the bag up to her. "Take the books, will you? I'm just going to drop this at the postbox where I found my package this morning."

"Ye are goin' down there?" asked the boy through narrowed eyes. "Where all thon men have gathered?"

I looked down the steep incline to where some of the men could be seen standing near the boathouse. "Yes, that was my intent."

"Are ye gonna talk to them?"

"I very well might. That is generally the kind thing to do when one meets new people."

"Well, how lang are ye gonna stay and gab? I've promised my ma' I wouldna linger overlong with the men about."

"She'll only be a minute, Hughie," offered Kate, glaring at me to make it so.

"Yes, only a minute," I reiterated, and shifted my attention to the ill-looking cadre that had gathered beside the boathouse. I could sense the confrontation. The men were making no effort to launch the two boats, painted lighthouse white with a black stripe, which had spent the winter upside down on a bed of logs in the boathouse. They appeared, instead, to be engaged in a heated discussion. I shifted my attention back to our undersized, fledgling cart-driver. "Would you mind stepping down here, Hughie?" I beckoned him with a gloved finger to the edge of the road with me. Hughie, after a moment of suspicious hesitation, alighted from the cart while Kate patiently remained on the bench, casting a warning glance with her narrowed brown eyes. "How would you like to make a little wager with me?" I whispered, being extra cautious that Kate could not hear us. "If you win, I'll give you a guinea. If I win, you spend an hour with me this afternoon—on your best behavior—learning to read. No complaints or snide comments; no infantile attacks on my character or behavior. What do you say?"

"I get a whole gold guinea from ye?" he questioned, looking intrigued by the notion. I nodded. "Wha' do I have tae do?"

I left Hughie with instructions and started down the steep road, watching all the while the men who had gathered near the boathouse. There were seven new faces, along with the familiar person of Mr. MacKay, who was standing tall and broad-shouldered as he listened politely, with his fiery head slightly inclined, to what the men were saying. Coming closer, yet still unknown to the group, I caught snatches of the argument, deep voices with the thick brogue of the Cape countering Mr. Campbell and Robbie with cries of "Why should we risk it?" "Ye ken very well wha' happened last time we listened to ye!" "We're shepherds, no' sailors!" "Mariners know the risk and take it willingly. 'Tis wha' they're paid for, by Christ!" And then one man chimed, "I dinna gi' a rat's arse that Napoleon's on thae loose an' marchin' on Paris. He could be stormin' the continent for all I care and still I'm no' gonna row your wee boat, Campbell!"

I was less than twenty feet away, and still the men were too preoccupied to notice my arrival. I gripped the letter tighter, took a deep breath and said, "Napoleon?" rolling the distasteful name a bit theatrically in my mouth as I continued forward. Mr. Campbell looked up. Other heads turned and the talking died down.

It was my cue; I was on.

With an inward smile I relished the look on the light-keeper's face, knowing that he had been expecting a more auspicious entrance than a young woman with an old calash bonnet tied snugly over her hair, a tight-fitting riding habit that had seen better days—just visible beneath an unbuttoned men's boat-cloak. He was also not expecting my amicable greeting of: "Tell me, gentlemen, why do you mention that man's name, and on such a glorious day as this? Please, do not ruin it for me. 'Tis been a bleak enough winter. I cannot begin to tell you how much

I'm looking forward to spring and the promise of new ventures!" Then, shifting my smile and attention to the light-keepers, I waved my letter in the air. "Mr. Campbell, Mr. MacKinnon, good day, sirs. And Mr. MacKay, how fine it is to see you here! I ran into your charming son not a moment ago at the top of the road. Such a good lad you have there." Then, coming to stand before the man, I untied my bonnet and folded it back, letting my hair tumble out in a freshly washed, vigorously brushed, lavender-scented, auburn cascade. "Tell me, who are your friends?"

The Highlander looked suspiciously at me, then at Mr. Campbell, and finally replied, with a polite bow, "Miss Stevenson, how nice it is to see ye here today. Allow me to introduce some kinsmen of mine." The introductions were brief and cogent, yet I listened intently to what Mr. MacKay said as he went around the ill-formed circle of mates, filing the names and faces away in the recesses of my memory.

There were a few with the surname of MacKay, I noted—an older man, Tosh MacKay, Mr. MacKay's uncle, who was perhaps in his fifties, and his son, Angus, both from a place called Inshore. Next was a ginger-haired young man named Jamie MacKay—another cousin, I assumed—who lived south of Kervaig along the river. There was Liam Ross, a small, rather shy young man whose wide, unblinking dark eyes were focused just below my neck. Next to him stood two other men, in their mid-twenties, Archie and Hector Gilchrist of Archiemore, both brothers smiling with a vigor I seldom saw. And then there was a Danny MacDonald of Durness, another family man, with a wife and children who lived cape-side now, a former-fisherman-turned-ferryman shuttling folks across the Kyle of Durness. Just how he got along with Mr. Campbell, I was uncertain, for I never heard the man spoken of before.

"Gentlemen, 'tis a pleasure," I said, acknowledging all the kind wishes by dropping into a courtly curtsey.

"Miss Stevenson," began the man named Tosh, a burly creature with deep-set brown eyes and a face reminiscent of a bear. He then pointed accusingly to the cliff where the lighthouse stood. "Are ye the daughter o' the man that puit that there?"

"The lighthouse, do you mean? I am, sir, though if truth be told, I was never consulted on the matter, so I'm as innocent in this as are you. Or were you, by chance, one of the masons on the project? I have to admit it's rather a fine-looking structure; wonderfully sound, and the lantern's pure genius. What's more, I was told the buildings are of granite quarried from nearby Clash Carnoch, and a finer granite I've never seen."

The man, taken aback that a woman could use so many words with nary a breath in between, shyly acknowledged that he wasn't. "I'm but a shepherd, is all. No mason, ma'am."

"A shepherd? You say it as if the responsibility demeans you. Being a shepherd is a fine vocation, Tosh. May I call you Tosh? Was not our beloved Jesus the gentle shepherd himself, tending his flock with brotherly love? I'm pleased to see that you are a man not only concerned with the wee beasties in your care but all who pass under your cautious eye as well." The rest of the men were speechless, looking rather nervous by this broad assumption. Mr. Campbell, I could see, was fighting a rueful smile. Robbie, wise man that he was, stood motionless, apparently sensing that something unseemly was about to unfold before his eyes.

"Mr. Campbell, dear sir," I said, coming beside him and taking his arm as if it were the most natural thing between us, much to his surprise. "I have a letter to post, as you well know, but before I do, tell me, what was this talk of Napoleon just now?"

He smiled dotingly, wonderfully convincing, and replied, "Why, my dear, Mr. MacKay has informed me the wee emperor escaped his prison in Elba in February and is now marching on Paris. Imagine that! And all of France is coming to his aid. 'Twould appear as if the war is not over yet. Ye should be safe enough, Miss Stevenson, never doubt it for a moment, but our shipping will continue to be harassed by French men-of-war and privateers alike, not to mention the increase in activity. All the more reason to be prepared."

"Oh yes, one must always be prepared. And speaking of such, why aren't the boats in the water yet? I thought you told me that was your task this morning. And you always have so much to do." I looked at the men. "Gentlemen, if you would be so kind as to give the keepers a hand, I would be forever in your debt. I have an appointment to keep, and I do so hate to be late."

"Ma'am?" began Mr. MacKay, looking crossly at Mr. Campbell, while Mr. Campbell, in turn, was looking curiously at me. "Hughie was waitin' for ye with the cart. He's volunteered tae take ye to our home."

"Yes, that was very kind of him, but I already sent him along with Mrs. MacKinnon." Robbie's cinnamon brows drew together at the mention of his young wife left solely in the care of the precocious ten-year-old; his deep blue gaze bore into mine unnervingly. "Oh, never worry, Mr. MacKinnon," I said with a knowing grin. "Young Master MacKay tells me he's an old hand at driving the cart. I just hope he stays on the parve road; these cliffs are treacherously high. Anyhow, I tell you this because Mr. Campbell, dear man, has already promised to pull me to Kervaig Bay in one of the boats. I was counting on a few of you good men to take a turn at the oars. I probably shouldn't mention this, but I've got a guinea riding on the fact that I'm going to beat young Master MacKay home." I looked around at the new faces; some regarded me suspiciously while others were watching the performance with open awe. I smiled mischievously. "And I'll put another guinea to every man of the boat team that can get me there first!"

Though it was a low, shameless ploy, it worked like a charm. The younger men, men eager and hungry for gold, bolted to the boats first, as if in a hill race, kicking up stones with their boot heels while their coattails flapped in the steady March breeze as they called for the others to help them launch.

I let go of Mr. Campbell's arm. "There, my end of the bargain is complete. Now, sir, I suggest you and Robbie each coxswain one of the crafts. I wouldn't trust shepherds with the task." And without waiting for him to answer, I escaped his grasp and headed down to the end of the pier, letter in hand, where I intended to place it in the postbox.

In truth, I had little hope that it would be picked up before Friday, but I felt compelled to give it a chance. The mysterious little package had blindsided me this morning, wounding me beyond words, yet it intrigued me as well. And there was a driving force within me that needed answers. I would not rest until I knew how and why the watch had been returned, and where on earth Thomas Crichton really was. My hand came away from the postbox as I uttered a little prayer for its swift delivery to Mr. Alexander Seawell of Oxford, England. Unconsciously my hand went over my heart. I felt the little John Roger Arnold chronometer ticking away, tucked deep within the confines of my swollen breasts, the steady rhythm giving me a small comfort.

By the time I headed back to the strand the lighthouse boats were already in the water and the men were taking their places on the benches as if they knew the drill quite well already.

"Miss Stevenson, come with us!" cried the Gilchrist brothers excitedly as they sat on the first bench in front of Robbie, hands on their oars, with Liam Ross' and Danny MacDonald's on the other set. "We're your men! We'll get ye there first!" I smiled and was about to take them up on the offer when I looked and saw that Mr. Campbell was about to take his seat in the stern of the first cutter, much to the chagrin of the oarsmen—all of them MacKays. The oars, having already been shipped in the pintles, were standing at the ready. The men fell silent. Hands came away and the oars dropped unceremoniously into the water. My eyes held to Mr. Campbell then, as he sat by the tiller, straight-backed and with stoic calm. If he was disturbed by the behavior of the MacKays he didn't show it. In fact, I could tell that his focus was not on them; it was glued to the dangerous breakers that rolled just beyond the cove. And in my silent study I saw what the men of Cape Wrath feared. Though the face of the light-keeper was strangely blank as he peered at the open water, there passed just beneath the surface of the blanched skin a dark tremor. It was the shadow of doubt—perhaps fear even—and it made the pale eyes all the more spectacularly wild and chilling.

Mr. Campbell was revisiting the demons that plagued him.

The silence in the first cutter was not lost in the exuberant mood of the second boat. They too became quiet, watching and waiting.

Pity, a feeling somewhat foreign to me, arose. And strangely I felt my heart go out to the lonely recluse. "Gentlemen," I began, almost reflexively, turning to the men of the first boat. "I thank you kindly for the offer, but I believe I shall have to decline. I promised to go with Mr. Campbell, and in Mr. Campbell's boat I shall go. Do forgive me."

"'Tis an unwise choice if ye do, lassie!" Archibald Gilchrist warned, and I could see by the look on his face he meant it. "Ye'll be lucky tae get there alive!"

The mood had so quickly shifted. Gone was my triumphant wager and in its place reared the ugly head of Highland superstition. And Mr. Campbell's sudden recidivism to a darker personality was not helping his cause whatsoever. Without much choice I retorted with, "Well, bless me, but I am a gambling soul. And I will double the wager that I not only arrive safely at Kervaig Bay, but also be in the boat that touches first. I put my faith and my life in Mr. Campbell's capable hands!" I looked pointedly at the light-keeper. With the slightest of movements he shook his head, his lips pulled into a grimace, silently warning me to rescind the offer. I ignored him and added, purely for the sake of spite, "The first boat to touch the sands will receive two guineas for every man, coxswain included." And then, without another thought on the matter, I ran to the first boat and climbed aboard. There, I took my place beside Mr. Campbell, with the tiller between us. I looked at him and tried to convey through a smile all the confidence I had mustered for my speech. His eyes, haunting and lucid, only darkened.

"By God, what kind of fool are ye?" he uttered, a mixture of puzzlement and pain in his words. "Ye should not be here at all, Miss Stevenson. May God have mercy on your stubborn, foolish wee soul! I know what you're doing, but you obviously do not. I insist that ye leave the boat at once." His words, thankfully, were inaudible to the others, due to a crashing wave. The surf was picking up.

"You've uttered many such sentiments since I've come to Cape Wrath, and you are undoubtedly correct, sir. However, I am not leaving this boat. We made a bargain the other night . . . remember?"

"You know very well I never asked for this."

"You asked for help . . . likely the hardest thing you've ever done, asking someone like me for help, so I know how important this is to you. And it's important to me as well. You think me frivolous and weak-willed. Well maybe I am, but once I make a vow I take it seriously. You *need* me beside you. These men need to see it too. So, if you're quite done berating me, I'll thank you to say not another word on the matter and order the boat to shove off. I've a lot of money riding on this little venture and I'd be hard-pressed to part with more than I can spare."

The look he cast, one of pinched incredulity, was strangely fortifying, likely so because he knew I was right. Without another word, or look in my direction, he gave the order and the boat was pushed off the strand and into the cold waters of the cove. The four rowers pulled on the oars with an energy spawned by captive fear as they fought to clear the growing surf with a pariah at the helm. They knew the next hundred yards would be the hardest won.

When the boat was coaxed onto a course where her bow was

pointed directly into the oncoming waves, Mr. Campbell leaned over and inquired with feigned politeness, just after cold spume hit my face: "Are ye comfortable?"

"Very," I replied prettily, wiping my face with the sleeve of my coat.

"I don't mean physically, Miss Stevenson." Although he offered a polite smile, his eyes were hurtfully sardonic. "What I mean is, are ye comfortable gambling away money ye don't have?" At that moment the tiller lurched, and he paused to correct our course, crying out as he did so, "Angus, lad, pull harder, aye?"

"What makes you think I don't have money?" I replied sweetly, unwilling to let him see how his indifference hurt me. "I'm a fallen woman, not a pauper, you know." My boldness shocked him, as I suspected it would. And, God help me, I liked shocking him. "However," I continued, smiling not at him but the men at the oars, "I might have overestimated my funds. I'm not quick with numbers. So, I believe it would be best if we arrive first or I'll have to take a small loan from you, and I should warn you, I might not be able to pay you back."

He gave me a sideways glance, uncertain how to respond to this, and then, as if fighting the urge, a glimmer of a smile touched his lips. This weakening of his impenetrable defenses was enough to compel me to continue. "You'll recall that I'm not exactly in good *standing* with my family? I'm sure Kate has told you that I was about to run off to Gretna Green with a sailor—the same man I gave the timepiece to. It was convenient for my parents that he didn't have the nerve to show up and coerce me into a foolishly unsuitable marriage. But they're still plenty disappointed. And after having been 'saved' from one evil, I doubt very much they'd send me money to perpetuate another, like gambling. But you're a working man, and a pinchbeck spendthrift, at that. You'll have some gold put by, I'll wager?"

"Some," he said, and although he didn't smile, I could tell that my frank admission, under the pretext of idle chatter, had touched him a little deeper than he imagined it would. "And I'm not a pinchbeck." It was said a little defensively. "I prefer the term 'frugal.' But all the same, I don't like losing money in foolish bets."

"Well then, you best get these men to pull harder."

I was awarded a begrudging smile, and then, as the mesmerizing aquamarine eyes turned with reluctance from me to the men at the oars, Mr. Campbell set his whole being to navigating the rescue boat.

It was roughly a three-mile pull to Kervaig Bay. The wind, thankfully, was at our backs on this day, one oddly reminiscent of the first time I had sailed along under the shadow of the spectacular Clo Mor Cliffs. The temperature was nearly the same as it had been in early November; the day just as gray but without the cloaking fog. And the seawater, much to my chagrin, was still freezing. Yet it was my mood that was much altered this time. No longer was I afraid of Cape Wrath and isolation. No longer did I detest my sorrowful plight and the presence of Kate. And most unsettling of all was the knowledge that the man sitting next to me was becoming oddly familiar. And I'd be lying to myself if I said I didn't now relish having the upper hand on him. Yet an unwavering fact remained, and that was, try as I might, my heart and soul still belonged to Thomas Crichton.

Once both crafts had safely cleared the breakers, and were beyond the point at which the waves broke in upon themselves, I had time to marvel at the skill of both crews. For if Mr. Campbell was correct, most of these men were shepherds, living on the undulating moorland high above the sea. Yet he must have had some inkling they were familiar with these waters or he never would have induced them to ply the oars. The sea was relatively calm, but in a storm it would be a different matter.

Cutting through the breakers, the second boat, with Robbie at the tiller, had pulled ahead, the young men having more muscle and vigor than the MacKay men. Their strokes were coming at a quicker cadence, their rowing deep and synchronized, and being caught up in the moment, and knowing I stood to lose fourteen guineas on the bet (not an insubstantial sum), I could not help myself from standing up and cheering my team on with a cry of: "Heave! Heave! Heave hearty, MacKays!"

This, I immediately realized, was a terrible mistake. For my excitement, imprudent and unchecked as it was, caused the boat to rock dangerously. At the same time a mighty swell hit us on the larboard side, shifting the precarious equilibrium of the boat that much more. My balance, compromised all the more by my burgeoning pregnancy, was not what it once was and I stumbled to starboard, taking the whole boat with me. My legs gave out. My hands flung wide to brace myself for the impact against the gunwale. My hip crashed against the tiller on the way down and my bonnet was thrown from my head. In a wild tangle of clothing and loose hair I toppled sideways toward the frigid water. Yet before I ever reached the sea I was grabbed from behind in a bone-crushing grip. And before I could take another breath I found myself firmly seated in the lap of Mr. Campbell.

His hold on me was so tight I could barely breathe, but I was grateful for it. And when I turned to look at him—thankful, relieved, yet with a heart still lurching wildly in my chest—I caught a look of fear in his eyes that made mine seem pale by comparison.

Whether it was from the thought of losing me, or the thought of another unfortunate accident before these suspicious witnesses, I could not tell. The truth was, his fast actions had saved me. I was about to utter my sincere thanks when I realized that as quickly as his fear had risen, it had turned to white hot anger; and it was only natural that I was the recipient of his wrath. But before so many watching eyes—eyes wide with unholy suspicion—the wily light-keeper chose another punishment for me, and that was the punishment of his forced affections. His grip tightened, preventing me from taking a full breath. "I think," he began while fighting his raging breath, "that I shall keep ye on my lap so you will not get it into your pretty little head to stand in my boat again." And then he smiled mischievously for the sake of the men.

"I think . . . I've learned . . . my lesson," I insisted, pushing against his solid chest while fighting for breath, all the while attempting to appear as if I liked the man.

"Have ye?" Although he was smiling, there lived in his eyes a private warning. "Good. Then ye can think of it as my reward for not letting ye go into the water. It's deathly cold, and ye gave the men a great fright."

"If that is your wish, than I shall let you," I replied, hoping I sounded convincing enough for the attentive ears pricked in our direction. My fingers were covertly attempting to break his viselike grip on me so I could breathe again. "But I'm afraid you won't be able to navigate with such a great weight pinning you down. Look," I said, pointing to the other boat, which was pulling far ahead. All heads turned. "They're beating us."

"Gentlemen," cried Mr. Campbell with renewed purpose, his mind, no doubt, on his own wallet. "What are ye waiting for? Grab hold of your oars and pull!"

This, thankfully, the men did, for they too, no doubt, were thinking of their wallets. And once the hearty men of clan MacKay were again on course, Mr. Campbell turned to me and whispered in my ear, "Your impulsivity has managed to widen the gap for the lads nicely. And every attempt you made to ease their minds about embarking on such an endeavor with me nearly went by the boards. I shall pray ye use better judgment in the future, Miss Stevenson." And then, with one final squeeze to emphasize his words, he released me.

There was nothing I could say, because it was true. And so I took my seat and remained quietly brooding, knowing for a certainty that I had lost any ground I'd made with the light-keeper, as well as a good deal of money.

I did, in fact, learn one thing as I sat chastened in the stern of the little oar-boat, aside from exercising prudence when travel-

ing in a small craft, and it was that when given a chance, pro-
moted by steadiness and pacing, experience prevails over youth.
As the bay of Kervaig opened up before us—her welcoming waters glittering in the sun as the first rays of the day were just
poking through—it became evident that the men in Robbie's
boat were growing tired. They had worked the oars with such
strength and vigor that after the long pull—the first of the
year—they were exhausted. Hugh and his kinsmen were also
tiring, but not nearly at the same rate. They had experience on
their side. I watched as all four oarsmen gritted their teeth—
Tosh uttering guttural words of encouragement to his son—
while using their heads as well as their arms to close the gap
that had been present from the start. Robbie's boat was drawing
closer as we entered the bay, and once the younger men noticed
our boat gaining on them they leaned on their oars with redoubled vigor. The problem with that, however, was that not all the
men pulled with the same strength and the boat began to veer
off course in spite of the coxswain's corrections. Mr. Campbell
saw the gap and took it, urging the men on with a steady calm in
his voice, a voice that revealed the reclusive lighthouse keeper
had at once the confidence and experience to guide his fellow
man. I was as much in awe of his handling of the situation as I
was with the fact that we were pulling ahead of the other cutter.

"By God, they're doing it, aren't they?" I uttered, and found
myself smiling at the man next to me. Without waiting for him
to answer, I shouted encouragingly from the safety of my seat,
"Keep pulling, MacKays! You're doing it! You're going to take
the lead!"

At the sound of my voice Robbie looked at me from across the
way. The grimace on his face, the narrowed eyes, combined with
urgent cries delivered to his men in such a competitive way,
made me realize that he was hell-bent on fleecing me, likely for
the shoddy way I had tricked his wife into the care of a suspect
minor. I had never seen him like this before. I glanced at Mr.

Campbell. Sensing my eyes upon him he turned and delivered a darkly disarming grin.

"I believe Mr. MacKinnon is intent on making you pay for years of torment to his dear wife."

"I was just thinking the same thing," I said, and offered an apologetic smile. "I'd be lying if I didn't say there's some justification there too. But if I do appear to torment her from time to time, it's because I have my reasons."

"It's more than your spiteful nature?" he offered, and assumed he was being clever.

But for some reason his words of accusation hurt more than I cared to admit, largely because Mr. Campbell thought me the unscrupulous one. Out of pique, and with the threat of tears at recalling how Kate had betrayed my trust, I said, "Do you really want to know why I'm here?—thrust on your promontory of hell and a constant burden to your self-imposed isolation?" This got his attention. I continued. "I'm here because I told Kate about my sailor and she promised she would keep it a secret, but she told my parents anyway. Perhaps it was a blessing he never came for me; they would have never approved of him. But my heart dies a little every day because of it, so you'll just have to forgive me if I sometimes appear cruel or unduly mean. She was my dear friend once, you know."

I could see him weighing this information behind his piercing eyes, and he looked at Robbie in the other boat. "Did ye . . . ever consider that perhaps it was for the best?"

"No," I said plainly, looking into his guarded face and feeling the familiar sting of tears that came all too easily. "And I'm surprised that you could even ask such a thing. I live in hell for my sins, Mr. Campbell, just as you do for yours. The only difference is that I was hoping to avoid this hell by seeking a little bit of heaven. I overreached myself."

"I'm sorry" was all he said, and strangely, I could see that he meant it.

With a new and driving force, Mr. Campbell set to guiding our rowers, and no one could doubt his desire to win. It was a harrowing, heart-pumping pull to the finish. Past the magnificent sea stacks that rose out of the water like the spires of sunken cathedrals, and straight to the approaching beach. No one spoke a word for the last hundred yards of the race. It was only when our boat touched on the sands, just seconds ahead of the other boat, did a cheer go up. The MacKay men were bent over their oars, mouths open and breath coming heavily. But it was the look in their eyes that lifted my spirits. For they were looking at Mr. Campbell, and this time there was no derision or fear, as there had been at the jetty, but something akin to respect. I too turned to the man, who both unnerved and intrigued me. His eyes, burning with the same intensity as the lighthouse he tended, held to mine, and then he nodded. Although in a rather unorthodox manner, and one not without some glaring flaws, I had upheld my end of the bargain . . . and rather successfully too, for Mr. William Campbell could not complain that he had lost any money in the bargain, as I had.

. . .

It was agreed that I would pay the men from the winning boat their two guineas apiece when they were to gather next, a week hence at the same beach, due to the fact that I was not in the habit of carrying that kind of money on my person. It would also bring them back to Mr. Campbell's cause for another go-round. I threw out the concept of a nominal pay for their continued efforts, somewhere in the vicinity of one shilling per week. Friendly greetings went around and everyone proceeded to the MacKay croft in much higher spirits than when they had first gathered at the lighthouse jetty.

It was at the croft, only a short jaunt from the beach, where I learned that I had lost yet another gold guinea. Apparently the Duchess of Sutherland, when properly coaxed and duly prodded with a rod, was a faster beast than I had given her credit for. And from the scurrilous glare from Kate I deduced that she felt blessed to have arrived at all.

Not only did I lose my bet with Hughie MacKay the younger, but I had also lost the opportunity to introduce him to the world of reading. He would not be pressed upon to spend time learning his alphabet with me when all the men were about. The ban of infantile attacks on my character was also lifted, though strongly tempered by the lad's mother.

Mr. Campbell had already headed back to the lighthouse, and most of the others were on their way home, when I finally was able to sit and visit with Mary and Kate.

"Angus told me how ye almost swamped the boat," wee Hughie gibed, speaking loud enough for all to hear. "Sent the fear o' God through 'em, it did. Ye stood up an' the whole boat began to topple. I heard 'twas Mr. Campbell what saved ye, and kept ye in his lap until he was certain ye'd not stand up again." The boy cast me a rather condescending look.

"Well, it wasn't nearly as dramatic as that," I corrected with a flippant wave of my hand. "And it was a wave, not me, that gave us the fright."

"Really." He narrowed his eyes skeptically. "Not the way I heard tell. Perhaps if ye lost some weight the boat wouldnae tip? I noticed ye've grown a wee thick since the last time ye were here."

"Hughie! That'll be enough out o' ye! Is it no' enough that ye scared poor Mrs. MacKinnon to death with your wicked driving? An' now ye insult our dear guest like the ill-mannered besom ye are! Another word and I'll see your faither bend ye ower the rail and take a stick to your backside!"

"But Ma, I'm only commenting on a fact," he pleaded, the damnable blue eyes wide and guileless.

I held up a hand to stop Mary and replied softly, "You're right, Hughie, and very observant; I am getting thicker, and I'm likely to get thicker still until I'm thin again. But I'll thank you to not mention it. Women are very sensitive about their weight."

"But why are you getting thick?"

"Because I'm with child."

This he was not expecting. His face, usually filled with mischief and good humor, grew sullen. His round, boyish features became pinched with incomprehension as he stared at me. And then he repeated his question: "But why?"

"Well now, that's a long story. And if you ever want to know it, you're going to have to learn to read. For mine is a story best told on paper, with words scribed in ink and not passed down orally from one person to the next, where the facts get lost and twisted in personal interpretation. I'd not wish that to happen. So, if you want to know, the next time I come here, ask me to teach you to read."

He stared at me silently for a long while, as if what I told him had somehow altered how he thought of me. And then, abruptly, he nodded and stood to leave, heading outside where his father and Robbie MacKinnon were talking.

Mary MacKay looked thoughtfully at me from across the table and then she mused, "Perhaps I shall learn to read too."

· · ·

Later that evening, well after supper and while Robbie was nearing the end of the first shift in the light-room, I heard Mr. Campbell's door creak open. He had been sleeping, I assumed, and had kept to his room since our return from the MacKay croft. We had not seen him, nor did he appear for supper. Kate suggested we wake him, yet I countered her advice by offering some of my own, namely that it was best to let a sleeping bear lie. This she agreed to, but only under the condition that I handle the task of feeding said bear myself when he awoke. And so, merely to bide the time, I sat in my room with the door open, writing a cursory letter to my parents—purely a courtesy to let them know I still lived, that the child I carried seemed to be thriving and therefore was still a black mark on their sterling name.

I heard his footsteps progress only as far as my threshold. And then came a soft knock on the stout oak door frame.

"Mr. Campbell, you're awake," I greeted, turning to face him as he stood silhouetted in my doorway. "I've saved your supper and will have it ready for you in a moment." He gave a small nod in acknowledgment, yet from the way he looked at me, the way the glowing eyes held to mine, made me to understand that food was not why he had come. I made no move to get up as he walked into the room, silently closing the door behind him. Kate was still awake, I consoled myself as he approached. She was darning stockings in the main room while awaiting Robbie. Mr. Campbell could do nothing to me while she was awake. Yet all the same, my hand, still holding the dripping quill, began to tremble. I stuffed the pen back into its holder and brought both my hands to my lap, willing them to be still.

Mr. Campbell stood very near to me. I could smell the essence of sweet tobacco mingling with the more antiseptic smell of the local whisky that was wafting off his black coat. The entire room seemed to come alive with his dark, masculine presence.

He clasped his hands behind his back and bent his head slightly forward, looking down on me. "I . . . I wanted to thank you for what ye did today, Miss Stevenson. But never again do I want to see you in one of those boats. Do I make myself clear?"

I pushed back my chair and stood, not coming exactly eye to eye with the man, as he was a good deal taller than I, but at least on somewhat more equal terms. "I did what had to be done. And for what it's worth, I quite agree with you on account of the boats. Charming as they appear, being rowed in one of your little skiffs is not my chosen form of travel."

"Ye prefer a coach and four, perhaps?—with a heated brick at your feet and a fur mantle pulled around your shoulders?"

Although he was making sport of me, it did sound rather wonderful, and I couldn't help but smile at the thought. "Ah, how well you know me. Before you held me captive on your lap I would swear you were only able to discern the subtle shifts of objects mechanical or scientific. And here I thought you were only trying to torment me, but I see the experience gave you some valuable insight."

"I was hoping it would give *you* some valuable insight so you'd be able to think more clearly," he countered with the same insincere smile.

"But I do think clearly," I replied, and looked at him earnestly. "I bought you more time, Mr. Campbell, and another go with those men. They need leadership, and perhaps a little incentive."

"Incentive? You bribed the men. You already owe the MacKay men eight guineas, and all of them are now expecting coin every time they show up."

"Why shouldn't we pay them?"

"With what? Outfitting two rescue boats with eight men's not exactly in the budget for a lighthouse so far from civilization. And where are ye planning on getting the eight guineas you promised the men?"

I huffed, wondering how he could maintain being such a boor, and pushed him slightly out of my way so that I could go to my chest. After rootling around a bit I pulled out a white canvas sack, unremarkable in all aspects with the exception of its weight and the way it jingled as I shook it. It was another of the heavy objects I thought to pack.

"Ye have the money?" he marveled, looking suspiciously at me. "Your father gave ye a great sack of money?"

"Gave me?" I replied. "Not exactly." And I tossed him two of the gold coins, his payment for winning the bet. "I was planning my elopement with a sailor, remember? Just what kind of fool do you take me for?"

He looked at the coins in his hand, the gold glowing brilliantly in the lamplight. And then his focus shifted to me. "I have never thought ye a fool, Sara," he said, using my Christian name for the first time. "Only foolish. And may God help me, but I suffer fools ever so much better than idiots. Keep your money," he said, tossing the coins back to me. "You owe me nothing. But I would be much obliged if you could see it in your wee foolish heart to make me some food. I've a muckle long night ahead of me and a little kindness from you, I find, never goes amiss."

. . .

Over the next few days it became obvious to me that Mr. Campbell's attitude toward me had softened. There was even something as foreign as respect coming from his many covert glances. And, not to embarrass the man, I pretended not to notice. But I did notice how he began to regard Kate.

It was no secret that from the start of our stint on the Cape he had thought Kate the paradigm of female virtue, never lashing out at her with a cross word or glaring her way in disapproval. Those reproaches were reserved solely for me. But things had altered slightly since our conversation on the boat. He was still polite and courteous where Kate was concerned, yet I could see he began to watch her more closely, and took a more objective interest in our relationship and how we treated each other. But not until Kate aired her pious thoughts during Thursday night's dinner about the irresponsibility of my choice to correspond with a stranger from Oxford did Mr. Campbell, uncharacteristically, defend me.

"Miss Stevenson deserves to know the truth," he said evenly. And before she could reply, before she could even counter with the improprieties of such scandalous behavior, he gently cut her off and advised her to keep to her own affairs. And then, without so much as a glance in my direction or at Robbie, he left for his duty in the tower.

All throughout the week I kept an eye out for the mysterious little skiff I had seen the morning my package was delivered, but I never did spy her. And not until Friday morning, directly after the great light had been snuffed out and the horses hitched to the wagon as we made ready to embark on our trip into Durness, did I ask Mr. Campbell if I could retrieve the letter I had left at the jetty. I wanted to make certain it would reach Mr.

Alexander Seawell of Oxford. With a show of chivalry, Mr. Campbell volunteered to retrieve the letter himself and dashed down the steep road to the end of the pier while we sat in the wagon, waiting for him at the top. When he finally came back I could see that his hands were empty, his expression perplexed.

"The letter's gone," he declared with the air of wonder. "By God, I never saw a boat pass this way. I must have missed it." And I could tell the mere thought that he had troubled him greatly.

Yet what troubled me was not the mysterious boat or her skipper. It was that my letter was gone; my only thought, my only prayer, was that Mr. Seawell, the antiquarian from Oxford, would answer it.

# EIGHT

# Mr. Seawell's Reply

 $\mathcal{T}$ he village of Durness was certainly no Mecca, nor was it a thriving hub of civilization. In fact, *village* was perhaps too lofty a word to describe the shocking paucity of whitewashed cottages that dotted the vast and austere landscape. Yet it was more civilization than I had seen in a great long while, and sorry though it was, Mr. Campbell did let on that there was a house that acted as an inn of sorts where a meal could be ordered and a room procured. We had traveled a long distance indeed, and the thought of ordering a hot meal and having it served by an unknown procuress was titillating. Yet the meal, however wonderful it would be, was not why we had come to Durness. We had made the journey to the little cluster of cottages by the sea just so I could have the local doctor glance at my swelling midriff. I would have liked to profess that such a visit was unnecessary, but as the child within me grew, so too did my fears. I knew only too well it was a mortally dangerous prospect with both the child's life and mine hanging in the balance, yet one I was undoubtedly obliged to make. And as our wagon trundled over the undulating moorland, across the still frozen streams and the Kyle of Durness, I was struck with a bit of an epiphany, and that simply was that no matter how long my labor was apt to be, it was highly unlikely a doctor would ever be fetched in time. This thought left me with the distasteful realization that Kate would be the one to help my child into the world; hers would be the first face my child would see. I was not well versed in the folk arts and had little knowledge of omens good or bad. However, I did strongly feel that if my baby's first glimpse of the world was Kate's great haughty glare it could not bode well for the child. I would just have to pray that Mary MacKay, bless her good-hearted soul, might be gotten as well.

I believed it was purely for peace of mind that Mr. Campbell insisted I make a visit to a midwife or an accoucheur; for, aside from his predilection for naked, dead pregnant women—a fact I shuddered to think on—I believed that the mere thought of childbirth, to one so far removed from humanity, was likely repugnant. We passed along the few cottages lining the main street, each one advertising on a little wooden sign the service, or multiplicity of services, to be found within. I spied the dwelling advertising that there was a surgeon to be had. The wagon slowed down, Mr. Campbell said something to Robbie, and Robbie along with Kate jumped out. Mr. Campbell, however, did not stop. He kept the team walking on, traveling farther down the rutted path, slowly moving away from the small cluster of civilization.

"I thought . . ." I began, touching the sleeve of his coat, "I thought the whole purpose of this trip was to visit the doctor?"

"Aye, and that man there is no doctor. He's a surgeon . . . a barber-surgeon and tooth-puller forbye. And, not to be coarse on the matter, but I'd no sooner put a young lady before him than I would the crown jewels. He'd have no scruples pinching either."

"You don't trust him," I said, finding that little morsel of fact intriguing. And then, studying him further, I asked, "Then why are we here?"

"Not to see him." He gestured with a back nod of his head. "There's another down the way."

"But where are Robbie and Kate off to? Should they not come with us?"

"Mr. and Mrs. MacKinnon are off to enjoy a well-deserved respite. Unfortunately, that wee village is the best I can offer the man and his wife at the moment. I highly doubt either one of them would relish going where we're going."

There was indeed another soul Mr. Campbell had in mind. This particular "practitioner of the arts" dwelled in a little bothy that appeared from a distance to be a good deal shabbier than even the term implied. It was a squat, whitewashed stone hovel. One could almost mistake it for a pile of rubble, but for the tuft of yellow thatch that capped it off, and the gray smoke wafting from the chimney carrying a hint of sage to our nostrils. The whole little homestead was set at a prudent distance from any other dwelling, I noted, and was nestled in the bosom of a vale that protected it from the tenacious winds of the sea. Just the sight of the forlorn little place induced me to believe that I should have taken my chances back in the village with the surgeon, inappropriately roving hands or not.

A large rowan tree was the first sight to greet us as we turned on to the little drive leading to our questionable destination. It was the only tree I had seen for miles, purposely planted and boldly guarding the entrance to the property from evil, I supposed. I watched Mr. Campbell intently as we rolled past, noting with some dismay that the magical tree hadn't thwarted his arrival; he was still very much alive and breathing. A few curs, upon hearing our approach, barked and harassed the horses, loudly heralding our arrival. But like most intelligent dogs they stayed at a cautious distance from the dangerous hooves and then, losing interest altogether, headed back to the plethora of other domestic animals that rooted under the bare branches of the tree, nibbling unseen delicacies scattered about the grounds. It was then I took a closer look at the suspicious dwelling, getting the strong impression that Mr. Campbell was tormenting me again. The thought of the creature that lived here placing their gnarled hands on my naked flesh invoked a real sense of fear, but I said not a word; I would never give him the satisfaction. Instead I sat stone-faced on the bench beside him, steeling my nerves and readying myself for another bout of his perverse inclination to humiliate and abuse me.

Without a word, or further explanation, he pulled to a stop before the door and alighted from the wagon, coming around to take my hand. I could tell by the mischievous look in his eyes as they delivered to mine a challenge that he was enjoying my discomfort.

"My, this is fitting, isn't it?" I quipped, stepping down, pushing the disdain from my voice and vowing to play my part upon pain of death. "A fallen bothy for a fallen woman. How charming of you."

"Is that what ye think?"

I smiled, ignoring his question, and walked on. He grabbed my arm and jerked me roughly around to face him.

"I'm doing you a great favor, Miss Stevenson," he seethed, apparently affronted by my ungracious attitude. "This, however paltry it may appear, is the best Sutherland has to offer."

"If that's what you would have me believe, then I shall believe it. After all, I'm well aware that I'm entirely in your care. However, if anything untoward should happen to me in there, or as a result of what I'm about to endure, I swear, Mr. Campbell, I swear that I shall be another poor soul to add to your long list of plaguing ghosts. I'm committed to that," I averred with a punctuating look. And then, responding to his extreme glare of displeasure with a smile, I added, "Now, let's get on with it, shall we?"

I got no more than a few steps away from the light-keeper before the cottage door flung open, and there, standing on the threshold, was a woman—an old woman, round-faced and jolly, wiping her hands on a bright purple apron while beaming graciously at the dark, glowering man beyond me.

I was taken aback, even more so when she declared: "Why, Willy Campbell!" and bounded forward to greet him, her sprightly calico frock and sunny greeting looking even more out of place than the smile on my chaperon's face. Her eyes, I noticed, were even paler than his, appearing almost silver in the full light of day. They were mesmerizing—she was mesmerizing—and aside from her motherly aura and effervescent personality, which was slightly contagious, her eyes were definitely the first things one noticed about her. "'Tis been an age since ye last cropped up on my stoop, and with a wife forbye! Och! And such a pretty child! Well, come along, then, come in, my sweeting, and let auld Maura take a keek at what that randy devil has done tae ye!"

I was about to protest her gross assumption but had not the opportunity. Pressing my arm in the fold of her meaty one, Maura, or auld Maura, as she referred to herself, whisked me away toward her lair.

Thinking I should know more about her than what my imagination had conjured, I politely asked after her surname, yet she was hesitant to give one, cheerfully explaining that she had seen five husbands to the grave, all fine men, and out of respect to their memories refrained from calling herself anything but Maura—although, she did add that her last two husbands had been of the surname MacKay.

I cast a glance behind me and saw Mr. Campbell standing between the team of horses, watching me with his unfathomable azure gaze. Sensing my reluctance yet guessing wrongly at its cause, Maura kindly added that her five husbands had blessed her with fourteen children, ten surviving infancy (a fairly remarkable number), and that she had helped scores of others into this world. Nurturing life was her passion, she said, birthing was her calling; and I believed her. Feeling somewhat comforted by her sheer motherly presence, not to mention her stellar qualifications, I entered her abode.

It was like entering the realm of some twisted fable or nightmarish dream. Cleverly carved, brightly painted, oversized furniture abounded, filling the small space with a surreal air. Add to this the astounding variety of dried plants and weeds that hung in great bunches from the low beams of the ceiling, and the effect was dizzying. The air was especially pungent and tickled the nose with an amalgamation of spices that took one aback at first. While trying to adjust my eyes and nose to these new surroundings, I was brought to the fire, where, to my amazement, a hefty pig with a yellow kerchief tied around its neck, and a black and white collie, lay snuggled together. "Och, Millie, get up, ye lazy sow," said my hostess, yanking the creature up by the ear. There was a squeal of protest, followed by an ear-splitting snort, before the order was obeyed. "You too, Geordie, ye randy wee de'il. Get! Poor dear is in the same boat as ye, I'm afraid," she explained to me, patting my cloak at the height of my belly in a knowing way. How she was able to tell my condition was still a mystery. She commented on the sow's great appetite, how it had broken into the larder and did real damage to a barrel of apples, all while placing me in a chair by the fire. She ordered me to prop my feet on the cushion-covered stool; I felt compelled to obey. "What ye need is tae rest your weary bones a spell and tae have a nice hot cup o' tea!" This she declared while swinging a blackened kettle over the fire. Then, with the same exhaustive flow of energy, she excused herself to have a private word with the man responsible for my current predicament.

Mr. Campbell had reluctantly followed us into the cottage. He stood just inside the doorway, hat off, head slightly bent as he quietly addressed the midwife. They conducted their conversation in a soft murmur, barely audible but for a few words that slipped out, causing the light-keeper to glance my way every so often. What was said, I had no idea, yet it became very clear what Mr. Campbell failed to deny.

"Sara, dear," came his rich voice, pulling my wandering gaze to him. It was the second time he had used my Christian name. The use of it here shocked me, but only for a moment. He delivered a touchingly sincere smile. "I shall wait outside for you, aye?"

I nodded rather dumbly then watched as he passed the old woman some coins before slipping back outside.

A cup of tea found its way into my hands, tea that was certain to have a touch of something darker in it, something suspiciously like the local whisky so liberally in use. I sipped it politely as the old midwife sat watching me and felt almost at once a heavy warmth enter my empty stomach. I sighed audibly, reveling in the feel of it as it radiated throughout my limbs, and then, wanting yet more of it, I tossed the rest back in one hearty gulp. The result was that my head, and all my troubling thoughts, lightened pleasantly.

"There, now," she began in soothing tones, her very presence making me feel surprisingly comfortable. I marveled at her plump cheeks as she talked and how the papery soft skin seemed to glow with rosy good health. "What a pleasure it is to have a new face to gaze upon. Let us natter a wee bitty before I examine ye, my dear. Tell me, how do you find life on the Cape?"

"Aside from the isolation, I find it rather pleasant," I replied, and delivered a convincing smile.

"And Mr. Campbell, how does he treat ye, dear?"

I thought on this a moment, and then decided to plunge on ahead with the lie. "Why, Mr. Campbell is kindness itself. Very kindly indeed," I added with a soft smile. Yet the old woman was gifted in ways that went beyond my understanding and she gave out a soft chuckle as she patted my thigh.

"You're quite skilled at deception, almost as good as himself.

But I wouldna be very good at the art I practice if I dinna see it."
She tapped her forehead with an old, though capable, finger.

"How is it you know . . . ?" I was about to say "Mr. Campbell,"
but thought better of it and said, "William?"

"'Tis all right, dear, I know he is no' the father of your child,
nor are ye his bride. But 'tis a deception that ye should consider
for your own good here. And to answer your question, he came
to me shortly after his arrival on the Cape, and then again last
autumn."

"After Mr. Duffy, the other keeper, died?"

"Yes. But it was no' only the other keeper that was lost that
day. Three others, good men with families, were also part of the
loss, not tae mention the entire crew of the imperiled ship."

"But why come to you, a midwife?"

"Because I'm no' only a midwife, dear. Some seek me out for
my other abilities; I'm known tae be a healer and at times I have
the sight."

"You're a seer?" I blurted, staring at the kindly woman disbelievingly. "You can really see the future?"

"Sometimes it comes upon me, aye," she admitted frankly, and
then her eyes narrowed. "But I'm no' the only one who has it.
Many do. Your Mr. Campbell also has abilities, I do believe."

At this absurdity I chuckled. "Mr. Campbell sees the future?"

"No, no' the future, per se," she clarified while holding me in
her mesmerizing gaze. "But he does see, and what he sees, my
dear, has a chilling effect on him."

As these words were spoken, and their meaning inferred, the
hair on the back of my neck prickled, traveling all the way down
my spine. Reflexively, I glanced at the door where Mr. Campbell
had so recently been. The old planks had been painted a bright
red to hide the fact they were splintered and rotting; yet still, be-
twixt and between the bright boards a few shafts of daylight had
snuck through, illuminating the dusty air. My eyes held to these
rogue rays of light until a shadow crossed on the far side of the
door, obscuring them. I took a sharp and sudden inhalation of

breath. "What . . ." I uttered in a mere whisper, drawing my attention back to the midwife, "what exactly does he see?"

She cocked her head to better study me. "Ye dinna know?" she asked cautiously. She watched me a moment longer, holding me in her odd silvery gaze. And then, coming to some conclusion, she offered, "Willy Campbell, my dear, sees the past. And the past he sees is full of ghosts."

It was a frightening admission coming from her lips and I had to ask, "Do . . . do you believe that he really does?"

She took a moment to poke the fire while pondering her reply. Another brick of peat was added before she turned to me. "I believe Mr. Campbell believes he see them, yes."

"Then . . . is he mad?"

This question provoked another spell under the silvery eyes—eyes, I noted, that matched the wayward strands of hair that had escaped her cap. I could not look away as she said: "Mad. Brilliant. Lost. He is all those things, but he is especially diligent; and because he is, he did voice a particular concern for ye."

"For me?"

"Aye. He mentioned ye received a package the other day; its contents had a particularly jarring effect on ye. I believe he is concerned that the shock of it might have affected the bairn ye now carry."

I looked down at my hands, folded neatly in my lap, and recalled the horrific shock of seeing the watch, knowing its connection to the man I loved. My hands trembled slightly. It was then an old hand came over mine; the touch, the warmth, the confidence it relayed consoled me. "Come," she said, pulling me to my feet. "Ye shall lie on the cot while I have a wee keek at ye and determine for myself the health of your bairn. Ye do understand you'll have tae remove your clothes?" I nodded. "Ye dinna wear stays or thae corset, I presume?" To this, I shook my head. "Good. Ye look a might too sensible a lass for all that!"

While the examination took place, the midwife asked more

questions specific to my condition and to how I was feeling. She talked as she poked and prodded, her voice always calm and distracting. And when the experienced hands began a vigorous campaign on my stomach, inducing a small foot to retaliate from just under my rib cage, she said, "Och, splendid! Let me guess, five, nearly six months?" I nodded and smiled at the accuracy. She continued to press and palpate the swollen mound, all the while stirring the tiny life within me, when her hands suddenly stopped. She was still, unmoving. So too was the baby. Her eyes, I noted, seemed brighter, yet distant. This change in demeanor frightened me and I asked her more than a few times what was amiss. At length she looked at me and slowly, softly, she uttered, "There's nothing amiss, Sara." A forced smile appeared on her thin lips, a smile that did not entirely reach her eyes. "'Tis just that I thought I felt a wee something."

"Felt something? The baby? Is something wrong with my baby?" I gasped, struggling to sit up.

"Nothing is wrong with the child, my dear," she was quick to console. "It appears quite healthy."

"Then . . . what was it? What did ye feel?"

There was sadness in her bright, pale eyes as she spoke. "I felt . . ." she began, and then halted. When at last she had the will to look at me, I could see on her face an overwhelming empathy, and perhaps the welling of tears. "I felt," she began again, and smiled kindly, "a great and abounding love." And that was all she said. The examination was over.

I was left to arrange my gown along with my colliding thoughts before joining her at the little cupboard. She was working industriously, her stout hands grinding dried herbs for a mixture I was to take with me. She turned and handed the little cloth sack over. "Give this to Mr. Campbell, he'll know how to mix it for ye. Ye are tae take it twice a day, six weeks before delivery. Starting immediately I recommend ye take a glass of wine in the morning—warmed claret, if ye can, port if ye canna procure it—and a glass or two before bed. Also, I must insist ye indulge in rest. A brisk walk in the morning is fine, but nothing strenuous, aye? I've already had a wee word with himself on the matter. I know what a taskmaster he can be. Also," she said, looking purposely into my eyes, "he must pay particular regard to gratifying your every desire."

"My every desire?" I repeated, and giggled at the thought. For Mr. Campbell, unbeknownst to the midwife, would go out of his way to begrudge me even the meanest request. "I'm sorry," I said, clearing my throat when she failed to see the humor of this statement. "It's just that perhaps I'm a bit unclear by what you mean by *my every desire?*"

"What I mean, dear, is that pregnant women—young, healthy women, in general—have particular desires that should be gratified by their menfolk. 'Tis in your own best interest to do so."

I was taken aback. The way she looked at me, her knowing smile and the long list of husbands attached to her name, confirmed for me her implication. "Are you suggesting . . . ?"

"I am," she confirmed with a nod of her head. "Intercourse, sexual intercourse, I highly recommend for a young woman; 'tis good for the health and complexion. The vigorous exercise will also improve your chances of having a successful delivery."

My hand flew over my mouth. I was aghast; the mere thought was scandalous . . . repulsive. "But . . . I'm not married to that man! He's not my husband! He's . . . he's . . ."

"Weel, that dinna stop ye before!" she interrupted with a pragmatic, poignant stare. "Or perhaps ye were married?" she mused with a tilt of her sage head. "Tell me, do ye ken anything about Scottish law? If it will ease your mind, all a man and woman need do tae be legally bound is tae have mutual consent on the matter. Witnesses, however, are a might helpful too."

Truthfully, I wasn't listening to her ramble. I was having a hard enough time swallowing her latest tidbit of advice. "Did he . . . did *he* put you up to this?" I demanded, growing beyond indignant.

"Nay, he did not. 'Tis just that such a physical release—as ye both could use—might help ease some of the mental torment and pain you each suffer in kind. Why, I wouldna be worth my weight in salt if I dinna see that!"

"Well, and I hate to be the one to contradict you, but you are very, very wrong in your assumption! And I do not suffer!" I declared with a passionate huff. Then, grasping the little sack of herbs in my hand, I turned to go. I hesitated, then looked back at the midwife. "And as for a successful delivery, I believe I'm prepared to take my chances!"

I was still in a rather viperous mood as I left the cottage, searching for the light-keeper while attempting to clear my mind of all repugnant thoughts. The midwife had been doing remarkably well up until the last moments of our interview, when she spilled her audacious seed—trying to convince me that a romantic interlude with the man that tormented me would be beneficial to all parties involved. I didn't see it! I would never see it! Yet ironically I was in search of the very creature that caused me such discord. The yard, but for the animals, was empty. After taking a few deep breaths, filling my lungs with the cool air, I headed over to the wagon and thought to wait there until he returned.

Yet it was there I found him, sleeping peacefully in the bed of the wagon. He was lying flat on his back in the loose hay, his dark coat wrapped snugly about him, an arm thrown over his eyes, exposing only the end of his aquiline nose and the firm set of his clean-shaven jaw. The collie called Geordie slept curled beside him. It was such an incongruous sight. His breathing was deep and relaxed. And although just moments ago I wanted nothing more than to berate him, I found, staring on his recumbent form, that I was loath to wake him; for he looked more at peace than I had ever seen him. Beneath the dappled shade of the rowan branches he looked very young and vulnerable, not at all the brooding recluse that battled his demons alone at night in the light-tower. It occurred to me then that I had no idea who this man even was. With this thought clouding my head—even getting the best of my better judgment—I cast a glance back at the bothy and was in time to see a lacy curtain drop back into place. The old woman had been watching me.

It was the dog that stirred first, sensing my presence. The head came up, the brown eyes focused and the great fluffy tail began thumping the hay-covered boards. It was then the name William came to my lips, and I whispered to the man beside the dog. I whispered his name: "William."

The arm did not move, nor did the body, but the lips, finely shaped and rather full, pulled into what one might almost call a beatific smile. Mr. Campbell was still asleep beneath the warmth of the late winter sun. I was mesmerized by this smile, a smile only the name William seemed to elicit. I had never seen such a thing before. There was no spite or malice in it, only a purity of happiness. And it was the first time I ever considered that this man, at one time in his life, might have actually been happy. The thought touched me. Again, to keep the emotion affixed to this stranger's face, I leaned over and whispered, "William."

The dog, feeling that this was an invitation to play, stood, and prancing over to me whacked his tail repeatedly against the face of the sleeping man. The arm came away. The eyes focused and the body sprang up with alarming speed.

"How . . . how long have you been there?" he questioned gruffly, glaring at me with his pale, piercing eyes.

The change was disappointing. I frowned in response and lied. "I've only just come."

He looked at the sky, noted the sun, and then pushed the dog out of the wagon. "Och! I must have drifted off," he said by way of an apology, rubbing his hands over his face in an attempt to wake up. He turned to me again, his eyes less accusing. "Are ye done, then? Is everything all right with you?" I could see his question was genuine.

"For now I believe everything is fine, sir; and I believe I owe you an apology. Your midwife, with the exception of one or two wild notions, was quite knowledgeable. Thank you. Now," I said, climbing onto the bench, "if you don't mind, I'm ready for that meal you promised me."

. . .

As spring approached, things picked up on the Cape. Strong winds and the hint of war kept us on our toes at the lighthouse, and the sudden willingness of young Hughie MacKay to read lent a sense of importance to my role as nominal keeper-of-the-light.

Since our visit to Durness, Mr. Campbell had been very cautious of what he would allow me to do. I believed the midwife had conveyed to him her insistence that I indulge in rest. Minimal housework was allowed, cooking as well, and so too was my tutoring. But I was not allowed to ride the horses, nor was I permitted to climb the lighthouse stairs or journey to Kervaig Bay to watch the men with their boat practice. This last precaution was added in order to avoid any wild inclination I might have gotten to ride in one of the lighthouse boats. He had also insisted that Mary and her son come to the cottage for tutoring. I countered this by stating that a brisk walk would suit me fine, and so I should be allowed to go to the MacKay croft once a week. He argued against this, hinting at my proclivity for foolish behavior. I took offense and lashed out with a defense of my own, and so a bargain was finally struck somewhere in the middle. Although Mr. Campbell never said as much, and although he was still rather distantly polite where I was concerned, there was a part of me that did wonder what other suggestions the sly midwife might have made to him; for there was something in his manner that hadn't been there before. I couldn't put a name to it. It was just a feeling. But I did notice, as well as did Kate, that Mr. Campbell took particular care to avoid me whenever possible.

This, Kate surmised as we walked to the MacKay croft, was because Mr. Campbell had been instructed not to upset me. "It's not good for the baby to have you upset, and everyone knows how you and Mr. Campbell upset each other. It's very unseemly, and in your case, unwise," she offered sagely.

"You upset me too," I told her plainly. "Perhaps you should learn from his example." This caused an amusing glower along with a huff of indignation.

"Only because you draw it out of people, Sara," she riposted. "Your own mother saw it, your father learned of it too. Why, only a saint could put up with you."

"I knew a saint once," I said, smiling pointedly at her, "and he liked me just fine."

"*He* was no saint, Sara, but a horny wee devil! And you the devil's maiden, carrying his devil seed!"

My eyes widened at this venom, and I stopped walking. "Come, now, Kate, that's harsh, even coming from you." And then I took a good look at her, the high color touching her cheeks, the flashing, accusatory look in her eyes and the pursed lips. "Dear heavens, you're not jealous that I'm with child, are you?" It was the first time the thought struck me; unfortunately I had given voice to the impulsive notion. Kate, ignoring me, kept on walking. "Is it true?"

"Never. Everyone knows children come of their own accord, in their own time."

"And you've been married over a year now," I uttered, looking at her again. "You are doing it correctly?" I asked, hoping to be helpful, and then instantly regretting my impulsivity.

"I'm a married woman!" she cried, indignantly. And then, turning on me with her characteristic show of spite, "Which is more than I can say for you! God have mercy on ye, Sara Stevenson."

"Do you not think I'm paying for my sins?" I asked, beginning to lose my hard-won self-control. "Look at me! I didn't ask for this," I said, and placed a hand on my swollen belly. "I will never tell you what you want to hear, Kate. I will never tell you that loving Thomas Crichton was a mistake because it wasn't. Can't you take enough satisfaction in the fact that you were right?

That he perhaps was using me?" I implored her with my eyes, trying again to make her understand what I was about to tell her. "I gave him my soul, and gladly, and if this child is all I have to show for it, then so be it. But I still believe, in my heart of hearts, that Thomas will come for me someday."

I could see the pity thick in her eyes, and the look was so distasteful. I could not abide such a look coming from her. It was cruel of me, to give voice to what I did, but I was driven by six months of pain and hurt. "Have you ever considered that God is punishing you and not me? I am the one, after all, carrying a child."

Her response was pure hatred, and a hatred that deep could only come from some vast insecurity . . . or perhaps even repressed guilt. With eyes that let me know just what she thought of me, amoral reprobate that I was, she still felt inclined to lash out. "Your behavior with that sailor was no better than an animal in heat . . . a weak-willed, wanton animal in heat! Mr. MacKinnon and I observe the proprieties of the marriage bed!"

This *was* surprising, and I'm sure she saw what I thought of her admission written on my face. "Never on Sundays, nor Lent, and the twelve holy days following Christmas?" I supplied. "Nor on fast days, feast days, the week before and after each solstice and equinox, and those special days reserved each month solely for the female curse?"

There was silence.

"You should try being a weak-willed wanton, Kate."

"I am no animal!" she averred, her brown eyes flashing, her countenance oozing self-righteousness.

"Maybe not, but I'll wager Mr. MacKinnon is. Poor, poor Mr. MacKinnon."

·  ·  ·

It was no secret that my skills with mop and broom, try as I might, were less than legendary, nor was the food prepared at our hearth worthy of the trip out to the precarious point, but I did relish my role as teacher, and my two pupils, though just beginning to discover the magic of the written word, positively glowed when they deciphered their first three letters strung together. It made me smile.

Hughie was still mischievous as ever, but a surprising, and rather touching, proprietary behavior toward myself tempered his wilder notions. He made certain there was no need for me to get up from the table unnecessarily when we worked on his lessons. He checked my tea every few minutes to see that it was still warm and had the addition of milk and honey in the proper measure. He even, much to his mother's amazement, offered to sweep the cottage for me whenever he came out for a visit. Yet it was after his third visit to the lighthouse that I began to wonder if the boy had other reasons for coming to see me.

This third appearance of Hughie's was unbeknownst to any of us until Mr. Campbell discovered the little creature, shortly after breakfast, up in the observation room of the lighthouse. Hughie had come alone, and was caught looking through Mr. Campbell's prized telescope. I had no doubt harsh words transpired, and it was a quiet, rather sullen Hughie that sat before me, diligently copying the letters on the alphabet cards I had made for him into a thin film of flour put out specifically for that purpose. I watched him form the letters, *CAT, RAT, BAT, SAT,* and for my own amusement, *Miss Sara smells better than Miss Kate.* I smiled at his progress, corrected a few mistakes and instructed him on how to better form the letters. Yet I could tell Hughie's heart wasn't in it. Something was bothering the boy. He was normally mischievous in my presence and his blue eyes never failed to sparkle whenever he addressed me. But his look, ever since his discovery, had been guarded, his boyish thoughts distant. Finally, he looked up and very softly said, "I suppose you'll be marrying the man now. 'Tis only right an' proper that ye do."

"Excuse me?" I replied, and stilled his hand, forcing him to look at me. "And exactly which man would you be referring to?"

His eyes flashed. "Mr. Campbell, of course." It was said with a derisiveness that was meant to wound.

"Well, and it would only be right and proper if your infantile assumptions were correct; which, as usual, they are not! I suggest you withhold judgment and stop making wild assumptions about me until you can read. And you'll need to read very well if you're planning to decipher the tale that I'm going to write. I'll not use many three-letter words, I assure you."

"Have ye given a thought tae drawin' any pictures, then?" he sneered. "Ye ken, making sketches and such? I find pictures more telling by far. Besides, they're a might less befuddlin' than anything ye might write."

"Befuddling? I shall make it especially so," I promised with a wink and indicated with a finger for him to continue writing. He cast me a sideways glance then did as he was told.

While Hughie worked I got up and poured another cup of tea. I looked out the window and saw Kate filling the washtub, making ready for the linen. Then, without so much as suffering a pang of guilt, I turned back to Hughie and watched as he traced a few letters into the shallow pan of flour. I sat back down at the table.

"I'm curious, Hughie, why Mr. Campbell? Why do you think I should marry him?"

He didn't look up; he didn't need to. I could see the bright flush of red in the alabaster skin of his neck, reaching all the way to the tips of his round little ears. Something had made the precocious child blush. He swallowed in the silence and continued ignoring me, feigning to concentrate extra hard on his letters.

"Hughie, I asked you a question. Why him?"

He wouldn't look at me. It was most unusual for the boy to back down at a chance to skewer me, and quite frankly, I found it unnerving. "May I remind you that you were the one who brought up this subject in the first place?" I pulled the tray of flour away, watching his fingers trail in a serpentine pattern through the hard-won letters. He turned to me, his face as red as his effulgent hair.

And then, very hesitantly, he said, "Because I saw a sketch of ye . . . in one of that man's books. And ye, Miss Sara, were mother-naked!"

. . .

Hughie's lesson came to an abrupt end, but not before I cajoled some information out of him first. The poor lad had been traumatized by what he had seen in the tower, perhaps even more so than I was after learning of it. I did my best to set him at his ease, smoothing the matter over as best I could before I saw him to his horse (the beast had been stabled in the barn with the others) and sent him on his way, suggesting that next time he should come out with the accompaniment of a parent.

I was in turmoil. My insides were racing. And to calm myself until I could get at the insidious book in the tower—the one the poor boy had seen, with images a child of that tender, impressionable age should never have glimpsed—I rolled up my sleeves and helped Kate with the washing. I plucked out of the pile a shirt of Mr. Campbell's and wrung it so fiercely—imagining it the man's neck—until not a drop of water was left and I felt I might pass out from the effort. Kate, oblivious to the world around her for a change, commented, "Well done, Sara. I see you are finally getting the way of it."

I waited until the men had finished their work in the lighthouse and had retired for the afternoon to their own quarters, Kate disappearing as well, and then I ventured up to the lightroom in search of the book bound in red leather. The stairs were much harder going with the additional weight I carried, but I would not be stopped. I would find the book, rip out the offensive page Hughie had seen and burn it. And then I would confront the monster. Yet when I reached the landing and ventured inside the observation room, I found it immaculate. Everything had been cleaned, the lens polished, the windows translucent as fine crystal and the table cleared of everything but for the spirit stove and pot. I searched the room, going over the whole structure for any sign of the book. And then I realized that of course he would have removed it. He would never leave it up here again. Not after this morning. The man might be dark and twisted, but he was also clever; brilliant, the old midwife had said. No. The book was no longer in the lighthouse. The book would be in his room.

Again I waited, busying myself with the preparations for the evening meal. Yet after about an hour of working in the quiet cottage, the stew ready to go over the fire, I decided to retire to my own room and wait until I knew for certain Mr. Campbell's room was vacant. I headed down the back hallway but stopped suddenly when I saw that the door to the light-keeper's room was ajar, but only just. What were the odds of him being in there?—of this being another one of his clever ploys? But then, my anger getting the best of me, I realized it didn't matter. An opportunity had showed itself, and I was going to take it.

Standing before the door, I coaxed it open . . . just enough for me to have a look inside. The blasted thing creaked, and I held my breath, waiting for Mr. Campbell to spring out at me. Thankfully, he never came. Growing bolder, I pushed it again, this time creating enough of a gap for me to peer in. The room was messy, just as I remembered, and I scanned the unmade bed until I was satisfied it was empty. Mr. Campbell was not inside. He must have gotten up and slipped out unnoticed. But that thought I would not ponder. His room was beckoning to me; a cluttered den of secrets awaited, and a book bound in red leather was soon to meet its end.

Not wishing to be too obtrusive, I confined my search to his desk and bookshelves. The desk, I saw, had been recently cleaned and therefore gave over nothing but for some black ink smudges, indicating that the man had written something not long ago. But it was a book I was interested in, a specific book, and so I turned my attention to the bookshelves and began scanning the spines, feeling slightly unnerved by all the ghastly creatures in their aqueous prisons glaring down on me.

At length I found what I was looking for, that oversized, nameless volume bound in vermilion. Truthfully, amongst the respectable titles and some rather scandalous novels indeed, it stood out like an ambitious courtesan in a Quaker church on a Sunday. I pulled it out and brought it to the desk, my sole purpose to descry the page wee Hughie had seen. I closed my eyes, preparing for the distasteful display, and opened the book.

It was the same horrific images that confronted me. I should not have been surprised by the sketches of naked women, but I was, and found myself even more horrified by the thought that this form of entertainment was a predilection of Mr. Campbell's. With eyes shielded by my left hand against the lurid display (leaving only enough space between my fingers to identify the picture I was in search of), I turned the pages. I gasped. I cringed. I even exclaimed aloud, "Heaven save and preserve me . . ." while the taste of bile burned the back of my throat. I scanned them as quickly as I could, flipping through page after page of women who unknowingly had laid themselves bare for this perverse voyeur. And then, near the end where some unfilled sheets awaited the master's pen, I saw her . . . or me.

My hand came away from my eyes as a knot seized my stomach, nearly taking the breath from me. The page in question contained a plain charcoal sketch, like all the others, but the face was familiar; the body, although quite flattering, was pure fantasy. Begrudgingly, I had to admit that it was a well-drawn image, more tastefully done than all the others. The woman, a remarkable likeness of me, was indeed naked, though it was her backside—high, full and round—that was featured. It was a pose of me looking over my shoulder, an inviting smile on my lips, one that the artist had captured with remarkable accuracy. It was a taunting smile, one designed to tease a man, and I suddenly wondered if this was what he really thought I was doing to him, preposterous though it was. A thick tumble of hair cascaded down my charcoal image's back, ending just below a narrow waist—one decidedly not pregnant. My, Mr. Campbell's imagination was good! And my arm, depicted gracefully by my side, made a feeble, yet largely unsuccessful attempt to hide a pair of very full breasts, plump and ripe as summer peaches, complete with pert erect nipples. With a growl of indignation, and eyes watering with burning anger, I steadied my trembling hands and gripped the edge of the page. With one mighty tug I attempted to rip it from the filthy book, only the paper was thicker than I had bargained for.

The whole thing came away, tumbling off the desk, and me with it, nearly taking out the chair as I went down. It was not quite the stealthy operation I had planned on, but I was determined in my effort to rid the book of my image and I grabbed the offending page once again.

The sound of the door shutting stopped me.

I spun around, our eyes met and caught, and then, before he could reach me, I yanked the page with redoubled force. Again I failed. He fell on me then, and we battled like two squabbling children in a schoolyard brawl, although, admittedly, I was the one doing all the kicking and fighting as he successfully pried the book out of my hands.

"Are ye aware that you're destroying private property—and in my private room, no less?"

"How dare you!" I seethed through gritted teeth, demanding he release me.

The order was finally obeyed, accompanied by an astounding: "No, how dare you, Miss Stevenson! You are in my room, nosing around! I'd be in my rights if I turned ye over my knee this instant and beat ye for it—pregnant or not!"

"You wouldn't dare!" I cried.

"Oh wouldn't I?" he seethed, his aquamarine eyes burning with anger and a challenge. The way he said it frightened me.

"And what about this . . . this vile book of yours?"

His dark brows pulled taut, accenting the remarkable color of his eyes beneath, as he replied, "What about it?"

"It's positively vile . . . filled with all manner of filthy images!"

For some reason this seemed to amuse him. "Vile, filthy images? And here I was thinking ye already knew about this book." As he spoke he lifted the object in question. "This is, in fact, the very book you were perusing so thoroughly the day I found you in the light-room—uninvited. Perhaps you are the one intrigued by it? After all, this is the second time I've caught ye looking through the pages when ye thought no one was about."

My hand came over my mouth, it was so scandalous. "How . . . dare . . . you!"

"How dare I? You, lass, should be the one asking yourself that very same question." And he smiled darkly, assessing me with his crystal gaze. The light-keeper was enjoying my discomfort.

I steeled myself. "You have no right to have such a book, sir! It is unseemly, unprofessional and downright amoral!"

He cocked his head and studied me further, his lips pulling into a taunting, sardonic grin. "Amoral? Unprofessional? Forgive me, but I find it fascinating how your mind works."

"My mind! You're the disgusting, vile, perverted recluse!"

"Is that what ye think?" he breathed, and the smile, although not gone, paled measurably. "You do know that I'm a grown man, dear lass? And surely you are not so ignorant . . ." he said, looking at my swollen midriff, "of the needs and desires of grown men. That being said, I think there is a misunderstanding here."

"I assure you, there is no misunderstanding!"

"You are aware, then, that this book is not, apparently, what you think it is?"

"I'm well aware of who and what you are, sir! And what . . . what do ye mean by *not what it appears*? I have eyes, you know, and those pictures are salacious. I'm not stupid!" I glared at him, still seething with anger.

"I never said that ye were. Meddlesome, however, intrusive

and astonishingly ignorant given your past behavior, have sprung to mind. And just so we are on the same page, this is no ordinary book, Miss Stevenson, nor was it devised to arouse a man sexually, although I think it interesting you jumped to that conclusion." This he punctuated with a very insulting look. "This book here, for your information, with perhaps the exception of only one picture, is a book of anatomy."

"A book of anatomy?" I looked at the nondescript vermilion cover in his hands, suddenly ashamed that the thought had never occurred to me.

"Aye, anatomy; the science and study of the human body." And then, noting my great, confounding embarrassment, he offered a soft, placating smile. "Forgive me, but I thought you knew."

My face, I'm sure, was as red as a poppy. "But . . . why should *you* have such a thing . . . a lighthouse keeper?"

There was a moment of hesitation. "I wasn't always a lighthouse keeper," he said, his voice plaintive. And then his smile faded, and a distant wistfulness touched his stoic features.

With a need to redeem myself a measure, I offered, "I know. You were a sailor."

His eyes found mine again. "I was never a sailor," he stated matter-of-factly.

This reply confused me. "But . . . but Mr. MacKay said . . . I heard him say that you lost half your crew on that ship?"

"Aye, he was correct. But still, I was never a sailor."

"Really?" I looked closely at him, confused all the more by this admission. Oddly enough he was studying me with a look of equal incredulity.

"You really don't know? Your father never told ye?" He squinted, and it appeared as if his pale orbs were peering into my soul. "You really have no idea why you are here?"

"I'm here . . ." I stated a little defensively, feeling very like a fool under this man's scrutiny. "I'm here," I started again and lowered my voice to something akin to contrition, "to be punished for my sins, which, sir, I must tell you, I am not ashamed of."

"Aye," he breathed, amusement touching the corners of his mouth. And then he came closer with the questionable book in his hands. He stood mere inches away as he whispered, "And so, I find, I too am here for sins of my own. For I, Sara Stevenson, am a physician . . . was a physician," he corrected. "But I find I'm nothing of the kind any longer; I'm barely even a man, for all that."

His proximity, the feel of his warm breath on my skin, made me nervous. I pushed him away and countered, "I beg to differ with you there. On the contrary, sir, given that you study pictures like these," I indicated the book in question, "I'd have to say you're very much a man. Did you draw them . . . the women? And are they really dead?"

"Aye, and aye," he answered haltingly.

"Did you kill them?"

Here he hesitated. My gaze was intense upon him and he had the decency to look away. "No."

"But you have killed?"

This question was met with silence, yet his look was telling enough.

The silence grew to an uncomfortable level as we studied each other like the strangers we were. The thought that this dark and brooding man standing before me had once been a physician was shocking enough, but that he had actually embarked on a career to help humanity and now shunned all contact with the very souls he had vowed to save was beyond remarkable. Either he awoke to the truth of his debased nature or something catastrophic had occurred to change him entirely. I tried to remember if I had ever heard anything on the matter at home—but then, I recalled, my parents seldom spoke of such things to us children. I forced myself to look deeply into his eyes again and suddenly remembered the curse.

Mr. Campbell believed he was cursed.

And because of the picture I had found—the drawing of me—
I was in no mood to tell him otherwise, and so I prodded. "Perhaps you would be so good as to tell me why it is, if you are no
longer a man of medicine, that you insist on looking through
that vile book?"

He scowled. "Vile? This book is not vile, Miss Stevenson. I
pulled it out in an attempt to . . ." he began to explain, then
halted. "What I mean is that I needed to . . ." I realized that this
pointed question troubled him, and I had to admit, I liked seeing
him so harried and flustered. I crossed my arms, tilted my head
and waited. He frowned and blurted, "Well, damn it! Because it's
been a muckle long time since I've . . . I was only attempting to
familiarize myself with the female body again."

I raised my eyebrows at this—a very bold admission. "And
what, pray tell, makes you think that's necessary?"

"I was hoping to be prepared when the time comes, as it will
inevitably come!" His dander was up; his dark, lustrous hair billowed about his head like a woolly storm cloud.

"Oh really?" I huffed, growing irate again. "Well, that's awfully presumptuous of you. Besides, why study? I thought such
things came as second nature to a man. Oh, but you said it yourself, you're barely a man any longer. Tell me, did sketching that
picture of me help you in any way?" It was delivered as it was
meant: all spit and vinegar.

"That picture is none of your business! And don't fool yourself, lass, 'tis nothing I want any part of. I was merely instructed
that I would be the one doing it." And noting my further outrage he grinned rather maniacally.

"You say you were *instructed* that you'd be the one to do it? By
whom, sir, were you instructed!?" I demanded in a voice far too
loud. Yet before he could answer I cut him off. "No. Don't tell
me. That midwife of yours put you up to this, didn't she?"

"Midwife?" he blurted, looking just as crazed as I felt. "No,

Maura never said aught to me on the matter. It was I who told her I'd be the one."

"Now, that *is* presumptuous!" I cried in outrage. "And here I thought it was all her idea; after all, she did go to great pains to fill my head with the unsavory notion . . . said it would be good for us both. Ha!" I nearly spat the word. "Let me tell you something, Mr. Campbell, regardless of what you think of me, I let no man touch me without my consent, and you, sir, I'm sorry to inform, are way down on my list!"

He stepped closer, grabbed both my arms and looked smugly amused by it all. "And I hate to inform you, dear lass, but I believe you have little choice in the matter, bottom of your list or not! I'm the one!"

"Over my dead body!" I declared, and shoved him away. He stumbled backward and hit the bookshelf, causing his disgusting collection of creatures to shudder. One jar toppled over. He caught it in time. I continued, "Or is that the way you prefer your women? Dead, so they won't have the will to fight you? Well, you can bet I'll be fighting you! And if you try to force me to it, that, sir, I believe is termed rape! I'll see you hanged!"

"Rape?" he bellowed, stopping my rant. His expression, eyes wild with confusion and pain, told me he was anything but pleased. "Jesus God!" he uttered in a burst of air. "You have it all wrong! We are not talking about the same thing here, I'm afraid."

"Are we not?" It was my turn to look alarmed. "If we are not talking about *that*, then what *are* we talking about?"

"Sweet Jesus!" he blasphemed again, this time looking truly vexed. And then he raked his fingers through his dark curls in that habitual manner of his. Looking back up, he uttered disbelievingly, "He never told you, did he? Your father never explained to you why you're here. Jesus God, the bastard! Well, then I'll be the one to do it," he said, looking pointedly at me. "You're here, Miss Stevenson, because I'm the one that's to deliver your child."

"You?" I uttered, covering my mouth with my hand to stifle the horrifically unpleasant sound forming in my throat.

"Yes, me," he affirmed, looking equally affronted. "And I'm afraid I feel much the same as you on the matter. Because 'tis a veritable death sentence . . . for all parties involved."

.   .   .

This new revelation was astounding and it shook me to the core of my being. The matter of the drawing that had driven me to his room in the first place and the notorious "book" fell from my thoughts. Mr. Campbell could sketch my naked image a hundred times over and still the affront would pale in comparison to the knowledge I had just learned. I had been sent here for the sole purpose of being under his care. That my father had knowingly put the life of his daughter and unborn grandchild in the hands of a pariah who not only was responsible for the death of half the crew of a ship he served on, and was party to the death of the previous light-keeper and three locals, but was unconscionable and cruel beyond measure. Was my behavior so appalling that my parents believed I actually deserved this? Did they revile me that much? Would they even care that my image was being manipulated and exploited for the perverse fantasies of the very man made to deliver my child? The punishment seemed cruelly disproportionate to the crime. I had only fallen in love with a man who I believed wholeheartedly loved me in return. Thomas Crichton, for the span of those few shining months, had been everything to me. And that I should suffer this . . . this death sentence, merely for the sin of disgracing my family, was a thought so ineffable I could barely conceive of it.

I would die here.

My baby would die here.

And I would never have the chance to tell Thomas that had he loved me, I would gladly suffer the same a thousand times over.

Later, alone in my room, I clung to the watch, feeling its beating heart against mine. I read and reread Mr. Seawell's letter, praying a truly fervent prayer that he would be able to shed more light on the mysterious return of my watch.

. . .

And so it was that I found myself again standing on that windswept precipice in the shadow of the lighthouse in the moment of dawn—that elusive, transitory moment dividing the night from the day. The last day of March was upon us; again there was a prevailing fog and I stood facing the sea, as I always did, praying for the life of my child, praying that Mr. Campbell, however cursed, would find the means to deliver us both safely. When at last I opened my eyes I saw it again, that odd little skiff, shooting out of the bay that guarded the lighthouse jetty. There was not enough light to see much, just the shape of the thing— the cut of her sails that seemed to shimmer slightly against the murky gray of the morning. And then, just as before, the fog swallowed the boat. I looked up at the windows in the observation room, just under the great lantern, and saw that Mr. Campbell had seen it too. He was out on the balcony looking intently in the direction where the little skiff had disappeared. His eye was to the eyepiece on the telescope, but apparently he was too late. Mr. Campbell then turned to me.

Of course he knew I was standing there. He had often seen me in the same spot, and since the incident in his room he had been evermore understanding of me. He knew that I came out to the precipice when I had difficulty sleeping, just as I knew he rarely slept at all.

Our eyes met.

The mere language of his body told me what I already knew: he had seen what I had seen. A moment of absolute stillness followed. Neither one of us had the will to move; yet both of us sensed the possible meaning. I was too far away to see the expression on his face, but I could tell what he was thinking. However, I was the first to move, large and cumbersome as I was, and before he could stop me I bolted off in the direction of the jetty.

I was still within the lighthouse bounds when he found me. Mr. Campbell moved surprisingly fast and caught up with me just as I reached the stables. His voice was mild as he offered, "It appears we've had company."

"Yes," I agreed, and kept walking briskly. "Did you recognize her?"

"No" was his reply. And then a hand on my arm stopped me. "It is a long way down that road. I'll saddle Wallace and ride there myself. Won't take but a moment."

"I want to go too," I insisted.

"Aye, I realize that, but ye are not supposed to be astride a horse, or have you forgotten?"

"Did I say I wanted to ride? I was planning to walk. The exercise is good for me; I find it relaxing."

He looked at me, undoubtedly to see how determined I was. Mr. Campbell might have been socially inept on most accounts, but he had learned enough of me to know that I was a very determined young lady. "It relaxes you, does it? All right," he relented. "But I'm going with you."

It was odd indeed for the light-keeper to leave his post during his watch. But I could tell he considered this trip to be very much a part of his business. The reason became clear. "Did you happen to notice anything chancy about that wee boat?" he inquired as we paced along in the light of the growing sun.

"Not really. I had a hard time making out much of anything at all."

"And are you at all familiar with the art of sailing, or does your knowledge of the sea only extend to sailors?" I turned on him, only to find him grinning.

"Is that your idea of a joke? You're lucky I'm in a benevolent mood this morning. To answer your question, yes I do know a little something about sailing, and for your information it was only *one* sailor I took a particular interest in, not sailors in general, so don't get your hopes up. Another aside for your private ear, I don't particularly fancy men in the medical profession either."

This made him chuckle. "The reason I ask is not to pry, but to see if you understand the improbability of what we just saw."

"We saw a little sailboat at dawn, heading out of the jetty and right into the fogbank . . . didn't we?"

"Aye, we did indeed. And that is what's even more intriguing, because, Sara dear," he intoned familiarly, a deep penetrating look on his face as he did so, "that cannot be. The wind's not right for such a thing."

I stopped and turned to look at him. "William Campbell, what are you saying?" I asked, using his first name just as he had used mine. Yet whereas I merely accepted that he should use my Christian name, given that he would, one day soon, be delivering my child, my use of his name made him wince and nearly come to a halt. "I'm sorry. That was impertinent of me. I should not have said that."

He recovered quickly and kept his pace. "Forgive me, but most just call me Willy."

"You do not like the name William?"

"I like it fine, Miss Stevenson . . ." He trailed off.

"Sara," I corrected. "Since you have been, unbeknownst to me, appointed my personal physician, I believe you may call me Sara."

"As I was saying, *Sara* . . ." My name elicited a charming grin from him this time. "I'm just not used to hearing *that* name. Now, back to the wee skiff. What I'm getting at is that either that craft was built to defy the wind—sailing right dead into the eye of it—or that wee boat is not of this . . ."

"Go on," I urged, noting how his eyes glowed with an eerie penetration. "What is it, William?"

He thought better of what he was going to say, shook the thought from his head and smiled. "Well, and maybe I'm wrong too. Lately it seems I've been wrong about a great many things."

"That, dear sir, is a common affliction of the male sex, I'm afraid." And I smiled triumphantly as he walked beside me in silence.

William Campbell was not wrong about one thing; someone had indeed paid a visit to us, and that "someone" had left another letter from the antiquarian—the Oxford man. Holding it in my hand I felt my skin prickle with anticipation, and I carried it back to the cottage as calmly as I could. Mr. Campbell was also intrigued, but the letter did not seem to hold quite the amount of interest for him as did the little skiff. Perhaps, I offered, the craft was the personal tender of the antiquarian himself? This seemed the most logical explanation, and no more was said on the matter.

Kate was there to greet us at the door and was clearly puzzled that we had both disappeared together. Robbie was up and about too when Mr. Campbell explained what had happened. It was then Kate noticed the letter in my hand. "Is that another letter from the Oxford man?" Mr. Campbell answered for me, and as he did I saw a look pass between the MacKinnons, the meaning of which I could not venture a guess. I looked at the table and saw that breakfast had been laid out. There was the typical watery porridge, a plate of runny eggs and blackened toast that could just pass for edible. I plucked a slice of the burnt bread and made a polite excuse before heading to my room.

After pulling the rocking chair near the fire I studied the letter, pausing to marvel at the handwriting a moment while attempting to conjure a vision of the mysterious man to whom the writing belonged. On impulse I sniffed the paper, dismayed to find it smelled only like paper with lingering traces of the sea. When I actually mustered the courage to break the seal I found that my heart was beating a little faster at the sight of his words, neatly formed, yet boldly staring at me in black ink. And I'm sorry to admit that I delved into it with the hunger of one who had been starved of humanity for a very long while.

*My dear Miss Stevenson,*

    *I am truly sorry for the raw nerve my last letter seemed to have
struck, and for the perplexity I seemed to have caused you. For I'll
have you know that was never my intent. The circumstances
surrounding the beautiful timepiece are certainly a great mystery,
and one, I am sorry to say, I am unable to expound upon. Yet there
is one matter I would like to address, and it has to do with a
certain disdain you seem to harbor for the name Crichton. It
appears that a man named Thomas seems to have wronged you,
and for that I am truly sorry. Yet I feel it is my place to explain
and defend the character of the extraordinary young man James
Crichton, who sacrificed his own promising young life so that one
unworthy, undeserving, wretched soul such as myself should live . . .*

And there began the most extraordinary tale I have ever
read. Mr. Seawell explained how he, a man of learning, had
thought to submit his body and soul to the rigors of war. Driven
by the loss of his beloved wife and child, both taken from him
during a complicated childbirth, and succumbing to a level of
grief and suffering that no man should ever be made to suffer, he
attempted to end his earthly existence. But even at this he had
failed, proclaiming that after every sorry attempt visions of the
Church loomed large in his consciousness, and the thought of
spending all eternity in hell was too much—even for a wretch
like him—to contemplate. Finding himself without hope, having
nothing on this earth to anchor him any longer, he began his
slow descent to the seventh circle of hell. Half-drunk, half-mad,
he lost his chair as a professor of history at the university. That
was when he decided to join the fighting on the continent. For
although he was too much of a coward to take his own life, the
enemy, he figured, would have no qualms on the matter.

He volunteered for service on the front line, entrenching himself in a war that would forever scar the face of the world. He
placed himself in harm's way time and again, yet after each bat-

ite he found that somehow he had survived the day. His bravery
as rewarded, he climbed the ranks, and slowly, very slowly, he
ealized that God had given him a purpose for living. He would

It happened when his regiment found themselves at the forefront of a terrible battle. It was a hopeless situation, he had said.
And just when he was ready to make the ultimate sacrifice for
the sake of his men, a selfless young Scot, newly come to his regiment, came forward and committed an act of undaunted bravery, giving Mr. Seawell a new lease on life. Yet it was a lease he
felt wholly undeserving of. He should have been the one lying
dead; it was supposed to have been his blood soaking the ground
of France that day and not that of young Jamie Crichton.

I was in tears by the end of the letter. My heart went out to
Mr. Seawell, this strange and lost soul. But mostly I cried for
Jamie Crichton, for to me there could be no mistake: he was my
Thomas. In my mind's eye he resembled the same brave, selfless
man that I had given my heart to, had celebrated his love with
my body and now carried his child. I fought hard to come to
terms with the meaning of Mr. Seawell's letter. The return of
the timepiece indicated that Thomas was dead; the words of this
latest letter confirmed it. Yet why would Thomas join the army
if he had been a sailor born and bred? It really made no sense,
and this incongruous detail was all I had with which to console
myself.

At length, when all my tears had been cried out, and while
still clutching both letter and beating timepiece in my hands, I
was determined to write a reply to Mr. Seawell's letter. Awash
with sorrow, yet driven by an indescribable need, I plucked out a
quill and attempted to apologize for the venomous tone of my
last correspondence. I sought to console the poor man any way
I could, and even found myself sharing a sliver of my own sorry
tale and why I had been perhaps a little chuff where the name
Crichton was concerned . . .

*Dear Mr. Seawell,*

*Thank you for the candor of your last letter. Your plight was moving indeed and I don't mind telling you it brought me to tears. My own sorry tale pales in comparison, seems frivolous and childish even, yet the hurt is real enough. You have honored me with such openness and candor that I now wish to reciprocate in kind, praying that you reserve judgment on one you have never met while at the same time hoping to shed some light on why the name Crichton induced a tad of vitriol from me.*

*The reason, quite simply, is because I fell madly in love with a young sailor of the name Thomas Crichton—against the rigid principles of my family and, perhaps, my better judgment. My only excuse is that I was young, foolhardy and infinitely happy. Yet in the end I believe Thomas betrayed me, leaving me not only with a broken heart but in a delicate position as well. For this sin I find myself isolated from the entire world, living in a lighthouse of my father's design on a place known as Cape Wrath. And believe me when I tell you, the name is a fitting one. For I've been made to feel the wrath of this paltry existence every day, and with every gust of arctic wind. Yet in actuality the locals tell me Cape Wrath was not named for the condition of this coast, but for a word the Vikings gave to this point when they ruled the sea. The word* hvarf *in Old Norse was the term used to denote the point of turning, and this lonely Cape marked the southern-most boundary of their empire at that time. Oddly enough, this part of Scotland is still known as Sutherland for that reason. So there's a bit of history for you, Mr. Historian!*

*I hope, dear Mr. Seawell, you can see it in your heart to forgive me my harsh treatment of those who bear the surname Crichton. The young man you described to me in your last letter was certainly the noblest example of mankind regardless, or perhaps as a result of, the name he carried. Do not, for a moment, feel cheated that you lived as a result of this young man's bravery. For I too at one point believed death was a more fitting punishment than total*

*banishment from society, but I have come to see it otherwise. I may*
*never know the real story of my Thomas, or be certain that your*
*James and my Thomas are indeed one and the same. That they*
*both carry the same surname is, perhaps, beyond coincidental. But*
*the fact remains that I am carrying the man's child and if indeed*
*he is dead, then this, to me, must be his final blessing, just as your*
*final blessing from him was your life. It is odd to think that death*
*has delivered your sentence, Mr. Seawell, and life is the cause of*
*mine—the life of Mr. Crichton's unborn child. I pray you shall find*
*reason enough to live, just as I intend to see this through to the best*
*of my God-given ability. May He bless us both in our endeavors!*

*If you would be so kind, I must ask one more favor of you. I*
*would like to learn more of this soldier who carried my timepiece,*
*namely what he looked like. If you would please describe his*
*physical characteristics I might better be able to judge the man and*
*his motives. It may be impertinent of me, but you may even have*
*some inkling as to why joining the army for this man was a more*
*favorable alternative than marriage to me? I'd be obliged for any*
*response you feel you can give.*

> *Sincerely and with the utmost regard,*
> *Sara Stevenson*

. . .

Writing the letter, purging my soul to a complete stranger, felt
oddly cathartic. I found it as soothing to my mind as the now
medicinal port (taken three times a day) was to my fecund body,
both helping to ease a burden unseen yet ever present. What I
had learned of Mr. Seawell also had a strange effect on me, for I
was the sole confidante of his very personal and hellish plight.
All in the space of those two correspondences, an outpouring of
words, there had grown a bond between us—two lost souls
linked forever by the watch-chain of Thomas Crichton.

By the time I emerged from my room the men had already
gone off on their duties. The kitchen had been tidied and Kate
sat knitting a blanket by the fire. She looked up. She noticed the

letter in my hand, the fresh wax seal containing my initials, and asked very softly, "Is he dead, then?"

"Excuse me?" I replied, thinking I hadn't heard her correctly.

"I asked if he was dead."

I looked at her, my eyes burning with the tears I had shed, yet I saw not even a glimmer of remorse in her own eyes. "I don't know," was my feeble reply. "The matter is still unclear."

She got up then and came over to me, guiding me to another of the wing-back chairs by the fire. Once seated she then forced a mug into my hands—the steaming liquid, I noted, was light brown.

"Mr. Campbell said to give it to you. Said it would help calm your nerves in the case you'd be needing them calmed."

"What is it?"

"That coffee of his . . . with a dousing of cream and a touch of what he terms 'Scotch hospitality.'"

I sniffed it, and then took a sip. Scottish hospitality indeed. There was more whisky in the mix than coffee, but it was good, and it went down easily as my companion studied me.

"It is for the best, you know," she consoled at length. "It would never have worked, even if you did manage to carry it off."

"What are you talking about, Kate?" I said, for I was in no mood for one of her lectures.

"Your sailor. It's better this way; it's better that he's dead instead of you waking up one morning wishing he was. Maybe now you can turn your attention to more important matters."

I was incredulous. That Kate could even think that the unnecessary death of a man—a good and decent man—was justified! And as for more important matters, there wasn't one. I looked at her, knowing my anger frightened her. "I never imagined you to be so cold-hearted. You still don't understand, do you?"

"I understand duty," she replied unbendingly. "And I was speaking of your unborn child. Stop thinking about that sailor for once and focus on the problem at hand! I received a letter from your mother while we were in Durness. If the baby should happen to live, she has made arrangements for it at the foundling hospital."

My heart stopped. All I could do was stare at her disbelievingly.

"Oh, don't pretend you didn't see this coming. The father's gone. They shall never let you back, unwed and with a child, nobody would be that foolish. And don't even think of taking this to Mr. Campbell. When I told him of your family's arrangements, he said he was already well apprised of how the situation stood. The man was a wee snappish about the whole affair, but it seems to me that your father had it in mind all along. There is another bit of news your mother wanted me to pass along, and that is that Mr. Talbot's second wife passed away shortly after Christmas. He's always been fond of you, and by summer's end he'll be looking to wed again. Perfect timing, if you play your cards right."

Again it was so perfidious that all I could do was stare dumbly at her.

"You could have had an easy life, you know, if you had just behaved like a lady. Poor Mr. Graham was a fine gentleman, and infatuated with you as he was, even he had the good sense to know that such a marriage would have spelled disaster for him. But as this would be Mr. Talbot's third marriage, a good deal can be overlooked, including taking for a wife a silly girl who once got it into her daft wee head to run off with a poor nobody of a sailor. Put the sailor behind you now, Sara. And start to think for once of your future."

My hand holding the letter was squeezing so hard that my knuckles had turned white. A wave of nausea washed over me and settled in the pit of my stomach, causing my whole being to sicken and shake with renewed hurt and anger. And all the hatred I had ever felt for this woman came flooding back tenfold. It was with great effort that I restrained myself from strangling her. I slowly stood up from the chair. "His name . . . is Thomas . . . Crichton!" I issued defiantly.

"Who, dear?" she remarked with raised eyebrows, looking smugly ignorant.

"He is not 'a sailor'!" I cried. "He has a name, and his name is Thomas Crichton! And I shall never, ever put him behind me!"

And I meant every word as I left the lighthouse cottage, heading straight for the jetty, my vision blinded by tears once again.

# NINE

## *Neighborly Secrets*

❧

*A*gain I had been betrayed. Only this new wave of despair was a direct result of my own foolishness, because I had never questioned the future of my child—I just accepted that I would be the one to love it. But without a husband, it would never work. Written in the dark history of my sex, there has never been a place for unwed mothers. Children of such unfortunate wretches were given over to the Church, or to foundling hospitals, or drowned outright by those less discerning. In fact, I never knew of anyone, never heard of anyone, in the same predicament as myself, and that thought alone revealed to me what an outcast I was. Certainly there were other women as headstrong and foolish as myself? Certainly I was not the only one to fall under the sublime spell of love? But I was pretty confident that I had been the only one to have been banished to a desolate lighthouse for the sins I committed. No other family could be so devious as to enlist a cursed light-keeper to dispose of their daughter's bastard while the rest of the world remained largely ignorant. But they, none of them, had ever bargained on the fact that I very much wanted to keep my child; for we two alone shared the secret of Thomas Crichton's love.

Without much choice, and finding myself on the underside of hope, the only prayer I had left to cling to was the safe return of my child's father. But even I knew how unlikely that was.

After Kate had revealed the "arrangements" that had been made for me, I had not the stomach to even be around any of my companions. I hated them all, even poor innocent Robbie for his mere association with Kate. Really, he could have done so much better for himself! Yet he had made his own bed, as the saying goes, so he, of course, was just as much to blame as Kate, my mother's tool. My renewed hatred for Mr. Campbell, among the more obvious reasons, stemmed from the mere fact that he had agreed to the absurd arrangements all along. Yet he was used to death and killing people. My hatred for him only made his job that much easier; it released him from the odious emotion of guilt should I not survive the ordeal.

At first I believed that Mr. Campbell hadn't even realized that anything had changed between us, for he was just as withdrawn as was I. We had come to a sort of placable understanding of each other after the dumbfounding scene in his bedroom over the "book." We each, I believe, in our own way felt rather sorry for the other, each of us so ignorant of the other's circumstances, and I especially looked the fool. Mr. Campbell had the good grace to overlook my assumption that he had wanted me as a man wants a woman. I believed he was too troubled to want anything but peace now, and having me around offered none. He often went to great lengths to avoid me, and I respected that. He even took more of his meals in his room, or in the tower. He too, I noticed, avoided Kate, and once we even took the same circuitous route around to the backside of the cottage just to avoid being seen by her. It was the first time our eyes had met since the day the second letter from the antiquarian had arrived. And all I could think to greet him with was a churlish "Good day to you, Mr. Campbell. I hope you and your netherworld friends are faring well?" At this greeting he pulled up, allowing me to slip right past him through the seldom-used back entrance of the cottage.

As April came, bringing with it a burst of warmer air, I found I was finally able to garner my thoughts enough to pen a venomous letter to my family, thanking them once again for all the kindness shown to me in my time of need. Certainly Scotland had never seen such a shining example of Christianity abound from her verdant shores! What a gift to the nation was the family Stevenson! I begged them not to lose sleep over my health, as I was blooming, literally. I glowed. I danced. I frolicked. I told them the Cape was just lovely this time of year, and how lucky I was to experience such extremes of weather! Certainly not many young ladies of my acquaintance had such a chance— more's the pity. Kate was charming as ever and was becoming quite a hand at keeping her husband happy (here I underscored "happy" several times). Lastly, I let slip how I had seen so many handsome sailors cruise past the lighthouse since I had been in residence, and how one in particular was now carrying on a correspondence with me. I wished love to all and signed only with initials before smashing my seal into the glob of hot wax. Then, before I took my letter to the jetty landing, along with another for Mr. Seawell, apprising him briefly of my latest setback, I took a moment to scribble a note for Mr. Campbell. It was only two lines, short and to the point! I finished packing some things into my basket, pulled on my best pelisse and slipped the note under Mr. Campbell's door, certain he would find it come morning. And then I left the cottage.

I never gave a thought to running away, for there was really no place to run. But I did feel it necessary for my continuing health that I get away from the lighthouse and her noxious inhabitants for a spell, and for this little holiday I knew I could count on Mary MacKay for a fortnight of kindness.

It was a clear dawn, the sun just beginning to make its presence known as I started down the road. Flocks of migrating birds had begun to fill the skies and as I walked along, watching black wings obscure the fading stars, the music of a thousand feathered voices kept me company. At the jetty, after navigating the steep road, I deposited my latest batch of letters, noting with an inward smile that my missive to Mr. Seawell was gone. I had not spied the little craft that had carried it away myself, but that, I rationalized, was due to having been preoccupied and fretful over my own predicament. And then, battling the weight of the wiggling protuberance that was Thomas' child, I climbed out of the cove and made for the MacKay croft.

Wee Hughie was the first of the family to spot me as I came over the rise that brought the homestead in view. He had been out front stalking the many chickens that ran harum-scarum before him, when he happened to look my way and, leaving his sport for the sake of hospitality, came dashing over with the speed only those raised in the hills seemed to possess.

"Have ye come to deliver me one of your lessons? I thought we were done with a' that?"

"Never." I smiled and handed him my basket to carry. "You're far too bright to give up on, and I'm far too stubborn to do so. Sorry, dear boy. You'll just have to put up with me for a while longer yet."

He paused a moment, falling back a few steps, and then bounded forward again. "You've run away, haven't ye?" he challenged with boyish zeal.

I kept walking, cast him a sideways glance and replied truthfully. "Something very like that; but only for a little while. I shan't burden your family overlong, but I would very much appreciate your company for a while. By the way, you're a very perceptive young man."

"Only because I knew you'd run away. Ye dinna belong there, Miss Sara. Ye dinna belong there wi' that man!"

The child was undoubtedly wise beyond his years and just

for voicing what I knew to be true I felt the urge to give him a great hug, but I refrained. I did, however, turn him to face me. "You do know that the book you saw the last time you were at the lighthouse was a book of anatomy? 'Tis the study of the human body. It appears that Mr. Campbell was, at one time, a doctor."

"Mr. Campbell was a doctor?" I could see he was having a hard time wrapping his wee head around that one. "Weel, what about it?"

"Well, doctors are required to study such things," I told him. "It's how they familiarize themselves with their art. They need to have an intimate knowledge of how the human body works if they're going to fix it. Most anatomy books are of men, but sometimes the need arises for a specific study of women. We're different from men, you know."

He cocked his carrot-topped head. "Aye, I know. Ye say doctors are required to read such books?"

"Yes, I believe they are."

"Well then," he proclaimed with a grin that could only be termed roguish, "I shall be a doctor for certain when I grow up!" And then he bolted forward, heralding my arrival boisterously to the house.

As luck would have it I was just in time for breakfast. Hugh, with his daughter squirming on his lap, was already seated at the table; Maggie assiduously attacked a piece of buttered toast that was held protectively in both hands.

"Why, Sara," said Mary, arising from her stool by the fire where she'd been stirring a pot of porridge and came to greet me. "What a pleasant surprise. Are ye come alone, then?" Her pretty face, with its fine dusting of freckles and wide blue eyes, had a puzzled look as she held me at arm's length after a welcoming embrace.

"I am," I replied. And with a tone to my voice that was meant to set her at ease, I explained how I had been out early walking, and how it felt so good to be moving that I had decided to con-

tinue the entire way. She smiled politely at this, glanced fleetingly at the unfamiliar basket in her son's arms and demurred to
me how honored . . . how pleasured she was.

"Hughie, did ye fetch the eggs yet?" she directed to her son.
The boy, having been disturbed in the midst of his task, set
down the basket and dashed out again. "We'll have tae take those
daft birds in yet," Mary mused, watching his retreating back, "as
there's likely tae be a wicked storm before long."

"A wicked storm?" I questioned. "But it's a glorious morning,
by all accounts." At this statement husband and wife looked to
each other.

It was Hugh who spoke first. "Aye, 'tis glorious enough for
the now, Miss Sara, but did ye, by chance, happen tae take notice
o' the wind?"

"Of course. It's still blowing, as it always is."

This elicited a smile from the handsome Highlander. "Aye, but
did ye notice how 'twas backing?"

"Backing?" I questioned, sitting down to a hot cup of tea. "I
don't believe I'm familiar with the term."

"The wind has shifted direction, Miss Sara. Which means
that by evening a storm will likely be upon us. Perhaps," he
added, a charming smile touching his lips as his eyes caught his
wife's, "'twould be wise if ye stayed here with us for a spell . . .
that is, if it wouldna be too much of an inconvenience?"

"How kind of you, sir," I replied sincerely. "And I will take
your advice, but only if you can assure me that it won't be too
much of an inconvenience to have me here."

"Inconvenience?" he chided, setting down his mug with a sly
grin. "Nay, Miss Sara, 'tis no inconvenience tae have ye here.
Mary could use the company, and as for wee Hughie, I believe
that havin' ye for our guest might stop his gob for a bit. The
lad's been verra worrit about ye of late." Hugh glanced at his
wife, who responded with a softly concurring smile. Then he
looked back to me and added with a wink, "If ye havena guessed,
Miss Sara, the lad's a might taken with ye."

. . .

I thoroughly enjoyed my breakfast with the MacKays. Sitting at the little table, a table made with love by the man of the house, I watched how this family interacted with one another, how they smiled, how they teased, how they laughed. It was such a change, such a welcome change.

Maggie was undoubtedly the center of attention, parroting in her toddler language nearly everything that was said, her cherubic face beaming with delight. She loved to eat, especially toasted bread. It was a huge game with her, for every time she'd pluck a piece off the platter and set it on her own plate, she'd make a show of reaching for the jam. This was Hughie's cue to steal the toast from her and eat it himself. Once the jam jar was in her chubby grasp, she'd look down on her empty plate and exclaim with surprise, "Toos! Where toos?" Then she'd look to her brother, cheeks stuffed like a squirrel, and cry with chagrin, "Ewee! Ewee eat ma toos!" Then the little hands would reach for another piece, and the whole game would start again, only sometimes it was "Da" who took her toast, or "Ma." It was silly; it was charming. And in the end little Maggie not only got a whole plate of her own toasted bread to eat, but also a whirl up into her father's arms and a kiss on the cheek before he headed out the door for the day.

To my surprise he set the child in my crowded lap; gladly I took her. She was surprisingly heavy, and warm, and irresistible. Instinctively my arms came around her, I pulled her to me and began a nonsensical conversation while the man of the house, arms now empty, took up his wife in a playful embrace. As I whispered a silly rhyme about the Duke of York into the child's ear, my eyes strayed to the couple. Hugh MacKay was a tender man, a good man and a husband who was inclined to kiss his wife warmly on the lips—as if she was his most beloved treasure. I watched covertly as he tilted her head up to his, and then bent to whisper something in her ear that made her giggle.

I knew that kind of smile.

I had smiled like that when I was with Thomas Crichton. And suddenly, selfishly, I wanted what Mary MacKay had . . . I wanted her life. She was with the man she was meant to be with—the man she loved, the father of her children. She lived in a shabby little bothy on the edge of nowhere, and yet she projected a radiance that many of the wellborn were lacking. I watched as Hugh turned to go, the look on his face serene and placid. He was a man comfortable in his own skin, a man satisfied with his lot in life. He ruffled the hair of his boy as he passed, their resemblance unmistakable. He instructed the lad to come out and assist him once he had finished his chores. And then, plucking his hat from the hook while performing a quick nod to us ladies, he left the cottage.

It was only after the house was quiet, Maggie put down for her nap and wee Hughie out with his father, that Mary pulled me to the table and asked pointedly, "So will ye tell me now, Sara, why 'tis you've come? Dinna tell me 'twas for the sake of the walk. For even a blind man could see that something's troubling ye. Hughie's also let on that something might not be quite right up at the lighthouse."

I sat back, taking a moment to form my thoughts. Then, throwing all caution to the wind, along with any pretext to dignity I might have had left, I asked, "Your son, for his age, is mightily perspicacious. Tell me, Mary, what would you do . . . what would you do if someone told you they were going to take your baby from you when it was born and give it to a foundling hospital?"

She didn't speak for a long moment. The little bothy was dead quiet but for the soft crackling of the fire as she sat staring at me in reflective silence. And then she inquired, "Would I happen to be married?"

I slowly shook my head. "No, unfortunately you may have overlooked that little detail along the way, although if it's any consolation, it was in the forefront of your mind." Unable to look her in the eye any longer, I lowered my gaze to the table.

"Unwed." The word alone sounded forlorn coming from her gentle lips. "Well then, 'tis easy." I looked up; her face was alarmingly blank. "Were anyone meaning tae take a bairn from me I'd scratch out their bloody eyes, I would." A wicked grin appeared. "Of course, that would only be after I had already cut out their cold, black heart!"

. . .

Mary MacKay was a good listener, and as the winds backed and shifted out on the bay of Kervaig, and as they grew in might and wrath with every gust, I poured out my story to her. I told her about my love for Thomas Crichton. I told her about my family and how they reviled such as he. I told her how we planned to elope and how I had waited and waited in the rain for Thomas to come, but he never did. I told her of Kate's betrayal, whereupon hearing this tawdry complaint from me she nodded her head and uttered sagely, "I might have guessed some bad blood stood between ye." There was my banishment to Cape Wrath, my relationship to the puzzling Mr. Campbell and the latest affront by my family: to be rid of the child and the stigma I carried. It was only the second time since falling in love with Thomas that I had a sympathetic ear, the first being, of course, Mr. Scott those many months ago. But here on Cape Wrath was another female, with a woman's heart, a woman who relived my tumultuous affair with her own emotions lying close to the surface. Her empathy was the motherly understanding and concern I craved but had been denied.

When I had told her just how matters stood, I lastly, without any mention of the odd little skiff, told her of the letters from Mr. Seawell—how enigmatic yet comforting they were.

"Ye say ye never met the man and yet he was in possession of your timepiece?"

"Yes, that's right. Here," I said, and pulled from my bodice Thomas' magnificent silver chronometer.

She held it gently in the palm of her hand then turned it over to stare at the inscription on the back. She looked up; her eyes delivering a now familiar questioning look.

"Try sounding it out," I coaxed.

Her lips formed the words slowly: "To . . . my . . . be . . . be . . ."

"Beloved," I offered.

"Beloved," she repeated, and looked up, "Thomas?"

"Yes. Very good. Go on." The next word was a bit of a struggle for her, but she read the last two with little problem.

She repeated the inscription aloud, still marveling at the engraving. "To my beloved Thomas, eternally yours, Sara." She looked up again, this time her eyes glistening with moisture. "Oh dear, dear child," she bemoaned. "Do ye truly believe he's dead, then?"

"I don't know what to believe. I pray not . . . and I hope to learn the truth eventually."

With maudlin eyes, she handed back the watch. I tucked it home.

"Could . . . did ye ever think that maybe Mr. Seawell is really your Thomas?"

I came alive at the suggestion, but then I shook my head. "I don't see how he could be. Besides, the writing is all wrong. I know Thomas' writing very well. He has a unique style . . . a poet's gift with words. He used to write me poems and letters. No. I'm afraid the letters are not from him."

"His writing was different, ye say?"

"Very," I assured her, vividly recalling each and every word he had ever written to me in the bold, round hand, meticulously practiced to cover his humble beginnings. "Besides, Mr. Seawell is a scholar, a man who had the very good fortune to be well educated. My Thomas was never afforded that sort of chance. And Mr. Seawell appears to have suffered quite traumatically himself."

Mary leaned forward on her elbows, her blue eyes cunning and mischievous, very like her son's. "Ye say he's well educated and suffered cruelly? Does this mysterious letter-writer of yours also happen tae keep a lighthouse and harbor a fancy tae draw unmarried women . . . naked?"

"So . . ." I swallowed. "So you've heard about that, have you?" It was my turn to be embarrassed, and I could barely look at her, hanging my head in shame. "I suppose the man has his reasons for what he does. But what is it you're suggesting, Mary?"

"I'm suggesting, dear, that perhaps your mystery man doesnae dwell so verra far away after all. Mayhap he's very near but wants ye tae think the letters come from a man very far removed from it all. Perhaps . . . perhaps 'tis an easier way for a recluse tae make contact with a beautiful young woman? After all, he did have in his possession a very intimate drawing of ye."

"He did indeed!" I huffed, going red at the thought. "And he had no right to draw that!"

"But he did," Mary added softly. "Although I highly doubt he intended for ye, or anyone else for that matter, to find it, dear. But my point is that a man only draws what captures his imagination. And ye, Sara, have captured his."

I looked at her as if she'd gone mad. "I was forced on him!" I stated defensively. "He despises me! And what you're suggesting is utterly preposterous! Mr. Campbell is nothing like Mr. Seawell! Mr. Seawell appears very literate, very soulful. He was a man once deeply in love and when his wife and child died he tried to kill himself. Mr. Campbell doesn't appear to be capable of loving anything at all, and as for killing himself, ha! Out of the question. He's a man who'd rather kill than be killed. Besides, how would he have gotten hold of my watch?"

"Somebody could have sent it to him, somebody who knew

about the watch or knew Thomas," she suggested. Then, think-
ing on something else, she asked, "Well, what about his writing?
You said your Thomas had distinctive writing; wouldn't Mr.
Campbell's be distinctive as well?"

I paused to look at her. "Dear God, the writing!" And then I
recalled that there was indeed something odd about it, something familiar. Both Mr. Campbell and Mr. Seawell had small,
neat handwriting. But it had been a while since I had seen Mr.
Campbell's. Yet I knew he wrote daily in the log up in the light-
room. I would have to compare the two to be certain. But why?
Why would he go to the trouble? What end would he possibly
be hoping to serve? Or was it merely for the pleasure of tormenting me? Was it another game to him—baiting my already
volatile emotions? I felt anger rise at the thought of such a cruel
prank. My eyes blurred with tears. How dare he toy with me!

"Sara, dear, please calm yourself," came Mary's voice, pulling
me back from my plaguing thoughts, her eyes wide with concern. "'Twas only a suggestion, and likely wrong. I'm certain ye
are in the right of it. Mr. Campbell and this Mr. Seawell sound
nothing alike." Yet although she revoked the thought, retracting
it coyly from the conversation, the seed had already been
planted.

• • •

I stayed with the MacKays for an entire week while the storm
raged outside, hitting the Cape with the most ferocious winds
and pelting rains I had ever witnessed. We were perpetually wet
and cold; our fire smoldered and sputtered, yet thankfully we
never lacked food or good cheer. There was plenty to eat and
drink, and surprisingly I was treated to my medicinal allotment
of the same high quality claret Mary had given to Kate and myself on our first visit. Hugh often insisted that I have as much as
I needed, regardless of what auld Maura (his great-aunt, who
also happened to have delivered Mary's two children) had advised. Hugh, apparently an expert on breeding women, pro-

claimed that rest and claret—in the proper measure—brought about healthy offspring. It was his secret, at any rate, he told Mary and me one evening as we sat by the fire, long after the children were snuggled in their rain-damp beds. We had all been dosing ourselves a bit heartily to keep away the chill when Hugh gave over his advice to me. "Auld Maura is full of suggestions for all who seek her. Some, as in the case of a wee dosing, are quite sound, others, one in particular she's aught tae mention," this he said catching the eye of his wife and delivering to her a lascivious wink, "is quite grand and should be followed tae the letter, as often as one can." As he spoke, the room fell silent. His singular focus was on his wife, and she, blushing like a young bride beneath his gaze, gave him a look of pure adoration. Suddenly I felt very out of place and secretly wished I were back in my own little room at the cottage. I was an intruder here, an uninvited guest forcing myself on the hospitality of this family. The MacKays were a gracious and kind lot, and although they went out of their way to make me feel at home, there remained that unseen chasm between us that suggested I didn't really belong.

Mary, sensing my discomfort, cleared her throat and proclaimed, "I highly doubt, Hugh, that the auld witch would give that particular advice to Miss Sara."

"Well then," he smiled again, this time his charming gaze directed at me, "and maybe she dinna. By God, I pray she dinna!" he declared, and let out a hearty chuckle.

"Actually," I admitted softly, drawing their attention, "I believe she did. But the advice she gave to me I flat-out rejected, as it had to do with Mr. Campbell being the one to 'satisfy my every desire' and you must know, we're only just . . . friends."

"Campbell!" they cried in unison. This passionate outburst gave me a start, yet I noticed that while Mary's face merely held a pleasantly scandalous grin, Hugh's did not. A flash of primal anger appeared behind the crystalline eyes and, pointing his near-empty wineglass at me in lieu of his finger, he advised,

"Never heed advice, lass, from a canny auld crone what has ye dancing with thae devil! In fact, I gave yon devil of yours an earful on that verra matter just the other day, thon randy wee fool! And what man, guardian or no', would let a lass in your condition wander out here all by her lonesome, the weather turning dark and in the gloaming forbye!"

"You saw William?" I interrupted. "I mean, Mr. Campbell? When?"

"Why, the very day ye came. Shortly after breakfast I found him racing that team of his right across the parve. He was all riled up that ye left and was meaning tae fetch ye back before the storm blew in. I told him you were safe with us and would be staying for a spell. He was about to argue that point, was verra insistent that ye return, but I must have convinced him otherwise on thae matter!" Here he cast a wink at his wife, but her meditative countenance hardly changed. His focus shifted back to me. "However, just tae put that wee dark mind o' his at ease, I told him no' tae worry about ye, and that I'd return ye in a week's time. I think he was square with that."

I looked the rugged Highlander directly in the eye. "You . . . you never mentioned to me that you saw him."

"Nay, I dinna see the need. After all, 'twas you that ran away from the man in the first place, aye? I figured ye had good reason . . . perhaps a verra good reason, at that. And I'm no' a man tae argue with a woman, especially a breeding one." His eyes, deep set beneath the cinnamon brow, studied my face intently.

"Again, I'm sorry to correct you, but it was from Kate I was running this time, not Mr. Campbell."

Mary, knowing ever so much more about the mind of men than did I, placed her hand gently on her husband's arm. His head turned, their eyes locked, and she delivered that all-knowing look. It was a puzzle, that look, but one Hugh seemed to understand. He gave a small nod in return.

"Aye, perhaps I should have told ye. Forgive me. An' perhaps there's a wee something else ye should know as well. Campbell, he wouldna race across the parve for just anybody, lass." The cinnamon eyebrows raised in a knowing manner.

"I am, after all, his charge, in a manner of speaking, Mr. MacKay," I replied dispiritedly.

"Och, I'm well aware o' that! But I'm also well aware that a man coming tae fetch back his charge seldom reveals such desperation. And Mr. Willy Campbell, racing hell-for-leather across the parve, why, he was fair desperate!"

• • •

As I lay in the little makeshift cot by the fire, I found myself unable to sleep. Truthfully, I was awash with guilt. The storm that had raged for a week was finally diminishing, yet I knew by now that during such storms the duties of a light-keeper never subsided. The light would be going day and night, the fog bell would be tolling continually and eyes would be ever fixed to the sea. It was not a time to abandon one's post, even if that post merely required one to produce warm meals and offer kind words of encouragement every now and then. Yet I had abandoned my post at the worst possible time. And the thought, along with learning of Mr. Campbell's efforts to retrieve me—even after reading my letter that should have explained everything—caused an unseemly amount of guilt to well up within me.

And guilt, on such a level, was quite foreign to me.

Could it possibly suggest that I was growing used to this life? Could I ignore the feeling that arose whenever Mr. Campbell went out of his way to find me? No man had ever tried so hard to find me.

Not even Thomas.

And as the fire dwindled, my mind had time to wander—to meander the tangle of convoluted thoughts, turning them over, examining them, attempting to make sense of the insensible. What was happening to me? What did I even think anymore? With whom did my loyalties lie? And why did I long to be back in the cottage, sleeping snugly in the very bed I had fought so hard to despise? The answer, quite simply, was that I was in limbo; for I could hardly make sense of anything at all. But I did know, come daylight, I would ask Hugh MacKay to take me home.

Dawn broke and the house came to life in the manner that houses do when there's work to be done. I sprang up and lent a hand in the kitchen while the men—or, rather, man and boy—tended the livestock. Breakfast was served up in the usual MacKay style, and after all had been sated I thought to make my request to return to the lighthouse. Yet the storm had created an ungodly amount of work, and both Hugh MacKays headed out the door before I ever got the chance. The day progressed as every other I had spent in Mary's company. She was perhaps hell-bent on preparing me for motherhood, but she was a font of knowledge. I learned the art of nappy-wrapping and how to apply one on an unwilling toddler. I cooked. I sewed. I mixed salves. Wee Hughie, whose sole mission in life was to teach me patience and humility as I fought to impart his letters to him, was out for the day. So Maggie was my charge, Maggie with the beaming smile, who made me understand how precious was the gift of life.

As midday approached, another meal under way, I was prepared to make my request again, when visitors, unannounced, began to arrive. It was a bright sunny mid-April day, and the passing of the storm had brought the neighbors out in surprising number. They came to pass along gossip about damage done, livestock lost and any unfortunate ship that got caught unawares. It was mostly men from the boat crews that came, old Tosh and his son, Angus; Jamie MacKay, with the signature MacKay hair, also sauntered in and made himself at home. The men had gathered around the table drinking and talking pleasantly when the Gilchrist brothers bounded in. Seeing me there without the benefit of my austere and churlish light-keeper guardian brought out their more flirtatious side, and they pre-

ferred to make small talk with me by the fire, while the rest of
the men attended to matters of the Cape. In honor of our guests,
a young lamb had been sacrificed for the evening feast. The poor
creature, dressed and spitted, was hung over the fire. Wee
Hughie, doing honors at the spit, turned to me, interrupting
both Gilchrist brothers, who were recounting some wild Highland tale, and said, "Miss Sara, see this here lamb? I killed it myself. One blow and he was done for." Pride oozed from the boyish
voice as his head gave a knowing nod. "I should tell ye also, the
woman what marries me, she'll never go hungry," and the conspiratorial wink was delivered. This caused the Gilchrist brothers to laugh heartily, slightly wounding the lad. They made
gibing remarks, teased the boy and declared that stalking a
penned-up beast chained head and tail to a fence, with his father's sharpened axe in hand, was no sort of test of manhood. I
took wee Hughie's trembling hand in my own, not only to
steady the lad's growing anger, but to save him from striking
out at the young men, making an even greater fool of himself.

"Tell me, Archie, Hector, what did you bring to this feast besides your hot air?" The brothers' smirking faces went blank.
"Why, you didn't even stop to pick a head of cabbage for the pot,
did you? And this young man here, half your age, has gone and
provided his father's fattest lamb for the feast. You should count
yourselves lucky he did so too, for now you'll have yourselves an
honest meal and not the mean black broth I would have served
you."

And that was wee Hughie's cue, for he chimed in, as I knew he
would: "Och, she's bloody right, lads, for I've done saved ye! I ate
what Miss Sara made once and no' only did it come back out, but
I had the shits *for weeks!*"

As evening drew near a few more men arrived at the MacKay
croft to squeeze themselves around the table and partake in the
good cheer. It was a wonderful diversion, a rare chance to talk
and get to know these people who lived and worked beside us,

and for the duration of that enchanting evening I forgot about my desire to get back to the lighthouse.

Liam Ross, the small, dark-eyed man whose quiet demeanor belied a great wit, pulled out a fiddle and began to entertain the little gathering of crofters with traditional airs and songs sung in a language I did not know. He was a Gaelic speaker, as were many others gathered there, and Mary sat beside me near the fire, translating ballads written when the Highlands had kings of their own. Spirits began to flow, for Hugh MacKay had quite a stock, and before long many slightly intoxicated voices filled the low rafters of the little dwelling. I was swept away as the deep, melodic voices joined together, honoring the land of their ancestors with the melancholy airs. Darkness came and the visitors stayed. More food was laid out, some little cakes, cold meat and cheese, more drink was poured round and the dancing commenced.

Mary and I were the only females in the croft, and I had grown rather large, but not so large that I couldn't dance a jig or two. By the time the visitors retired to the barn and outbuildings to sleep, for most were too drunk or just plain spent to even contemplate the journey home, I was dead tired—my guilt driven from me by pure exhaustion. And what was more, having so many men around vying for a dance, I felt very like the belle of the ball!

It was in the wee hours of the morning that I awoke suddenly, driven once again by the desire to get back home. Dreams of Thomas had come again, and so too did dreams of another man, but whether it was Mr. Campbell or Mr. Seawell, I was uncertain, for in my dream they were one and the same. But the dream was vivid, the emotion sharp, and it left me feeling empty . . . wanting. The cot by the fire contributed to this feeling, for although it had been lovingly made for my comfort, it was not a proper bed. My body, young though it was, was not immune to the aches and pains brought about by dancing with a turgid midsection, aches that were only exacerbated by the hard floor. Try as I might, I was still a spoiled, self-centered young lady who longed for her own bed in her own room—a room not so heavily infused with the scent of sweaty male.

I knew that I should wait until dawn to leave, but I was impelled by an inner drive. I had been away too long; I had been burden enough on the gracious MacKays and the family would have plenty of company to contend with come morning. Hugh hardly needed the added burden of seeing me safely home.

A swift note written clearly, using words and pictograms I knew Mary could decipher herself, told of my heartfelt thanks, my appreciation for all they had done and that I felt it was time I return to my duties at the lighthouse. Thomas' pocket watch, steadily ticking away in my bodice, revealed the time to be three in the morning. Dawn was a good ways away yet, and I just might make it back in time for breakfast. Still in the dark of night, I gathered my belongings and left the croft, heading for the road through the parve that would lead me home.

It was my good fortune that a full moon had appeared to guide me, risen late yet throwing a strong enough glow to cast a shadow. The night was quiet and still but for the low rustle of the nocturnal creatures who rummaged through the heather in the dark. A light breeze came at my back to help me along as I picked my way gingerly through the undulating landscape, atop the tender grasses and bell heather just springing to life. And as I walked farther away from the little croft that was the last outpost of civilization for a good long while, my body fell into a comfortable stride, a cathartic rhythm, and my mind began to wander.

I hadn't gone very far before my gentle musings were shaken by a sudden sound that split the air. It was the whistle of a man, high-pitched and shrill, and it came from no great way off. At the sound I dropped where I was, pressing my swollen body to the earth, afraid that I had been spotted. My heart tatted away with the rapid beat of fright, and I silently cursed myself for my impulsiveness—my stupidity. I was alone on the moorland at night, and God only knew what specters and banshees claimed these wastes as their own! I remained hidden, attempting to meld with the landscape, while thinking I was a fool of the worst kind. Yet as I waited, it seemed eerily quiet, and I thought that perhaps the sound I heard was all in my imagination. Minutes passed. I grew restless, and lifted my head again to peer into the moonlit darkness.

At that instant the sound came again, closer this time, and it came in three quick bursts instead of the lone one. I dropped to my former position, heart beating, skin tingling, and curled into a protective cocoon around my belly. Another moment of silence followed, and then, somewhere far out in the distance, I heard an echoing call. Three haunting whistles floating on the cool night air, sounding as if they were bouncing off the cliffs far below.

Quiet settled over the moorland once again. Curiosity got the best of me, and I decided to move to a place where I might better see this creature that called so boldly in the night. I left my basket and proceeded on hands and knees to a little rise, my cumbersome frock and cloak making the going slow. And there, as I crouched in a thick clump of heather, my breath coming quick and short, I peered over the rocky embankment, only to see the entire bay of Kervaig open up before me far below. High cliffs sheltered the cove on three sides while the dark, softly undulating water shone like polished onyx under the full moon. The tide was in, greatly reducing the length of the gentle beach at the head. And though it was a spectacle of wonder on such a night, it was nothing compared to the sight of the magnificent ship ghosting at anchor just inside the protection of the cliffs. Upon spying the vessel, so near the dangerous coast, I inhaled sharply. My hand flew to cover my mouth and I prayed that I hadn't been heard. But what in God's name was it doing here?

Just the sight of it, sitting there at anchor, was mesmerizing. She was a sleek craft with two masts supporting a spectacular array of both square and triangular sails, most of which were

furled. Had I any knowledge of the sea other than that one particular sailor, as Mr. Campbell had accused, I might have been
able to identify what type of ship she was. But my knowledge,
unfortunately, did not extend so far. Yet I was in awe; and in my
awe a great and terrible vision flooded through me. I became
convinced Thomas was on that ship.

I watched intently, searching for any movement—searching
for a glimpse of the person I longed to see. I caught a glint in the
moonlight. Some activity was taking place on the ship. And staring with eyes strained to the point of pain, I saw that a small
boat was being lowered into the pearly black water.

My heart soared.

Thomas was coming for me . . . Thomas was finally coming
for me!

I could wait no longer. How odd it was, after all this time—
all this waiting—that I should be so anxious to see him. I should
be mad. I should be boiling with fury at the way he had left me,
but I wasn't. I was overjoyed at the thought that he had finally
come for me—that he had searched for me and now was here.
My child would know his father after all.

I stood up from my place of hiding near the precipice, intent
on backtracking to the bay, where I would meet him on the
beach. This thought filled me—the wondrous reunion of lovers
torn apart. I would throw myself in his arms and beg him to
take me away. I saw it so vividly in my head—his warm embrace,
his hungry kisses . . . his soulful murmurs of apology. With excitement coursing through me—an excitement I hadn't felt in a
great many months—I turned to go.

I didn't see it coming.

I never heard a sound.

A hand, sudden and hard, hit me, covering my mouth while
the furious weight of the stranger's body forced me back to the
ground. The weight crushed painfully on top of me. Fear and
frustration burst forth and I screamed—or tried to, but the iron
hand stopped me from uttering a sound. It was then a mouth

pressed close to my ear. A hiss of hot breath came, demanding that I be quiet. It came again, this time gentler yet ever insistent. "For God's sake, Sara, it's me. Hush now! Hush, lass! For God's sake, be quiet!"

Recognizing the voice, yet positively stunned that he should be here, I nodded. The man, having considerable experience with me, kept his hand pressed to my mouth while his warm body remained very close to mine. He then gently rolled me to face the bay. It was then I understood. Just beneath us, on a lower rise, so close that were I so inclined I could have reached out and touched their heads, came a procession of men. They were silent but for the sound of their muffled feet on the soft ground, and they came one by one over the rise and to the pathway leading down to the beach. It was in the dark of night, and their faces were hidden from view, but the moon, lending its full intensity behind the silent army, revealed quite stunningly their silhouettes. And these, to my great astonishment, were familiar.

The first to pass beneath us was the unmistakable effulgent head of Hugh MacKay, the tall, broad-shouldered, stalwart Highlander. He was followed, quite remarkably, by every other soul who had descended on the bothy unannounced—our reluctant boat crews—making me understand that it was no coincidence they had been there on that very day.

The men of the Cape were up to something.

This clandestine meeting—this lonely, sheltered bay, in the dead of night, under a full moon—and the strange barky sitting at anchor, waiting, was more than chance serendipity. With questioning eyes, I looked at the man next to me. He held his finger to his lips, indicating that I continue to watch in silence.

When the men had finally reached the beach and were out of earshot, Mr. Campbell turned to me with eyes flashing dangerously and hissed, "What the devil are *you* doing out here? For God's sake, Sara . . ." But he couldn't form the rest of the words that tumbled into his brain. He was too angered.

I glared just as darkly. "I might ask you the very same question! It's three in the morning and you're out here . . . wandering the moors near Kervaig Bay? What, were things too quiet at the lighthouse for you this evening? Or, perhaps, one of your ghosts chased you out?"

His pale eyes glowed in the moonlight. "Stop it!" he seethed, and squeezed my wrist tightly, inflicting a small dose of pain. I flinched. Realizing that he was hurting me he let go. But his breathing came heavy; he was all worked up with the night's exertion. And turning to me he asked, "And what do you mean by running off like that? Leaving at the crack of dawn with nary a word. By God, did ye not see there was a storm coming? And what's this supposed to mean?" he questioned, passion gripping his voice as he pulled out the note I had written to him before I left and waved it under my nose. "Huh? Or do ye not remember, it was so long ago? Well, let me remind you, then." And he proceeded to recite the two hastily written lines with jaunty mockery in his voice. " 'Gone to the MacKays for a holiday. Will return when ready'? What the hell were ye thinking?"

I stared at him, unwilling to speak.

"And since when do Edinburgh lasses take their holidays in a run-down Highland bothy? Isn't that a wee step down in the world for the likes of you?"

"I don't know what you're talking about," I replied, shifting my attention to the beach and the men below. "I had a lovely time. And their bothy is not run-down. It's cozy. Very neat and tidy."

He grabbed my arm, forcing me to look at him again. "This is not a game, Sara! My point is . . . why do ye insist on running away like that all the time? You make it a habit, and it eats away at me when ye do. For God's sake, I'm the one who has to answer for ye in the end! Do ye not understand that?"

I looked closely at him, remembering what Hugh had said, how he had come to fetch me back—how he had been persistent in the matter. And then, only with the benefit of the moonlight,

I saw the dark, mottled skin around his left eye. It was faint in the darkness, but it was there. Willy Campbell was recovering from a black eye. Reflexively, and rather touched that he should suffer the likes of this on my account, I brought my hand up and gently touched his cheek just beneath the eye, where the darkness started. He froze at my touch, yet he did not turn away. And then I asked softly, "Why do you feel you have to answer for me in the end? Why do you feel the need to fetch me back all the time? Is it duty that drives you, Mr. Campbell, or is there . . . something else?"

His eyes, dark and liquid under the night sky, searched my face, and then, quite unexpectedly, his hand came over mine, pressing it securely to his warm flesh. His hold on me was firm, desperately so. "I know why it is ye left." His voice, usually deep and a bit gruff, now came as soft and hesitant as the night air. "Kate told me of your mother's letter . . . what it said. But I thought ye knew . . . I thought ye understood that . . ."

"That I would be giving up my child?" I finished for him, sadness touching my voice as I tried to pull away from his grasp.

He squeezed tighter, unwilling to let me go. And then he slowly brought my hand protectively to his chest. His pale eyes, catching the light of the moon, widened. "No! God no!" he averred. "I thought ye understood that if you or the baby . . . survives . . ."

"You're afraid that we won't?"

"Deathly" was his pained reply. And in that moment I could see this was his greatest fear. William Campbell, the unlucky physician, the man with the palpable pall of death surrounding him, feared for my life and the life of my child. It was touching but wholly unnecessary. I was about to reassure him that I would fight every ounce of the way, when a sound from below caught our attention. Boats were being launched from the beach.

Our boats.

Willy, seeing this misuse of lighthouse property, unceremoniously let go of my hand and popped up. "By God, they're not really doing it!" He looked at me in astonishment. "That Highland devil is using my boats for his own gain."

"His own gain?"

"Aye. Just look at them down there!" he commanded, and I did.

Boats were plying to and fro in the still waters—lighthouse boats, to be more specific—and expertly handled, at that. They were carrying some type of cargo that the ship was unloading in them, but they were not making for the shore with their payloads. Instead, they were pulling for a spot along the cliffs, where they suddenly disappeared from view. Mr. Campbell pulled out a spyglass and, after looking through it a moment, handed it over to me. It was hard to make much out, dark as it was, but I could see there was a cave hidden in the cliffs, a cave that was only accessible by boat at high tide. I looked questioningly at Willy.

"They're smugglers, lass. Surely ye knew that. And here I was convinced that he was against bringing the boats to this bay on account of principle. But all along he wanted this."

"What do you mean? Mr. MacKay was indeed against you when you suggested training the men for the rescue boats. I was there, William, remember? I was the one who helped you convince them, talking Mr. MacKay and his men into rowing around to the bay in the first place. I even paid them to do it, if you'll recall."

He glanced at me, his eyebrows pointedly arched. "So ye did. But no, Sara, it wasn't you who talked them into it. It's what that red devil wanted ye to think. He used ye, Sara, just as I used his boy. Damn me," he uttered aloud, appearing fleetingly amused by it all. But then he wiped the grin from his face.

"How did you know they'd be here?"

"Believe it or not, I happened to spy the cutter. She's a fast sailor. *Le Temeraire*, she's called."

"You know that ship?"

"I know of her," he corrected. "She's French built, captained by a well-known French privateer by the name of Etienne Flambaux. A canny devil, isn't he? Our Hugh MacKay had a vested interest in her too. He's a relative that's Captain Flambaux's partner. But I've never been on time to witness their wee covert operation before tonight. Impressive, isn't it?"

"Very," I uttered with a blatant lack of enthusiasm.

"Well, now you know why it is I'm here. I spied her in the offing as she rounded the point, which, by the way, is hard to do, and then I woke up Robbie to take over the watch. He's got the light now." He was watching me, waiting for my sorry excuse.

"You want to know why I'm here?"

His reply was a curt nod.

"Very well. I was growing a bit homesick." This caused an incredulous expression on his face. "No, it's true. I wanted to leave yesterday, but the men began showing up."

"Really? You were homesick? And which home was it ye were longing for?"

"My home at the lighthouse," I replied honestly. I was pleased to see this made him grin. "But then I saw that ship. And for some inexplicable reason I believed Thomas was on board. I know it sounds daft, but right when you tackled me, which, by the way, scared the wits out of me, I was convinced I was going to find him—I was convinced he was coming for me."

At this admission he grew quiet again, his face still and contemplative. "You still . . . love him?"

I didn't need to reply. He already knew the answer.

A soft, plaintive smile appeared on his face and he held out his hand to me. "Come, Sara," he said, "'tis time to go home. And, for what it's worth, I'm glad you want to come back to the lighthouse."

William Campbell patiently guided me along the uneven ground as Kervaig Bay dropped from view. And once back on smoother ground he turned to me and said, "'Tis just not the same without you. Kate's positively frantic. I now understand a little better what it is that lies between you, and I say this only for the sake of living peacefully in the cottage, but you will have to try to get along with her." I nodded solemnly. "And one more thing: I am not your enemy, Sara."

"You won't force me to give up my child . . . even though my family wishes it?"

"Not if you don't want to, which, by the by, I'm glad to see ye don't."

We came to a horse—Bruce, I believed it was—hobbled to a scrubby little bush near the road. The animal whinnied softly as its master approached in the darkness, and Mr. Campbell, after greeting his horse with kind words and a loving rub on the nose, helped me into the saddle. I watched as he took the reins in hand and led us both down the road to the lighthouse.

"What will happen to the men?" I asked, still awed and bothered by what we had just witnessed.

"What will happen to MacKay, do ye mean?" he replied, walking closely beside my leg, his tall form brushing against me every now and then. I found it oddly comforting. "I'll likely kill him," he said evenly.

"William!" I cried, pulling on the horse's halter to stop both man and beast. He turned to look at me. I could see the hint of amusement touching his luminous eyes.

"However, on account that ye fancy the man's wife and children so, I suppose I shall find other means to punish him." He continued walking.

"Why do you hate MacKay so?"

"Who said I hated him?" he replied, looking questioningly at me as he walked. "Aside from the fact we squabble now and then, sometimes even coming to blows over particularly touchy matters, if you must know, I rather like the man. If we were both on the same side, I might even be inclined to act a wee more neighborly."

"Will you report him?"

"Why would I do that?"

"Because he's a smuggler and smuggling is against the law, you even said so yourself. And lighthouses have a responsibility to uphold and protect maritime trade."

"Aye, so ye do know a thing or two about the trade? Yes, smuggling carries a heavy price, and I wonder at why they would risk it. But then, I'm reminded of how hard their life is out here, how they eke and struggle just to make a living off this old rock. Yet they choose this life and their freedom over being at the mercy of a capricious landlord who might toss them off their land at any time if the lord should so choose. MacKay and his men are intrepid. I respect that. It's one of the reasons they're so loath to rescue other imperiled ships—on account that they profit from the pickings. That, for my own reasons, I don't respect. I also don't appreciate the flagrant use of my boats. That will stop now that I know what they've been up to. But this enterprise, smuggling claret from France without paying the heavy duties attached to such a drink, allows them at the very least to feed their families during a harsh winter. That is survival. For that I will not report them, nor am I required to. The lighthouse, however, is forbidden to harbor smuggled goods. Since we don't harbor anything, there's no issue there. But my boats? By God, that does burn me!"

"How long have you known about this?"

"Oh, I've had my suspicions for some time now, and the claret you brought back after your *first* foolish visit to their croft confirmed it. Alasdair also knew something was up, and even had a word with MacKay on the matter. Did ye happen to know Alasdair Duffy?"

"I met him briefly last summer," I replied, trying hard to recall the man, for my mind was heavily encumbered with other matters back then. "He was an older gentleman, was he not?"

"Aye, a bit. But he was also a bit of a meddler too. He had a habit of sticking his nose into other people's affairs. He also happened to have a thing for a certain Mrs. MacDonald, the same lady who lost her husband and son on that day last fall. Her

menfolk were fishermen; Alasdair had an amazing gift for knowing just when the herring were running."

"He was having an affair with a married woman?" The
thought was scandalous indeed.

"That was the rumor. I never pried much. I never asked the
man his business. But I did find it odd that all three of them
should die on the same day."

"Did only those three men go into the water?"

"There were five men in the boat that day, the same as we run
now. Alasdair was at the steering oar, the MacDonald men were
in the bow. There was, however unperceivable, some bad blood
between them, I'll grant ye that. The other rowers that plied the
oars were Tosh MacKay—Hugh's uncle—and Danny MacDonald, a cousin of the deceased men and a fisherman as well. The
seas were rough that day, Sara. It was a hard pull to the ship that
was wrecking. I was in the other boat when I happened to see a
wave come and swamp them. Alasdair had the bow at a dangerous angle to the surf, there were some who say 'twas spite or
malice that he did so. But no matter how foolish he might have
been, he was no murderer. It was an accident. The two MacDon-
alds, father and son, were taken out of the bow by the wave.
The rest of the men were merely swamped. I was fighting to
keep my own men afloat while it all transpired so I didn't see
what happened next. But when I did chance to look, Alasdair
was gone. Only Tosh and Danny remained, and they were frantically searching for their mates while trying to stay afloat. The
whole affair was a disaster from the start. The surf was too
rough to have even considered a rescue. But I did. Danny and
Tosh lost their heads entirely, and if it were not for fear of losing
them too, I might have pressed on. As it was, we ended up turning back to save our own lives. We were still too far from the
ship that was going down, but close enough to hear the voices of
the men calling to us . . . begging that we come save them. Jesus,
but it was bloody awful! And the pain of it, Sara, was that it
wasn't only the three men who died that day. A whole bloody

ship went down, every one of her crew dead. That, to me, was unbearable."

"I'm sorry," was all I could utter after such a heart-wrenching tale. And I did feel sorry for this man; for I knew that the death of others truly haunted him. But then I asked, "Still, it is odd that Alasdair should have gone in too, isn't it? Do you think the men pushed him—perhaps for what he knew . . . or for what he was doing with Mrs. MacDonald?"

"I wouldn't like to believe the men of the Cape are murderers, if that's what you are asking. Perhaps it was the will of God that he died? Perhaps he was being punished for the liberties he was taking with a married woman? Who's to say? Only God sees fit how to punish the sins of men. We are not to question the methods, only accept them as they come."

"And you accept them. Tell me, did you and Alasdair get along well?" I asked, curious at his devil-may-care attitude about his former employee's death.

"I got along with Alasdair about as well as I get along with anyone, I expect."

"William Campbell!" I chided again, watching him start at the name as he walked undeterred beside me. "And is it any wonder? You, sir, can be intolerably abrasive!"

"Aye, I can," he concurred. "And you, Miss Stevenson, have a habit of being intolerably foolhardy."

"Aye, I do," I agreed with a wry smile. "Though truthfully, it's only one of my many faults."

The look on his face further charmed my melting heart.

. . .

Just as the lighthouse was coming into view, dawn was breaking. We had been traveling the last few miles in companionable silence, each of us contemplating our own particular thoughts as Bruce trudged along beneath me. I watched Mr. Campbell walk beside the horse, his faultless, purposeful strides falling in time with the animal's, his dark hair, a mop of chestnut-brown curls,

now neatly queued. His black three-caped cloak fluttered in the
wind, and suddenly I felt an overwhelming rush of gratefulness
that he had found me on the moorland. I was tired, and doubted
if I could have made the journey so swiftly on my own. I longed
for my bed. I longed for sleep. My heavy body ached and yearned
for the release only sleep could give; and I knew that he had
likely not slept at all. I marveled at how he could manage. I
found myself watching him, oddly drawn to the effortless way he
moved: the solid build of his body, the complexity and perplexity of his mind, and so absorbed was I in him that I for once took
little notice of the glorious dawn that was awaking around me. I
heard the sound of birds taking to the air but paid them little notice. And I was staring at him still when he came to a grinding
halt.

He spun around. Our eyes met, his were unusually bright.
And the bruise I had detected in the night made itself known. I
felt a pang of guilt at the sight of the yellowish-green skin as he
cried, "By God, do you see it?"

"Hmm?" I uttered, my mouth touched with sleep. I then followed his gaze to where, out on the open water, my odd little
skiff sailed. The sight of it shocked me fully awake, and I marveled again at the beauty of it.

"Ye do see it, don't ye?"

"Of course I do. That's the boat that delivers Mr. Seawell's
letters," I replied.

His eyes narrowed suspiciously at me.

"Well, what I meant was, he delivers my post, but I don't need
to tell you that now, do I?" Yet as I said it, I had to squint to see
the boat clearly. It was hazy out; the little craft was hovering on
the indiscernible horizon with the vaporous image of a mirage.
It wavered. It came into view. It wavered again. And then, as the
light from the sun grew brighter, climbing the waves—moving
ever closer to where the boat was—it finally touched the billowy
sails. A bright flash of light appeared as if the sails themselves
had caught fire. And then the little craft vanished—just van-

ished—in the brilliant light. When I finally had the will to look away from the awesome spectacle, I saw that Mr. Campbell had been studying me. I raised my eyebrows; he narrowed his in reply.

"I suppose," I began haltingly, "that we should check the jetty now to see if there's a letter?"

"I suppose that we should" was his guarded reply. Mary's suggestion that he was the letter-writer had plagued me ever since she had uttered the ridiculous notion. And now, after having learned a bit more about him, I had to wonder. "Do you think, sir, that there will be a letter awaiting me at the jetty?"

"I think," he began, staring intently at me, "that there just might be."

"And have you, William Campbell, ever been to Oxford?"

He raised his dark brows at this but did not answer. It was apparent that he was just as intent on getting to the jetty as I was.

Making it to the treacherous path that sharply descended to the landing below, he stopped. "Stay here," he said, and turned to go.

"No, let me go," I countered, and watched his face as he processed this.

"Don't be foolish, Sara," he replied as his dark cloak billowed in the wind behind him. "You've had a long night, and you're not supposed to overexert yourself."

"Very well," I relented, "but only if you're certain you don't mind."

Apparently he didn't, for he had already turned his sights on the jetty and was well on his way.

I sat patiently on the horse until a bobbing head appeared, followed by a tall, lean body clad in a fluttering black three-caped cloak. Mr. Campbell's head was bent in silent reflection as he climbed the last bit of road coming out of the jetty landing. And then he came to me, his hands empty. My heart sank at the thought of not having word from the antiquarian—who might possibly be a work of fiction concocted by this perplexing man.

Either way, regardless of the motive, I found a solace in the letters, it was my private refuge, and I was sorry to think that perhaps the mysterious letter-writer had lost his muse.

Mr. Campbell walked up to the horse and took hold of his halter. "Why so glum?" he asked, peeking over Bruce's glossy brown neck. I believe he could see that my hopes had been dashed, and before I could express my disappointment, he reached into his coat and drew forth a letter.

My reaction to the sight of the paper pleased him, and with a gentle look of amusement he quipped, "Did you really think it would not come? After all, ye saw the skiff same as me."

"I was unsure," I replied truthfully. I read the familiar inscription, noting the neat, precise handwriting, and placed it inside my pelisse, pressing it close to my body for safekeeping.

"So what does he write, this Oxford man?" he inquired rather nonchalantly as we continued to pick our way through the spiny heather and soft mosses that led back to the cottage.

"It's rather personal," I replied, looking at the back of his dark head. He didn't turn around but kept walking. "But as you've been so kind as to retrieve this for me, I shall tell you why I like receiving Mr. Seawell's letters. I like them because I find them very revealing . . . not so much because of his connection to Thomas, which is still rather unclear, or the other man who appears to have carried his timepiece . . . but Mr. Seawell has revealed to me a rather heart-wrenching personal story. And like you, William Campbell, he is a man battling his inner demons."

The lighthouse keeper, ignoring this pointed remark, kept on walking.

I continued. "It's rather ironic, but he too is plagued by death, and . . . and I believe Thomas Crichton might just be one of those poor souls who haunts him."

At this, he faltered. The horse came to a stop and he slowly turned around. It was something in his eyes, the way they burned with a frightening intensity, causing the spectacular bruise around his left eye to appear more vivid. The sudden change in him frightened me. "Do you still not know if he's dead?" he inquired harshly.

"I . . . it's uncertain."

Without another word he turned his head toward the sea, facing the direction we had seen the little boat disappear over the horizon. His breathing was coming in short quick bursts now, as if something had riled him.

Concern swept through me. I felt that in some way this change in his demeanor, this quicksilver shift from pleasant company to atrabilious recluse, was somehow my fault, but I didn't see how. And so, cautiously, I asked, "Is something troubling you, William?"

"Yes," he said, but would not turn again to face me.

·  ·  ·

William Campbell said not another word as we traversed the brooding waste the rest of the way to the lighthouse. Even the sight of a lone puffin nestled in the bracken near the cliff's edge failed to excite notice from him. He walked with head bent, his gait near drudgery as the orange-billed auk followed us with its jet black eye amidst a ring of downy white. The chubby bird, with its splash of color and humorous appearance, was a sharp contrast to the current mood of the man and the Cape. Sensing this, the puffin gave a cry and flapped its slick black wings before disappearing over the edge of the cliff. Bruce and Mr. Campbell continued on.

Kate was laying out the table as we arrived, a table set for three. I would have liked to say that she was happy to see me back, but there was no warm embrace or kind word from her as I came through the door. Mr. Campbell was finishing up in the stable and had sent me ahead to warn her of our arrival. He had been gentle as he pulled me from the horse, warning me to keep the peace in the cottage, and he struggled hard to offer a smile, but it was a smile that did not reach his eyes. The astonishingly pale orbs were still lost and distant, and they were very much on my mind as Kate practiced her rough exercise on me.

Her face, as I first came through the door, was one of astonishment. But then she darkened, glowering in my direction before stomping back to the cupboard where after noisily retrieving another bowl and spoon, she slammed them both on the table. The quiet cottage came alive with her hot anger, and I marveled that the earthenware hadn't cracked. "So, you've finally come to grips with your lot, then, eh, and now you have returned? Or do you still feel the need to run away?" she sniped, her dark tendrils bobbing from beneath her linen cap like Medusa's snakes. "It would have been easier on us all if you and your devil's spawn had just gone off the cliff—put an end to the misery that plagues us all. That would have been easier to explain to your mother than this . . . this shameful display!"

Such asperity was disturbing and deserved a reprimand. I was tired, snappish and could have lit into her as she was begging me to do, but then I heard Mr. Campbell come in behind me. One look at him and I could see that the last thing he needed was more problems to add to his already addled mind. The man needed sleep, and for his sake alone I replied, "It's nice to see you, Kate. And I'm truly sorry for the trouble I caused."

Her answer was chafing silence.

"Listen," I began, hoping to ease some of the tension between us, "you don't need to trouble yourself on my account. I'm exhausted and will retire immediately."

"Trouble?" The word oozed from her drawn lips. "Don't go to any trouble on account of you? You have no idea what sort of trouble your little escapade has caused us! Dear Mr. Campbell here was beside himself with worry. Your disappearance near drove him daft, not to mention the added stress of the storm. My Robbie was as bone-weary as a man can be and still be alive! But you are too self-absorbed and spoiled to even see it! God have pity on you, Sara Stevenson, for being the thoughtless creature that you are!"

I looked at Mr. Campbell standing solemnly behind me. The bruise maligning his stoic face, the dark circles under his eyes, the tousled hair, and the guilty demeanor suggesting that I had indeed gotten under his skin, made me feel like crying. Remorse came sure and swiftly, yet so too did anger. "I do pray that God pities me, Kate," I said, turning back to her. "I pray the good Lord takes pity on us all. And I'm truly sorry for the trouble I caused everyone, especially Mr. Campbell. But back to your earlier reproof, why the devil are you still answering to my mother, Kate? Do you really feel the need to report my every fault and failure? Do you not think the woman knows by now what I am? What I can't understand is why you two insist on believing I will ever be that same person I once was." Our eyes met, her doe-eyed gaze widening at the question in my own. Yet before she could answer, I turned to go.

"Do you really want to know why?" she called to me. I did not turn around. "Because we still have hope for you, Sara. God knows why, but people often make a habit of clinging to it, even when, by all accounts, they have little left to hope for."

• • •

I was relieved to be back in my own room again. The soft downy bed, with its mountain of pillows and beautiful quilt, called to me, but I was too worked up to sleep. The knowledge that the good people of the Cape, people I had grown to care deeply about, were involved in illegal smuggling was hard to swallow. Mr. Campbell's sudden appearance had shocked me as well, but not as much as the knowledge that he perhaps had a deeper attachment to me than pure responsibility. The black eye, given to him by Hugh MacKay, no doubt, was very telling, although Mr. Campbell, of course, had avoided further discussion on the topic. I did find him intriguing; that I could not deny. But it was only, I believed, because I was here—in this vacuous land where even the most peculiar of men might spark a young girl's fancy. And then there was another letter from the antiquarian. I had secretly been longing to delve into it ever since the odd little skiff had been sighted. Yet Mr. Campbell had pulled it from the depths of his own coat. He could have had it in there all along, and I would have been none the wiser. After all, he was known to frequent the jetty. But was he indeed the letter-writer? Similarities existed between the two men; in dreams I even pictured them one and the same. But why go to the trouble? And how had he gotten the chronometer? It was all too much to contemplate, and I was too tired to even think on it any longer. Instead, I pulled Mr. Seawell's latest missive from the bodice of my gown and climbed into bed, intending to read the letter.

I found it odd that the sight of the handwriting alone should raise my pulse. The neat, confident hand had become the only link I had left to the one man I undeniably still loved. And Mr. Seawell was going to tell me now if the brave soldier who had saved his life was indeed my Thomas.

This thought alone was crushing. There was a part of me that didn't really want to know. Logic declared that the young Scottish soldier had to have been Thomas; it was his timepiece that Mr. Seawell had sent to me. But the facts were all wrong. And why the devil would he run to the army when he could have spent eternity with me? With trembling hands, and a heart that I feared might give out, I broke the bloodred seal and read Mr. Seawell's latest letter.

*My dearest Miss Stevenson,*

*Let me first tell you how your letters brighten my day and my unbearable loneliness. You are an angel, my dear, my angel, and yet you are not an angel without some demons of your own, I find. Allow me to be the one to comfort you, and to tell you that you did nothing wrong where Mr. Thomas Crichton was concerned. You had the promise of a man; you believed he loved you and you gave*

*him your heart in return. I've seen many a woman fall for a good*
*deal less than that. But now the child you carry takes on the*
*greater importance. Your latest letter revealed the pain and*
*torment you suffer at learning of your family's plans to give the*
*child over to the foundling hospital. After years of love and*
*nurturing, you saw your own family turn you away for a mere*
*slight upon their name. And now, you must consider, should you do*
*the same to one that is innocent?*

*I will be honest. I would have gladly traded my own life so that*
*my child and wife might have lived. I know of no man, no parent,*
*who would do less, and I believe, knowing what I do of you*
*already, you are too warm and kind a person to deprive your child*
*his proper place in this world. I now pray every night for your safe*
*delivery and the health of your child. And when it comes—this*
*child that bears the name of Crichton—keep the child. Love the*
*child. And should you wish it, Alexander Seawell will stand by*
*you. It would be an honor, for this war, and this cruel world, has*
*made too many orphans already . . .*

Mr. Seawell, due to his past experiences, had a reverence for
life that bordered on the sacred, and it was hard for me to think
of Mr. Alexander Seawell without calling to mind Mr. William
Campbell. Although their stories were quite different, there was
a similar chord, a familiar echo, and it puzzled me all the more.
The light-keeper was still a mystery to me, and we seldom
talked of his past at all. But could Mr. Campbell be trying to
reach me, delivering me his thoughts and message through this
innocuous and enigmatic persona? If indeed he was the letter-
writer, it honored me that he would go to such lengths, and at
the same time it angered me. Why go to such lengths?

But it was apparent that whoever Mr. Seawell really was, his
hard-won energies were now focused on the welfare of my unborn child—a life he had convinced me he would fight to preserve.

The last paragraph of the letter was devoted to describing

the physical features of James Crichton, just as I had asked. Here my hands shook so terribly that I had trouble deciphering the words. But to my utter astonishment, and joy, the man who saved Mr. Seawell's life was not Thomas. Whereas his James Crichton had been of a tall and slender build with dark, wavy hair and crystal blue eyes, my Thomas was of a medium build and fair, like a blue-eyed Apollo, complete with golden curls. Thomas was a fine, handsome man indeed . . . and, according to Mr. Seawell, he was not the man who had died.

It was this revelation that pushed all other quandaries aside as I set the letter on the bedside table. I lay back, resting my head on the pillows and vowing to learn more about this Mr. Seawell in order to determine if he was indeed Mr. Campbell. There were so many puzzling mysteries here; mysteries seemed to abound on Cape Wrath. But at the moment, none of them mattered. Nothing mattered anymore but the joyous news that Thomas had not died saving Mr. Seawell's life. That was the selfless act of some other unfortunate soul who carried the name Crichton.

I released a deep sigh, savoring this thought as I caressed my swollen belly; for it meant that there was still hope. A glimmer, perhaps more. But it was something. And as Kate had so recently reminded me: people often make a habit of clinging to hope, even when, by all accounts, there is little left to hope for . . .

# TEN

## Willy's Prayer

❧❦❧

It didn't take long for Mr. Campbell to recover his senses from the long night in which the smugglers had first made their presence known; nor did he have to reach back very far to feel the same outrage he had felt as he witnessed his boats being used to ply their goods. That was the needle that pricked him, again and again and again. It was that thought that denied him any more than four hours of sleep. It was that thought that kept him pacing back and forth during both his watches in the light-room. In fact, the thought was so execrable to the light-keeper that it only took a mere twenty-four hours before he set off again for another rash visit to the MacKay croft. This time desperation wasn't in it. It was retribution, I believed, and I silently pitied the intrepid Highlander Hugh MacKay.

"Please, let me go with you," I begged, following Mr. Campbell out of the cottage after watching him wolf down his oat porridge, scooping it out with a military economy that could have only been for the sake of keeping him upright. I alone knew where he was off to. I could see the thought behind his eyes, and he knew it. He didn't mention a word of his intentions to Robbie. We had briefly discussed the situation and thought it best never to mention the smuggling activities of our neighbors to either Robbie or Kate. Robbie, dear man, could be trusted, but Kate (as I very well knew) could not. And she had ways (we both were in agreement here), of making her husband spill all his secrets. Again, while he readied his horse, Wallace this time, I vocalized my wishes. "I think it would be best if I went too. Not so suspicious, you know. I often frequent the MacKays. And besides, you even said so yourself, people actually *like* me."

This caused him to pause in midpull while cinching the girth of the saddle. His lips twitched into a smile, but he was fighting it, until, settling on a mildly rebuking grin, he turned to me. "Only the good Lord knows why, but they do. 'Tis one of your more endearing traits. But, lass, I don't want MacKay to like me. I want him to fear me. I want him to loathe me. By God, I want to see him sweat! And with you along that's not likely to happen—with your winsome, carefree smiles and charming light natter and such. This is not what ye might term a neighborly visit."

"Yes, I understand that, and that's exactly my point. He has a wife and two children . . . children who should grow up knowing their father. I like Hugh MacKay, in spite of the fact that he tricked me."

"Us," he corrected, and gave one last, mighty tug on the strap, securing the saddle once and for all, and then tied it off. "For Christ sake, I'm not going to kill him. But I am going to make him pay for using my boats. And you," he said, turning to face me again, "you will be a good lass and obey my wishes, and those are that ye stay here. You still need to smooth over all the feathers ye ruffled on Kate—don't look at me like that!" he chided, and then added, "I know the woman's a tempest, but I, for one, am tired of storms. Like it or not, we all have to live under the same roof." And from the look in his eyes, including the dark rings that encircled the spectacularly compelling irises, I could see just how tired he was.

"I'm well aware that I have some work to do concerning Kate. I am also well aware that the MacKays are our neighbors here, just as are the other men who colluded to row your boats out to the ship the other night. We all have to live here, William. Please, try to remember that when you exact your revenge on Mr. MacKay." And with a fervent look in my eyes, I let him go on his errand—alone—obeying his wishes for once. Not necessarily because I wanted to, but simply because I was too big and cumbersome to follow on my own.

After watching Mr. Campbell ride off, I was left to find some shred of decency on which to repair the fractured relationship between my former companion and myself. Truthfully, there was little left to even work with there, things had grown so disagreeable between us. And since my return from my wee holiday, and after our bout of heated words to each other, she took to ignoring me. This was all well and good, for I didn't feel much like talking to her myself.

I walked back inside and silently took up the chore of scrubbing the breakfast pots beside her. Noticing me standing there, she dunked a bowl into the tub of hot water, creating an unsightly splash. She pulled it out, letting the water drip all over the floor, sprinkled a little sand in it and scrubbed the bloody thing so hard I thought she might reduce it to rubble. I picked up a bowl of my own and did the same thing.

Robbie, clean-shaven and freshly scrubbed, emerged from his room. He then noted our silent engagement in the kitchen. Robbie was a sagacious creature and knew how and when to pick his battles. This was one he wanted no part of.

"Ladies," he uttered, purely for the sake of civility, and made a dash for the door with eyes peeled to that lone bastion of male security: the light-tower. Kate watched him go with a regretful look in her eye, making me believe that she didn't relish the thought of being left alone with me either. A quick look in my direction, and she dispelled all illusions of containing a humane emotion, and dunked her bowl again, with the obvious intent of drowning it.

"You could go with him, and I'll finish here," I offered sincerely.

Her eyes, a disarming liquid brown, grew wide as her fine brows arched with suspicion. It was hard to believe such anger and spite could live behind something appearing so lovely and docile. "Even if I wanted to, I wouldn't be welcome just now."

"So," I said, drying my hands on my hopelessly stained cotton apron. I turned fully to face her. "You have been instructed to find some way to live with me as well. My, how men grow skittish when their domestic tranquillity is threatened. Very well, let's have it out, shall we? Do you wish to start or shall I?"

She turned to face me, drying her hands on her own, much cleaner apron, ignoring the pile of dishes on the board behind her. She narrowed her eyes warily; her lips, flushed as red as her cheeks, were pursed in a look of extreme consternation, and then, rather calmly, she tilted her white-capped head in my direction.

"Very well, I'll start," I began, and set out on a course that I prayed would make her understand. "Let me start by commending you on your loyalty to my family."

This elicited a skeptical quirk of an eyebrow.

"No," I said, "I'm not making sport. I'm being sincere. You have a moral sense of obligation from which you never waver. You know your duty; you know your mind, Kate, and once you set a course, nothing can throw you from it. I find that very commendable. I, however, have never been anything near to such discipline of principles. You have chosen for your friend, Kate MacKinnon, someone who has ventured way beyond the reach of moral soundness, family obligation and perhaps even common good sense by now, and for that deception and the pain it must have caused you, I am truly sorry. That being said, I am not sorry or ashamed I carry this child. And no amount of hardships I suffer for it will cause me to marry a man I do not love. I made a choice eight months ago, and it was a choice I made consciously and willingly, in spite of what you may believe. Whatever happens in the end, I want you to know this above all else: I did truly love Thomas Crichton, and I truly believe that he loved me in return. Let me hold on to that, Kate. Please. Do not take that from me. If the child should live and I should not, then I will entrust it into the care and discretion of a person of my choosing—not my family. They have suffered enough. Yet if both the child and I do survive, you may consider telling my parents otherwise, if you wish. Perhaps that would be a kinder service to them. Because I intend to keep this child."

Her face blanched. All the color, all the high spirits she possessed in such great quantity, left her as she stood listening to me. Her mouth moved but no sound came out. She swallowed, her lower lip quivered and she began in a voice that croaked as if the wind had been choked out of it. "You . . . you would really give up everything . . . everything for the bastard you carry?"

"That is, I believe, what I have been trying to tell you."

"You would suffer poverty, hunger, banishment from your family and all good society for it?"

"If I had to, yes," I responded levelly. "And it's not an *it*, Kate. We're speaking of a child here; my child."

Her hand came over her mouth. She looked at me as if hearing for the first time what I had been trying to tell her for months. "Dear God," she uttered when she could. "You really will do it, won't ye? Dear God . . . Oh God! Sara?" And then, unable to bear the naked truth of it any longer, or the sight of me, she ran from the room, sobbing uncontrollably.

Kate MacKinnon now understood what it felt like to suffer defeat.

Her mission to save my wretched life and character was over, as was her dream of being returned to the bosom of my family a hero. And as I heard the door to her room shut soundly behind her bitterly weeping form, I felt a twinge of sorrow, knowing that I had been the one responsible for crushing her dreams.

. . .

I was never so anxious for the return of the light-keeper than I was that day. I kept watch for him while going about all my duties as well as Kate's since she remained sequestered in her room, my eye seldom leaving the road. Robbie had tried a few times to console his wife after hearing of what transpired in the kitchen. Yet he, like me, returned to the parlor every time with a look of utter astonishment. This induced me to be extra kind to him, taking special care to fix him a good hot meal and seeing that he had plenty to drink. And after he was consoled as well as he could be, I encouraged him to get some rest. And thus with Kate and Robbie sealed in their own quarters to ease each other's sorrows, I went outside to wait for William Campbell.

It was shortly after noon that the light-keeper returned. After finishing all my chores I then, primarily for the sake of keeping myself occupied, began rummaging through the kitchen garden, a little plot of land nestled between the high walls of the courtyard and the barn, and not far from the cottage refuse pile. It had been a hastily planted garden, I surmised, noting the random budding scion of last year's crops amidst a goodly tangle of weeds. But then, two men had lived here, I recalled, and I doubted very much either one of them had a green thumb. The soil would need to be turned, of course, and replanted, but until that could be done I busied myself pulling weeds. I was absorbed in the task; I found it rather cathartic after such a tumultuous morning. And as I turned my mind to the budding green tangle, I heard the sound of a horse approaching. I grabbed a handful of the invasive green nuisance and gave a mighty tug.

"That," spoke the familiar voice in its rich, melodious brogue, "'tis nay weed, my dear lass."

I looked up. I scanned the strong face, clean-shaven that morning. The original bruising around the eye remained, but there were no others that I could immediately detect. I tilted my head to look at him, still holding the clump of broad-leafed stems in my hand, and said, "Excuse me?"

"That . . . in your hand," he pointed, "'tis nay weed but *Rheum rhaponticum*—or rhubarb, if ye like." He smiled. "But it's long from being ready."

"Oh yes, of course. I know that," I lied. "I found it just lying here." And I gave him an earnest stare, noting with some dismay that dirt still clung to the roots. "I think . . . I believe the hares were at it."

His eyes, glowing with mirth, held to mine; yet he was making a great effort to frown. "Hares? Is that so? Tell me, Miss Stevenson," he said, swinging down from the saddle and pausing to secure the reins to the little post that guarded the entrance, "do ye happen to have a knack for the gardening?"

"I'm unclear exactly what a 'knack' might be, sir, but I have read many books on the subject." This, to a man who gleaned a good deal of knowledge from books himself, was not an entirely flippant statement. He gave a nod of approval and gently took the fleshy stems from my hand, inspecting them with half an eye.

"These are uncommon hares what did this," he stated, turning the plant in his hand while palpating the stringy roots with the other. And then he tilted his head at me, awaiting an answer.

"Yes," I uttered in agreement, feeling the heat rise to my cheeks. "I know for a fact they were uncommon. I also know for a fact that they will know better next time than to go after this particular plant."

"Uncommon hares what learn?" he quipped, and then a slow smile lit his face. "I would almost welcome such enchanting creatures into my garden." His eyes came up, locking on to mine. And he added very softly, "For I've a great deal of respect for besoms that can mend their ways."

"I never said the hares would mend their ways, sir," I corrected with the same soft tone. "I was simply stating that they have a capacity to learn."

This elicited a broad, truly heartfelt smile. It was a remarkable look for him, lighting his entire being and causing his mesmerizing gaze to appear purely incandescent. "I find that learning's a start," he said, holding to my eyes with a heated gaze while tossing the wasted leaves onto the rubbish pile.

"Learning is all well and good," I agreed, and looked away; for his gaze was too bright and heady by far. And then, consciously changing the direction of the conversation for my own sake, I asked, "And maybe you could tell me, Mr. Campbell, did Hugh MacKay learn of your displeasure at watching him degrade your boats with his illicit cargo?" Feeling bolder, my eyes traveled back to his, curious to see how he would react to this line of questioning. "Does Mr. MacKay, in fact, still live at all?"

"Och aye, he lives," the man breathed evenly. "But he lives a might meaner now, knowing I know what I know. He was also not overly joyous when he discovered you'd gone missing either." Here he delivered a particularly pointed look. "I leave it to your own overly active imagination as to just how that conversation went, but I will tell you plainly, he got an earful. For what man in his right mind would let a young woman—a very pregnant young woman forbye—sneak away in the dark of night to walk across the parve alone? I believe he has a better understanding of the matter now, and he now wears a black eye to prove he's learned his lesson." Here he was quick to add a nod at the irony of such folly. "It had him fair flummoxed that ye would do so, Sara. And MacKay, for his part, was very contrite on the subject. So contrite, I might add, that he was inclined to strike a wee bargain with me."

"A bargain? What kind of bargain, sir?"

At this a mischievous grin split his face and he turned back to the horse. After a moment spent rummaging through the saddlebags he returned with two dark green bottles in hand and a knowing look in his eye—the same variety of green bottles, I noted, that Mary MacKay had given to me on that first momentous visit.

"What's this?" I questioned, eyeing both him and his bargain curiously.

"Retribution," he replied with a slightly wicked grin. "This,

Miss Stevenson, is payment for the flagrant debauchery of my boats."

"Payment? He's paying you for . . . debauching your boats? You're not actually going to let him continue to . . . debauch them, are you?" This was a curious turn of events indeed, and I stared with wonder at the light-keeper.

"I'm not exactly going to say what's to happen to the boats beached at Kervaig Bay, for they're out of sight from the tower, aye? All I'm saying, dear lass, is that from now on our table will be provided with pure, fine quality, unadulterated French wine, and I will have a rescue team at my beck and call whenever I have need of them. Whatever else may occur in that bay is, from this day forward, between Hugh MacKay and his maker."

"Even if your boats happen to fall into the hands of those that might . . . misuse them?"

He shrugged at the notion rather nonchalantly.

This news—this change of heart—startled me so greatly that I cried aloud, "William! William Campbell, that's wonderful news! I'm so proud of you!" And before I could stop myself, being swept up in his triumph, I found my whalelïke body racing to his arms. Surprisingly, and without hesitation, he opened them to me.

It was an awkward embrace, for I had never held a man with my belly protruding so greatly before, and at once I was very conscious of what I had done. Mr. Campbell, for his part, was quick to overlook the impediment, yet not so quick to release me. And that, in spite of the fact I found his embrace warm and comforting—a bit wonderful even—was awkward indeed. William, finally sensing the unsettling calm, gently released me and I quickly stepped away, putting a good four feet between us. He made a show of studying the nascent garden, his hands thrust deep into his pockets, head bent forward while a tuft of his chestnut hair obscured his eyes. I too studied the paltry plot of earth, while covertly studying him. And to break the awk-wardness that had grown up between us, I softly offered, "It ap-

DARCI HANNAH

pears you have upheld your end of the bargain nobly and have done more than I could have ever asked to keep peace on the Cape, and for that I truly am proud of you. But I should tell you, I tried my best to uphold my end of the bargain as well today." I glanced to see if he was following. The mixture of cautious curiosity playing about his features told me that he was. "I'm sorry to inform you, sir, but my unpleasant task didn't turn out nearly as successful as your own."

. . .

In the days that followed Mr. Campbell's triumph and my less than notable cease-fire with Kate, there was a gentle sort of calm that settled over the lighthouse and all her inhabitants. Mr. Campbell exhibited the greatest change, in that I believed for once he could actually sleep. After our little conversation in the garden he went inside, hung up his coat and asked if I would mind waking him for supper. And then, without another word, he retreated down the hallway to his bedroom and quietly shut the door. That he needed me to wake him suggested that he was actually contemplating giving in to what his body craved most, and I was glad of it.

Kate displayed the oddest behavior change amongst us; whereas she had always shown a fiery disposition, verbose and bossy even, she now was a mere shell of the woman she once was, going about her chores quietly, her demeanor humble and reticent. Whenever I made light of a subject, attempted to engage her in small talk or offered a direct challenge merely for sake of a direct challenge, she backed right down without even the courtesy of a questioning look. And when she did happen to look at me it was with large, maudlin brown eyes, very like the look of a dog that lost its master. Kate, from all appearances, was now the one having difficulty sleeping. Robbie, with a fortitude belonging only to those men with a deep and abiding love for their spouse, was patient and gentle with her, yet he was just as puzzled by this change in her demeanor as the rest of us. And truly, it broke my heart; for Kate now walked the cottage like a woman abandoned by her most cherished dream. Only when the MacKay family came for an unexpected visit did she show any signs of her true self again.

This unexpected visit was, of course, under the guise of learning. Mary explained as she alighted from the wagon, a squirming Maggie in her arms, how wee Hughie had lamented the fact that I had gone without saying so much as a good-bye or leaving further instructions on his letters, and they felt it their neighborly duty to check up on us to see if aught was amiss. I took the squealing toddler in my arms and gave her a welcoming hug before setting her free, assuring Mary that all was well. Maggie, I knew, was indeed happy to see me, for she was too young to have learned the fine art of schooling her emotions. Wee Hughie, on the other hand, sat glowering at me from the safety of the wagon. It was proof enough that I had hurt him, and for that I was deeply sorry. I was sorry too for leaving the hospitable family with the capricious temerity I had. But suggesting that wee Hughie missed me solely for the pleasure I took in tormenting him with informal schooling was a bold-face lie. And it was a lie I gladly accepted. I walked over to where he sat on the wagon and took his reluctant hand in my own. I then forced him to look at me, and when he begrudgingly did, I vowed sincerely to make it up to him. To start with, I implored him to take the first slice of the apple tart Kate and I had worked hard on all morning.

"I'm so glad you've come, Hughie, and you're just in time, for I've need of a brave lad to have the first slice of what Kate and I are proud to call an apple tart."

"What would I want tae do that for, Miss Sara?" he challenged, blue eyes flashing daggers at me. "I ken verra weel ye have no art in the kitchen."

I could see his mother bristle behind me, and I passed her a look that begged her to let the boy speak his mind.

"I think," I began again earnestly, "that you will find, just as in learning to read, that if one continues to put forth the effort, one's skills will greatly improve. I'm not going to claim my tart will be the best you've ever tasted, because that would indeed be a lie. But I can honestly tell you that your stomach will not rebel from the effort of eating it. And I would like very much if you would. I'm sorry for leaving your family in the rash manner I did, but I had my reasons, just as you have every right to be angry with me now. Yet just because I left that night doesn't mean I'm giving up on teaching you your letters. I have faith in you, Hughie, and I'll ask you to put a little of the same in me. Taste our tart, and see for yourself how gifted a teacher your mother is."

The ice was broken and the boy accepted my apology with a shrug of his shoulders and a half-hearted frown; so too did his mother, though responding with her signature winsome smile. Hugh, with a purplish bruise marring the beauty of his right eye, had a purpose of his own for such a visit, and learning to read wasn't it. Alighting from his wagon after his wife and children, he came over to Mr. Campbell and, looking levelly into the man's eye, said, "I've got a wee something for ye, Campbell," and went to rummage in the back of his wagon.

It was a cask, and not just any cask, but one bearing a cachet of the fleur-de-lis. "This washed up in the bay a few nights ago. I thought ye, being the all-knowing eye of these parts, would be interested in it. God only kens what it contains. I'm only doing my duty here, ye understand. But I have it on good authority that more are likely to wash ashore before the spring storms blow in."

"A cask, ye say?" inquired Mr. Campbell with a good show of curiosity. He then grazed a finger lazily over the imperial seal, and slowly nodded his head. "Well, ye did the right thing here, MacKay. And I thank ye for respecting lighthouse authority. I shall see that this gets into the right hands." And as he spoke these words his magnificent gaze settled on me.

"Aye, see that it does. Mayhap it will even ease someone's anxieties a wee bit. Ye ken, cozen the troubled mind of one who might be expecting . . . something small and wriggly tae appear?" And Hugh MacKay, with one twinkling eye (the other too bloodshot and purple to twinkle properly), gave me a wink. Mary knew very well what her husband was about.

"Aye, I'm certain sure it will. In fact, this cask will improve matters greatly for the ones who are destined to receive it. And that brings to mind a fine-looking tart the ladies made. If you'll bring the cask to the storage room for the now, MacKay, I'll go fetch a pitcher and we can celebrate this find of yours with a wee drink while we sample the latest culinary achievement to come from the lighthouse kitchen. I'm not brave enough to brag about the quality of the vittles that grace our table, although I find them perfectly suitable myself, but I do believe I now have something quite proper to wet your lips with."

And with that said, the two men, along with their suspicious cask, disappeared into the lighthouse while the rest of us made for the table.

The apple tart was surprisingly good, the crust flaky and golden to perfection, and the drink the adults used to wash it down with was piquant and heady. Wee Hughie even dove into the dish for another helping and begrudgingly told me that it would do. And thus the day unfolded with an easy companionship that went beyond even my wildest dreams.

· · ·

Another dream of mine, one not yet realized but ever present, thrusting its tenterhooks into the forefront of my mind with greater urgency every passing day, was my dream of finding Thomas before the birth of our child. My only tool for this purpose, besides the hours spent patiently watching the ever-increasing shipping that took place out in the lanes, just beyond the reach of the lighthouse, was my correspondence with the antiquarian, Mr. Seawell. I don't really know why I thought this was a connection, for he had told me in each letter that the man who saved his life was not the same man that I loved. But for some inexplicable reason—call it the chronometer, that time-piece with a steadily beating heart of its own—he was my link, and oddly enough, he was also my channel for understanding the intricate mind of Mr. Campbell; for the coincidences between them were too great to ignore.

With a dogged determination, I stepped up my letter-writing to the man, consciously probing, strategically questioning—purposely driving to unlock the very soul of the antiquarian so that I might know him intimately. And as I delved into the inkwell, scribbling away with a haste brought about by my absurdly burgeoning figure, my gallant champion, Mr. Alexander Seawell of Oxford, illusorily transformed into the winsomely dark lighthouse recluse, Mr. William Campbell of Cape Wrath—and the man, through this odd circumvention, was slowly being drawn out of his tower.

The connection that drove me to a better understanding of Mr. Campbell, besides Mr. Seawell's letters, became his odd little garden, that paltry patch of earth on the rocky outcrop that was our home. Yet in spite of the harsh weather and the poor soil, it appeared as fertile as myself; and I found that I liked visiting the little plot every day in order to see what the sun had slowly coaxed from the stone-cold darkness. Mr. Campbell made a habit of visiting the garden too, and he would tell me about each plant, what it was commonly used for and of others he intended to plant once the *Pole Star* arrived with his seeds. Besides collecting dead creatures in glass bottles and drawing naked, dead ladies, the garden appeared also to be one of his hobbies—one of his more benign hobbies. Along with providing the kitchen with fresh greens and vegetables sorely lacking from the "winter lighthouse diet," it was his scientific outlet, his place of observation and study, and many of the herbs and plants he cultivated had uses for healing the body.

His face visibly relaxed whenever he entered the little sanctuary, and as I watched him kneel on the ground, gently examining one of the tender young greens, I understood that this was a place where even the most tormented of creatures found peace. Perhaps that was why I liked it too, that and the fact that William Campbell was willing to share this special place with me.

Mr. Seawell, I learned, also had a hobby: collecting antiquities. He wrote of it with the same passion as William talked of his garden. In fact, I could almost see the stranger's eyes light up as I read the words that explained his obsession in a way William Campbell could never explain his to me.

> 'Tis odd for a man who has shut himself away from all human contact to be so moved by an inanimate object that it nearly brings him to tears. I don't expect you, my dear young lady, to understand—you who are still so young and vibrant—but that was the way I felt about your timepiece. Holding it between my hands gave me a rare pleasure, a pleasure very like the sight of your round, womanly script, and I'm sorry to think that I ever harbored thoughts of not returning it to you. But I was moved to do it, and God has blessed me for the heartache it caused, for your letters are an even greater treasure to me . . .

The words the man wrote were like a balm to my wounded soul, and although I had no idea what I was playing at or to whom I was even writing—so boldly, so tenderly, so honestly— I found that I could not break the connection. A fear was driving me forward, causing me to engage this lonely man because he was my only link to Thomas Crichton, however elusive it was. My own mother even found it necessary to warn against the evils of corresponding with unsuitable males, in a venomous letter she deigned to write me in reply to the only one I had written her. And her closing was especially poignant, instructing that I was also expected to do my duty concerning a certain orphanage in Edinburgh. It was delivered in the middle of May, the day the tender came to the lighthouse jetty to drop off the next six months of supplies. Ironically, my mother's warning came just after Mr. Campbell had taken to the jetty the last letter I ever planned to write the antiquarian. He would see to it, just as he had seen to the others, assuring me that it would be in the postbox awaiting our odd little skiff to appear.

I did not go to greet the ship. Only Robbie and Mr. Campbell went down to the jetty that day to meet Captain MacDonald and his men; for the sight of me, as Kate softly suggested, so near to bursting with child, would certainly have shocked them all.

• • •

After the supplies had been logged in and properly stored away (a time-consuming, laborious task), after all the chores had been seen to and the evening meal cleaned up, I retired to my room, exhausted and sleepy, with a tiny glass of the medicinal dosing the midwife had instructed I take. It was perhaps just a talisman to ensure a safe delivery; and I wanted a safe delivery. With glass in hand I opened the door, having every intent of falling into a dreamless sleep, but the sight of a box placed atop the quilts of my bed stopped me. And when I saw the little note attached, a note written in the now familiar hand, I began to shake uncontrollably. I glanced again at the box, quaffed the heady, pungent liquid in one gulp and set the empty glass on the bedside table. With growing trepidation I perched myself next to the curious delivery and picked up the little note. To my utter astonishment and delight it was not addressed to Sara Crichton, as Mr. Seawell had always addressed his letters to me, but to another appellation of that seemingly whimsical race, an appellation that brought a smile to my face.

*Dear Canny Wee Hare,*
  *Enclosed you will find a very thorough book on horticulture, along with a new delivery of seeds. Might I beg of ye to read up on*

*these particular specimens and how best to care for them? And
maybe ye'll agree to sit upon a wee stool in the garden whilst
instructing me on how they should lay? I find I am not above
taking advice from a knowledgeable wee creature, especially one
that happens to add a rare beauty to a place that has been bereft for
so long. The roses, a hearty, thorny, tenacious variety, are for your
pleasure alone. Again, I would be ever grateful if you might advise
as to where I should put them. I give you free rein, with but a few
necessary exceptions.*

*William Campbell*

With proof in hand that there could be no mistaking the distinctive script that told me William Campbell was indeed one
and the same as Alexander Seawell, I smiled triumphantly, yet at
the same time confusion reigned. There ensued a contrary flood
of emotions so befuddling to my current state of mind—a mind
further addled by advanced pregnancy, the liquid elixir and the
gift—that I was at a complete loss as to what course of action I
should take. Did William know Thomas? How did he get the
watch? Why hide behind the mask of a stranger to confuse me?
What the devil was he thinking? How dare he do such a thing to
me! How dare he toy with my emotions! Then I saw the infant
rosebushes, woody stemmed and covered with thorns, and the
way they were tenderly swaddled in brown burlap and thoughtfully placed beside a leather-bound volume inscribed *Treatise on
the Complete Kitchen Garden Including Identification and Care of
Edible Plants and Herbs,* moved me.

"Damn him," I uttered in a voice wrought with total helplessness. "Damn him!" And this time I knew very well which him I
meant. I also knew the course of action I would take for the time
being. And so, churning and quaking from more than the powerful elixir, I climbed into bed, turned up the lamp, picked up the
cumbrous volume and vowed to read every last word of it before
the night was through!

In truth, I didn't get more than a few pages turned.

. . .

It was sometime in the dark of night when I heard the latch to my door rattle and softly click, as if in a far-off dream. The sound of booted feet came light on the floorboards, and at once the room was suffused with the scent of the sea and the cold night air, with just a dark hint of coffee and a sharp tang of expensive wine. With lids still too heavy to open, I lay in a dream-like state on the bed, fully asleep yet partially awake. In my mind the entity had not a face but a presence, a solid masculine presence, and I could feel him standing beside the bed. The book, still between my two hands, was gently removed, and my arms, limp with sleep, were placed with great care at my sides. The light coverlet was drawn to my chin, and the lamp glowing brightly on the bedside table was extinguished.

Quiet settled over the dark room, yet I could still feel his presence beside me. And then, gently, a light pressure came over my swollen belly. Warmth radiated through my taut skin, and the fecund mound began to tingle pleasantly. My sleeping body knew not to be afraid of this presence, for he was now, with a telltale pop of a knee and the soft groan of the floorboard, kneeling beside me. I imagined the head bent in supplication, when the voice, soft and pleading, began speaking in an Edinburgh burr. The first words uttered echoed through me, and I could feel them surround my unborn child like a downy blanket, bringing a sense of warmth and peace that I had not felt for many a month; for the voice had invoked the name of Thomas Crichton.

My lips, reflexively, pulled into a smile at the sound of it, and the face of the man floated before me in my sleep-drunk mind. Then, in a voice barely discernible, came the name again, and with half a mind I listened to it speak.

"Thomas Crichton, I beg of ye, lad," came the utterance in a fervent tone, "with the help of your maker, bring this child safely into this world. The Lord knows I am an unworthy soul for the task. And I have little enough to recommend me for such a prayer, but this: see this child safely to its mother's arms and William Campbell will vow to protect them with his life for as long as he shall live."

I didn't know why the words were spoken, for what was conscious in me was entirely focused on the image of Thomas that swam before my mind's eye. But then the gentle pressure on my belly slowly came away, and with it the image of my love. The warm, tingling sensation had also subsided. And that presence of male, so comforting in the dark night, was gone as well, leaving the room silent once more.

·  ·  ·

I had been sitting on a chair, brought specially to the garden by the man I was now infuriating with my indecision, when the men arrived. We hadn't heard them approach, being too busy squabbling about the placement of the peas, a vegetable I doubted would do very well on the Cape, and one I wasn't particularly fond of in the first place.

"You're going to have to dig those up, I'm afraid," I said, disapproval thick in my voice. "I thought *that* was where we decided the cabbage should go, not the peas. The peas would look best over there."

"Did ye, by chance, even bother to read the book?" he questioned, looking at me from his ignoble stance on hands and knees in the dirt, doubt dripping from his piercing aqua eyes.

I lifted my chin. "Of course I did, and I should tell you, the man who wrote it was rather vague on the proper placement of such things as legumes. The cabbage he was quite fond of and stated that it will come up in big, round, happy faces, totally outshining all in its path. They should be in nice, neat rows all down here," I indicated with the edge of my hand, "and the leeks and onions beside them. The turnips and carrots can go over there, and your precious herbs along that wall. There are better things to take up dirt than peas, William."

He narrowed his eyes skeptically at this. "Ye dinna like peas, do ye?" he accused thickly, rising slowly from the dirt he had worked so hard to prepare. He brushed off his hands and squared to me with that annoying disapproval clear on his face. "You are forbidding me to plant the wee peas merely on account that you do not want to eat them! Am I correct?" He didn't wait for an answer. "Because that is very selfish of ye, Sara Stevenson. If ye don't want to eat peas, I will not force ye to do so, but for heaven's sake, don't deprive the rest of us of the pleasure!"

I never was one to take accusations kindly, and unfortunately for him, pregnancy did nothing to temper this default in my nature. "Are you accusing me of being selfish, William Campbell? Are we to go down that inglorious road again, sir?"

"Aye, if we must," he challenged bravely. He was not a man who lacked courage, I knew. "And I believe I'm only telling it like I see it."

"Well then, let me tell you a little something, sir; you are seeing it all wrong! The reason, if you must know, why I suggested taking out the peas and throwing them away in the first place is simply because they will attract hares. Everyone knows that, Mr. Campbell . . . everyone with the exception, perhaps, of renegade lighthouse keepers with a penchant for peas. Hares love peas! Plant the peas and all else will be eaten by those seemingly innocent, though catastrophically damaging, rodents! One tenacious hare in your garden can cause real damage, sir!"

"Aye, and don't I know it well!" he replied, glaring at me with perhaps a deeper pleasure. And then, with a smile bordering on malicious, he recovered with, "Well, and hares are good eating too. Did ye bother to think on that? It might be a sound practice to plant the peas, aye? In fact, I shall plant them all over here, and over there," he said, indicating the same large portion of the garden as I had. "I shall lure the canny wee besoms into my pea-garden, and then, whilst they're nibbling away on the sweet wee fruits, growing ever fatter with the effort, I'll grab 'em up, snagging 'em from behind, and wring their wee flea-bitten necks!"

It was in the middle of this rather juvenile tirade of Mr. Campbell's, where he demonstrated with great pleasure his prowess at snuffing the life out of innocent creatures (and I had every reason to believe that he would relish doing so), that the newcomers made their presence known. We both turned to look at the two men, their ominous dark coats fluttering in the steady wind as they rode two shaggy black mounts, horses bred for rugged duty. They were armed, these men, and made no effort to hide that fact and, I noted with some alarm, they were heading directly for us. With a feeble lack of heart, I turned back to the light-keeper and rescinded softly, "Very well, Mr. Campbell, have it your way. Plant the peas wherever you like."

Normally, I believe the man would have gloated over this victory, no matter how small it was, but there was no time to do so. One of the men, a baldheaded, pugnacious creature, had pulled just beyond the garden entrance and called out to William in a ragged voice that suggested he had smoked more than his fair share of cheroots. "Are ye the keeper here?"

"I am," came William's cautious reply.

"We're from the Excise, sir, and we'd like to have a word with ye. It seems that there's been a ship sighted on several occasions making for this coast."

"I hate to be the one to inform ye, sir, but many a ship makes for this coast. 'Tis why the good gentlemen of the Northern Lighthouse Board thought to put this lighthouse here."

The man, narrowing his dark, bulgy eyes with displeasure at this remark, added, "This is a French ship, sir, and is well known tae dabble in illegal trade!"

"Aye, don't all the French?"

The man failed to smile at this flippant remark.

"Very well, you're in search of a Frenchman, and you believe this ship of yours has business here?" At this Mr. Campbell beheld the man with faint amusement lifting the corners of his mouth.

"And what do ye find so amusing about that, sir? Do ye think it impossible that men smuggle goods here?"

"Not impossible, improbable," he corrected flatly. "Had ye ever taken a good look at this coast—from the sea, where a ship is likely to approach—then ye would understand why such activity as ye speak of sounds absurd. These waters are inherently dangerous. This coast is too great a hazard to attempt such a thing. One wrong move or the wind not quite right and a ship would be smashed to pieces against the rocks. Why risk it? What kind of captain, Frenchman or other, would dare such a venture?"

"You believe our questioning tae be unsound?"

"No sir. My place is not to question the ways of the law. I'm only here to illuminate the coast, which is what we do."

"And ye keep a precise logbook of every ship that passes."

"Aye," Mr. Campbell replied levelly, before adding pointedly, "and of every vessel that was unlucky enough to wreck among these rocks."

"That is exactly why we're here. We would like to see this logbook of yours, Mr. . . . ?"

"Campbell, Willy Campbell," he said, making no effort to extend a hand to either man.

"Well then, Mr. Willy Campbell," said the leader, repeating his name while sizing up the light-keeper with a lingering glare, "and whilst I take a look at this logbook of yours, Mr. Liddle is gonna have himself a wee keek around. I hope that willna pose a problem for ye?"

"Only if Mr. Liddle manages to disturb the great lens; otherwise, sir, I don't see that there'll be any problem at all." A disarming smile appeared on his lips and then he turned to me. Although he was trying hard to cover it, there was trouble in those pale eyes of his, evident perhaps only to one who had made a habit out of studying them. I knew exactly what he was thinking, for I was thinking the same. And with a gentle nod he turned to the storeroom and called out for Robbie MacKinnon. Within moments the ginger head appeared and Mr. Campbell beckoned him over.

"Robbie, these are men come from the Excise. They've asked to have a look around."

"Certainly," Robbie responded with his sanguine grin. "And what might the gentlemen be looking for, Mr. Campbell?"

"Smugglers, Robbie lad, the men are looking for smugglers." Both light-keepers grinned at this wild notion; the Excise men failed to find any humor in it. "Take Mr. Liddle here and show him around, if ye please, Rob."

"Aye, sir. This way, if ye please, Mr. Liddle." And Robbie led the surly Excise man to the storehouses.

Mr. Campbell then turned to me. "Please excuse us, my dear, and thank you for your patient direction in the garden." There was a teasing smile attached to this remark, but it was soon gone. "I shall be only a moment. You may wish to wait in the cottage until we are finished." This he phrased as if it were a suggestion, although I knew enough to understand it wasn't a suggestion at all. "Perhaps you might tell Kate to put on a pot of tea for these gentlemen." He knew what I would do if left to my own devices. I fought hard not to glance at the stable. His gaze was willing mine away from even thinking of it. I understood although I did not agree. Nonetheless, I performed an awkward curtsey to the men and made my way to the cottage, just as William was beckoning for the baldheaded tax collector to follow.

Kate could sense my nervousness and I hastily told her of the men who were now searching the lighthouse.

Swinging the kettle over the fire, she looked at me. "Well, why so nervous about that? They are only doing their job, same as us."

"Yes, but we don't look nearly as intimidating when we do it."

Kate arched one of her fine brows at this. "You used to be frightened of Mr. Campbell. Are you telling me now that you no longer fear the man?"

"I was never afraid of him!" I lied blithely. "Perhaps I just understand him a little better now." She nodded slowly and continued to busy herself. I looked out the window. Mr. Campbell and the Excise man were coming to the cottage with the logbook.

As the two sat at the table discussing ships and possible connections to the one the government man was looking for, William, quite knowledgeably and wily I might add, purposely led the man astray, confusing him with other ships—possible links—while never acknowledging that he knew very well what ship the man was talking about. When I saw Robbie returning with Mr. Liddle, my heart stopped for a second. For in the man's hands was a familiar small cask with the damnable stamp imprinted with the fleur-de-lis.

Coming through the door Mr. Liddle set the barrel down with a bang on the table. "Tell me, Mr. Campbell, are these part o' your standard provisions at the lighthouse or are ye hiding something?"

Mr. Campbell froze. His eyes, glowing beneath the dark brows, narrowed dangerously. He was backed into a corner and he knew it. The possession of the cask alone was incriminating enough to cause problems. But Mr. Campbell had enough problems, and I would buy his way out of this one.

"Sir," I chimed up in my most engaging parlor voice, breaking the momentary silence. "Why, goodness me, that would be mine!" And I gave the man what I hoped would be as disarming a smile as any I had in my arsenal. "Of course that's not part of our standard provisions. Why, bless you, sir, but the Board would never be so frivolous!"

Both men, as well as my fellow keepers, stared incredulously at me. William, however, was catching on. The man Liddle gawked at my very pregnant form, so did the other man, and he asked, "And why would ye have such a thing as a cask o' French wine in your possession, young lady?"

"Why, my father sent it to me, of course, knowing how important it is for a woman in my condition to have such a thing at hand, while also knowing what dreadful gut-rot the local drink can be!"

"And just who might ye be, Miss . . . ?" the man asked coldly, derision dripping from his voice as he stared unnervingly at my protruding belly. He never bothered to look me in the eye.

I stuck out my chin and declared, "My name is Sara Steve—"

But here the light-keeper broke in, adding, after theatrically clearing his throat, the name, "Campbell. Mrs. Sara Stevenson-Campbell, sir," he said in a firm tone, while holding the Excise man in a cold, steely gaze. He did not chance a look in my direction, nor did he look at either Kate or Robbie. He merely continued his deception. "She's my wife and the daughter of the man who built this lighthouse. *That*," he said, pointing to the cask, "came from his private stores in Edinburgh, bought when the ban on French imports was lifted. It was his gift when he heard the blessed news that he was soon to be a grandfather. Mr. Robert Stevenson, you must understand, has a real soft spot where his youngest child is concerned."

The Excise men regarded what he was saying. William was silently warning them to let the matter drop. And with a show of reluctance they finally backed down, acknowledging that the lighthouse had won this round. But they relayed through suspicious eyes that the Excise would be watching us closely.

When they had left, William turned to Robbie. "So, you let the man Liddle into the stables."

"He was insistent, sir!" Robbie defended vehemently. "I had no idea it was wrong. I had no idea *that* was in the tack room! And I had no idea ye and Miss Sara were married!"

William stood up from the table and, looking at his employee with a hint of sorrow in his clear eyes, said wanly, "I have asked a lot of ye already, Robbie man, and I'm likely to ask still more of ye yet, but I will not encumber you or your wife in matters that might lead to trouble, and because so, I ask that you bear with me awhile longer. As for *Miss* Stevenson . . ." he added, turning his electric gaze on me. I could tell in an instant that his mood had changed. Gone was the capable lighthouse keeper who stood cool under pressure. Gone was the pleasant and charming

gentleman of the garden. In his place, the brooding dark creature reappeared. His gaze bore into mine with frightening intensity as he quietly said, "Miss Stevenson is not my wife. But
I'm afraid she has entangled herself too deeply in matters already. I believe the lass has gone so far beyond her understanding that even she will not be able to disengage from events
already set in motion. But that, as she must know, was always
the danger of pursuing such an unchancy course." And without
another word he turned from me and left the cottage.

I watched in stunned amazement as he walked through the
courtyard, head bent in silent torment while his long black cape
fluttered on the wind behind him. And then, without a look
back, he turned and disappeared into the black cavern of his
tower.

·  ·  ·

Mr. Campbell, for all my efforts and strong will, was still a mystery to me, as was the elusive Mr. Seawell. Things had been
going smoothly between us until the visit from the Excise men.
They had disturbed our banter in the garden, and in the garden
was where William Campbell and I came together. At first I assumed that he was merely angry because I had forced him to improve relations with our brethren on the Cape. We both agreed
that it was not our business that the men we relied on to effect a
land-based rescue also happened to engage in illicit activities.
He had even been the one to strike the bargain with MacKay and
his men resulting in the cask of claret. And, rather gallantly, he
had protected me with his name when the Excise men had found
the smuggled goods hidden in the stable. For that I was grateful. Yet I thought we were on better terms than for him to brood
so privately.

Mr. Campbell, without a doubt, was a diligent and capable
lighthouse keeper, never stepping a toe out of line, always master of his domain . . . until, perhaps, I happened along. It had
been a rough beginning for us both, neither one of us willingly

accepting our being thrust together. But we had finally breached the wide chasm that stood between us, or so I had thought. And I had been proud of him too, for the effort he had made in showing signs of humanity—for the subtle transformation that suggested he actually liked spending time in my company and the company of others. But ever since the Excise men had come and found the contraband drink, he had become withdrawn again.

I had done my best to defend the presence of the little cask, grasping at whatever I could that would sound viable, within reason. For this diversion I knew he was grateful. But he had become aloof again, tormented by those things unseen that seemed to haunt him in the night; and my baby, with every passing day, was making itself ready to be born.

I was scared.

I was desperate.

And I needed to be on good terms with Mr. Campbell, for I believed my child's life depended on it.

For days I deliberated on the encounter I knew must come. I was hoping Mr. Campbell would have stepped forward long before it came to this, coming to my room in the dead of night as was his habit, frightening me, comforting me, telling me he had actually been the one to fabricate the story of Mr. Seawell. I longed to know how he had come to possess Thomas' watch in the first place, and why he had decided to send it under the guise of a stranger. I waited for him while the child in my womb grew to the point of bursting, writhing and wriggling, wreaking havoc on my tender insides until the time was ripe for it to come into the world. And on the very last day in May I felt I could wait no longer.

The wind was picking up, a storm was coming and I knew I must encounter the one man I had left to rely on. Fortifying myself with a generous glass of the contraband claret, I made my approach, knowing very well he wasn't sleeping.

I knocked on Mr. Campbell's door. It was long after supper, and he had retired to his room directly, sitting in that den of death to await his first shift for the night. Robbie was already on watch, and so Mr. Campbell, instead of using the time to sleep, waited. Certainly he had heard me coming, for I never bothered to attempt a quiet approach. I marched down the hall with my boots still on. With proof of his duplicity in hand, I knocked firmly on the door and bravely waited. I waited a good minute, bracing myself for the abrupt opening where he would be standing in front of me in a sorry state of dishevel. I waited, but still there was not a sound. I knocked again, harder, urgently, and this time I was rewarded by a voice softly calling out for me to enter.

He was sitting with his back to me at his desk, intently cutting into something with his knife—something that looked suspiciously like a puffin. I could see the jet-black velvet wings pinned outstretched on a board as the man attacked it with his blade. He didn't turn around. He kept his back to me and continued his macabre exploration.

"I know all about you, William Campbell," I boldly stated. "You can't hide it from me any longer."

At the sound of my voice the knife quieted in his hand, yet still, he didn't turn around. I continued, deciding to press where it would hurt him the most—deciding to use the very impetus that had driven poor Mr. Seawell half-crazed. "You were married once, weren't you, William?" I stressed his name, knowing how the sound of it had once made him flinch. "But your wife died, didn't she? She died giving birth to your child, William, and the pain of it . . . why, the pain of it nearly destroyed you."

He spun around. His pellucid eyes set beneath the spectacularly dark brows pierced mine. He looked at once alluring and dangerous. "How?" he croaked, his voice sounding unnatural in his constricted throat. "How the hell would ye know about that?"

I walked toward him, emboldened by this newfound weakness in his nature, and ignored his question. "Unable to bear the pain of her death, and the heartache it caused you, you were driven to join the army . . . or in your case, the navy. Am I correct?"

"What are you talking about?" he whispered dangerously. "How could you possibly know anything about that?"

"Because you told me of it yourself, didn't you, William?"

This had him. He was clearly distraught, and I watched as the glowing eyes roved wildly as he fought to recall doing so.

"In your letters, William," I simply stated.

"What letters!" he demanded. "I didn't write you any letters but one. And that I remember very well! I only asked for your help . . . in the garden."

"You have asked for my help long before that day, in the letters you write under the guise of being a reclusive and suicidal antiquarian."

"What?" he uttered in raw disbelief, and made ready to refute this.

I stopped him with my hand. "Don't," I said, advancing on him. Months of anger and frustration were coming forth, boiling within me like an unholy brew. "Don't try to confuse me, William. You're very adept at that! Just tell me, why did you do it? Why did you feel the need to toy with me so? By God, William Campbell, tell me how Thomas' watch came to be in your possession!" This last request sounded frightfully desperate even to my own ears.

He stood, abandoning his mad dissection of the bird, finally seeming to understand what I was accusing him of. "Dear God, you actually think . . . you actually believe I was the one who wrote those letters?"

"I don't think. I know!" I shouted, and pulled from the folds of my gown the note he had written to me and signed, matching it up against the writing and signature of Mr. Alexander Seawell. "Deny it if you can, William. But please, please do not insult me with paltry excuses or this two-penny chicanery of yours any longer!"

"Sara . . . for God's sake, lass, listen to me! I swear to you I did not write those letters . . . not one of them!" he averred, pointing to the one from Mr. Seawell in my hand. "I have never even met the man. Nor have I ever been to Oxford!"

"I don't believe you. You're lying!" I cried with hands firmly planted on hips while another wave of white hot anger took me.

"I would never lie to you," he defended, his own eyes burning with frustration. "However, the same could hardly be said for you!"

"I lie to you purely out of necessity. You lie to me for the mere pleasure of seeing me hurt!"

"That is, in itself, the most damnable lie yet! I have never lied to you, Sara. Nor am I lying about this now." And with that he ripped the letters from my hand and brought them under his scrutinizing gaze.

And then he stilled.

He was deathly still. "By God . . . how can that . . . ?" He looked up, holding me with the question. "That does indeed resemble my hand." He studied the note awhile longer, marveling at the similarities. "It is remarkably similar, but you must believe me when I tell you that I did not write those letters. Nor do I have any connection to this . . . this enigmatic Mr. Seawell of yours."

There was something convincing in his look. Perhaps it was the way his eyes softened as he beheld me, or the sadness that was clearly in them. Whatever it was, I believed him.

"Could . . ." I began, grasping for some explanation, "could you have possibly written them while you were in one of your . . . darker moods?" I suggested softly. "And not have even realized that you did it?"

"What?" Obviously this suggestion offended him. "Are you suggesting . . . that I don't know exactly what I'm about?" There was a chiding incredulity about him that almost shamed me from uttering what I just had. Yet before I could explain myself better he continued. "Could you, in fact, really be daft enough to think that I wrote those letters assuming another persona? I may have my darker moods, Miss Stevenson," he whispered with a wry grin as he advanced on me, coming so close he was mere inches away. "Aye, very dark and dangerous moods indeed. But unfortunately I'm always frighteningly aware of exactly what I am about. Oh, what I would give for a half hour where I did not know what I'm about."

I put up my hands to block him from stepping any closer, but my belly, protruding even beyond my amazement, did that for me. He stopped at the feel of it pressing against his own hard stomach. Yet he did not back away, he stood firm and then looked down, marveling at me and the bulging entity I carried. "You really did not write those letters, did you?" I conceded, feeling the familiar upheaval of defeat. He shook his head slowly. "But the story . . . Mr. Seawell's plight is familiar to you?" And to this he was forced to respond with a nod. "Then will you tell me, William, will you please tell me your story? You already know mine," I uttered, staring into his liquid-crystal gaze, "but I, Mr. Campbell, am no wiser about you than I was when I first came here. Please," I uttered desperately, "please at least give me this one thing. Tell me what horror has driven you to be out here, living on the very edge of the world, shunning all humanity that crosses your path."

For a moment I wasn't certain he would comply, but something in him changed then, and that wall of dark isolation slowly dissolved. He reached down and took my hand in his; there was nothing shy or tentative about it. He was warm, solid yet gentle, and I liked the feel of the way he held on to me, as if he too needed to be held. And then, without further hesitation, he led me over to his bed. I watched as he fluffed the pillows and attempted to smooth the covers that likely had never been smoothed before, and then, sitting on the edge of the bed, he gently guided me next to him.

The story of William Campbell was a hauntingly familiar one, but for the names and places.

He had indeed been married when he was a younger man, fresh from medical school. He had been somewhat of a prodigy at Edinburgh University, passing exams with flying colors, and had looked forward to a promising career as a physician. He married his longtime sweetheart and started work as an attending physician in the Royal Infirmary. Yet for all the hard-won knowledge he attained in medical school, he soon found that in reality his skills were not nearly as effective as they had been on paper. There was more to the sick and poor than a standard procedure. And even when he had fought and struggled to save a life, he became only too aware that the poor had little resources to improve their health. They might survive the day, but the conditions they lived in, the only food they could afford, were all sadly inadequate. And he struggled with the failure he was met with nearly every day. His only solace back then had been his wife. And he had loved her dearly.

But the real pain of life started the night his beloved went into labor with their first child. It should have never happened, for she wasn't due for over a month. And he wasn't even thinking she would have need of him when he answered a call for assistance. It was a call from a midwife delivering the bairn of a poor woman in the country on a frozen night in January. The woman had been ill, the messenger boy said, and was still battling this illness when she went into labor. The poor thing was expected to battle both.

The cottage he was brought to where this laboring woman lived was cold when he arrived, not only from poor design, but from lack of means to even buy fuel for the fire. The woman in labor, after he examined her, was found with a high fever which compounded the trauma of childbirth. William questioned the husband and asked him why there was not a fire set to warm the house. But the man had seemed indifferent to both his wife and her discomfort. After doing his best to reduce her fever, and dosing her as he saw fit, William needed the use of hot water. That's when he gave the husband some money and sent him to buy fuel.

The husband never returned.

It wasn't until the next day, long after William had returned home, that the man was found in a tavern, drunk and oblivious to the world and the fact that his wife had died shortly after giving birth. The child, already sickly, lived only but a few hours. After this long, sleepless night, and likely contracting chills himself in payment for his fruitless struggle, he returned home, tired, disillusioned and wanting only the comfort of his wife's arms. But he found that while he had been battling for the poor woman's child, his own wife had gone into labor.

It was far too early for the child. And when he had found her wracked with pain and sitting in a pool of blood on the floor he knew he would need to recall everything he had ever been taught to bring his child safely into the world. But he was not trained to be a midwife, or accoucheur, and by the time one could be gotten it would be too late. After a heart-wrenching struggle, he realized that the child was stuck and because it was not coming out, it was killing his wife. He was forced to make a decision to save one of them, and his logical choice was to save his wife. Desperation and inexperience drove him to try to take the child by cesarean, a risky surgical maneuver that had been performed successfully on many accounts. But that was with assistants, with instruments, and the help of strong opiates; he had nothing at hand. William was alone. And it was his only choice.

In truth, he knew little about what he was attempting, but his wife's fervent pleas drove him to do it, she pleaded for him to take the child, and with little choice he pulled out his knife and cut into her.

It was a horrible, bloody mess. As soon as he reached the womb he knew what a mistake he had made, for his wife was bleeding profusely. He worked quickly, furiously; but the blood, the screams, the blue fetus stuck in his wife's pelvis, overwhelmed him, and he knew that all the while he was working in this furious manner, his wife was slipping further away. He grabbed the tiny fetus—his son—and dislodged it from its

mother. The bairn was still alive, but just barely. And he abandoned him, hastily wrapped, to the floor and began cauterizing
the vessels he had severed. By the time he had finished, the great
incision sewn closed, his wife was already unconscious. He did
everything he knew to save her, but he still could not stop the
bleeding. And in this helpless despair, alone with his wife in his
arms—a woman he had butchered with his own knife—she had
died. The baby, small and weak, and unable to take a full breath
of air, had also died.

And that destroyed him.

In that one terrible night he had lost the very impetus that
drove him. He lost his will to be a doctor; he lost his will to live.
Short of killing himself, which he would not fathom to do, being
one who had learned the value of life and had taken the Hippo-
cratic oath, he made the decision to escape all his memories of
Edinburgh and took a job as a naval surgeon.

As Mr. MacKay had alluded to earlier, the voyage was met
with an overwhelming medical disaster. Just two weeks out of
the harbor, yellow fever had been brought aboard by a pressed
convict and spread unchecked throughout the crowded lower
decks. In a matter of weeks the crew was reduced to barely even
enough men to work the sails, let alone fight her. And that was
only the beginning of his private hell afloat . . . that was when
total isolation called to William Campbell.

When his spectacularly disastrous commission in the navy finally ended, and he miraculously found that he was still alive, he
went to my father's office. He knew his father had gone to school
with my father; the two had been old friends. It was out of duty
to this friendship that William Campbell was given the appointment on Bell Rock—that forlorn sunken reef in the Firth of
Forth. It was on the Bell where his penance had begun, and in
the long, lonely nights of his duty, the ghosts had started to appear. Every one of them, every man, woman and child he had
ever laid a hand on under the guise of healing, called to him from

beyond the grave. And slowly, very slowly, they pulled him into an unworldly existence; and he, for his part, accepted his lot.

"That was why I did not want to see you here, Sara," he whispered when he could, looking beseechingly into my eyes. "That was why I resented you showing up the way you did: so young, so full of life, so careless with your charms. And, God save me, but I didn't want your death, or the death of your child, on my hands. I wanted to hate you. And when I found that I couldn't do it, I tried to make you hate me," he uttered, his luminescent eyes becoming moist with emotion. "Oh Sara," he gasped. "You have no idea the torment I suffered for it."

I could see it. It was still there, clear in his magnificent eyes, and it broke my heart. I reached up to him, putting my hands on either side of his trembling face, and pulled his head to my body, holding him tightly against my chest as he wept, my rotund belly acting as a pillow to absolve his long overdue tears. I crushed him to me with a force driven as much by heartache and sorrow as it was by mutual need.

"It's all right now, William," I whispered into his thick chestnut hair as my own tears dripped off my cheeks into the soft nest of curls. "And never, never you worry about me. I give you my word; I swear I will not be another ghost to haunt you. You may think me foolhardy and selfish, and perhaps I am, but I will tell you this, no man yet has ever driven my will from me. And I have a very strong will, William, to live."

"Aye," he uttered, still in the throes of his sorrow. At length he sat up, and while I dried his tears with the back of my hand he studied me. And then he whispered, "'Tis just, at times, ye remind me so much of her."

"Am I like your wife?" I asked with a soft smile, my hand still caressing his stubble-covered cheek.

To my surprise he shook his head. "Nay, in truth ye are nothing like her."

This was not the answer I had been expecting, for the dear

creature he had described to me had sounded like a beautiful and charming woman, and secretly I wanted very much to elicit admiration from this man. He must have seen my disappointment because he felt compelled to continue, "My wife obeyed me without question. You, on the other hand, have a habit of not minding me at all."

"Well then," I replied softly, fighting hard not to smile at this taunt against my character. "I shall just have to try harder. But I'm not promising any miraculous change."

I received a smile for this, a heartbreaking, genuine smile, and the mood in the room became somewhat electric. I was still sitting close to the man, on his bed—holding his hand—and I realized then that I was drawn to him just as, perhaps, he was drawn to me. We sat in silence, reveling in the comfort that had settled between us, thousands of questions and curious thoughts still swirling in my mind, waiting to be given voice, and while I was thinking of what to say to him a rather untimely, unpleasant thought occurred to me. Quite suddenly, and rashly, I blurted out, "Oh dear God!" and yanked my hand from his grasp.

This startled the poor man greatly, and he narrowed his eyes at me, thinking, perhaps, I had gone daft again. I explained, "The letter . . . the last letter I wrote to Mr. Seawell . . ."

"What about it?"

"Well, I was certain it was you who was writing me. Remember? And he promised me, just as you had, that he would protect my child. And then I asked the man . . . no, William, I implored the man to come for me before I was to give birth!"

At first he didn't see the importance of this and looked deeply into my eyes, questioning my sanity. I placed my hand over his and squeezed fervently. "Don't you see? He's coming for me. Alexander Seawell of Oxford is coming to Cape Wrath, William, because I asked him to!"

"Well, how do you ken that? Why would the man come all the way out here to champion a strange woman who could, for all intents and purposes, be a loon?" he queried, while smiling slightly at the way he had enunciated the word "loon."

But I was not smiling. "Because," I averred nervously, "I received his reply. It was a very short missive, William. Hasty even, as if the man were in love . . . and I was certain it was from you!"

"You said the man sounded as if he were in love with ye? By God, lass, what did the note say?" His curiosity was obviously piqued, although I could see he didn't like the sound of this at all.

"It said, quite simply: 'My dear Mrs. Crichton, I am on my way!'"

## ELEVEN

### The Storm

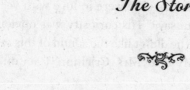

It had grown dark and was well into the night when William brought me back to my room. We had spent a long time in his room talking, and he seemed intent on putting me to bed in mine, showing all the tenderness of a lover as he did so, seeing me into my night shift and tucking the quilts high under my chin. He then sat on the edge of the mattress and beheld me under the soft glow of the oil lamp. "I promise, we shall sort this all out," he assured, "and very soon, at that." And then he bent to place a chaste kiss on my forehead, whispering as he did so that I should get some sleep. "There's a right storm brewing out there, lass, and it's likely to be a dirty night. Sleep now and I shall see ye in the morning."

He was about to sit up when my arms came around him. It was on impulse; I couldn't help it, and suddenly I felt myself pulling him back down to me, bringing his fine lips to my mouth. It was a temptation the light-keeper could not resist.

He came to me willingly, warmly, and it quite took the breath from me. It had been a long time since any man had done so. If

Thomas Crichton had left me and was never coming back, then at least William Campbell was here—and he was tender, and urgent, and sensual. He was a man as destitute and lost as I, yet he had vowed to stand by me and had gone through great personal pain to do so. Thomas had also made a vow, but a vow forsworn; he had failed me.

My heart was still of two minds on the matter, but my body was pathetically, and quite willingly, responsive to William Campbell. He was like the dark of night to Thomas' bright shining day: saturnine light-keeper against sanguine mariner. Two more different men from totally different worlds there could not be, and, God help me, but my heart was overwhelmed with the want of both of them.

I was awkward and pregnant. It had likely been a long while since the light-keeper had felt the arms of a woman around him. And he tumbled into the bed beside me, pulling me to him with a hunger that left me breathless. His kisses were cathartic; his lips, full and supple—and the sound they elicited from my constricted throat surprised even him. It drove his need; dear God, he was as ravenous as I. And though he was tender he was unwilling to wait any longer. Forgoing all the finesse of a surgeon, he yanked the tie of my night shift and threw it wide open, pausing to stare at what lay before him. There was an animal-like hunger in his eyes tempered by a look of breathless awe. His gaze was as potent and erotic as his kisses. "Dear Lord," he uttered at last, breathing as heavily as I. "But ye are a creature of rare beauty, Sara Stevenson." And then slowly, very slowly, he began his exquisite assault. His mouth moved from my lips to caress the tender skin beneath my chin. My head went back in ecstasy as he slowly explored the taut line of my throat with his sublimely sensitive mouth. And the delicious torture he practiced on me continued working its way down, all the way down, to the soft swollen mounds of my breasts. They were larger than they had ever been before, and very sensitive. And the suddenness of his warm mouth over my erect nipple caused a wave of throbbing pleasure that nearly rendered me senseless. I cried out, unable to help myself.

My pleasure inspired him—ignited him—and with a skill I could never have imagined, he drove every thought from me with his hunger, his insatiable tongue and his cleverly exploring lips. I could not stand it. My body, huge and cumbersome though it was, cried out for him with an untrammeled desire I never dreamed possible. And to make him fully understand what it was that I wanted, what it was that I ached for, I removed a hand from the tangled chestnut curls of his head, and reached down to the swollen hardness straining to break free between his muscled thighs. I tried to find the buttons on his breeches to release him, but gave up—with a mind too distracted by his expert assault—and instead slipped my hand under the waistband of his pants. It was my turn to feel the thrill of his sudden, surprised, pleasure-laden gasp.

He was magnificently built, smooth, hard and urgently ready. And with my hand thus making him readier still, reveling in the feel of him, the pleasure he took from my touch and the eagerness of his need, I begged him to love me, having no doubt that he would.

"Please, William," I uttered to his splendid dark head, my breath dispersing through his thick silky hair. "Dear God!" I half cried, half pleaded. "I know it's a bit awkward but I'm afraid I'll die if we don't."

He looked up from between my breasts with eyes afire, matching the heat in my own. One arm was gently draped over the swell of my belly, the other still taunting a sensitive nipple. "*You'll* die? Dear God, lass, have a care for me," he breathed, and I watched with dark pleasure as his eyes rolled back in ecstasy as my hand continued to stroke his sensitive, very ready maleness. And then, stilling my hand with the one so recently employed on my wanton breast, he said, "My dear, you've already made me your slave. But are you sure . . . ? I dinna want to hurt ye." And I could see in his mesmerizing gaze that he was utterly sincere.

His stoic self-control touched me. But I didn't want self-control; I wanted to feel the wild, unheeded passion I saw in his eyes. "William Campbell," I uttered in a breathless moan, my body aching with a torturous unfulfillment from the want of him. "If you never listen to me on anything else, please, please, listen to me on this. Love me, William Campbell, for the love of God, make love to me now!"

We both struggled with the buttons of his breeches, our fingers clumsy with the frenetic need that drove us; all the while his lips were hungrily kissing my own. I gasped, he moaned, and when he was finally free to help satiate the raging fire that consumed us, the blasted bell began to toll.

William ignored it.

Finding my lips again, he kissed and nibbled me in a wild attempt to regain the frenzy that drove us, but all the while the damned bell kept on ringing, growing louder and more urgent. I was annoyed. I was angered. It was so cruelly unfair! Yet try as he might to distract me, the bell had thrust its way between us, reminding us that we were not free to pursue our selfish needs.

"William, darling . . . your bell," I croaked, stupid with pleasure and highly discomposed. "Your goddamn untimely bell is tolling!"

He stilled beneath my hands. A heartfelt "Goddamn it!" exploded from his lips, and then, shockingly, he resumed his work on my nipple. William Campbell, paradigm light-keeper, was ignoring the harbinger of his calling. The thought was endearing—and it was all my fault! How would I ever explain it to Kate?

"William. Please . . ." I uttered in a pitiful moan. "You know you have to go."

"I know," he breathed heavily, and laid his head helplessly on my swollen bosom. "And God help me, but for once I dinna want to. For once I want to stay here. I want to stay here with ye, Sara. I want nothing to do with that goddamned tower!"

This heated admission made me smile, it was so unlike him,

and gently, pushing his heavy head off my chest, I made him look me in the eye. "Go. Robbie needs you. He's tired, and I'm not going anywhere. Go to your watch, William; keep your eyes sharp, and come to me when you're through . . . that is, if you still want to," I added, putting a hand on the huge ball that was my midriff, the only thing still modestly covered. "I'm as large as a cow and likely not what you dream of at all."

"But you are what I dream of!" he uttered passionately, and pulled me into his arms again. "Don't ye know it? Ye, my dear, are the very thing that torments me!" He flashed an ironic grin. "And now, when I have you here . . . and *you* finally ready and very willing to reward me for *all the hell* you've put me through . . . and might I add ye were doing amazingly too. I've forgiven ye everything . . . and then some." He raised a brow to make his point, causing me to smile in return. "Now the goddamned bell pulls me back!" And with a touchingly deprecatory grunt, combined with eyes that glowed with unsated wolfish hunger, he eased himself away from me. The bell kept tolling. "Stay here, just like that, my canny, wee, beautiful hare," he commanded gently, teasingly. He hastily fastened his clothes and left me with one last tingling kiss, stating: "And God willing, when I return we shall finish what we've started here."

. . .

I must have fallen right to sleep, for a feeling of warmth and serenity surrounded me so completely, and for the first time since arriving at the lighthouse I was at peace. I dreamed of William Campbell. I dreamed of running my fingers through his thick dark curls. I ached to caress the new-sprung stubble of his jaw. I was positively bursting to feel his hard body against mine. But mostly I hungered for his mesmerizing eyes. And in my dream, only in my dream, we finished what we had started.

But somewhere out there another waited, and in the dark of night, carried on the wings of a storm, he came. My blissful dreams subtly turned harsh and painful. The warm caresses of the lighthouse keeper turned to a deathlike cold, while the pale blue-green eyes that had once haunted me shiftily morphed into those of another. Vibrant and chilling, the blue gaze cut into me, and the face of Thomas Crichton obscured all other thoughts. It was a nightmare, painful in its reality, heartrending in its purity.

I could hear the wind driving against the ship he sailed with unrelenting force, the sails being ripped into ribbons on their yards before my eyes, while the father of my child called to me, pleading, swearing anew his undying love. The ship was wrecking, breaking around him in a black and violent sea. He was going down, and men were drowning. The bell was tolling for them, calling into their nightmare without mercy as they struggled to stay alive. And while the wind drove the ship onto the rocks, driving the waves and rain into them without mercy, I could take no more of it; I screamed.

I was still screaming when I sat up in bed, drenched with cold sweat. It was all a dream, I realized, but the wind and rain were not. Neither was the continuous tolling of the bell that had invaded my nightmare.

I jumped up and pulled a robe around me, suddenly realizing that a squall had hit the Cape. The bell was tolling far too long and too fervently for it to be the mere changing of a watch. Something was happening, something very wrong. And the dream came flooding back. I had no idea how long I had been asleep, but it was still sometime in the wee hours of the night, for William had not returned to me as he had promised he would. I ran out of my room. In the hall I could hear the men's voices shouting in the courtyard. But when I had reached the door to the cottage, and flung it open, only Robbie was still standing there. William had ridden off. I pulled on an oilskin coat, sea boots and a weather hat, and bounded into the courtyard to see what was wrong. Kate, I noticed, was following closely behind me.

"What's happening, Robbie?" I yelled to the man who was also making ready to mount his horse. He spun around.

"There's a ship in peril down the coast, Sara. She's just off Kervaig, holding ground with an anchor, but she willna be able to hold for much longer. She's starting to break up. Willy's off to gather the men. I'm to meet him at Kervaig Bay with lifelines ready!" And indeed Robbie had been busy securing thick, coiled ropes and a few unlit lanterns to his saddle.

"There's a ship lying at anchor off the bay?" I questioned, yelling to be heard above the wind while having the distinct feeling that I knew the very ship he was talking about. He gave a curt nod. "I believe Mr. Campbell knows that the men have already gathered there?" Again came the nod. "Then you must go to him, Robbie; ride as swiftly as you can! There's not a moment to lose!"

"You stay here, Sara, you and Kate!" he shouted, looking over my shoulder to his wife. "Keep watch and make sure the bell keeps tolling, aye."

"We've got it, Robbie," I assured loudly. "And Godspeed to you now." He paused just long enough in his duty to deliver his wife a mighty hug and tender kiss, and then he turned and mounted up. Both Kate and I watched speechless as he rode away in the driving rain, not removing our gaze from him until he had cleared the lighthouse grounds. Once he was out of sight, I turned to her.

"You need to get up to the observation room and keep watch. I cannot do it. You need to keep the bell going. And the lantern needs to be wound every two hours. Can you do that?"

"Yes, I will. But what of you, Sara, will you be all right down here?"

"Of course," I replied. And with a glibness she was known to overlook I added, "I shall just wait here, in the cottage, until I hear otherwise."

"Very good," she replied, and fighting the gale force winds and driving rain, she went directly to the tower. I too went directly to my task.

I had grown so large that the going was not easy. Compounding my great girth with the wind, rain and darkness, it was perhaps a miracle I could find my way at all. But I was driven by determination. The MacKay croft was only a few miles away. The men would bring the survivors there, and Mary would need all the help she could get tending to them. That was my drive. I would not let my friend down. And at the back of my mind stirred the belief that Thomas Crichton would be among them. I needed to get to Kervaig Bay in time!

This thought propelled me into the rain-soaked darkness, heading down the rutted road that would take me through the parve; and it was with me still as I rounded the point that over-looked the jetty. But when I actually happened to glance down into the cove I had every intention of passing, I saw a sight that drove all thoughts from me. For there, floating in the sheltered waters, impervious to the raging squall, was the mysterious lit-tle skiff of Mr. Seawell's. My heart nearly stopped beating when I recognized it. And without another thought to my previous task, or the reason I was out wandering the open moors in the bosom of a storm to begin with, I turned and gingerly began picking my way through the rivulets and ruts that made up the treacherous descent to the lighthouse jetty.

Miraculously, and with great effort on my own part, I made it to the bottom, noticing with some amazement that the weather down here was vastly different from the driving rain above. It was calm, the waters still, the rain no more than a light misty nuisance. And although my vision was slightly obscured by this foggy darkness, it did nothing to diminish the awe of seeing the ghostly outline of that familiar boat sitting at the end of the pier.

I walked forward, drawn by some unseen power to reach it, my eyes never leaving the little skiff—a beautifully made boat with rigging that seemed to glow with an unearthly brilliance. I was about to put my foot on the dock when I happened to notice the figure of a man standing at the far end.

The hair on the back of my neck prickled, yet still I advanced. Tentatively, I placed a foot on the wooden dock and felt the jolt of a thousand tiny hatpins prickling my skin at once. It was the same familiar tingling I had felt before, only this was far more intense. Still, the figure stood at the end of the pier with his back to me. I took a few steps closer, my curiosity driving me—any other sane creature would have known better, any other creature would have run away. But I was not any other creature, nor, perhaps, was I entirely sane. And throwing all caution to the wind I uttered aloud the name: "Mr. Seawell? Mr. Alexander Sea-well?"

At the sound of his name the dark figure began to turn, and slowly, very slowly, he stood facing me. The breath caught in my throat; it was so unbelievable. My heart lurched with a star-tlingly painful beat and I found I was unable to move or utter a sound. For there, at the end of the pier, stood Thomas Crichton.

"Dear God," I uttered helplessly, my hand covering my mouth as the hot sting of tears began, and then they flowed unchecked in great salty rivulets. "Oh, dear almighty God!" But that was all I could utter, for the power of speech had now left me entirely.

I watched in this state of speechless wonder as the man I had loved so completely, and with such wild abandon, slowly came toward me, looking brilliant, looking godlike with his golden-bronzed image. He looked as handsome as he ever had, as hand-some as the first day I had laid eyes on him—long ago in my father's garden. My insides were in knots, the baby in my womb seemed to drop exceedingly low in my body from the shock of it and I was finally able to speak the name—"Thomas . . ."

"Why?" came the heart-rending voice that sounded as if he had uttered the words next to my ear. "Why did ye no' wait for me, Sara?"

"What?" I uttered in an equally pained reply. "But . . . but I did wait for you, Thomas. Oh, God, but I did! I waited for hours . . . for days . . . for months. By God, Thomas, after all this time, after all you put me through, I am *still* waiting!" And even I could hear the hurt and anger in those words.

His was a look of puzzlement. "I'm sorry," he said. "I was

waylaid and thrust out to sea. But I wrote ye letters—many letters telling ye that I'd come for ye as soon as I was able, but ye returned them all, Sara, unopened. Why?"

Although his voice was oddly calm during this speech, mine was not and I was nearing hysterics. "Letters, Thomas? I never received any letters from you! And God as my witness, I would have never returned them!"

He continued to advance, moving ever toward me with a look on his face that broke my heart. "I told ye once, Sara, my love, that I would move heaven and earth so that we could be together. Have ye forgotten it already? Have ye lost all faith in me, lass, believing that I would no' do it?"

I couldn't believe what I was hearing. Thomas Crichton, the man I had given my heart to those many months ago, the man I had sworn to love forever, had returned. And for once I was utterly speechless.

"Well, at long last here I am, my love, my heart," he said softly, standing directly before me with a look so bittersweet that it made all the torment and heartache I had ever suffered for this man seem pale and insubstantial by comparison. And then he uttered the words written so plainly on his face: "I have been to hell and back for you."

The way he said it, the conviction in his voice, made me believe that he had. And then, holding me in his compelling gaze as the odd prickling consumed my flesh, he continued. "I have suffered greatly for my devotion to ye, Sara, causing me to make a deal with the owner of that boat. He knew you were here, ye see, but I didn't know it, not until I was made to deliver that first package to you. I wanted to come to you then, but I needed to fulfill my end of the bargain or I was told I'd never see ye again. I could not take that chance. It was pure torment knowing ye were here yet I forbidden to do anything about it—delivering another man's mail forbye, a man by the name of Alexander Seawell."

"What?" I uttered, feeling the world sway beneath my feet. "You were here, all along?"

"In a matter of speaking. But today I have fulfilled my obligation to the auld sailor. I have done all he's asked of me, and he has released me from this hell I've been made to suffer. He has let me come to you, Sara, and yet I find you calling to him."

"No, Thomas . . ." I cried, feeling sick and confused at the thought. "I had no idea. I swear!"

"Were ye expecting Mr. Seawell?"

"No!" I cried, then added truthfully, "Well, yes, I suppose. I told him to come . . . but only because I thought you were dead."

"Dead?" he repeated, and then added with that disarming grin of his, the one I loved so, the one I carried with me in my heart: "Death could never part us, love, providing ye still loved me. Do ye still love me?"

"Oh yes," I cried as anguish and joy collided in one debilitating burst of tears. "Oh yes, Thomas, my love, I do! Very much. I've never stopped. Even when I thought you had abandoned me. Even when everyone else said you had. I never gave up. By God, I would have given my life just to know you still cared!"

This admission, this true and heartfelt admission, pleased him and his face broke into that glorious smile, with eyes dancing and that inner glow perfectly exploding from his very essence. It was as if the sun, in this dark and foggy little cove, had finally appeared, and it warmed me, radiated through me— giving me that burst of life-sustaining bliss that told me all would be well again. And then he came to me, the man with the face that would always melt my heart.

He opened his arms, ready to embrace me, beckoning me to join him, and into these I gladly went. But just as his warm, familiar arms should have come around me, holding me and the child I carried in his protective embrace, there came a rush of cold air. The frigid burst shot straight through my body, chilling me to the marrow of my bones and traveling all the way to the pit of my womb. And with this cold rush of air there came a feeling of heartrending loss, and of panic, and of horridly chilling surprise. I spun around and saw him standing behind me with a look on his face that matched the shock on my own. "NO!" I shouted when I saw that his glorious golden body was fading. "OH GOD NO! THOMAS NO!!"

"SARA!" he cried with all the urgent desperation I felt. I saw that his eyes were registering the same shock and horror I felt, and he reached out for me as I reached for him, both of us unwilling to believe it—the sickening cruelty of what was happening. I tried to touch him, to pull him back, to grasp and hold on to that essence uniquely his own: what made him Thomas Crichton, the man that I loved. But then, understanding touching his beautiful eyes at last, he uttered almost disbelievingly: "I'm . . . I'm dead."

"Thomas, NO!" I cried as great wracking sobs began taking hold of me.

An odd sort of smile crossed his face then, and I felt his warmth, and a wash of what could only be pure, radiating love. "Oh, Sara, how I love ye. Oh, how I wish I could spend the rest of my days with ye and our bairn." His eyes, like living pools of regret, rested on the great swell of my belly as he spoke. I knew then that he had felt the child I carried. "But I've gone and died, lass," he said, as if explaining this to himself as much as to me. "Please . . ." His voice was soft and plaintive as his body, so young and heartbreakingly beautiful, began to fade. "Please do not be angry, love. Never ye fret for me. I died, Sara, and it was your love that kept me from seeing it."

"THOMAS! THOMAS, PLEASE COME BACK! DON'T LEAVE ME!" It was a last, desperate plea, bursting from my body with a violent force that brought me to my knees. I fell onto the hard wood of the pier, crying uncontrollably, convulsing with so much pain and heartache that I felt I too would die. He was gone. After hoping all these months that he would come, he was now finally and eternally gone. I could not bear that thought. I could not bear it! I wanted to die and go with him.

And then I felt again that unworldly tingle.

I felt, rather than saw, the light, for my tears were so blinding.

I felt it directly over me, and when I looked up I was startled to see a man standing over me. He was an older man, a kindly-looking man dressed for the sea. His sudden presence should have startled me, but it didn't. I wiped the tears from my eyes, however useless it was. Yet even through my tears I could see a radiance about this man, and a beauty so pure that he could have been Thomas' father. But this man, this new apparition before me, I knew was not of this world. The thought did not frighten me. I was far beyond feeling anything, let alone fright. "Are you Mr. Seawell?" I asked him.

"No," he said kindly. "Mr. Seawell is not born in your time. But when he does come here someday, as he will, he will be touched by the love both you and Thomas share."

"I don't understand. If you are not him, who are you, then?" I demanded, angered and confused; which I felt it my right after the heartache I was made to suffer.

"Only a messenger," he replied gently, and I knew then he was an angel.

"You're the owner of the boat, aren't you . . . and the one who tormented him!"

"Love," he began, looking serenely at me, "especially one born of such purity of heart and held together by unyielding devotion, deserves a second chance. That was my gift to Thomas. Live your life, Sara Crichton, yet always keep him in your heart the way you will always be in his. And when you are ready, many years from now, he shall come for you. That is my promise."

As the old sailor spoke these words, I was overcome by a feeling of peace and serenity. It was consuming, and relieving in an odd sort of way even though I was still unwilling to fathom what had transpired. And then, just like Thomas, the angel too was gone. The cove turned dark and the rain fell once more. I looked to the end of the pier and saw that the little skiff—my beautiful little skiff—had vanished as well.

It hit me then, what I should have realized all along, but never could: the letters from the stranger Mr. Seawell, the reappearance of Thomas' timepiece, the haunting presence of the man who convinced me to believe that he still loved me. Thomas had died, and I didn't even know how or why, and it broke my heart beyond measure. But what I did know—that daft thread I had clung to for all these months—was that beyond doubt, Thomas Crichton had truly loved me as I loved him. And then it hit me: he really had moved heaven and earth for this one last, heart-breaking meeting.

Tears poured from my eyes, silent, helpless tears that mingled with the rain and coursed down my cheeks unchecked. I was filled with a debilitating sorrow that I believed would never go away, because Thomas was dead and he was never coming back. I sat on the pier recalling his face, his voice, his smell, the feel of his warm body next to mine as we made love. I wanted to remember every detail of him, to recall every moment we had spent together. And I grieved the fact that he would never get to hold his child. I let it consume me, these thoughts of him, while trying to make sense of what had happened . . . knowing I could never make sense of what had happened.

It was only when a terrible gripping pain seized me that I finally moved. And then it came again, squeezing my stomach with a force I had never felt. When it subsided, I stood, and I knew that my baby was preparing to be born. Thomas Crichton was gone. He had told me so himself. And there was nothing this side of heaven I could do about it now. But I would be damned if I didn't do everything I could to save our child. Tears were still coming, and that I could not help, but I did fight the fatigue and heartache long enough to climb the jetty road. I fought the gush of water as it tumbled down the muddy incline in great rivulets; I fought the wind and the driving rain—and mostly I fought the bone-chilling knowledge that I had been visited by a ghost . . . and an angel.

Slowly I made my way back to the lighthouse, not only harboring a devastating sadness, but also gripped with fear. The men were attempting a hazardous rescue out in Kervaig Bay.

They would be gone all night, and I doubted my child would wait that long to be born. Kate was my only hope—Kate, dear Kate. It was true that at times she drove me to despair, but I needed her now and I knew she wouldn't disappoint me.

I came into the courtyard, pausing only to suffer the urgent pains that were increasing in strength and frequency, and made my way to the lighthouse tower. On a gust of wind I threw open the door and called up to her, my urgent voice reverberating up the spiral stairs, bouncing off the heavy stone walls. I yelled to her again and again, nearly crying with hysterics. But Kate did not answer.

"Kate, for the love of God, please answer me!" I cried, sobbing, on my knees at the foot of the steps. "My child is coming!" Yet again I was met with silence. I sobbed helplessly as another painful contraction came. And then I realized that even Kate would have answered my call. My heart sunk at this very thought, for it meant that she had likely seen me leave for Kervaig Bay and thought to follow.

I was damned.

Kate was gone.

I was utterly alone.

I made my way back to the cottage and stood by the fire, gripping the mantelpiece tightly in order to keep my body upright as I attempted to get warm. But I feared my body might never be warm again. Nonetheless, I held to the mantel out of sheer will and felt the peat fire slowly permeate my wet clothes. I stood there dumbly, confused and bewildered, heartbroken and destroyed as the impact of what had occurred at the jetty sank in: Thomas had finally come to me—Thomas' ghost.

But I did not believe in ghosts, even Mr. Campbell's ghosts. They were just stories, allegories for darker things. Yet mine had been real enough. I had truly seen Thomas; he had spoken to me. And it was that strange encounter that continued to haunt me.

And then I remembered the letters.

They were real; they had to be. What the angel said about Mr. Seawell made no sense. I released my grip on the mantel and made my way to my room. I went straight to the desk, pushed aside the pile of papers and opened the box where I had kept all Mr. Seawell's letters.

The box was empty.

I searched frantically, overturning every scrap that lay there, pushing aside books and papers, but none revealed the many letters Mr. Seawell had written. They had vanished . . . just like Thomas. I had no proof. I had nothing to validate that the man ever existed, that he ever wrote the heart-wrenching tales that brought me closer to the troubled light-keeper. Yet I knew, deep down inside, that he had been very real.

I wanted to cry. I felt my child coming but didn't know what to do. I didn't want to be alone, and so I went back to stand near the warmth of the fire, fighting the painful contractions that wracked my body, praying that I would be delivered of a miracle.

It was in between these body-splitting pains, when I was standing at the hearth, held upright by stubborn determination and a white-knuckled grip, breathing deliberately and heavily, that the door suddenly burst open.

The sound alone shocked me, for I hadn't expected anyone to come. And when I turned to look, indeed there was no one. A gust of cold air and rain hit me then, driving the damp sea air straight through me. I would have blamed it on the storm and the high winds if I hadn't felt his presence, that calming, familiar presence accompanied by a tingle of anticipation that I had felt whenever I held one of his letters. A smell of paper and ink infiltrated the room, and there was something deeper, muskier; something like the essence of male. I closed my eyes. Tears came again, coursing down my cheeks as yet another ghost surrounded me: another ghost beyond my reach. Poor, dear, lost Mr. Alexander Seawell.

It was then that the warm water gushed between my legs. I watched in horror as it pooled on the floor, just as another excruciating pain gripped me. This one brought me to my knees, nearly splitting my body in two.

I was scared.

I was going to die.

And I didn't want to die—not alone, not with so many ghosts calling to me.

That was when I began to pray for the one man who could save me. The man I had learned to put my faith in; the man I realized I had grown to love. It was a long shot, I knew. But then again, I always believed in long shots. Crouched hands and knees on the floor, my body arching protectively around the baby that was fighting to be born, I implored God to bring him swiftly to me; for William Campbell did not need another death on his hands this night.

I have no idea how long I stayed like that, curled around the pain of birth, crouched like an animal in labor. I was breathing heavily. I was sweating. I was mumbling prayers under my breath, gritting my teeth with determination. Time had no meaning any longer. And just when I believed I would succumb to both the pain and the ghosts that had engulfed me, I heard my name.

It was soft but urgent, uttered with fear, and it was enough to penetrate my private cloak of suffering. I turned and cast a pleading eye at the open doorway. He was standing there, wet, windblown, looking positively tormented. A fleeting smile crossed my lips as recognition hit me. I was alone no longer. My prayers had been answered.

"William . . ." I uttered, unable to say anything more. The pain had started again. It was nearly nonstop.

"Sara! Oh dear God, lass!" he uttered, and scooped me up in his arms. "How long? When did it start?" he questioned, carrying me swiftly to my bedroom.

"How . . . did you know?" I asked him as he gently laid me on the bed we had almost made love on half a night ago. He now began the process of making ready for the birth. "How did you know to come?" I asked again with gritted teeth, following him with my eyes.

He came beside me and took up my hand. He pressed it tightly to his chest—so tight I could feel the frantic beating of his heart. He was as scared as I was. "Because I saw him, Sara," he replied softly.

"Saw who?" I uttered, fighting to sit up. "Who?"

"Thomas Crichton," he whispered, easing me back down. "I've been seeing him for some time now, same as you."

"What do you mean, William, seeing him? Is he . . . is he one of your ghosts as well?"

"Nay, he's not my ghost, love. He's yours. But he did reveal himself to me on several accounts. Remember your wee little skiff? The one only you and I could see?"

"Only you and I?" I uttered, because the thought that only he and I could see it never crossed my mind. And then I said a little accusatorily, "You knew he was dead?"

"Aye. I thought you did too, but then I realized that you didn't, and, God forgive me, but I didn't want to be the one to tell ye. I know how ye loved the man; I knew it would break your heart to learn of it. And I didn't want your heart to break, not for all the world."

I reached a hand up to touch his cheek.

"I also know that he loved you." And the tears in his eyes told me of his fear. "But I too have grown to love you, Sara. You know that by now. I tried to fight it, but God help me, I'm not that strong a man."

I pulled his hand to my lips and kissed it. I then squeezed him so tightly I made him flinch, while awaiting another pelvic-splitting contraction to subside, and then I kissed him again. "I . . . love . . . you too, William. And like you, I also fought it. But I'm afraid . . ." I waited until the pain passed. He too waited, hanging on my every word. "But I'm afraid I shall never be able to give you *all*

my heart." It was an honest fear. Because I would always love
Thomas Crichton, and William Campbell deserved better than I
could give.

Another contraction came. I grimaced, and fought with all
my might not to cry out in front of him. He held me, pulling me
to him and whispering into my ear while pushing the sweat-
soaked hair off my brow, "I swear, I shall never ask it of ye. But I
will ask you, although this is hardly the time, to be my wife."

I looked at him, his pale eyes, his unreadable face, and
grunted, "You are joking!"

"Never." He was sincere.

There could not have been a greater shock to me at that moment. And he knew it; he took a perverse pleasure from it. The
smugly mischievous grin on his face made me want to hit him.
"So now ye must live, Sara Stevenson-Crichton-Campbell, ye
must live and love me as best as ever ye can. I'll accept no other
way."

"Really?"

"Aye."

I nodded my acceptance—attempted a smile even as my own
eyes filled with tears. "Oh William," I uttered, feeling like I was
being torn apart, both physically and emotionally. "I'm honored,
truly . . . and so sorry to put you through this . . . all this, and
without any . . . formal . . . more pleasurable . . . introduction." I
grunted again, going almost dizzy with the effort. "But . . . dear
God! I beg you, please get yourself down there. My baby is coming!"

· · ·

Two remarkable things happened that stormy, windblown
night. The first was the successful birth of my son, delivered
safely into this world by the capable and gentle hands of
William Campbell. The child, the infantile image of his father
with his tiny ruddy face, rosebud lips, blue eyes and halo of
golden fluff atop his head, was instantly named Thomas Crich-

ton after the man who would have loved him but was somehow deprived of the chance. There was another man, however, who I knew would do his best to honor the memory of the man by loving his child, and he sat beside me on the bed, gazing at the tiny infant in my arms, the pale blue-green eyes never leaving the little boy's face. It was perhaps William Campbell's greatest achievement to date.

The other remarkable thing occurred shortly after wee Thomas entered the world, and that was a visit from a man named Jeb Stewart, one of the sailors rescued from the imperiled privateer *Le Temeraire*.

Dawn had already broken when the man arrived accompanied by Kate and Robbie MacKinnon. Every man on the Cape had played his part in the rescue, and though the ship suffered, no souls were lost. Mr. Stewart had been one of those rescued, but he was no ordinary member of her crew. He was a former sailor with the British Navy, and he was intent on seeing me. He understood that I was tired, having just given birth, but was insistent I hear him, for he had risked much to find me. And so he entered my bedroom, carrying in his great, muscular arms a sea chest that he had been charged to deliver to me.

One look at it and I knew. Unfortunately, it was my time for tears. I had cried so many in the past twelve hours, more than I prayed I would ever do again. But I could not help them now, and so, in front of this stranger, they fell once more. But Mr. Stewart had expected this to happen, bringing such a thing to me, and he smiled consolingly as the shock of seeing Thomas' belongings subsided.

The sailor, Jeb Stewart, had a kindly round face, heavily lined by the sun and many years at sea. His clothes too were those of a mariner, his colorful gingham shirt checkered in red and blue, the stout, loose-fitting breeches and a thick braid of brown hair that reached to the middle of his back. His brown eyes were intelligent yet kind as he pulled a chair beside my bed and gently set down the chest. He then took a long moment sizing me up, scanning my puffy, tear-streaked face as well as the sleeping baby in my arms. The others were in the room with us as well, William sitting quietly on the bed beside me, Robbie and Kate pulling up chairs at the foot. And then Mr. Stewart softly spoke the words in his thick Scottish brogue, "Sara Stevenson. At lang last we meet, lass, and God how I wish 'twere under a more cheerful set o' circumstances. But I have traveled far and wide tae see ye, an' bring to ye no' only the effects, but the heroic tale of the man wha' loved ye . . ." And there began the explanation of why Thomas had failed to show up at Calton Hill on that day so long ago.

It had been nearly eight months since the young man had been carried aboard his ship, the HMS *Majestic*, unconscious. This poor wight, Mr. Stewart had said, had been knocked over the head while on his way to a tryst with a certain Edinburgh lady, and he had been the one instructed to lash him into a hammock lest the lad should awaken before they were safely into the Firth of Forth. At this I exclaimed with a hand to my mouth, "Thomas was kidnapped?"

"Ma'am," he said to me, kindness sparkling in his brown eyes, "in the service we prefer thae term 'pressed.' But aye, your man, why, he was a special case. He was a marked man, if ye get my meaning. An' I ken this weel, due to the fact that his dunnage came aboard ever afore he did. The lad's sea chest came from a man working on the tender belonging tae the Northern Lighthouse Board. 'Twas one of Captain MacCrea's gents wha' brought it."

"But . . . but why?" I questioned, thinking it impossible. "Why would Captain MacCrea do such a thing? He liked Thomas very well."

Here the man looked around the room, eyeing the couple sitting at the foot of the bed. "Aye, he liked the lad fine enough. But somebody else did no'. And that somebody was the lass' father." His eyes then settled back on me. I understood.

As soon as Mr. Stewart spoke these words, a horrible, terrible feeling arose in the pit of my stomach. If what he was telling me was true, then my father had been the one who took my young man from me. But my father didn't know of our plans! Certainly Thomas never would have said aught to anybody about what we were planning to do, and he was painfully afraid of his employer. That day on Calton Hill was our own affair.

"But sir," I uttered when I could, still waiting for this information to sink in. "My father would have had no idea that Mr. Crichton and I were planning to elope. He never even knew we were in love, let alone that we had been seeing each other secretly."

"Fathers ken more than they let on forbye, especially when important information is being leaked to them from one close to the young lady in question."

Kate.

My eyes flew to hers. The look on her face, the pain in her eyes, was her answer. Even her husband looked at her as if he had never seen her before. I knew Kate had told my parents of Thomas, but I thought it was after I had gone missing that day on Calton Hill, not before. And no one had ever told me otherwise . . . until now.

"How . . . how could you do such a thing?" was all I could utter, disbelievingly. And then another bout of great wracking sobs tore through me. It was William who comforted me, pulling me to him, holding me tightly in the shelter of his arms. For he alone knew just how much I hated Kate at that moment.

"Sara . . . I'm truly . . . sorry. I thought . . ." she said helplessly, her own tears obstructing her speech. "God as my witness, if you only knew how sorry I am! I tried to tell you! It was all a mistake! I never realized how much you really . . ."

I looked at the brown eyes; the whites around the dark irises were bloodshot with pain. Her usual look, the haughtiness, the self-righteousness, was entirely gone. And then I slowly began to realize that the change in her demeanor over the past few weeks had been not that of a woman who'd lost sight of her dream, but a woman who knew she had entirely crushed the dream of another—another she had once deeply cared for. There was nothing either of us could do now but listen to the rest of Mr. Stewart's tale.

"Mr. Stewart," spoke William softly, once he realized the worst sting of betrayal was over. "Perhaps, sir, ye will continue your story?"

"Aye, aye, I will," and with a visible gulp to steel his nerves he picked up the thread of his narrative precisely where he had left off. "As I was saying, sensitive information was given to this lady's father and that man, having great pull with the mariners on account o' the work he did, made a deal with Captain Babbington of the HMS *Majestic*. And so it was that the lad found himself lashed into a hammock, swingin' in the half light on the lower decks of a man-o'-war. What I dinna bargain for was how much his sorry plight would affect me." And the look in the man's eyes as he spoke reflected all the pain in my own.

Thomas, according to Mr. Stewart, was no ordinary case. Of course pressed men rebel, but Thomas did so with such relentless fervor that even Captain Babbington began to take notice. "He was a right good sailor, ye had tae give thae lad that, an' knew his trade well as any. But he made a rare habit of defecting, and every attempt he made tae go over the side was met with due consequences. At first the captain merely had his grog and tobacco stopped indefinitely. This would have sorely chaffed any ordinary sailor, but young Mr. Crichton hardly took notice at all. Next time the lad tried tae go over the side he was given the lash. And yet he still persisted in this foolishness. In fact, young Tam made such a point o' defectin,' 'twas almost a game between him and the marines what keep order on the ship. Every night marine guards were posted to keep watch—every fishing vessel that pulled alongside was checked, and every trick in the book was tried and duly thwarted. The lad was denied all liberties except his work, and even at that he had to be monitored by a watchful eye. 'Twas I that was given this unholy job.

"Young Mr. Crichton received more excruciating discipline than ever a man was meant to receive, and still he persisted. When I had brought him down to the ship's doctor tae have his back anointed and wrapped for the seventeenth time in nearly as many days, I finally asked the lad, why? Why did he persist so? It was then young Tam turned to me, and as he's lying there facedown on the doctor's table, he says with that steely blue gaze o' his mocking me, 'As I've told ye before, I have commitments, Mr. Stewart, commitments to a lady. I doubt very much if ye ken what either word—*commitment* or *lady*—might mean.' Well," Mr. Stewart remarked, smiling at the memory, "young Tam always had humor about him, ye had tae give him that. An' a right way with words too. And I will tell ye this, he took his punishment with as much goodwill as any man could. Even auld Captain Babbington began to take pity on him and offered to send the particular woman he was trying to reach sae desperately a letter.

"Tam, seein' that he was being given an inch, began a string o' letters that day, quite inundating the poor captain. And when he was no' writing letters, or doing his duty, he was plotting his next attempt to divest himself of thae auld *Majestic*! Might I tell ye, ma'am, how his heart broke every time one o' his letters was returned unopened? It drove even the most hardened auld salt tae tears."

"But . . . but I never received any letters, Mr. Stewart!" I averred, feeling a frantic, helpless despair. "I swear, had I received but one, I would have likely commandeered my own ship and attempted to find him!"

"Aye," he said with a soft smile. "I believe that ye would too. And so must have your parents. For poor Tam dinna even ken where ye were but for your home in Edinburgh."

"And my mother had returned all Thomas' letters unopened!" I added dejectedly, quite overcome myself with the heartache he must have felt.

"Now, my dear, it just so happened that when all this came

about, old Bony was startin' up his tricks again. And we found ourselves pitched for battle with a Frenchie. Every man jack o' us was itching for a fight that day, but none so more than your Thomas. In fact, I believe it fair drove him, and for once he gave no thought tae jumpin' ship. For he was in so much pain already, both physical and mental, that only the heat of battle could soothe him.

"The captain knew that young Tam would fight with every drop o' blood that flowed through his fiery veins, and so he put him on the boarding party under me. That was when Tam asked of me his favor.

"He told me all about ye, Miss Sara. So good was his description that I would ha' known ye had I met ye on the crowded streets o' London. And once he had described a bit of what lay between ye, he asked, should he be knocked on the head, would I find ye and give to ye all his belongings. I promised him I would, but I also swore on my life that I would make certain he would be the one to find ye once the war was over.

"Your Tam fought like a lion that day, and the bloodlust was full on him. He killed many a Frenchman before he answered my sorry call. We had been fighting side by side on the enemy's decks and got separated. Seven frogs had me in a corner when young Tam came to my aid and pulled them off me, flinging them here and there with an unworldly strength. And only when the deck had been cleared did I realize the great gash on his head. For Tam, caught up in the moment, dinna even feel it himself. But he saw the look in my eye, and I believe 'twas then he grew a wee frightened. He noticed for the first time the blood running down his face in great rivulets, and says to me, 'Och! Jeb, 'tis nothin'! Never ye worry 'bout me,' right before collapsing into me arms. I carried him down to the surgery, that poor fisherman's son, and he looked me in the eye, his own moist with pain, and said, 'Ye remember your promise, Jeb. Ye find Miss Sara Stevenson and tell her how I loved her. Never forget, man. Never forget . . .'"

There were tears in the old sailor's eyes as he uttered these words, and they fell down his sun-wrinkled face, leaving great salty streaks that glistened in the soft morning light. But his were not the only cheeks that were wet. There was not a dry eye in the entire room, nor was there a sound uttered. We were all transported by Mr. Stewart's story.

The old man-o'-war's man cleared his throat and continued. "I says to the lad, thon poor beautiful boy, 'Ach, ye daft mannie, ye tell her yourself!' and to that Tam smiled. 'Twas a glorious smile on that boy, an' that was how he died, smiling in my arms, all the while thinking of ye, Miss Stevenson."

It was while the HMS *Majestic* was refitting at Gibraltar, after the battle Mr. Stewart had described, that he ran into some old mates newly employed on the privateer *Le Temeraire*, a ship whose very name meant *reckless*. These men, cast-offs from the navy during the decommissioning of a great many ships when the war looked to be over, had landed themselves in a lucrative venture. They told him how they frequented a coast, a forlorn coast on the northern tip of Scotland, where they had heard tales of a beautiful young woman who had been sent to live in a lighthouse there, built by her father, one Robert Stevenson. Mr. Stewart, upon hearing the name Stevenson, knew fate had intervened.

"And that very night I achieved what poor Tam had failed to do ever since coming aboard. I defected right there, never a look back, and joined the crew of the *Le Temeraire.*"

And in this way Mr. Stewart made good on his promise to Thomas Crichton; I now felt moved to make a promise of my own.

While the brave sailor sat teary-eyed in the chair beside my bed, I handed him the tiny child in my arms. "This, Mr. Stewart, is Thomas Crichton's son, born this night of June first in the year eighteen hundred and fifteen. You once held his father, and for that I am eternally grateful; now you honor me by holding his son."

Mr. Stewart looked at the newly born infant in his arms as the tears continued streaming down his cheeks. And with the tenderness of a proud parent he bent and kissed the downy head. "I never met a braver man than your father, laddie," he cooed in a voice as tender as a nursemaid's. "An' I was blessed tae have known him. When ye get old enough, auld Jeb Stewart will tell ye more of the man whose name ye now bear."

Mr. Stewart heartily agreed to be godfather of Thomas Crichton's only child, and he made good on that promise too.

·   ·   ·

It was some time before I felt strong enough to look at all of Thomas' worldly effects neatly packed into the little wooden sea chest bearing his name, which Mr. Stewart had gone to such pains to deliver. I was surprised by how little there was, just some sailor's slops, a comb, a tin pannikin and spoon, a knife, a Bible, an Edinburgh edition of *Poems, Chiefly in the Scottish Dialect* by Robert Burns and a little sack of money that he had been saving, all of which took up only half the chest. The other half, to my astonishment, was entirely filled with letters addressed to me . . . all of which had been returned unopened. That simple truth broke my heart.

William Campbell and I were finally able to finish what we had started in my bedroom on that stormy night at the end of May, yet it was a good six weeks before we did. That was when my baby was christened, legally bearing the name Thomas Crichton II. For it was proven, beyond a shadow of a doubt, that he was no man's bastard but the legitimate son of a dead man. Because of the letters, the irrefragable mutual consent on both our parts and the peculiarities of Scottish law, Thomas and I were man and wife under God for those few weeks when our child was conceived, even if no one ever knew of it but us. Kate bore testimony, working hard to repair the friendship we once had. I was not a begrudging soul, but I was stubborn, and slowly Kate MacKinnon became a woman even I could be proud of. On that same day, after the christening of wee Thomas Crichton, another ceremony was held at the old church in Durness, and that was the marriage ceremony joining me, Sara Stevenson Crichton, to William Campbell.

William was a fine man and a good husband. The successful and blessedly uneventful birth of wee Thomas did much to lift that veil of death that so plagued him. And though he never embraced the vocation of physician again, he did have an astounding amount of knowledge on the subject. This drove the scientist within him; his intellect and curiosity were great, and the natural world held a kind of fascination for him that at times bordered on irksome. When he wasn't busy preserving mariners' lives he turned his passions in the direction of amateur naturalist and studied, as no man before him had ever done, the flora and fauna indigenous to the Cape. Wee Hughie was his first apprentice in the art, the boy knowing instinctively where to find the creatures William sought out, and he, more often than not, took his knife to the poor beasts that intrigued him so, drawing his findings meticulously in one of his leather-bound sketchbooks.

However, one creature I absolutely forbade William to dissect and examine under his microscope was the hare; for that guileless little besom abounded in our garden (much to his chagrin), validating my theory on peas. The hares of Cape Wrath loved peas as much as I did not, and they had eaten every last one of the fleshy plants down to the nub. William suffered duly for this, first because he liked peas, and second because the victory, however small, went straight to my head. But he, being the canny man he was, was thoroughly adept at trapping hares, and caught them by the score. We ate of them gladly, but William was forbidden to take them beyond the stewpot!

We chose to stay at the lighthouse on Cape Wrath, a place that in those early days resembled more of a nursery than any proper place of business. And slowly, the ghosts of William's terrible past left him. The only time I saw fear in those pale, haunting eyes of his was whenever another child was about to be born. It was only after the successful delivery of our fourth son (William Campbell only knew how to give me sons; Kate and Robbie had all the daughters) that I suggested, perhaps mockingly, that he just stay in his tower if he preferred and I'd handle the matter myself, calling him down at the "all clear." I could see that he actually entertained this thought, a wistful smile flitting across his handsome face at the suggestion. But William had too much of the physician about him yet to pass up such a learning opportunity and delivered every one of our sons and Kate's daughters with his own capable hands. He was also remarkably adept at mixing his own elixirs!

Although Cape Wrath was to always be our home we did make the trip south to Edinburgh a few times. The first of these was the November after Thomas was born. William was required to make a visit to Baxter Place, duty drove him; nothing nearly so honorable drove me. My parents were quite pleased with the match I had made, for William Campbell came from a good family, but even they knew that from their previous actions I was lost to them as a daughter.

Yet there was another reason we had traveled to Edinburgh that November besides seeking my parents' blessing, and for this purpose William and I found ourselves wandering through a little fishing village on the Leith estuary. And when the man opened the door of the little hovel we had knocked on, I knew instantly I had come to the right place, for there could be no mistaking who he was. The magnetic blue gaze, the disarming white-toothed smile and the hair once golden but now white; he was the image of his son, only older, grayer . . . sadder. And as instantaneously as I had recognized him, he had recognized me, for Thomas, after that glorious tour around the coast, had gone home and made his peace with his father at last. He had moved back there, choosing the hut of a poor but kindly fisherman over his crowded lodgings in a questionable section of Edinburgh. And there, under the roof of the only other person who had loved him as much as I, he had lived. It was there he strove to be a good, honorable man. And it was there he had ended up telling his father all about me, including our plans to elope.

When the man saw his grandchild in my arms, he cried. They were tears of joy and sorrow in equal amount. He then took his grandson in his arms in a meeting that touched both William and me beyond words. I knew for a certainty we had done the right thing by finding him. Just as both William and I knew that James Crichton would play an important role in his grandson's life.

William and I often talked of the night that had changed both our lives forever, but never around the children. The rescue of the men from the privateer *Le Temeraire*, though thoroughly successful in every way, was never formally noted by the lighthouse, nor was it ever mentioned by the people of the Cape, except for during those long winter nights spent huddled around the hearth, where fantastical tales were spun and retold year after year, purely for the entertainment of young and old alike. The elusive craft *Le Temeraire* was never to be seen (officially) again, yet oddly enough, claret was still the preferred drink of the locals!

From the moment wee Thomas arrived on Cape Wrath, the letters from Mr. Seawell had stopped. His identity was always a great mystery to us, and why he had chosen to contact me through Thomas was an even more puzzling incident for us to comprehend. We knew we never would understand. We had even traveled to Oxford once to find his lodgings, but were told, on several occasions, that no one by that name had ever lived there. The trail was dead. There was no information anyone could give us on the man's identity. And William and I were both in agreement when we surmised that we had both been touched by something special and unearthly that year—something that only the two of us had been able to share. I never heard from Mr. Seawell again. Yet I knew, deep within the core of my being, that one day Alexander Seawell would come to

Cape Wrath. And I prayed that what he would find once he arrived would be enough to restore his faith in humanity once again, just as his letters had helped to restore my faith and had brought William Campbell to me.

And that unearthly little skiff, owned by an angel and sailed by the man who forever had a hold of my heart? The ghost of Thomas Crichton never again appeared. It was only that once. And it was that fleeting, unearthly encounter at the jetty that forever changed my life and the way I would look at life from then on. No, Thomas Crichton never came to Cape Wrath again. But I never could bring myself to stop searching for him. Never . . .

# TWELVE

## Alexander Seawell

### MAY 31, 1915

*I*t had been a hellish journey, and one he was glad was nearly over. Yet getting to Cape Wrath posed problems of its own. After taking that crowded, smoke-filled, meandering train route north from Oxford, changing once in Edinburgh and then again at Aberdeen, he finally made it to Inverness, that glittering capital of the Highlands. Yet there he found his journey was just beginning. Another rail was in order, heading north yet again, across the River Ness and into the Highlands proper. Yet the old steam engine could only take him as far as a little village called Forsinard. Thankfully, he was in Sutherland.

It was there he attempted to hire a taxi to take him to the northern village of Durness. Arriving at the little station he questioned a local man. The man, like many he had encountered north of the border, speaking a form of English he barely understood, comprehending only five to the dozen words and even then he was only guessing, smiled at his naïveté. He inquired of the man again, asking after a lorry for hire, and this time he was directed to another soul dwelling on the outskirts of the little village.

Alexander found the croft without incident, being the only one for miles. And it was there he met an old peat harvester named Hamish MacPhee, a weather-beaten yet apparently cheerful gent who seemed overjoyed at the prospect of company. After taking a glass of the local whisky he inquired of the man about hiring transportation to carry him as far as Durness. The old crofter smiled and disappeared into a lime-washed building, returning a moment later with a short, portly, ill-looking donkey.

Alexander waved his hands in alarm at the sight of the mange-ridden creature, and told the man he was in search of an automobile, or bicycle, or horse-driven hayrick. The old crofter shook his head and beheld him with a near toothless smile, insisting the donkey was the preferred transportation of these parts. But Alexander didn't want a donkey, he told the man, not even at the cut rate of seven pounds. But he might consider the old plow horse for the same fee.

Here the old man balked. For the plow horse was his bread and butter; the plow horse he could not spare. It was the donkey or nothing.

Alexander, feeling despair and a keen desperation to press onward, knew his choices were few, and so, begrudgingly, he paid the farmer the seven pounds and found himself either the new owner or new leaser of a stocky, unmotivated beast of burden named Donkey-Odie. The farmer had said the creature's name with relish; but Alexander did not smile. He was too preoccupied with marveling at his own stupidity. The farmer, thinking the Englishman had not heard him correctly, for he knew the English to be queer folk without an ear for the local jargon, handed him the lead rope, saying the name faster. This time Alexander heard it correctly. The name sounded suspiciously like Don Quixote.

A frown crossed his lips at the same time the old man smiled cleverly as they stood in the doorway of the dark, hay-infested barn. Alexander chanced a peek inside and saw that it was lined to the rafters with thick bricks of drying peat. Shame flooded him as he stared at the smelly creature. A name so great in literature should not be degraded so, even if the beast that bore it would be carrying his luggage over moorland, and mountain, through peat bog and forest, to the relative metropolis of a town called Durness. The donkey, a suspect and notably unchivalrous beast, brayed loudly and proudly in response to his name. Alexander, not being one to question the ways of the aged or the infirm, nodded his acceptance of this new and trying torture, and attempted to lead his reluctant travel companion (which for reasons of his own he chose to call Odie) down the road, all the while the sound of laughter trailing at their backs. And just when he was out of earshot of the old man and his raucous hilarity, the rain started.

It was coming down in buckets by the time they entered the peat bog. That was pure hell. Even Odie, a loud though somewhat compliant beast, sat down and brayed in protest. Yet Alexander was on a mission, and come hell or high water—even treacherous spongy bog—he would make it to the lighthouse on Cape Wrath! And so, with the help of a willow switch industriously applied, man and donkey pushed on.

And that was when Alexander Seawell of Oxford questioned his sanity and his noble motives.

He had plenty of time to ponder his rash action too as he and Odie trudged along under a black cloud that seemed to be following them. And he traced it back, all the way back to that horrible day in France when that poor young soldier lay dying in his arms, young Jamie Crichton. The lad had given him that remarkable chronometer and had asked with his pleading blue eyes if he would return it to his pregnant wife. It was not an unusual request for a man who had just given his life in battle. And he had assured the young man that he would. But the watch was very fine—too fine for a young Scotsman to be carrying into battle. He was ashamed when he thought back on how he had toyed with the prospect of keeping it. Yet the lad's eyes had haunted him, and he pushed his greed aside and sent that young man's fine timepiece to a place called Cape Wrath. He had never even heard of Cape Wrath before, let alone harbored a desire to visit such a place. Scotland, with its rugged beauty and odd-speaking people, was for the Scots and hardly a place to interest a man like him—with, perhaps, the exception of Edinburgh . . . possibly even Glasgow. But they could keep the rest of the country to themselves for all he cared.

And truthfully he hadn't cared.

He hadn't cared about anything until he received that first letter. He never expected a letter in response to his, especially one that smacked of so much venom against some poor bloke named Thomas Crichton. It was from a woman, no less—a young, rather vibrant woman, and not at all the poor widow he had intended to reach. But this woman—this Sara Stevenson, as she called herself—had awakened something buried deep within him with her words; her passion was palpable. And he found that in spite of himself, and his stoic resolve to never be happy again, her words had made him smile.

And God, it had felt good to smile.

It was then he set out to explain himself a little better to this Miss Stevenson, and to assure the feisty creature that young, brave James Crichton was not at all the lecherous blackguard she inquired after. And he certainly did not bear the name of Thomas either!

Again came a letter, this one even more inexplicable than the first, and the sight of it had affected him more than he would have liked to admit. For that wall he had struggled so hard to erect, that impregnable mental structure designed to protect him from ever getting hurt again, was coming down, and all because of some spurned woman who had felt compelled to write him from a lonely outpost called Cape Wrath.

It was her letters alone that had kept him going when nothing else could. When his tour of duty fighting on the continent had ended he came home even more lost and dejected than when he had first enlisted. For so many of his countrymen had died over there. He even tried to get his old job back at the university, researching and teaching in the college of history, and was immediately awarded a seat in the department. But it was too soon, too rash, and his first time in the lecture hall was utterly disastrous.

He had been well prepared. Sparked by the beautiful timepiece of young Mr. Crichton, he decided to talk about chronometers, the art of horology, and the problem of longitude that had so plagued the mariner up until the early nineteenth century. He would talk about John Harrison, the brilliant horologist, and his quest to create an accurate sea-clock. He would talk of his predecessors, the intrepid Earnshaw and his contribution of the spring detent escapement, and the remarkable John Arnolds, father and son, both with an amazing gift to reproduce the chronometer like none before them ever had. And he had held one of their fine pieces, if only for the space of a few weeks.

But in that lecture hall, as he looked out over the young, impressionable faces that sat and listened to his oration, he saw that ghastly blue pallor of death that had so recently plagued him in France.

He tried not to look at the students, but that was not his style. Reflexively he looked up again, and that was when his eyes caught the magnetic blue of another. It was a young man, a hauntingly familiar young man who stared at him with James Crichton's eyes. But the young man was not James. He was a golden-haired Adonis; yet the blue pallor of death had marred his fine looks. But the eyes . . . oh how they had glowed! Alexander, unable to take his eyes off the young man, was shaking uncontrollably, and finally had to dash out of the lecture hall in a panic-sweat. He realized then that he could never go back there—back to his old life and his old ways.

He had changed.

He was a changed man. And the only comfort he found was in the womanly round hand of a strange young lady who lived at the far end of his island home. And he was sorry to think that he found himself fantasizing about her nearly every minute of the day. What did she look like? What did her voice sound like? How would they get along if they were ever to meet? It was wrong of him; he knew that much. But God help him, he was not entirely in his right mind these days!

And then came that little note. It was not her best letter, no heart-wrenching story of her lost love, nor did it speak of the ongoing fight against her family to keep the child she was carrying. No, it was nothing of the kind. It was short and urgent, and touchingly simple. She asked, quite plainly, if he would find it in his heart to be with her when the baby came, for she didn't think she could bear it alone.

Of course, his mind was already made up on the matter. This young woman had become everything to him, and he would see her child safely into the world. He believed it was fate that deigned it so; his journey north was inevitable. And in that instant, after reading that urgent last letter, he had dropped everything (not that he had been doing much), and took off for the place called Cape Wrath.

.  .  .

Alexander and the obstinate beast Odie finally made it to the little village of Durness, tired, hungry and positively aching with the effort of getting there. Yet again he was made to realize, as he quenched his thirst and sated his hunger in the local inn, that there was no transportation out to the lighthouse. There was a road, the boy who served him his ale had stated, though not a good one, but at least there was a road. And the boy smiled at this, finding it smugly amusing. He told the cold, wet man that if he was planning to get himself out to the lighthouse that night, as he had insisted on doing, then he was just going to have to walk the eleven miles himself!

Alexander paid for the meal and gave as a tip to the helpful youth his smelly, wet travel companion, Donkey-Odie. Whether the young man wanted the beast or not, Alexander didn't really care, nor did he wait around to find out. Instead he took his belongings from the donkey's back, slung them over his shoulder, fed Odie a few apples, and then gave a loving scratch behind the ears as a fond farewell. Before the sky ever thought of opening up again, spilling from the thick blanket of black clouds its wind-driven waters, he took himself off in the direction of the ferry at the Kyle of Durness.

In retrospect, Alexander believed he had never behaved with such temerity in all his twenty-nine years. He was getting older now, no longer a young man, and he would need to start to pull his life together if he was ever going to make anything of himself. And this rash trip to the far end of Scotland, character-building though it was, was not likely helping him gain that foothold on reality he so desperately needed.

Also, in retrospect, perhaps he should not have burdened the boy at the inn with the donkey. He might have need to eat there again someday, and soon, he mused while observing the rolling black sky. And he doubted very much if the service would be improved by his generous gift.

He had traveled no more than four miles when the rain began. However, it was not a driving rain . . . yet. He offered up a quick prayer to keep it so, even though he had lost faith in such things as prayer. But it had long been his habit to utter a wish to the God of his childhood, for that God had been kind to him; it was the God of his manhood that was wanting.

And strangely, crossing the damp, drizzly moorland that sat atop the highest cliffs on the Isle of Britain, he found himself desperately wanting to believe in something again.

It was late when Alexander Seawell arrived at the lighthouse after walking the many miles through undulating moorland, and once there the reality of what he had done began to sink in. He had traveled nearly the length of Great Britain, suffering extreme discomfort and even owning a beast of burden for a day, just to see a woman he had never even met. What if she had changed her mind? What if she really did not want him there?

What if . . . ?

What if . . . ?

But he knew there were a million "what ifs." He also knew that he was going to have to bite the bullet, as they say, sometime.

Alexander, pulling himself up to his full six-foot height, stood unmoving beneath the towering light that flashed its yellow beam, a beam that had beckoned him onward for these last many miles through rain and darkness. And though he had braved the hellfire in the trenches on the continent with nary a care, he felt himself shake like a newly foaled colt at the thought of what he was about to do.

Dear Lord, how his whole body shook and trembled!

He tried to steady himself; he made a mad attempt at courage. But in the end it was the air, swirling about him wet and cold, charged with the tingle of electricity, that finally drove him to the cottage door. For his body began to tingle and prickle with electric excitement and he truly believed that if he didn't move soon he would be struck by a rogue bolt of lightning for his stupidity.

Water was pouring off his hatless head in rivulets as he set his hand to the wood of the door. He gave one great, purposeful knock. It was a hard knock, for he was now determined, but not nearly so hard as to burst open the door in the manner it had. The oaken slab flung inward with such rapidity, creating a mighty bang as it hit the inside wall. It was as if a gust of wind had blown it open, and the shock of it stunned him.

Yet it was nothing compared to the shock of seeing her there, standing by the fire, holding tightly to the mantel as if it were the only thing keeping her upright. At the sound of the bursting door, the woman had turned to face him, and in that one moment all his fears were allayed.

She was beautiful, magnificently beautiful beyond even his wildest fancies. And she was as ripe as a melon, he noted with wan dismay, near to bursting with the child she carried; the child he would now see safely into this world.

Yet the surprise on her face startled him. Her look was one of shock, as if she hadn't expected to see him there. In truth, his arrival was untimely, and he could hardly blame her for the wild-eyed look of fright she had turned on him. Yet after all, she was the one who had asked him to come. And he had told her that he would. But still, the beautiful creature didn't utter a sound.

"Sara," he half whispered, half croaked. "It's me. It's Alexander. I've come at long last, my dear. Please, do not look so alarmed, love. T'will never do. I told you I would make it, and here I am." Although this speech was delivered with a disarming smile, much to his great dismay, it did nothing to calm the woman. In fact, if he was reading the situation correctly, she seemed even more frightened by far.

She turned fully to face him. Her eyes were as green as emeralds, he saw, silently admiring them as they flashed alarm, and the hair, the magnificent strawberry blond hair that framed her face, had tumbled about her shoulders in a cascade of loose curls. She was stunning! And the color, that soft apricot hue, almost matched the flush of her cheeks. Yet it was her pink rosebud lips that held his attention as they formed the word *Who?*

She tried again, looking at him as if she had seen a ghost. "Who . . . who did ye say you were, sir?"

"Why, I'm Alexander, my dear. The man you've asked to come? It was like traveling through the very gates of hell to get here, I tell you, but here I am." His heart—that sensitive organ that had just begun to beat again with a glorious purpose—had now nearly stopped beating within his chest. "Is . . . is that not what you wanted? Am I not what you imagined I would be?" he uttered in a near whisper.

"I'm afraid, sir, I dinna understand what the devil you're talking about."

It was too much, the pain of it—the heartache was too much—and he blurted, "By God, it's me, Sara! Alexander Seawell! The man who's been writing you these past six months! The man who sent you the timepiece from James Crichton? By God, I'm the very man whose heart you've managed to mend with your kindness!"

Recognition dawned in the green eyes that stared unblinkingly at him, and a wave of relief finally hit home. But then, just as he believed she finally understood, she surprised him yet again by letting out a loud, pain-stricken gasp. "You . . . you knew my Jamie? Your name is Alexander Seawell and ye knew my Jamie? Dear heavens above . . ." And then her eyes—those magnificent misty emerald eyes—rolled back in her head. It was all he noted before catching her unconscious form in his arms.

．　．　．

When the young lady finally awoke she beheld him with a look of awe and wonder, and uttered in a voice very like an angel, "You are Alexander Seawell and ye knew my Jamie!"

"Yes, my dear. I did know a young man by that name. He served under me in my regiment. But I thought you were not married to Jamie. In fact, you heatedly denied as much in your letters. You only spoke of a Thomas, if you'll recall, a Thomas Crichton. He was the man you loved," he reminded her gently, silently thinking that the advanced pregnancy had addled her mind.

Yet this did not have the desired effect on the poor creature either. For she, in her fragile state, swore emphatically that James Crichton was her husband.

"Sir," she began, sitting in one of the chairs near the hearth, "my name indeed is Sara, and your name is legend in our home. I dinna expect ye to understand, but I'm no' the Sara you came to find."

"What do you mean, you're not the Sara I came to find?" he questioned, beginning to feel like a great fool. "How many Sara Stevensons live in a lighthouse on Cape Wrath, Scotland, may I ask?"

She smiled kindly at him and gently took his hand, barely believing it herself. "There were a few women by the name of Sara who have lived in this place, but only one that bore the name Stevenson. I am Sara Crichton, wife of Jamie Crichton, who died in the Battle of Givenchy in France nearly eight months ago."

"Holy Mother," he uttered, looking at this young, pregnant woman anew. This was the woman to whom he had written that first letter. He had addressed his letter to Sara Crichton, Keeper· of the Light on Cape Wrath, just as Jamie had instructed. And she had kept the fine chronometer but had denied everything. What the hell was she playing at? "You say your husband died in the Battle of Givenchy?" Just uttering the name of the place made him shudder. It brought back all the horrible memories, all the men that had died over those four bloody days. He returned his attention to her, his brown eyes narrowing as he took in the size of her belly. "But . . . was not your lover one Thomas Crichton? A man you yourself called . . . How did you put it? Ah yes, a besotted, debauching sailor?" he accused, his ire rising.

At this description, her fine pink lips pulled into a rueful smile. "I'm sorry to inform ye, but no! The only man I ever loved was Jamie Crichton, an honorable man like his father, and his father before him. Mr. Seawell, sir, I dinna profess to know what the devil's going on here, or what it is that brought ye out to Cape Wrath on such a night as this, but I think ye had best come with me. For there's something I must show ye that I have no way of explaining."

She led him out of the cottage, walking rather slowly due to the great weight she carried, which also induced a charming little waddle. He found that it moved him strangely. The rain was still coming down, and they went as fast as they could into the lighthouse. They did not head up the spiral stairs but went instead down a dark hallway to a door at the end. This led to a storage room of sorts, he realized as his eyes adjusted to the wan light. And once they did, he noted that there were all manner of treasures that had been kept there. The antiquarian in him was spellbound by the array of antiquities, but the man in him pressed on; for the woman was intent on showing him something buried at the back of the room.

She brought him to stand before an old wooden chest—finely made, he assessed, and one very like what a sailor might have used a century ago, in the great age of sail. And then he noticed the name etched into the dark wood. The name, to his horror, was Thomas Crichton. He stood speechless.

"This is the sea chest of Jamie's great-great-grandfather," she said softly, running a reflective finger over the name while watching how the man reacted to the sight of it. She was not disappointed. "James," she continued wistfully, "was fascinated with this, for it was always shrouded in such great mystery. And it was always kept under lock and key by his grandfather, James Crichton the second. For auld James was the keeper of the chest, a responsibility passed down by his father, Thomas Crichton the second before him, whose own father was the man who owned this sea chest. It was always kept under lock and key, as I've told ye, not to be disturbed ever, until a man named Alexander Seawell should happen to come to the lighthouse." She looked curiously at him. Still he did not understand. She continued. "It was Thomas Crichton the second who was entrusted with this special duty, for his mother, one Sara Stevenson-Crichton-Campbell, had instructed him on her deathbed that it should be so. For to Alexander Seawell alone she had willed this auld relic. And you, sir, are the first of that name to ever have come along." Her eyes held to his as she said this.

He was stunned. His mind could barely make sense of what

she had told him. Yet one look at the old wooden chest, with the familiar name emblazoned upon it, made him slowly understand that something very odd and surreal was unfolding before his eyes. Perhaps it was the long journey through the Highlands? Perhaps it was the purchase of the unchancy little donkey from the old crofter? Whatever the cause of the unearthly incident, he was undeniably moved and horrified beyond words.

The woman, the beautiful pregnant widow of his former comrade, was speaking again. "Of course, no one knew of a man by that name," she informed him kindly. "And everybody thought the lady had gone daft in her auld age. Many, many years passed between Sara's time and my Jamie's, ye understand. 'Twas only when Jamie's grandfather took himself back to live in Edinburgh that my husband, who was then Keeper of the Light here, received the key and the duty of guarding this chest. But the temptation was too great. Jamie was such a dear lad, Mr. Seawell, such a dear lad indeed, and never a day goes by that I dinna cry for him. But he had an insatiable curiosity, and instead of just keeping the auld chest as is—as legend dictates it should be—he broke the lock and delved into the mystery.

"Ye see," she continued softly, "the legend of this family and this chest begins with Jamie's great-great-grandmother who was the daughter of the man what built this lighthouse. She was said to be quite beautiful, and was from an important Edinburgh family. But when she disgraced them by falling in love with a sailor, a poor sweet lad by the name of Thomas Crichton, they sent her here as punishment. For Sara had gotten herself with child from this man. And here's where the story thickens. Sara thought she had been abandoned, not only by her family, but also by the man she dearly loved. Yet she could not have been further from the truth! 'Twas her family what had done her a wrong turn. It came out that they had paid a man to knock her lover on the head and press him into service on one of the king's ships before they could ever marry proper; for there was a war on at the time. The lad died in a bloody battle four months later, but no' before writing to her every day they were apart. And here, Mr. Seawell, are all his letters to her."

The chest gave a deep groan of protest as she lifted the lid for him. Instantly, and with an unheeded curiosity, he bent his head to investigate the cavernous hold. The contents, he noted, contained some vintage, well-preserved sailor's slops, an old mess kit containing a knife, spoon and pannikin, a beautiful family Bible and a fine and quite collectible first edition of Burns' poetry. Although that was titillating for a man such as he, it couldn't hold a candle to what lay in the rest of the chest; for every last inch of it was filled with folded papers.

They were letters, he saw, yellow with age, and all the wax seals broken. He gingerly picked one up and saw that the edges were terribly worn and dog-eared; they were all like that . . . as if each one had been read over and over again. But they had all been carefully refolded and tied by lengths of red satin ribbon. He could hardly believe what he was witnessing, let alone what he was feeling. It made no sense. For if all this lady was telling him was true, then he had been communicating these past six months, and falling in love with . . . a ghost. And then he couldn't help himself; a tear slipped from his life-hardened eye.

"They say," James' widow continued in her pure, sweet voice, almost wistfully, "that when she learned the truth of what had befallen her, she broke off with her family and chose to live out her life here on the Cape. Only when her Tom was old enough did she send him to be educated in Edinburgh. He was a bright, honest lad, and her family was quick to take him into the family business. But he soon tired of it and came home, back to the Cape, where he married a local girl by the name of Maggie MacKay. They settled out here at the lighthouse."

"But what of . . ." he heard himself utter in a voice strained with sorrow. "What . . . what of Sara Stevenson?" There, it was out, and he fought the tightening in his throat while beholding the young lady, feeling his heart breaking yet again.

Her eyes held him with kind pity. "Why, never ye worry about her, sir. She lived a good life, Mr. Seawell. While she was serving out her time here, awaiting the birth of her illegitimate child and believing that Thomas had left her, she began to harbor certain tender feelings for the man who was the first light-keeper here, a man they say was appointed especially by her father for the job. His name was—"

"William Campbell," he finished for her.

She looked questioningly at him.

"I know. I know about him. She mentioned him once in a letter."

"What do you mean by 'she mentioned him once in a letter,' sir? Sara Campbell's been dead for nigh on fifty years. I highly doubt the lady would be sending any letters."

He smiled wanly at her, knowing that just as her mysterious little chest had been hard to explain—having been designated for him nearly one hundred years ago—his own letters from a dead woman named Sara Stevenson would likely also seem odd, but he would try to make sense of it. And he attempted to explain to Jamie's wife what exactly had brought him out to the Cape in the first place.

"So that's how she must have known you would come," the young lady said, her fine apricot brows drawn together in consternation as she tried to make sense out of a tale that made no sense at all. "If she was writing to ye, and ye were writing to her, but . . . Oh Mr. Seawell, how could that be? 'Tis impossible!"

"I can tell you, Mrs. Crichton, how I long to know it myself. All I know is that Sara Stevenson, or Crichton, or whatever she called herself, wrote to me in my time of need. I don't know how or why, but she did." He swallowed painfully, looking at the young woman who appeared the very image of what he envisioned Sara would have looked liked had she been alive. "And I, God help me," he uttered as tears stung at his brown eyes once again, "I fell in love with her."

Sara Crichton, the widow, attempted to console Alexander Seawell, kindly offering him a handkerchief pulled from the depths of her calico dress. "Never ye worry about her, sir. She lived a good, happy life here. She was much loved by all who knew her. William Campbell gave her many sons, most of whom decided to live around Edinburgh . . . some even in England. They were all such bright lads. But she and Willy, for some unknown reason, stayed right here. She helped the local men prosper respectfully, for at that time they were rumored to have engaged in a wee smuggling operation, running a whisky distillery here and smuggling their brew over to the French in exchange for wine. And she even started a school for the local children. If you like, if it will make you feel any better, I can show you where she lies."

"She's . . . here? She's buried here?"

The woman turned to him, her eyes looking suddenly strange and distant. "Aye, she's still here. Sara Stevenson-Crichton-Campbell has never left us yet." Her eyes focused on him again. Thank goodness they'd lost that misty-eyed distance, he thought. "I can show you, if you like."

"Yes," he whispered, fighting back the darkness that was closing in again. "I would like that very much."

Sara Crichton, the younger, then took out the stack of letters and handed them to him, suggesting he might want to read them to get a better picture of the woman to whom the letters were written and the man who had written them but was denied her love. Yet when the pile was removed Sara Crichton gasped, noticing something she hadn't before.

"Dear Lord," she uttered, crossing herself. He saw that her green eyes were filling with tears. "How . . . how did that get in here?" And before he could ask the source of her alarm she pulled from the bottom of the chest a silver pocket watch.

It was the John Roger Arnold silver detent chronometer, circa 1805. The one he had taken from James' hand as the young man lay dying in a trench, and promised to return it to his wife. Tied around the watch was a folded piece of paper, terribly yellowed with age, yet addressed to one Alexander Seawell of Oxford. Her hand shook. Tears filled her eyes.

"Jamie . . . my Jamie had taken that watch from the chest and carried it with him off to war!" she cried. "I warned him against it . . . said that it should not be removed! Family legend says it must stay! It must stay until a man named Alexander Seawell of Oxford arrived! But my Jamie dinnae believe in the legend, Mr. Seawell. He thought 'twas all nonsense. How . . . how is it possible?"

Like the poor widow, his hand also shook as he took the watch from her, and he noticed with some alarm that it was still ticking. But this he did not mention, nor was he certain of what to tell this poor woman. His eyes were then drawn to the note.

A note written in *her* hand.

The sight of it took the breath from him and he found, to his great dismay and astonishment, that he was again brought to tears. He itched to read it. He longed for her hand, for that round womanly script was like a balm to his very soul. Yet before he could read her last letter to him, the young lady let out a blood-curdling cry. He turned at the sound and saw that she was grabbing her pregnant belly. A gush of water then fell to the storeroom floor, darkening her long calico skirt in the process. He knew in that moment James Crichton's child was coming.

·    ·    ·

Alexander Seawell of Oxford delivered Sara Crichton of Cape Wrath a little boy early in the morning of June 1 in the year 1915. The mother instantly named her infant son, who sported a tuft of dark hair and blue eyes like his father, James Thomas Crichton, after the man who would have loved him but was denied the chance. Once mother and child had been attended to by the doctor—the man Alexander had wandered the lonely moorland through rain and driving wind in search of, and found residing at a little croft five miles away—and he saw that both mother and child lay sleeping peacefully in bed, only then did he pull a chair by the fire in the parlor and take out the pocket watch.

He carefully untied the note, taking great care not to tear the fragile paper. And then, instinctively, he smelled it. He didn't know why, but he had always smelled her letters, letting the faint hint of lavender and chamomile create a picture in his mind of the woman to whom the beautiful script belonged. His hand, he noticed, was trembling. He studied the watch for a moment, amazed that the old thing still worked—that it could still keep time—and comforted by that fact alone, he thrust it in his shirt pocket, pressing it close to his heart, where he could feel the steady, mechanical beat. And then, still with a trembling hand, he read the note.

*June 1, 1815*

*My dear Alexander,*

*During the month of May, in the year of our Lord, 1815, I waited for your arrival, but you never came. How could you? You had not yet been born. I don't know how else to explain it but for this: our lives were touched by the mysterious power of love causing our paths to cross the insurmountable chasm of time. And to what end, my dear Mr. Seawell, our unearthly correspondence will come to, I cannot tell you. But I do know that one day, many, many years from now, you will come to my home on Cape Wrath, and walk through my door, just as I have envisioned you doing many a time. I do not know what you will find when you arrive, but I do believe you will find what you are looking for, just as I have found the answer to my prayers this night.*

*I am giving to you the timepiece you once sent to me, the very one I once gave to the young man I loved. I know now that he never stopped loving me, and because of that love, I will raise his son and tell him of the fine and brave man who was his father, and of another brave young man from Oxford who helped in a no less poignant, yet utterly unbelievable way, to save his life.*

*Thank you for all your heartfelt words and kindness, and for helping me through a dark and lonely time. You were a godsend. Literally. And I hope you too will find the peace and love you so well deserve, just as have I. I wish for all that makes your life complete.*

*With my sincere and deepest affection,*
*Sara Stevenson Crichton, Keeper of the Light*
*Cape Wrath, Scotland*

Alexander gently folded the letter and wiped the tears from his cheeks, knowing they would keep on coming for some time. It was nearly dark and the storm had finally abated by the time he walked out of the cottage, intent on laying eyes on the grave of the woman who had touched his life from another place and time.

He found the little gravesite alongside another, bearing the name of William Campbell, the man she married instead of him. It was irrational, untimely even, but a flash of jealousy took him at the sight of the name beside her. "I hope you treated her well, old man," he stated plainly. "For she once told me what a bastard you could be. Of course she was too much of a lady to use such a word, but it was implied. How I do pray her initial impression of you was wrong." And then, feeling an unexpected kinship with the name on the tombstone he felt compelled to add, "I envy you, though, Campbell. God, how I envy you."

And then he remembered, Sara Stevenson never told him she loved him. How could he even think she had wanted him that way? He knew she had been in love with another man, Thomas Crichton, just as he had been deeply in love with his wife, Jane. But he had hoped . . . God, but it was useless! The woman was long dead, and so too were his hopes and dreams.

After saying a heartfelt, private prayer over the grave of the woman who had impelled him to journey to the end of the world—the woman he had fantasized about these many months—he then began walking toward the sea, in order to clear his addled, aching head.

His mind was a jumble of emotions and he was at a loss about what to do. He sought solace in the shadow of the great lighthouse, staring out at the vast darkness that was the Atlantic Ocean. Every now and then the light would come around, penetrating the darkness. But it was a misty night. A soft drizzle and low clouds obscured most of the heavens, but there was a breeze, and it felt good on his hot face.

He kept his face to the sea, his eyes closed, thinking of the woman Sara Stevenson while utterly unable to comprehend what had happened to him—and the damnable unfairness of it all.

At length he felt the wind shift. The suddenness of it caused him to open his eyes. And that's when he saw her.

It was the image of a woman, a breathtakingly beautiful woman, wearing a translucent gown in the style of an era long past. And she, just like he, was looking out to sea. She was not standing more than fifteen feet from him. His breath caught in his throat as he beheld her, and he wanted to call out to her, to tell her he had finally come. But he could see that she was not looking at him, she was searching for something, someone. He took a few steps closer, but still she did not look his way. And then he spoke her name. "Sara Stevenson . . ."

She turned to him, and a soft, wistful smile touched her full lips. It was breathtaking—heartbreaking—and without any warning at all she walked right through him.

The shock of it, the jolt of cold air, and the smell—the womanly essence of her—filled him completely. Emotions he had long buried came rushing to the surface again—absurd happiness, calming tranquillity, pure contentment—yet prominent above them all was the utter fulfillment of love. It washed through him; he wanted to bask in its heady glow. But then he realized it was not his love he was feeling. Nor were they his emotions. They were hers . . . they were the emotions of a ghost.

With the wetness of tears coursing down his hot cheeks he followed her, for she was intent on going somewhere.

It was by chance he saw it. It was so dark, no moon or stars to light the way, but the glow from the woman before him was enough. He had followed her gaze out to sea as she headed along the cliff's edge to a point unknown. And what he saw made him stop dead in his tracks.

It was a ship. A ghost ship.

The boat the woman was running to meet was not overly large, just a coastal sailing craft, yet of a make and model long forgotten. He was puzzled by the sight of it, but only for a moment, because that's when he recalled the sea chest. Thomas Crichton had been a sailor; he had also been her lover.

Alexander followed his ghost down to a little cove well below the high cliff walls, knowing all along that he was witnessing something transcendental. It was there, at the end of an old wooden pier, that the unearthly little craft had finally come to rest, and he marveled at it, watching it bob gently on the still, black waters of the narrow bay. And then he saw her again, that ghostly beauty. She was on the pier, heading straight toward the boat.

He stood at the landing watching with his heart in his throat as a young man sprang onto the dock. The mere sight of him caused another shock, for Alexander recognized the winsome lad. He had seen this golden youth before, in Oxford; he was the university student staring at him in the lecture hall with those eyes so like Jamie's. And now he realized that he had seen this image more than once, though it had been just the outline of the man, really—his fleeting shadow cast on the brick wall of the alleyway as he traveled past. He had only appeared whenever a letter from Miss Stevenson had been delivered. But he had never suspected the connection. Why would he? He had been too befuddled and daft trying to find the mere will to live, let alone take note of a ghost. But God, it was unbelievable, even to his heavily burdened mind! He had been seeing the very man that the woman of his dreams had been in love with, and he never knew. He had been visited by the ghost of Thomas Crichton.

His attention was held rapt by the couple, and with his heart thumping away too loudly in his ears he watched as the gallant lad took the woman's hand in his own. At the instant of their touch, a burst of joy and happiness hit him. It was pure emotion. He was spellbound by it, held mesmerized by it—and watched in awe as the young woman got into the boat that she had longed to sail in for over a hundred years.

His heart broke; and then he felt it stop entirely.

He thought that he too was dead, for he could no longer feel that steady beat in his chest. Reflexively he pushed his fingers into his neck and was reassured. His pulse was still palpable; his heart was still beating. And then he remembered the watch. He pulled it out of the little pocket next to his chest and held it tenderly in the palm of his hand.

It had stopped.

For a hundred years it had remained true and had kept ticking away without pause, and now it had stopped. He couldn't even see what time it was, it was so dark, but again he knew the watch was indeed very special. Special to them all.

It was then it hit him. Sara Stevenson, the woman *and* the ghost, had been waiting for *him* to come before she could leave. She had been waiting for Alexander Seawell to arrive on Cape Wrath. And he had finally come.

He grasped the stilled watch in the palm of his hand, unwilling to let it go. He was gripping it still, clutching it to his aching heart, as he watched the little skiff sail off into the cloaking mist and darkness, the vessel that held the woman of his dreams. It was only after he could no longer see the ghostly craft that he realized he'd been crying.

For she was gone. Sara Stevenson, the ghost of Cape Wrath, had finally gone home.

Alexander Seawell found himself alone once again and on the edge of existence. And he too harbored thoughts of leaving. For a great maudlin sadness had filled him, it depressed him; it crushed him to his very core. And it was with great effort that he made it back to the lighthouse at all. But the lighthouse had called to him, it beckoned him with that inextinguishable yellow light, and he, like a moth to a flame, had followed it.

He walked into the darkened cottage lit only by firelight and a few oil lamps that had been kept burning. And he found himself standing in the doorway of a bedroom. It was there, through his tears, he beheld the lovely young widow asleep on the bed with the newborn child at her breast.

He felt a strange tightening in his chest at the sight of her. She reminded him strangely of his wife, Jane, the first woman he had ever loved. It was when she died of scarlet fever before giving birth to their child that he felt compelled to join the fighting in Europe. It was there he had planned to die. But this woman's husband had foiled that plan. And now *he* was the one standing in her doorway, not James. He was the one staring at this young woman; so much like the other young woman he had journeyed across Scotland to save.

He felt the pulse of his heart beating in the back of his throat at the sight of her. And his breath came in short, quick bursts— as if he had just run the Kaiser's gauntlet with his life intact. He could not remove his eyes from her, and so he just stood there, watching as mother and child slept, the pair of them also alone on the edge of the world. It was then he felt a twinge of something very like hope well up from deep within him. It was faint, but it was there.

He was struck with the notion that he would not be leaving Cape Wrath anytime soon. For there was too much history here, there were too many ghosts. Yet above it all, there was the glimmer of something rare and alluring. He couldn't put a finger on it, but he could feel it all the same. It was here, and it was impossible for an antiquarian like him to ignore.

# AUTHOR'S NOTE

As this story is obviously a work of fiction, I took many historical liberties with my plotline, due in part to the timing of the two great wars that shadow this story: the Napoleonic Wars, from 1793 to 1815, and World War I, from 1914 to 1918. The first large leap of fiction was the lighthouse on Cape Wrath. This lighthouse was indeed built by Robert Stevenson (a remarkable lighthouse engineer and grandfather to Robert Louis Stevenson), but not until the year 1828, thirteen years after the setting of Sara's story. In order to make a love story traverse a hundred years (which, by the way, I'd like to think could happen), I had to put Sara in a lighthouse that did not yet exist. I also have no evidence that the Stevensons ever had a daughter named Sara. They did have thirteen children, of whom only five survived infancy, four boys and a daughter named Jane, and they would all have been very young indeed in the year 1815. Also, I do not have any solid evidence that the Stevensons ever banished any of their children to one of their remote lighthouse settings for anything other than education on the engineering of a lighthouse. Though, being a parent myself, I cannot guarantee that the thought never crossed their minds.

Another matter I'd like to clear up is my negligent indication that the entire population of Cape Wrath engaged in smuggling. This, of course, is not true. While it remains a fact that fewer people live in that region of Scotland today than did before the Highland Clearances of 1790 and onward, the livelihood of the people of Sutherland, perhaps of all the Highlanders, was the most affected. And those who lived on Cape Wrath at that time, in the heart of MacKay country, must have been hardy souls indeed. It was when large sheep farms moved in to replace the small clan farms that the local population was encouraged to move to the coast and become fishermen or kelp harvesters. And if some did manage to prosper in the land of their ancestors at the expense of the government, well then, my lips shall forever remain sealed!

Darci Hannah<br>
Howell, Michigan

DARCI HANNAH lives and plays in Michigan with her husband and three sons. When she's not playing, she's hard at work on her next novel.